MISTLETOE AND MURDER

LAURA STEWART

BLOODHOUND
— BOOKS —

ALSO BY LAURA STEWART

The Murderous Affair at Stone Manor

To Lindsey, who always thought a book dedication would be cool. This one's for you, lovely X

PROLOGUE

NOVEMBER

'Now then, Sadie, have you got everything this time?' Lorcan Flynn asked the elderly lady as he walked her to the waiting taxi.

Sadie smiled sweetly and nodded, her silvery white hair slipping loose of the kirby grips. 'You know what they say; if you leave something behind, it's your subconscious letting you know you want to return,' she said, then gave a small chuckle, 'or it could be dementia setting in.'

'Nonsense!' He chastised her fondly. 'You're more on the ball than I am.' Lorcan held the taxi door open for her, giving the local driver a friendly greeting.

Once she was safely seat-belted up in the front seat she wound down the window. 'Can you put my name down for the next course you'll be teaching? I feel I'm ready to work on facial features now.'

'Of course, I'll forward on the details. Now, you take care of yourself.' He patted the car roof and watched as it drove down the dirt track. Sadie was the last to leave the Lorcan Flynn Residential Art School and, much as he loved tutoring, he was glad to have the time to himself again.

He loosened the red spotted handkerchief which tied back his dark blond dreadlocks and turned to go back inside, feeling the bite of late autumn in the air. He stood for a moment taking in the view; the clouds skimming past the watery sun creating rolling shadows on the gold, green and browns of the patchwork fields. On a clear day like today Lorcan could see down towards the village of Glencarlach, with little glinting patches of the North Atlantic. Although still daylight, the moon was high in the sky, as if impatient for the day to end.

Lorcan hoped for a dazzling array of stars tonight. His telescope was always within easy reach in case the universe put on a show. With uninterrupted views all around him and no street lights around, Lorcan was constantly reminded of how remote this place was. And he wouldn't have it any other way.

Although originally from rural Northern Ireland, Lorcan had spent most of his twenties in Glasgow, at first studying at Glasgow School of Art then working in the same city, making a name for himself from the highly coveted paintings with equally high price tags. Yet, it seemed, the more successful he became, the more disillusioned he felt. Suffering from an 'is this it?' moment not long after his thirty-fourth birthday, he wondered if a change of scene was what he needed. He'd moved briefly to London, then even more briefly to New York, tried Berlin too, but despite the bigger and more vibrant art scenes, Lorcan felt emptier than ever before.

He moved back to the West End of Glasgow, reconnecting with his fellow artistic souls but by that point ennui had set in and he soon felt out of step with his contemporaries. He knew he'd become stuck in a rut, a little of his artistic spirit disappearing daily as he moved further away from the man he'd been in art college. A victim of his own success he found himself craving a simpler life.

His painting style developed into a more untamed free form,

he returned to the world of sculpture; to the art which no one really wanted or understood, that he'd put aside when fame and fortune came knocking. But those were the pieces that made him feel alive again. And although he knew it was desperately cheesy, he had an urge to give something back; he wanted to ignite the spark of art appreciation in others. After much hand-wringing and indecision, he'd spent a weekend holed up in his beautiful Glasgow townhouse watching reruns of *Grand Designs* and George Clarke's *Amazing Spaces* and, feeling inspired, first thing Monday morning he took a leap and bought a smallholding in the north of Scotland. He hired an architect and together they created a working art studio where he offered week-long, tutored, residential courses.

First, he'd converted the stable into a glorious art studio. He then transformed the scrub yard and derelict outbuildings into an oasis of calm, planting wildflowers to attract local wildlife and erecting cosy en suite eco-pods so he could have up to eight people staying at a time. Then he'd extended his own living quarters, turning it into a sprawling, spacious home, with glass down one side of the building, capitalising on the views of the surrounding dramatic glen.

There was plenty of living space but he always seemed to gravitate to the heart and soul of the house – the kitchen – with the log-burning fire and Aga cooker, where he could sit for hours watching the changing colours of the sky over the Torridon Hills in the distance. The kitchen seemed to be his guests' favourite place too, he'd noticed, as most evenings he had to practically stick dynamite under them to make them head off to bed in the wee small hours of the morning. But secretly he was delighted; as well as providing first-class tuition, the food and ambience had become as much of a crowd-pleaser thanks to the local chef he hired to cook the breakfasts, lunches and dinners for those on the course (allowing Lorcan to pick up some culinary skills at the same time). And his well-stocked cellar of rather nice wine and single malts played its own part in the attraction too.

The majority attending his courses were middle-aged couples searching out an alternative to a fortnight in Lanzarote, but Lorcan didn't mind, he loved witnessing the joy on their faces when they produced their first ever landscape or still life. He made enough money from the handful of courses he ran throughout the year to keep him going through the other months, allowing him to focus on his own work. He'd even started evening classes in the Glencarlach Village Community Hall and he helped out once a week at the local primary school. He finally felt fulfilled; life was good.

Lorcan went through each of the eco-pods to make sure no one had left anything and, finding them empty, turned the beds back, ready for his cleaner, Ruby, who was due first thing the next morning. He checked his watch – almost four – perfect time to head off into the village to the Whistling Haggis for that day's special and a quick pint. Or four.

Tutoring season was well and truly over and it was high time Lorcan joined the Glencarlach social whirl once more.

As he was heading back to the main house, his mobile started to ring. He was surprised at the name that flashed up on the caller ID.

'Hello! Long time no hear, how are you?'

'I'm well, Mr Flynn. Yourself?'

'Aye, I can't complain.'

'Is this a suitable time to call?' the voice down the other end of the phone said.

'Yes,' Lorcan let himself back into his house, closing the door over to keep the warmth in.

'Good. I do hope you recall the matter you assisted me on previously.'

'Of course.'

'Good, that's very good. I fear something has come to my

attention which would indicate a similar scenario and I may need to enlist your help again.'

Lorcan sat at his kitchen table, all thoughts of pints and a pie vanishing, and listened carefully to the man on the other end of the line.

CHAPTER 1

18TH DECEMBER

Amelia Adams lowered her brush and took a step back from her easel to critique her work. If she squinted just a little bit more, it vaguely resembled the assorted elements of the still life before her.

One thing was certain; she was no natural artist.

'Okay, everyone, that's enough for tonight. And this year!' Lorcan Flynn announced from the front of the class. 'I hope everyone has a merry Christmas and I'll see you back here the second week of January. Oh, and please remember to drop off your submissions for the art exhibition and let me know if you want to put them into the auction,' he added, shouting over the noise of chairs being scraped back and the other class members chatting as they gathered their belongings together.

Amelia started to pack up her paints and brushes as people streamed out from the village hall.

Lorcan came over and surveyed her painting and Amelia felt acutely awkward under his intense scrutiny. 'You can be as rude as you like about it,' she said.

Lorcan looked taken aback. 'Why would I be rude about it?'

'Because I have all the artistic ability of a blindfolded three-toed sloth.'

Lorcan pulled a face. 'I hear they're very skilled watercolourists. But seriously, don't be so hard on yourself, your proportions are good, the shapes are fine. If I was being super-critical, I'd say it's possibly a little flat, so yeah, you could work on your depth...'

'Are you trying to say I'm shallow?' Amelia joked.

Lorcan laughed. 'We just need to focus on light and shade to really bring out the dimensions. We'll focus on that next term.'

'So, have you got anything planned over Christmas?' Amelia asked as she slipped her canvas into her art folio and zipped it up.

'You mean apart from being the chief organiser of the Glencarlach art exhibition and auction?' he said with a twinkle in his eye. 'No, nothing else. Just a couple of weeks of bingeing Netflix and eating and drinking. Speaking of, we need to get a night planned.'

'Yes!' Amelia agreed heartily.

Lorcan had arrived in the village not long after Amelia and as 'new-comers' together, had formed a strong friendship. It wasn't long before Lorcan's easy-going friendly manner and Northern Irish charm had won over the residents of Glencarlach.

'In fact, Toby mentioned having a drink in the Whistling Haggis tonight,' Amelia said

'Ah, your brother can always be relied on for a quick half in the local! That sounds good!'

'As long as I can get away,' Amelia said, mentally going through her to-do list. She'd even swithered about making it along to the art class that afternoon, but despite not being very accomplished at art, Amelia did enjoy the two hours she spent clearing her mind and focusing on a charcoal drawing or a painting.

'You busy?'

Amelia nodded as they headed out the village hall together, Lorcan switching off the lights as they went.

'We've got a wedding planned, with the guests arriving from tomorrow and they're staying for the next ten days.'

'That's great.'

Amelia wasn't so sure. What had started out as a low-key event was morphing into quite a full-on affair! As the owner and manager of the luxury boutique Stone Manor Hotel, this was the first major wedding Amelia had been in charge of since opening. In fact, it was the first of any kind of wedding Amelia had been in charge of since opening.

When Carlo Todero and Lucy Carvalho had first got in touch a couple of months previously, they'd loved the idea of a simple, rustic wedding in the naturally beautiful spot of Glencarlach in the north-west of Scotland. They'd been enchanted by Stone Manor itself; an impressively grand Georgian mansion Amelia had inherited from her beloved godmother, complete with hidden passageways, priest holes and a folly. And there was the legend of the hidden treasure – a rare and priceless ruby that sent many of the previous inhabitants insane and murderous in their desire to find it. As a mystery fiction fan, it had become a dream come true for Amelia to star in her very own mystery, and she had indeed 'starred' thanks to a documentary crew filming her journey as she renovated her new home into a luxury boutique hotel.

Although the treasure had now been found and returned to the Cairo Museum and the saboteur that had almost killed Amelia in his desire to discover the treasure for himself had been caught and imprisoned, the mysterious Stone Manor had lost none of its allure for Amelia and she was determined to turn it into a successful hotel and wedding venue no matter the demands of the betrothed couple.

'Well, fingers crossed I see you and your brother tonight,' Lorcan said as he took out a big bunch of keys and locked the front door of the hall. 'And what about that boyfriend of yours? Is he back from his book signing tour yet?'

'Not yet,' Amelia said, trying to keep the disappointment out of her voice. She checked her watch. 'Although he should probably have touched down in London by now.' Jack Temple had been gone a couple of weeks, touring the States, and Amelia couldn't believe how much she'd missed him. Being busy at work helped pass the time but as soon as she finished her shift and headed back to the Gatehouse they shared on the hotel grounds, her loneliness was palpable.

The Gatehouse was on the compact side of bijou and Jack frequently drove Amelia to distraction by spreading his work out over every available surface, while his discarded boots tripped her up in the hall. His muscular six-foot-two frame took up most of the small double bed and when he'd left, Amelia had at first loved all the extra space and not having him cursing every couple of minutes as he bashed his head on the low beams. But now, over two weeks on, the novelty of having the bed to herself and the peaceful evenings had lost their appeal. The Gatehouse now seemed cavernous and void of life. Amelia had even worn one of his oversize woollen jumpers to bed, pretending it was for warmth but knowing deep down she really wanted to get a whiff of that familiar fresh air, outdoorsy smell of him. She feared she was at risk of turning into a soppy and simpering female from a romance novel.

November 30th marked the day Jack had flown to New York and the next day she'd opened up the first window of her chocolate advent calendar. But this year she wasn't just counting down to Santa. Each little Cadbury's Christmassy shape was one day closer to Jack's return when she could kiss that scratchy stubbly chin again. But however much she missed him she knew the wait was worth it because once he returned, he'd be home in their little Gatehouse for good. It was the reason he'd agreed to the exhaustive book signing tour, arranging with his agent that he'd take a couple of extra days in New York to tie-up his old life. One of the many perks of his being a bestselling thriller writer was that he could work anywhere, even at their wobbly kitchen table.

Another perk was that he'd penned some great murder mystery weekends, which the hotel offered as a special package: definitely another plus in the hotel's 'attractions' column. And if she managed to pull off the Todero-Carvalho celebration, she could add 'wedding venue' to the list too.

Lorcan tried the door handle of the village hall to double-check it was secured then pocketed the keys.

'Well, if I don't see you tonight for a drink, we'll try and all meet up soon. I can crank up the old Aga and get some grub on one night up at mine.'

'Sounds good!' Amelia said enthusiastically. Lorcan was a natural host and had held many a good party in his beautiful home with guests chatting and drinking into the wee small hours of the morning, sprawling out into the garden in summer or clustered round their host's log burner on the dark wintry nights, eating delicious stews and home-made soda bread courtesy of the old-fashioned Aga Lorcan had reconditioned.

With a cheerio, Amelia crossed over the road to the Stone Manor Jeep, throwing her artwork onto the back seat. She'd just put on her seat belt when her phone pinged at her and she saw it was an email from James, her deputy manager. He'd attached the updated list of requirements that had just been emailed from Carlo.

Scanning down the list, Amelia wondered how on earth she'd manage to get four dozen red roses in the north-west of Scotland six days before Christmas, source a string quartet and find white doves to be set free after the ceremony. At best Amelia thought she may be able to cobble together a couple of bunches of flowers, use the local folk duet for music and she had a dozen chickens. Maybe if she found some nice ribbon to tie in bows round their necks... *Just as well I like a challenge,* she thought as she started up the engine. She was just about to pull out when her mobile's *Tales of the Unexpected* ringtone sounded and all wedding woes disappeared when she saw the caller's identity.

'Hey!'

'Hey, gorgeous!' Jack Temple's sultry American voice drawled down the phone at her and Amelia felt the miles that distanced them melt away. 'How are you?'

'Just wondering if our laid-back betrothed couple are secretly harbouring Bridezilla and Groom of Doom tendencies.'

'Uh-oh.'

'It's fine, I'll work it out. How's it going?'

'It's going good. I just wanted to let you know I've landed in London.'

'Great! Did you manage to sleep on the plane?'

'Nah, not really, I'm sure the jet lag will kick in later. Just a couple of more days here for some signings then it's back home to you.'

'I'm so glad you'll be back by Christmas.'

'Hey, I can't risk you kissing someone else under the mistletoe, can I?'

Amelia could hear the smile in his voice and wished 22nd December was closer than four days away.

'As if!'

'Well, I know my charm is still irresistible, no matter where I am in the world,' he said with a laugh. 'I'd better go, that's the luggage coming through now. I've got a pretty packed day but I'll call you later, yeah?'

'Yeah, give my regards to Big Ben!'

'Love you!'

'Love you too!'

She hung up and chucked her phone into her bag on the passenger seat. With everything full-on at work, the four days would no doubt fly by and then she and Jack could have their perfect Christmas together.

Amelia sat for a moment, looking out the windscreen, taking a moment to appreciate her surroundings. She could hear the sea breaking against the rocks just a few feet away on the other side of the harbour wall, a few of the boats bobbing about with the swell of the water. At the other end of Main Street, behind the row of shops, lay a network of lanes and small roads which wound their way up the hill leading to the early nineteenth-century cottages in their charming higgledy-piggledy rows with larger stretches of greenbelt and farm land between them the further out the village they sat.

It was no wonder Glencarlach was frequently voted one of Scotland's prettiest villages.

And at Christmas, it became even prettier. Lights had been attached to the row of independent shops and strung up bunting-style between the old-fashioned lamp posts, twinkling invitingly against the darkening sky.

She sat watching as a group of men hoisted a large Christmas tree off a trailer to put into place halfway along the sea front. Amelia smiled, imagining how lovely it would look with the multi-coloured lights in place.

She turned on the radio, cranking up the volume as Chris Rea sang he was driving home for Christmas. Pulling away from her parking space she joined in with the festive classic, thinking how wonderful Christmas would be this year.

'Left a bit, right a bit, a bit more…'

Back at Stone Manor, Amelia got to the reception desk as her brother, Toby, resplendent in his chef's whites, was seemingly giving instructions to an eighteen-foot Norwegian Spruce which nestled into the curve of the grand, oak-panelled staircase.

'A bit more...'

The foliage quivered and inched slightly to the side.

'Perfect!' Amelia called out and James, the deputy manager, appeared from behind the Christmas tree. He blew the hair from his forehead, face red with exertion.

'Is this one a better size?'

'Much,' Amelia beamed. Earlier in the day she'd discarded the ten-footer which looked lost in such a grand hall. It had been sitting there for a week and annoyed Amelia every time she'd walked past it. Now, with Christmas being so close, Amelia decided to go bigger. The smaller tree now stood, glinting merrily with fairy lights and baubles, in the dining room.

'How's everything?'

'Great!' Toby said as she followed him through the 'staff only' sign which led to the kitchen and other areas the guests didn't get to see.

Amelia's eye lit up as she saw the Christmas pudding cheesecake just before one of the kitchen hands popped it into the fridge.

'Don't worry!' Toby said, tying a scarlet durag behind his head, flattening down his dark brown quiff, before he picked up a massive box of veg and carried it over to one of the prep areas, 'I'll make sure to save you some.'

'Thank you!' Amelia dodged out the way as another chef hurried past her with a large platter of seafood.

One of the unexpected positives of Amelia opening up the hotel was working with her brother. Growing up they'd been close despite annoying the hell out of one another; Amelia's organised and methodical nature was at odds with Toby's laid-back spontaneity and often Amelia would find herself falling into the older sister role and nagging her brother. Toby taking up the position of head chef could easily have been a disaster but it turned out they were the perfect business yin and yang, each making up for the other's shortcomings and both fiercely loyal towards each other. Her brother had proven to be a very skilled chef, having honed his talent in the years he'd spent travelling.

Amelia's main concern was that he'd get itchy feet and want to move on to another adventure but for the first time in his adult life, Toby seemed happy to set down his roots.

Just like Amelia, Toby had fallen in love with Glencarlach. He'd also fallen in love with the notorious actor Gideon Fey, the reformed hell-raiser and chief instigator of the Stone Manor documentary hit. In between filming, Gideon returned to Toby and the cottage they'd bought in the heart of the village.

'How many covers tonight?' Amelia asked.

'Thirty. Most are the group Christmas parties with the set menus.' Toby turned to shout over to Craig, who, as well as being a waiter doubled up as a sommelier and mixologist for the hotel. 'How's the Christmas cocktail coming along?'

'Made up in the pitchers and chilling in the fridge. I've also added a special dessert wine to go with the cheesecake,' Craig hollered back, holding up a bottle.

Toby went over to look and nodded in approval.

'Ames!' Toby shouted just as Amelia was heading back to the reception desk. 'You still up for a couple of drinks in the Whistling Haggis after our shift this evening, yeah?'

'If I've got time! I mentioned it to Lorcan too, after the art class,' she called back as she disappeared out the door.

'Right, get your coat, you've pulled!'

Amelia looked up from her leather-bound desk planner where Toby stood holding out her coat, hat and scarf. He'd changed from his chef's whites and was dressed for the outdoors. The cold outdoors, as he had on a giant padded parka, sheepskin gloves and a woollen deerstalker perched over his reinstated gelled quiff.

'But I've…'

'Nothing else to do tonight,' he interrupted her protestations, plucking her pen from her hand and closing over her planner. 'We have no guests tonight. Everything is prepped and ready to go in the kitchens for tomorrow and the back shift has everything in order and everyone knows what to do in the event of a last-minute booking, running out of milk, small fire, gun shoot-out, siege, kidnap or nuclear war thanks to your *very* thorough and informative staff update earlier,' he teased.

Amelia narrowed her eyes at him. Her thorough to-do lists, anxious overthinking coupled with a flair for the dramatic were an endless source of amusement to those close to Amelia.

Toby simply grinned back, handing her her coat.

'But it's just gone half six…'

'Which means more drinking time in the pub.' He rubbed his gloved hands together in keen expectation. 'And do you really want to be here when the village knitting and crochet group come in for their Christmas night out? You know how they get when they start on the Jägermeister shots! They're due at seven. Everything is under control, isn't it?' Toby addressed Craig who was coming out of the kitchens with the chilled pitchers of Christmas cocktails, one bright red, the other green.

'Yes! Don't worry, Amelia,' Craig nodded, 'we've got everything covered. I love the new tree, much better that size,' he said with a grin as he headed into the bar.

'He's such a suck-up,' Toby joked with an eye-roll.

'He's just getting into the Christmas spirit as much as I am!'

With one last look at her to-do list, with yet another email from Carlo Todero stapled to the top which confirmed the final guest list and arrival times, Amelia let Toby hustle her out the door and they walked companionably together along the pillar-lit driveway towards the centre of the village and heart of the community; the Whistling Haggis bar. Amelia had been worried about opening the hotel in what could be perceived as a direct business threat to the well-established bar. But the hearty pub grub favourites were not disadvantaged by the finer dining element of Stone Manor. In fact, the hotel had offered many job opportunities and even the Whistling Haggis's landlord's son worked part-time for Amelia whilst studying hospitality management at the University of the Highlands and Islands.

Business for the Whistling Haggis continued to boom after it became a favourite fixture of the documentary and the entire village was firmly placed on the tourist trail and many of the Whistling Haggis regulars never had to buy a drink for themselves in the summer months thanks to their television notoriety!

The pub was just under a mile away and even at a brisk walk, it was so cold that by the time they reached the village Amelia had lost the feeling in most of her toes. Opening the door to the pub, the welcome heat from the inglenook fire hit them. As always, the traditional bar was jumping, though slightly quieter than on the weekend nights when they usually had live music, courtesy of the local talent. Once the café on Main Street closed at 6pm, the Whistling Haggis was where the majority of the villagers congregated.

'I'll get these,' Amelia said as she stuck her coat over the back of a chair at the only free table and headed up to the bar. Archie, one of the older weather-beaten farmers, of whom she was very fond, gave her a wink in greeting.

'The usual, Amelia?' Big Davey the landlord asked, hand hovering over the glasses.

'Please.'

'It won't be too long until Jack's back now, will it?' he said as he pulled a pint of draught heavy.

'Uh, no, it's not,' Amelia agreed.

'Aye, 22nd of December will be here before you realise. Just hope he doesn't get delayed. Travelling at this time of year can be right problematic.' Big Davey nodded sagely as he left the pint to settle and reached up and got a bottle of Laphroaig off the top shelf and hand poured a double measure.

'Especially as the weather's going to turn too. There'll be snow,' Archie added.

'Oh? I didn't see that on the forecast,' Amelia said.

Big Davey gave a disparaging snort. 'Ach, yon folk on the TV know nothing. It's all in the berries. They're big and dark red which means....' He paused for dramatic effect as he poured water into a little jug and set it beside the whisky, '...a cold and snowy winter is coming,' he finished ominously.

'Maybe we'll get a white Christmas!' Amelia said, quite excited at the prospect.

Big Davey gave a non-committal shrug.

'Will it get really deep?' Amelia wondered how likely it would be if they got snowed in. Last year, her first winter in Glencarlach, unusually there hadn't been a single snowflake, much to Amelia's disappointment. Instead, they endured strong winds and torrential rain for most of January.

Davey shook his head. 'That happens much more inland towards Inverness and on the East Coast. We tend to be too close to the sea to get it bad, but I have a feeling we may get more snow than usual this year, so who knows. Don't worry, just settle up at the end of the night,' he added as Amelia reached for her purse.

'Thanks, Davey!'

Amelia poured a splash of water onto the whisky just to break the surface and took the drinks over to their table. She slid the pint over to Toby and sat down opposite with her Laphroaig.

'Is it weird that Big Davey knows my boyfriend's travel schedule?'

Toby smiled. 'MI5 can only look on in jealousy at the insider network of information that goes on in Glencarlach! The other day Archie asked me how Gideon's shoot was going and if his cold was better – he'd seen him buying Lemsip in the chemist when he was last here!'

Just then the door opened and Lorcan walked in and headed up to the bar as Davey automatically started to pour his drink.

'Lorcan!' Toby called and the tall Irishman turned round. Seeing them he waved and came over as soon as Davey put his drink in front of him.

'Jeeze, it's cold!' he said, stomping his Doc Marten-booted feet and sitting down with his pint of export.

'I see you've come prepared.' Toby nodded to the head torch Lorcan had wrapped around his woolly bobble hat.

'I know you mock, but I'd rather look a bit of an eejit than trip over a stone and break my leg in some remote spot!' He gave a laugh as he carefully removed his torch.

Personally, Amelia thought it a very sensible purchase and mentally added it to her to-buy list. Being so far out in the country there were no street lamps to light the way and if it was a dark, overcast night, no helpful moon or star constellations to light the sky either.

Lorcan took off his hat, releasing his dreadlocks which tumbled halfway down his back.

Big Davey came over with a pile of leaflets. 'Here you go, just thought you'd like a read. It's about the village Winter Festival.'

'The Winter Festival?' Toby repeated in wonderment.

Amelia sighed inwardly. Clearly, he hadn't looked at the leaflet she'd posted up on the staff noticeboard.

Big Davey nodded. 'Because of us now being a little more on the map, touristically speaking, the village council thought it would be a good idea to take advantage of the interest in our community and get some winter events organised.'

'Winter events? Like skiing? Bobsleigh? The skeleton?' Toby asked incredulously.

'Less Winter Olympics, more village fair but in the cold. I think my days of slipping into salopettes are over,' Davey said, patting his impressive stomach.

Amelia wondered at those days ever really beginning.

'We're organising a Christmas cake competition and a local scavenger hunt. And obviously we have the annual Christmas pantomime in January.'

'Of course,' all three echoed with due reverence. There was always a flurry of excitement when the Reverend Roddy McDade cast for the annual Christmas pantomime even though it was a foregone conclusion that Big Davey received one of the leads in return for all the free drinks the Reverend got throughout the month of December. To be fair, Amelia had heard Big Davey sing and she had to admit he was quite an impressive baritone and he clearly didn't shy away from a little cross-dressing in the guise of Widow Twanky or an ugly sister.

'And there's the art fair too with some of the pieces carrying on to the charity auction.' Big Davey patted Lorcan's back. 'Our very own village artist is chief organiser of that event.'

'Yup,' Lorcan nodded, 'it's coming along nicely. People have been dropping off their work up at my studio and the village hall for me to start hanging them. And people have been very generous in handing in some more antique paintings. We'll have a good mix.'

'Are you going to enter some of your work too, Lorcan?' Amelia asked.

'Yeah, I've already put a couple aside. And some photographs. It's not my main medium but I've got some nice snaps of the area and the locals.'

'It'll be great. All the proceeds are going to local charities.' Davey nodded happily. 'Amelia? I'm sure there must be some paintings up at Stone Manor you'd be willing to donate?'

'I've definitely got a couple!' Amelia said enthusiastically, knowing there were a few hideous paintings she'd inherited that she'd not mind parting company with. Most were hidden away in one of the storerooms off the cellar but there were a couple still hanging up which gave Amelia a bit of a turn whenever she passed them. 'I'll look them out tomorrow.'

'Message me when you've got them and I'll come in the van and pick them up,' Lorcan said.

'Great!' Davey clapped his meaty hands together. 'And maybe you can persuade your famous guest to pop along to the auction too, that'd certainly drum up more interest!' And with that bombshell, Davey left to drop some leaflets on another table.

Toby and Lorcan turned to look expectantly at Amelia.

'Clearly Wee Davey doesn't think guest confidentiality extends to his dad,' she sighed.

'So, spill, who's coming?' Toby asked.

Amelia leant into the table and kept her voice low. 'A couple of the guests of the wedding party are quite well known.'

Toby and Lorcan also leant forward, mirroring Amelia's body language.

'It's a film producer...'

Lorcan sat back, as he pulled on his goatee. 'Ah, clearly he's here to offer me the new Bond. It was only a matter of time,' he said, his turquoise eyes twinkling merrily.

'...and his wife. She's the *really* famous one.'

Toby gave a groan. 'I hope it isn't someone very famous, otherwise Gideon might sulk. You know he likes being the celebrity draw of the village.'

'It's Evangelina Wilde!' Amelia said, sitting back, waiting for their reactions.

Toby gave a low whistle and Lorcan turned quite pink and looked a little shell-shocked.

Evangelina Wilde was an icon. She'd been an ice-blonde, blue-eyed, willowy ingenue when Amelia was growing up and everyone wanted to look like her, although it had been a bit of a struggle for Amelia as she was barely over five foot, was already forming her more 1950s-inspired hourglass figure and had dark brown hair and eyes.

Evangelina Wilde had been on every director's wish list but she'd only made a small number of films in her early twenties when, just at the height of her popularity she'd married the producer of her latest film and disappeared from the limelight, never to be seen again.

Every so often there was a rumour in the papers she was going to do *Strictly Come Dancing* or *I'm a Celebrity Get me Out of Here*, but none of them ever came to be.

'Well, I'm impressed,' Toby said after taking a long swallow of his pint. 'To be honest, as someone very secure in my gayness I got some confusing stirrings when I saw one of her films once as a teenager!' He gave a laugh. 'I wonder what she looks like now, if she's changed much,' he mused, adding, 'how old would she be now? She's a little older than me as I remember.'

'Same age as me, thirty-seven… or, um, around that. I think,' Lorcan said tugging on his goatee.

'Well, we'll see them soon enough. According to Mr Todero's schedule, they're due to arrive first,' Amelia said, then drained her glass. 'And now, if you guys don't mind, I'm going to head home.'

'But we just got here! Do you not want to stay for dinner?' Toby said in surprise. 'They've got scampi on the specials board!'

'Tempting as it is, I'm just going to grab something at home, watch an episode of *Poirot* and have an early night.'

Toby's eyes narrowed at her. 'What's for dinner? Something other than Pot Noodles, I hope.' He regularly reprimanded Amelia for her often appalling diet. No one, especially Amelia, could understand how she could eat such rubbish and remain so slim. Amelia's best friend, Sally, regularly bemoaned this unfairness when she swore only looking at a slice of cake piled on another pound.

'I'm sure I've got green things…' Amelia said evasively. She did. A green packet of salt and vinegar crisps she planned on eating between two doorstops of white bread and lots of butter.

'I can't believe you're standing us up for a little French detective!' Toby said in mock outrage.

'He's Belgian,' Amelia said hotly before realising Toby was

goading her. 'Mainly I'm standing you up because you make fun of me all the time!'

'Want us to walk you home?' Lorcan asked.

'Thank you, but I'll be fine,' she said, standing up and sticking on her hat.

'What if the ghosts and ghouls get you,' Toby said, making a spooky 'whooooo' noise.

She gave him a withering look as she zipped up her coat.

'You're braver than me, walking into those woods by yourself. They give me the heebie-jeebies,' Lorcan said.

'It's all nonsense. I'm as likely to see Santa Claus as I am a ghost on the way home,' Amelia scoffed.

'Well, for tonight, the only spirit I'm interested in is a Jameson's chaser to go with my pint,' Lorcan said, standing up. 'Fancy one too, Toby?'

'Twist my arm,' Toby said with a grin as Lorcan headed to the bar.

'Text me when you're back safe, okay?' Toby said as Amelia pulled on her gloves.

'Ah, you do care after all!' She blew him a kiss and made her way back outside into the cold. She walked up the lane by the side of the pub and through the ornate gates which signalled the boundary of Stone Manor property, leaving the twinkling lights of the village behind her.

Despite her brave words in the bar, it was always at this point Amelia quickened her pace. Even with the subtle pillar lights illuminating the long drive, Amelia managed to freak herself out when she walked along it, alone, at night. Not that she'd ever let her brother know it, but her already fertile imagination needed no encouragement to ramp up a gear. Beyond the drive's verge, the darkness of the trees could easily give anonymity to someone; someone watching her, silently following her movements. Ghosts were one thing, but the living with murderous thoughts were another.

The wind whipped through the branches and the hairs stood up on the back of Amelia's neck as she thought she could hear someone calling out her name. She willed herself to keep looking straight ahead and not turn to look...

A fox took that moment to emit a cry... at least Amelia thought it was a fox... unless it was someone meeting a violent end. Or the ghost of someone who'd met a violent end. Lorcan wasn't alone in being spooked as Amelia knew most of the people in Glencarlach believed in the ghost stories surrounding the village. The vast grounds and dense woodland of Stone Manor was home to a multitude of hauntings if local folklore was to be believed. The estate held a fascination for the villager's teens, who often dared each other to go into the wood at midnight on full moons.

Amelia cursed her imagination as visions of ghosts now filled her head, especially the one of the headless horseman which was said to haunt the woods. She'd never seen anything but there were plenty of people in the village who swore they had, and Amelia often fancied she could hear hooves pounding over the land just beside her on the road.

She picked up her pace again trying to quell her unwelcome thoughts and just got to the Gatehouse when her phone started ringing.

It was Jack again.

'Hiya!' she said, delighted to have his company, even if it was through a phone from hundreds of miles away. She leant against the back door, the welcoming lights from the kitchen filling her with relief as her heartbeat returned to normal.

'Hey you! What you up to?'

'I just got home. I left Toby and Lorcan at the Whistling Haggis. What about you?'

'Well, this afternoon's book event was postponed until tomorrow which gave me free time so I managed to squeeze in some Christmas shopping.'

'Ooh, get anything nice?'

'I may have, but you'll have to wait a few days to find out.'

'Tease! So, are you going to try and fit in any sightseeing?'

'I did try, but the London Eye was shut for essential maintenance and The National Gallery was closed off and swarming with police due to a theft earlier. I tried to go to Ronnie Scott's, but it was sold out. I suppose I could always take in a show in the West End…'

'Ha! You know you won't. You're far more likely to find a quaint little pub full of interesting characters and spend the next few hours getting their life stories!'

He laughed. How she'd missed his laugh! 'You know me so…' there was a crackling noise and a clatter and Amelia could hear Jack shout 'WATCH IT!' There was more rustling and he was back on the line. 'Hello! You still there?'

'Yup, what happened?'

'Some asshole just barrelled into me, sent me flying. Honestly, I'd forgotten just how rude people are here. And it's so crowded! I've come to realise over the past few days I'm just not cut out for a city anymore. I've turned into a country guy. I want open spaces and rolling hills.' She heard him sigh. 'I'm really missing you and Glencarlach. Mainly you. In Glencarlach. Make me nostalgic. Tell me about home.'

She loved how he now considered Glencarlach home. 'Well, it's absolutely baltic here! Big Davey says it's going to snow. I really hope we get a white Christmas. And everyone is agog with excitement for the Winter Festival.'

'Really?'

'Not really, but it's mad enough to be good fun.'

'It all sounds blissful. It won't be long until we're snuggling up together in front of the fire in the Whistling Haggis, tucking into Big Davey's steak and kidney pie. So, how's all the prep going for the wedding?'

Amelia gave him a rundown on all the gossip as she let herself into the Gatehouse. Being small with thick walls, it retained its heat well and Amelia instantly felt herself thaw. But with the thick walls came bad phone reception and the line started breaking up. Reluctantly they said their goodbyes.

Hanging up, Amelia unwound her scarf and took off her bobble hat. It seemed a lifetime ago that she lived in London. She wasn't envious of Jack being in the bustling city; the crowded Tube, people never looking up, the constant quick pace of life. She didn't miss that lifestyle at all. Well, occasionally she had a pang for the shops, but really, her life now didn't fit with clothes from Harvey Nicks.

Although her wardrobe was nowhere near as stylish as it was when she lived in London, it was a lot more practical for the sub-zero temperatures and high winds blowing in off the sea. She did have to deal with hat hair more often too, she realised as she caught her reflection in the window, seeing her short, choppy dark brown hair sticking up at odd angles.

Going over to close the curtains Amelia cupped her hands over the glass and peered out into the darkness for a moment, just to confirm there were definitely no headless horsemen cantering past.

CHAPTER 2

19TH DECEMBER

Since finding out that Evangelina Wilde was going to be one of the wedding guests, Amelia had mused over what the actress would be like. With so many years out of the spotlight, had she let herself go? Had she been ravaged beyond recognition by a notoriously brutal industry? Had she turned into a spoilt diva?

Arriving at work the next morning, it was clear Amelia was not alone in having these thoughts. With the bride and groom having sent Stone Manor such a detailed itinerary, everyone working knew exactly when all the wedding party would be arriving. Close to Evangelina's arrival time, Amelia had never known so many staff needing to be around the front desk at the one time.

Just after eleven, she arrived. Despite her unassuming appearance of jeans and red polo neck jumper with a navy wool coat draped over her arm, Evangelina Wilde exuded charisma. Her long blonde hair was caught up in a messy bun and with very little make-up on she barely looked any older than when she'd made her last film. It was only when she smiled a warm greeting at Amelia and laughter lines crinkled around her eyes did she show any hint that a few years had passed since her last film appearance.

'Hi there, my husband and I have a reservation,' she said in her distinctive soft, husky voice. 'It's Ricky Varelli and Evangelina...'

'...Wilde, yes, welcome to Stone Manor.'

Just then the front door burst open and a smaller, slightly swarthy man with dark hair hurried in, looking thunderous. He was wearing a camel coat and Amelia didn't think she'd ever seen anyone wear one of those outside a gangster film. He also sported an expensive looking pair of tasselly brogues.

'See, Ricky, isn't it beautiful!' Evangelina said quietly to him as he continued to look around him.

Ricky conceded her point with a grunt as he looked up at the stained-glass cupola window. He smoothed down his gelled hair. 'I suppose my cousin wouldn't book anything shoddy,' he said in a strong South London accent, 'although why we couldn't stay in London is beyond me.'

Evangelina looked at her husband with barely concealed annoyance. 'I think it's a beautiful part of the world. I've always loved Scotland,' Evangelina said with a wistful smile.

'Fine if you like bagpipes and tartan. Thank God there's Scotch,' Ricky said dismissively. 'Did a parcel arrive for me?' he asked Amelia.

'No, I'm afraid we haven't received anything for you.'

Ricky swore. 'I need to make a call,' he said, bustling back out.

Evangelina turned and gave Amelia a warm smile.

'Is it possible I can book another room please? It's for a friend. She's not part of the wedding party but wants to come up here for a break.'

'Yes, we still have rooms available,' Amelia said as she brought up the bookings page. Heading out of summer, she'd had no idea how busy they'd be over the Christmas and New Year period. Christmas was always sold as a family time, films showing generations of the one family crowded round a Christmas tree and a dining table groaning with food, but obviously that wasn't the type of Christmas everyone had. With families dotted around the world and people being on their own, it wasn't always possible to have the festive period that Hollywood liked to perpetuate. Many chose to ignore the time of year, and many didn't have Christmas as part of their culture. Amelia looked down at the list of bookings and who was due to arrive over the next few days.

Apart from the wedding party, there was only a booking for a single man and an elderly lady who was the great aunt of her best friend's fiancé. Amelia's best friend, Sally, had met Hamish, a local farmer, when they'd been renovating the hotel. They'd been together ever since and were due to be married in the summer. The official line was that there was no room in any of Hamish's relatives' houses for Betty. Although evidently a lovely lady, it seemed she was best experienced in small doses. Amelia was intrigued to see just what she'd be like!

'What's your friend's name?' she asked Evangelina.

'It's Nisha Khatri. She hopes to arrive the 22nd and I'm not sure how long she'll be staying. Possibly just until Boxing Day or the day after.' She handed Amelia a credit card.

'That's not a problem, I'll leave it open ended.'

As Amelia took a swipe of the card Lorcan came out from the kitchens and headed towards the library lugging ladders and a massive holdall. Amelia looked up to see Evangelina staring at him as he disappeared down the corridor leading to the library.

'Don't worry, we're not getting any maintenance done. That's our local artist. He's picking up some paintings for an exhibition.'

'Who…?'

'His name's Lorcan Flynn. You may have heard of him as he's very well known.'

Evangelina turned back to Amelia and smiled as she slipped her card back into the front pocket of her jeans and Amelia could have sworn her hand shook as she did so.

Amelia handed her a large and heavy old-fashioned key ring with a tassel on it. 'You're in the Chandler Suite. It's about two thirds along, turn right at the top of the stairs.'

'Would you like me to show you around the hotel?' James piped up, from hovering around the Christmas tree, rehanging tinsel that didn't need rehanging. 'We've got a small gym and a sauna. We also have a local beautician who can carry out a variety of treatments. I know the bride-to-be has some booked but if you're needing anything else done... not that you *need* anything... but...'

'I'd love a tour of the place once I've unpacked, thank you,' Evangelina said with a smile and Amelia had to hide hers as James looked starstruck and seemed to melt a little.

'Why don't you recover from your journey first, with a trip to the bar,' Craig said, materialising at her side. 'We have a great Christmas cocktail list.'

'That sounds wonderful. I'll definitely have a look at that, but first I'll take my bags up...'

'Don't worry!' James said. 'I'll do that for you.'

With another smile that managed to envelop everyone in its warmth she thanked James profusely then followed Craig through to the bar. James watched her go, mouth slightly agape.

'Honeys, I'm home!' A clipped, haughty voice rang out behind them.

Amelia turned to see Gideon Fey standing at the end of the reception desk, hands on hip. With a supercilious raise of a blond eyebrow, he said, 'And I'm *very* disappointed to discover that nobody *ever* fawns over me like that!'

For the next hour Gideon held court in the kitchen regaling everyone with stories from his latest film shoot. With his ribald tales, acerbic wit and wicked talent for impressions and storytelling, he held everyone enthralled.

'I wasn't expecting you home for another couple of days,' Toby said as he got that evening's service underway.

'Anyone would think you weren't delighted to see me!' Gideon huffed in mock offence.

'Well, I would have made sure I had a bit of a tidy up first.' Toby grimaced.

Amelia knew first-hand just how untidy her brother could be and dreaded to think what mess awaited them in their cottage!

'Well, one of the camera guys lives quite close to here and was getting quite antsy about the weather as there's meant to be a cold front coming which will make the Beast from the East a few years back look like a pussy cat. He was winding everyone else up and then there was a bit of a falling out... nothing to do with me.' Gideon held his hands up, his golden-brown eyes wide with innocence. 'Turns out a couple of the cast were having a bit of a thing and it all got a bit intense and she screamed at him one day and the entire set was walking on eggshells and miserable so the director called an early halt and warned them that they need to have either made up or split up amicably by the new year when we continue shooting. Personally,' Gideon added, 'I'm bloody glad we got away when we did as I couldn't imagine anything worse than being snowed in with a bunch of temperamental actors!'

'Quite!' Toby said with a ghost of a wink. 'Imagine the horror!'

Gideon dramatically turned his back on Toby and patted Amelia on the hand. 'This means I can be of help around here.'

'Great!' From previous experience, Amelia knew Gideon's 'help' consisted of him swanning around, chatting to the guests and putting the staff off their work.

But Gideon clearly didn't pick up on Amelia's sarcasm and he trailed after her as she went to get her coat and hat while Toby shooed everyone apart from essential staff away.

'So, who was that blonde beauty Craig and James were running after when I arrived?'

'Evangelina Wilde,' Amelia said.

'No!' Gideon plastered his hands to the sides of his face. 'Wow! No offence to your darling little hotel, but what in the world is she doing here!'

'She's a guest at the wedding.'

'Oh my! Clearly I'm such a trailblazer I've started a trend of celebrities flocking to the village!' Gideon followed her to the back door. 'I shall have to get acquainted with her and find out why she dropped off the face of the earth all those years ago. Ooh! Maybe we could work on a project together. Imagine how good we'd look together on screen!' He plucked the Glencarlach Winter Fair leaflet off the noticeboard. 'We could even offer ourselves up as judges for the Christmas cake competition!'

'You may have to wrestle Jean Maddox to the death for that privilege as she's down as the judge.'

Gideon's face fell. Jean ran the little grocery store in the village, was a stalwart of the community and a fierce force to be reckoned with.

'Well, I'm sure there's something else we can help out with. What's her husband like?'

'Hmm, I'll reserve judgement for now.'

It was only when Amelia let herself out the back door that Gideon became aware she was leaving. 'Where are you going?'

'I need to get to the shop for some supplies.' Another last-minute email had arrived from Carlo requesting a specific chocolate bar Lucy liked for their arrival – which was now less than an hour away.

'What am I meant to do?' Gideon asked slightly peeved.

'Stick on an apron and get peeling,' Toby said as he walked past, heading to the storeroom.

Toby paused and frowned at Amelia. 'You're not getting any

more Pot Noodles, are you? I can easily make you some quick dishes to reheat at home.'

'You are obsessed with your hatred of Pot Noodles!' Amelia said, affronted. 'Of course I won't!'

'And we've a new flavour in, a limited edition, something like Oriental Spice.'

'I found it, Jean, thanks,' Amelia said, putting up her basket full of Pot Noodles and other supplies plus a few more packs of herbal teas for the hotel, alongside the requested chocolate.

'Wee Davey was just in. He said you're shaping up to be quite busy over Christmas with the wedding guests all arriving.'

'Yes, we are now!'

'That's good,' Jean nodded as she rang up the two-litre bottle of Diet Coke and multipack of crisps. 'You may end up getting a few more nights out of them if we get the dumping of snow we think is on the way. If they can't leave they'll have to stay with you longer. Extra money!'

Amelia chuckled. 'That's certainly one sales approach! But I'd prefer my guests to *want* to stay rather than be forced to.' She paused packing her bags for a moment. 'Do you really think getting snowed in is likely? Big Davey said it normally doesn't lie here.'

'Normally it doesn't but the berries never lie, neither does my arthritis and it's been *crippling* me these past couple of days. Mark my words, snow is on the way. It's why I got in a few extras,' Jean said as she helped Amelia bag up her purchases.

Amelia had thought the already cramped shop was tighter for space than usual. She had had to squeeze past boxes that had been piled up in the aisles until their contents could be put on the shelves.

'Oh aye,' Jean continued, nodding her head vehemently, her

steel-grey perm curls bouncing. 'I can't be running out of supplies if we get snowed in. I have a duty to the villagers.'

Amelia had wondered if Archie and Big Davey's talk of the snow was all for effect, but now Gideon had worked with someone also convinced bad weather was on the way, and Jean was certain too. Amelia had made a point of watching a weather forecast earlier in the day. The smiling weatherman had just waved his hands around the map of Scotland and talked about plummeting temperatures, wind direction and cold fronts; but there was no word of snow blizzards.

With a cheery goodbye to Jean who was now wielding a pricing gun and making her way to the first box of Baxter's soup, Amelia grabbed her bags and left the shop. Although just after four o'clock in the afternoon it was already almost dark and the sky had a heavy grey denseness about it.

It was only when she got to the corner and an icy wind almost knocked her sideways that she realised she hadn't put on her hat. Setting her bags down she rummaged about in her deep pockets when she heard a voice from round the side of the shop. The unmistakable London accent of Ricky Varelli.

She surreptitiously peered round the corner to see him, still resplendent in his camel coat a couple of feet away. He didn't sound happy. Amelia drew back into the shadows, pulling on her hat very slowly as she listened in.

'Of *course* I'm not happy!' he said exasperated. 'Trust me, this is the last thing I wanted to happen! No, I'm not backing out at all! ... We stick with the plan ... don't worry about that, I'll work out something ... We need to sit tight and wait ... No, no one will catch us if we're careful ... We'll remove that problem. Hopefully permanently...'

That sounded rather damning Amelia thought as she strained to hear more, but Ricky's voice got fainter. She glanced back round and saw him walking away, his phone still attached to his ear as he gesticulated angrily with his other hand, pacing the pavement. Short of going nearer, Amelia knew she wouldn't able to hear any more. She crossed the road, musing over his conversation, wondering who'd he'd been talking to, and what problem did he want removed and quite what did 'permanently' entail?

Back at Stone Manor the betrothed couple had just driven up as Amelia returned. Greeting them, Amelia now understood that when they'd booked and paid for all their guests to stay for the days leading up to, and then beyond the wedding, and told her money was no object, they really did mean it.

Carlo Todero oozed wealth, from his bright green Lamborghini parked outside to his designer jeans and tailored shirt. As he shook Amelia's hand warmly, she caught a glimpse of his Patek Philippe watch. Carlo was completely bald, well-tanned, well-toned and utterly charming as he greeted Amelia effusively. He was also at least double the age of his fiancée, Lucy.

Lucy, in her mid-twenties, was undeniably a beauty, with long wavy dark brown hair and stunning blue eyes. She had an enviably slim body which she was showing off in a tight bandeau style dress. From the vertiginous heels she was sporting, Amelia guessed she hadn't been the one driving the sports car. It also appeared that she was glued to Carlo's side.

'This is so romantic!' she said breathlessly, looking around her in delight. 'I can't wait to look everywhere! I loved the documentary! I was addicted to it! The hidden treasure and the folly and all the romances going on. I really *did* love it!' her wide eyes sparkled with sincerity.

Carlo chuckled benevolently. 'She did! And when we found out my favourite author also lived here, we couldn't imagine having our wedding anywhere else.'

'Oh, are you a fan of Jack's books?' Amelia asked.

Lucy giggled and clutched Carlo's arm protectively. 'He's *such* a fan! Carly follows Jack's blog ob*sess*ively!'

Amelia smiled. Since coming clean that he was the writer behind the nom de plume Denholm Armitage, the writer of the quintessentially British Detective Grayson series, Jack's agent had really cashed in on it, hence the book signings tour and blog. Despite Jack grumbling that writing the blog made him feel he was returning to his angst-driven teenage years when he'd kept a journal, he'd dutifully kept it up, especially when he'd been on his book tour. Amelia made a mental note to tell Jack it was clearly working and people were engaging with it.

Still holding Carlo's hand, Lucy pulled away to try and see into all the rooms. 'Oh, the drawing room is so pretty! What an inviting fire. Now, where's the billiards room?'

'It's just down there, the other side of the staircase.'

'Ooh, and that must be the bar,' Lucy said.

As if on cue, Craig came out of it to go into the kitchen. He glanced up at the reception desk momentarily as Lucy squealed. 'And this must be the barman! Oh, this is all so perfect! It's all going to be perfect.' She turned and buried her face into Carlo's chest, clearly overcome with emotion. Craig stood there for a moment as if unsure what to do then hurried off into the kitchens.

'Now then, *mia cara*,' Carlo said to Lucy. 'I have in mind we get into a lovely warm bubble bath together before dinner.'

Lucy giggled and snuggled in closer.

Amelia handed them two keys. 'You have the Christie Suite and the Vine room next door for your wedding preparations if you want to keep the tradition of the groom not seeing the bride from the night before.'

'Oh, we do,' Lucy said with a gasp, eyes wide. 'We don't want *any*thing to jinx our big day, do we, Carly.'

'We certainly don't,' he said before nimbly chasing her up the stairs, to her obvious delight.

Hearing Lucy Carvalho's giggling shrieks fade as the door to their suite closed, Amelia turned her attention to the reception desk and a Post-it note with her name at the top, just as James appeared through the entrance with a couple of cases. Amelia had no idea where the bags had fitted as Carlo's car didn't look as if it had much luggage space.

'Ah, yes, that guy called earlier,' James indicated the note Amelia was holding. 'It was a dreadful line. His name was Benedict, but I didn't catch his surname.'

'Did he want a room?'

'Nope, he just wanted to talk to you, wouldn't say why. We got cut off. I was about to call 1471 to check the number he called from, when the florist called.'

'And?' Amelia held her breath.

'Four dozen red roses will be delivered in plenty of time for the wedding.'

Amelia felt giddy with relief. Maybe everything would work out well for the wedding after all. She stared at the Post-it note and the name. She couldn't think of a Benedict. She knew a Ben, short for Beniamino, the director of the Stone Manor documentary, but he had her mobile number and wouldn't call the main reception if he wanted to talk to her. She crumpled up the little green square and threw it in the bin figuring he would call back if it was important.

CHAPTER 3

Lorcan added a few final brushstrokes and took a step back. His highly critical eye swept over the painting. It was good. But he knew it would be. He was not being big headed; it was why he'd been selected to paint it.

Since receiving the phone call in November, Lorcan had done nothing but work on this painting. All thoughts of his own work and any other commissions were firmly placed on the back seat. He'd still kept up his teaching commitments and working on the Glencarlach Art Exhibition, but the moments he wasn't focusing on those, he lived and breathed the piece that sat majestically on the easel in front of him in his studio.

He sat up on the work surface behind him and opened the bottle of red wine he'd selected to celebrate his final brush stroke. Of course it was Italian, a Chianti Classico. He carefully peeled off the foil and twisted the opener into the cork and with a few turns and a flick of the waiter's friend, Lorcan deftly removed it and poured a large glass of the dark red wine with a satisfying glugging sound.

He sat for a moment, nursing the glass, enjoying the dark

cherry aromas. The wine was possibly a little on the cold side, but he'd had it with him in his studio for the entire day, waiting for this moment, and the studio was chilly. He'd been so intent on his painting he'd forgotten to switch the heating back on when it automatically switched off at five.

He checked his watch. It was now half past nine. His stomach gave a cry of hunger, also recognising the time and flagging up that he'd not eaten anything for hours. Lorcan pushed himself off his worktop and took one last look at the painting. He still had the final layer of varnish to apply, but that was for tomorrow. The hard work was now done.

Lifting up the bottle and carrying it and his glass, he turned off all the lights on his way out the studio, closing the door behind him, hurrying over to the main house, shivering against the icy wind. His home was thankfully toasty warm. He looked through his fridge to see what he could forage. He had pancetta, parmesan and eggs. Spaghetti carbonara would go down a treat with the red wine, he thought cheerfully as he took the ingredients out the fridge and grabbed the tall storage jar of pasta.

Getting out the heavy based frying pan and popping it on the hot plate, he dropped in a knob of butter and a dash of olive oil, and watched as they melted and amalgamated, spreading over the surface. He tipped in the pancetta and watched as the little cubes heated up, rendering fat. Leaving them to sizzle gently, Lorcan filled up the kettle and while he was waiting for the water to boil, took his phone from his pocket and scrolled down his contacts list to the number he needed.

A text would suffice. He sent, 'It's done,' then switched his phone off, turning his attention back to his dinner.

As he separated the eggs Lorcan knew that now he'd finished the painting he was in a tricky predicament. Without this all-consuming task to deal with he now had plenty of free time on his hands. And just a couple of days ago he'd been looking forward to filling his time with Netflix and evenings in the Whistling Haggis. But with the bombshell news he'd received the day before, Lorcan had a horrible feeling he had nothing to properly distract himself from thinking about *her*.

CHAPTER 4

20TH DECEMBER

Amelia arrived early to work the next morning and found Lorcan's Jeep parked up at the hotel's entrance. He was leaning against the driver's door, arms folded across his chest, staring into the distance, seemingly lost in thought.

'Morning!' Amelia greeted him cheerily as she got level with him, and he jumped at her interruption.

'Hi, morning! Sorry, I was miles away there!' He pushed himself off his door. 'I thought I'd come get the rest of the paintings.'

'Yes! Come on in and I'll get you a coffee. You should have gone inside rather than wait out here.' Lorcan looked frozen and Amelia wondered how long he'd been standing there.

He followed Amelia round to the back of the hotel, his big boots crunching noisily over the gravel. She took him in through the back door and into one of the storage rooms. There, propped up against the wall were a couple of dozen assorted paintings in a variety of frames.

On moving into Stone Manor, Amelia had inherited a strange selection of paintings. There was a rogue's gallery of the previous inhabitants' portraits lining the walls, which she liked as she could put a face beside the historical stories, even if all the previous owners looked a little on the dour side. On renovating the house, Amelia had kept up the best of the paintings and taken away the rest, hoping to eventually cover up all the spare wall space with art more to her taste.

'Everything here is fair game?'

Amelia nodded. 'You can have them all, and if you don't use them for the exhibition you can have them for the frames or the canvases. I really don't want them,' she said, screwing up her face as Lorcan picked up a small oil painting of a dead pheasant hanging on a hook waiting to be plucked and cooked for dinner.

'But, I do have a favour to ask,' Amelia said. 'You know Jack's been on his book tour? There's a promotional poster that all the authors signed and I thought it would be nice to get it framed,' Amelia said as she retrieved a large poster tube and carefully removed the contents. With Lorcan's help she unrolled the poster.

Lorcan nodded appreciatively. 'That's a really nice memento. Ooh, he's in illustrious company, isn't he,' Lorcan noted as he read the other bestselling authors' signatures.

'It's a little extra for his Christmas, but thought, if you didn't mind, would you be able to frame it first?'

'Of course, he's going to love it.'

Just then, James poked his head round the door. 'Mr Varelli just called down. He wants to know if a parcel arrived for him. I've not seen anything.'

Amelia shook her head. 'There's nothing.'

'He's off to call Amazon and go to the post office to double check.'

'We'll be sure to keep a look out for it, thanks, James.'

'Oh, and Toby said there's a bacon and fried egg sandwich waiting for you; you too, Lorcan,' James said as he left.

'Great! Thanks.' Amelia turned to Lorcan. 'Make sure you get some breakfast and someone can help you load this lot into your Jeep, when you're ready.'

As she left, Lorcan looked a little distracted, pulling on his goatee absent-mindedly.

With the breakfast service over, a serene calm had descended on the kitchen, with everyone busy clearing up and none of the shouting out of orders and bustling around. Even when they didn't have many guests staying, there were always locals who liked to pop in for a stomach-bolstering cooked breakfast of smoked kippers, locally sourced sausages and bacon, or eggs Benedict, courtesy of the laying hens they had on the land they kept reserved for the hotel's produce.

Amelia found Toby sitting at the long table, coffee in hand, poring over a recipe book. He slid over a plate with a roll, stuffed full of bacon, with just a tantalising hint of golden yolk visible. Amelia pounced on it hungrily.

'Busy day planned?' Toby asked.

Amelia nodded; her mouth too full to speak. She chewed and swallowed before answering. 'We've got the rest of the wedding party arriving. And Betty is checking in today too. Evangelina Wilde booked another room for her friend last night; she'll be here in a couple of days' time.'

'Great. I've upped all the local orders. Everyone's talking about the weather. I figure it won't hurt to have a bit extra in the freezer.'

When setting up Stone Manor Hotel, Toby was adamant that they'd source local produce and grow their own where possible. As well as having hens roaming around, they had also set up many poly-tunnels which produced an abundance of herbs and seasonal vegetables. Toby had also been talking about keeping some goats and going on a cheesemaking course. Inspired by Raymond Blanc's kitchen garden at Le Manoir, Toby saw no reason that Stone Manor couldn't emulate his culinary hero's Michelin award-winning hotel, albeit on a much smaller scale.

'Another bonus of having our main suppliers local is that even if the snow does come, we can still get the produce back by sledge,' Amelia suggested, wiping a large dollop of egg and brown sauce from her chin.

'Imagine bringing home a haunch of venison like that!' Toby laughed. 'It appeals to the latent hunter gatherer in me!' He drained his coffee. 'Right, I need to get on. Just to warn you, Gideon's on the prowl. He wants to help out. Although I think he's just a bit bored and is hanging out so he can befriend Evangelina. He could always help you get the rooms ready.'

'Or he could be your sous chef?' Amelia suggested back.

'Heavens no!' Toby looked appalled at the thought. 'I suppose I could send him off to count the napkins?' he said uncertainly. With the hotel busy and Toby working a lot, they approached dealing with Gideon in the same way one would try to entertain and distract a toddler.

'Although I may *have* to get him to help with the service as we've got a couple of folk down with a nasty cold that's been doing the rounds. I stuck a note out at the front desk.'

'I'll re-do the rota,' Amelia said as she mopped up the last of the egg yolk with the roll and popped it into her mouth.

Leaving Toby in the kitchen, Amelia headed out to have a final inspection of the rooms. Being a boutique hotel there were only fifteen rooms, and each was named after one of Amelia's favourite crime and mystery writers.

The very first room, where Carlo and Lucy were staying, was the Christie Suite, named after Agatha Christie. It was Amelia's love of Agatha Christie which had started off her journey into finding the hidden ruby of Stone Manor. On inheriting the house Amelia had picked her best loved book from the library – *Murder on the Orient Express* – and there she discovered the first clue to the mystery, a letter, hinting at the mysteries and secrets of the old house. When moving into Stone Manor at first, this had been the bedroom Amelia had stayed in, where she'd also found an old diary hidden in one of the secret compartments in the wood-panelling. The original features of the room were in such good condition it needed little more than some TLC to get it back to its full glory.

Amelia had chosen rich damask fabrics and antique furniture to give the impression of being aboard one of the famous Orient Express carriages. There were other little nods to the undisputed Queen of Crime: an old-fashioned typewriter in the corner, a watercolour of Christie's house, Greenway, and a bookshelf full of the author's books. All the other rooms had décor inspired by the author they were named after as well as having a collection of that author's works close at hand to read.

Amelia was just leaving the Rendell Suite after checking the miniature toiletries had been replenished when Gideon caught up with her, his arms full of towels.

'I was told you needed these.'

'Ah, yes, for Nisha Khatri.' Amelia let them both into the Highsmith Room and went to open the window slightly to give it one last airing before occupancy and as she did she saw Ricky marching round to the front of the hotel from the guest car park, followed by Evangelina.

'He seems an odious little man, doesn't he?' Gideon said, dumping the towels on the bed. He came and stood beside her, arms folded, leaning against the window frame as they looked down, watching as Ricky paused to take a phone call.

'I haven't really had much to do with him,' Amelia said, as neutrally as possible.

'Oh, darling, don't go all professional and diplomatic on me!' Gideon huffed petulantly, flicking through the copy of *The Talented Mr Ripley* before returning it to the bedside table. 'I much prefer it when you're indiscreet and judgemental!'

'Hmm, well, I only met him briefly yesterday but I didn't exactly get a warm fuzzy feeling from him and I overheard him have a strange phone call.' She gave him a very quick rundown on what she'd heard Ricky say, then picked up the towels.

Towels laid out and en suite checked, Amelia let them back out the room and they headed downstairs.

'Evangelina seems so lovely and warm, far too good for that oily little man,' Gideon said as he followed her into the bar area.

'Shhh!'

'Oh, don't worry, she had her workout gear on when I came up the stairs to find you. She'll no doubt be heading to the gym. She looks like a cross-trainer kind of a woman, don't you think?'

Not having given one moment's thought to what Evangelina's preferred exercise would be, Amelia ignored Gideon and went behind the bar and ducked down to rifle through the cupboards.

Gideon hunkered down beside her. 'What are we looking for?'

'Cocktail accessories. We've got a Christmas group booking tonight and they've requested a cocktail theme and I know I have a stash of straws that fan out to be flamingos and parrots here somewhere.'

'Classy!'

She thrust a packet of cocktail umbrellas at him then reached further in, past all the cocktail shakers and jiggers while Gideon opened the pack and thrust one jauntily behind his ear.

Just then the door opened and Amelia heard Evangelina's husky voice say, 'Quick, close the door, I don't think anyone saw us!'

CHAPTER 5

Amelia was about to stand up to announce their presence but Gideon put a hand on her arm to restrain her and silently brought his index finger to his lips.

'Sorry to drag you in here like this. I saw you last night when I was checking in...'

'I heard you were staying here,' a familiar Irish accent spoke, and Amelia stared at Gideon in astonishment.

'Lorcan?' Gideon mouthed. Amelia nodded.

'Yes, I didn't know you lived around here,' Evangelina said. 'Ricky's cousin, Carlo, is getting married...' Evangelina trailed off.

There were a couple of beats silence then both started talking at once.

'How are you–'

'How have you been–'

Then an uneasy laugh from them both.

More silence hung in the air as Gideon looked at Amelia and mouthed, 'What the hell?'

'Look, I hope this won't be weird. You and me both here,'

Lorcan said eventually. 'Does Ricky know…?' Lorcan let the rest of the sentence hang in the air.

'No,' Evangelina said, 'he has no idea.'

'Right. Okay.'

'I really just wanted to say hello in case we bump into each other, and if we do, it'll be fine.' She gave a slightly nervous laugh.

'Ah, right. Yup. Okay. I'll maybe see you around.'

'Lorcan, you look well, the country air must suit you.'

'Yeah, it does. You look well too.' He laughed. 'What I mean is, you look beautiful. But then, you always have.'

'Lorcan, can we meet up? To talk?'

'Reminisce?'

'Something like that.'

There was another lengthy silence before Lorcan said, 'Yeah, that would be good.'

'Great, here's my number.'

Amelia heard the door open.

'It's all clear, give me a ten-second head start,' Lorcan said. A moment or two later the door closed.

Amelia and Gideon gave it a few more seconds before slowly looking over the top of the bar. The room was empty.

'I wonder what that was all about?' Gideon said.

'Clearly they know each other. I feel a bit bad about eavesdropping on them.'

'Oh, don't! Come one, you must admit, your spider senses are tingling!'

'I'll have you know I'm a professional hotelier!'

Gideon narrowed his golden tiger eyes. 'Don't give me that. I tell you what though, I'm making dammed sure I'm going to be lurking around here more to see what goes down between the two of them!'

For the rest of the morning Gideon hung around Amelia at the reception desk, clearly desperate to discover more gossip-worthy information, and to discuss the Ricky Varelli phone call Amelia had eavesdropped on.

Amelia was also keen to talk about it, but a bustling hotel wasn't the place to do it, especially when she had staff shortages to accommodate.

Ripping up the staff rota, she started again hoping some of the casual staff wouldn't mind earning a little extra by working overtime. She knew James would help out and Wee Davey would too.

Craig Cameron was also a godsend. He'd applied for a job with them at the end of September, being upfront that he only wanted to stay for three months before moving on. He said he only ever stayed that long in a job, keen to travel as much of the world as possible in his camper van.

This approach had certainly made for an interesting CV and he had worked behind the bar in some very prestigious hotels.

In a couple of weeks he would be gone and Amelia would be sad to see him go as he was an excellent mixologist as well as a valued member of the team, who didn't mind mucking in with anything that was needed of him. Amelia knew he'd be fine with taking on an extra hour or two.

She'd offered Craig a promotion and extra money if he'd stay but he was adamant he was moving on, citing France as his next stop. At least he'd be a few degrees warmer there. Amelia worried about him being warm enough in his camper van in the depths of a Highland winter. She'd offered him one of the rooms in the hotel but he'd laughed and said he'd survived much colder when he'd travelled through Scandinavia and had worked in one of the Ice Hotels. He assured her he was happy in his cosy little van, in the top field of a neighbouring farm which rented out camping spots in summer, with electrical points and fresh water connections. Amelia really did hope it was cosy as she didn't think a dose of hypothermia would look very good for her staff welfare record.

With Gideon almost bursting from the desire to gossip, Amelia finished the rota, hoping all other staff would remain hale and hearty or she really would have to rely on using Gideon as backup. Gideon, who was finally contenting himself with reorganising the decorations on the Christmas tree to be more aesthetically pleasing, as seasonal tunes wafted in from the bar lounge.

'Oh my! Well, isn't this just *beau*tiful!' The loud American voice boomed from the front door, breaking the harmonious stillness.

Everyone in reception looked up to see a vision in a scarlet trouser suit and long white fur coat framed in the doorway. With one hand on her hip, the other flicked out the long, jet-black hair which streamed down past her shoulders in a silky curtain. A pair of enormous dark glasses hid most of the woman's face, apart from her lips which were the same shade as her trouser suit. Waiting for a suitable amount of time to ensure everyone's attention, the woman sashayed towards the reception desk.

'And I thought I knew how to do an entrance!' Gideon said, impressed, dropping the piece of tinsel he'd been holding.

'This is all just so *quaint*! Isn't it, Terry? Terry?' She turned towards the door just as a man laden down with cases, bags and a hat box almost fell through the door.

'Let me help you with those, sir!' James said, hurrying over, steering him away from a large decorative vase holding an assortment of umbrellas.

'And you...' Amelia looked down at her list of names due to be checking in.

'Vanessa de Courtney,' Gideon sighed from beside her.

The woman practically preened. 'Oh, are you a fan?'

'You were spellbinding in *Cat on a Hot Tin Roof* on Broadway and your Lady MacBeth at the Globe has stayed with me,' Gideon pressed his hand to his heart.

She lowered her glasses slightly and peered at him more closely. 'I seem to be in equally exalted company, Gideon Fey! Are you staying here too?'

'Well, I'm more flitting in and out to bestow some glamour and sarcasm.'

She gave a delighted laugh. 'Well, this trip has suddenly gotten even more interesting! We need to catch up and talk shop over some cocktails.' She paused. 'Oh, wait, you don't drink now, do you?'

Gideon leaned in. 'Don't worry, darling, sobriety hasn't dampened my spirit!'

While this interchange went on, Amelia was frantically scanning the booking system for a V de Courtney but nothing was there, no matter how interesting or creative the taking down of the surname could be.

'It'll be under my name. Terence Maxwell. We're Mr and Mrs Maxwell.' Mr Maxwell was as softly spoken as his wife was loud.

'Ah yes, part of the wedding party. And it's two rooms,' Amelia checked.

'Yes, we don't pack very lightly,' Mr Maxwell said apologetically.

'Here is your suite key, the Conan Doyle and here's the one for next door, Vargas…'

Mrs Maxwell plucked the tasselled key fob from Amelia's hands. 'And this is definitely the double right next door?'

'Yes.'

'The one that's north facing?'

'Yes.'

'Lovely, I have my watercolours with me, I find art helps me relax.'

'For your information, there is an adjoining room to your extra room, but that has been booked out specifically and the Vargas was the only double next to your suite that was north facing,' Amelia explained. 'Obviously the rooms are locked on both sides so there is no way anyone could access your room without your consent.'

'Perfect!' With a gracious smile to Amelia and a little wave to Gideon, Mrs Maxwell turned and made her way upstairs, hollering, 'Bring up my handbag, Terry,' over her shoulder to her husband who was still trying to juggle the luggage into a more easily carried configuration.

'Don't worry, Mr Maxwell, someone will take your bags upstairs for you.'

'Thank you, I... um, I'm afraid there are more in the car.'

'Don't worry, we'll park your car around the back and fetch them too.'

'Super, thanks.' He turned and watched his wife reach the top of the stairs and wander along the gallery landing, stopping to exclaim in delight at the paintings.

'Is she a keen artist?' Amelia asked.

'Oh well, she likes to dabble,' he said, then taking the key for the suite, hurried up the stairs after his wife, taking her oversized Prada tote bag with him.

Gideon tapped the side of his nose. 'North facing for art, my arse. It'll be for her make-up.'

'Really?' James asked, agog at this snippet.

'Oh totally!' Gideon said, warming up to some gossip. 'I mean, she's a beautiful woman, very well preserved, but let's face it, her biogs don't add up mathematically! If they did, she'd have been making her debut on Broadway aged four! Any press release now just fudges her early years. I guess she must be mid-fifties now.'

'That's hardly ancient,' James said.

'It's practically Methuselah for a female in our profession!'

'So, what's with the marriage then, it seems a bit of an odd pairing,' James asked, clearly loving the insider information.

'Shhh!' Amelia warned, but only half-heartedly as she too wanted to know the gossip.

Gideon draped himself over the desk, and had a surreptitious look around, revelling in being able to spill the beans. 'Word is she was wild in her twenties and thirties. Her after-show parties were legendary. Then the usual happened, moth getting too close to the flame, yada-yada-yada, had to change her ways. Rumours of multiple affairs with producers, actors, directors; she liked to keep her options open.

'It all got a little heated with one high-profile producer when his wife found out and her management decided she should move in different circles, hence the move to the UK and conquering the West End and doing far worthier projects.

'She met the Queen at some variety thing and that then opened doors to the upper echelons, bumping shoulders with the aristocracy and then she met her very own viscount. It was like a discount version of the Prince and the Showgirl! That man is no Larry Olivier! Anyway, she married him and after a sell-out performance at the old Vic, decided to retire from the stage and reinvent herself as an agent. A very successful one I might add.'

'Terence Maxwell is a, a…?' Not being very up on peerage ranks, Amelia had no idea what Terence Maxwell's title should be.

'Lord. They are Lord and Lady Maxwell.'

'He seems so…'

'Weak-willed, trodden on and under the thumb?'

'I was going to say "normal"!' Amelia said, although she could now place slightly better why Vanessa was with someone as seemingly ordinary as Terence. Titles went a long way.

'Anyway! Turns out he doesn't like using his title unless it's for official things. Drives her mad as she'd use it all the time if she could. He's fabulously wealthy and owns acres of land that he likes to tinker about on. Into the whole organic scene, keeps bees and makes honey, that sort of thing.'

'How do you know so much about them?' Amelia asked in wonderment.

'I'm just a walking Debrett's, poppet!'

'Well, lord or not, he needs the rest of his luggage, I'll go park the car,' James said picking up the key Terence had left on the desk and heading out the door.

'But now, tell me who is the guest requesting the Simenon Room? Has he been before?' Gideon asked as he removed one of the Post-it notes Amelia had stuck on the computer screen and read it.

She took it off him and stuck it back where it had been.

'Nope, I don't have him as a returning guest.'

'Ooh,' Gideon's curiosity was whetted and he turned to give her his full attention. 'Is he a fan of Inspector Maigret? I mean, it's a nice room but they're all equally as nice.' He looked up at the bedrooms and counted along. 'Ooh, it's the eighth room along isn't it? Is he Chinese? It's a very auspicious number over there, means success and money, those kinds of things.'

'It's a Mr Griffin,' Amelia said, looking up the booking.

'Hmm, doesn't sound Chinese.'

'Maybe he just likes the number eight. Or maybe he also likes a north-facing room to paint in, or do *his* make-up in,' Amelia added lightly, although she had also wondered why he'd specified having that room.

'I wonder if he's just very suspicious and has a thing about the number eight. You should have some ladders up at the front door, see if he can come in! What else can you do? Break a mirror in front of him, see how he reacts?'

'The guests aren't here for your entertainment, you know.'

'I have to get my kicks somehow, darling!' Gideon peered over her shoulder as Amelia scanned though the bookings. 'When's he due?'

'Well, that's the thing. He's been a bit vague about it. He's had the room booked since yesterday but isn't sure when he'll get here.'

'How curious!' Gideon's eyes widened. 'You don't think it's because of the, you know...' he mouthed, 'secret passage!'

'I did wonder, but how would he know?'

Part of Stone Manor's mystery was that it was home to numerous priest holes and secret passageways which Amelia had unearthed through a combination of interpreting the clues she read in the old diary and plain, dumb luck. When undertaking the renovations and decorating she'd kept as many of these features as possible and made sure very few people knew about them. The Simenon Room did have a passage that went from behind the fireplace to the cellar but that exit was always locked.

Amelia sighed. 'Mr Griffin is probably just an overworked man who wants to get away for Christmas as soon as he can and possibly just likes Maigret novels! We often get requests for the Christie Room.'

Gideon narrowed his eyes. 'Yes, but that's because it's the grand suite with a four-poster bed in it. Come on now, are you telling me your mystery senses aren't tingling?'

'Well... a bit, but I'm also the owner of Stone Manor Hotel so have to remain discreet to all my guests' needs!'

'That sounds a lovely line to use for your marketing! And it's a good thing I'm here. I suspect everyone of having an ulterior motive. You're just far too trusting of people's innocence!'

Just then James reappeared with another assortment of luggage. 'They've packed a hell of a lot of clothes even if they are staying for a fortnight!' he said, struggling under the weight.

'Stage divas are never renowned for their light packing. Oh, is it snowing?' Gideon asked.

'Aye,' James brushed a few large flakes from his shoulders, 'and it's starting to lie.'

'Imagine if we get snowed in!' Gideon said gleefully.

Amelia looked towards the glass entrance doors and saw that the drive and grass now had an icing powder covering of snow. 'I'd like it a whole lot more once Jack gets home.'

Gideon patted her hand. 'Don't worry, poppet, if there's anything I'm sure of it's that Captain America will find a way through to you in any weather, even if he has to steal and drive a snow plough himself.'

CHAPTER 6

With all the checked-in guests settled in the bar for a light lunch, Amelia had just handed out the menus and was helping Craig behind the bar with the drinks orders when James hurried through from reception.

'It's that man who called yesterday. The one that got cut off. He's called back and wants to speak to you.'

'Benedict?'

'Yes, a Benedict Geissler.'

She turned to Craig beside her who was pouring champagne into flutes. 'I'll be back in a minute, but I've got to take this call. Will you be okay?'

'Don't worry,' he said, 'I've got this.'

In reception, Amelia picked up the phone. 'Hello, this is Amelia Adams.'

'Hello, Amelia. My name is Benedict Geissler and I need to speak with you about a matter most urgent.' The voice was very clipped with a slight accent.

'Of course. Would you like to book a room?'

'No. I need to speak to you about a very discreet matter.'

'Well, I'm here at the hotel all–'

'No.' He cut in. 'I cannot meet you at the hotel. Somewhere quiet. Where we won't be seen.'

Amelia pulled a slight face at the phone. He was certainly being mysterious but her curiosity made her play along. 'Do you know where the folly is? It's on our property but out of th–'

'I will find it.'

'Okay.' She glanced up at the clock. 'Is three o'clock okay?' She thought that would give her time to help with the lunches and clear some other jobs she needed to do.

He gave a clipped confirmation that three was suitable.

'Can I have your number, just in case I'm held up?' Amelia asked, knowing she still had the last of the wedding party to arrive as well as Hamish's elderly great aunt.

Benedict Geissler rhymed it off for her and she scribbled it down under his name on the top of her pad. 'Okay, I'll see you...' but she found herself speaking into a dialling tone as he'd already hung up.

As the guests disbanded after their lunch, Lucy caught up with Amelia at the reception desk.

'Miss Carvalho! How can I help you?'

'Well, please call me Lucy for a start, although you can call me Mrs Todero in a few days' time,' she said then gave a happy giggle. 'I just wanted to talk to you about a little hen party.' She glanced over her shoulder and then leant over the reception desk. 'I wasn't sure if Carlo had suggested something or not.'

'He didn't mention anything,' Amelia said warily. She'd never even brought it up assuming like so many engaged couples, the hen- and stag-dos would have been a month or so earlier, in some European city, giving everyone enough time to recover from three or four days of solid drinking.

'Oh, don't worry, I don't want anything too fancy. I know Carlo will like something fairly sedate for his stag with the boys, but I'd like to go a little bit wilder!' She gave Amelia a hopeful smile.

Amelia hated to break the news, but Glencarlach didn't have a nightclub or anything that could be remotely described as a wild evening.

'With the wedding planned for Boxing Day, I would imagine that...'

'Don't worry, I know you'll need a little time to get something organised but the twenty-third or even Christmas Eve would be fine.' Lucy clapped her hands. 'You have a lovely spa here, maybe we could start with some pampering and then a bar? Somewhere a little more rough and ready than this beautiful hotel. There's the one in the village, isn't there?'

'The Whistling Haggis? Yes, um...' Amelia didn't know how Davey would feel to hear his lovely village pub described as 'rough and ready'! 'Leave it with me,' Amelia said.

'I'd love to be able to have it planned soon.'

'Of course, I'll call Sally, our beauty therapist and then I'll phone Davey and see what we can come up with.'

'Thank you.' Lucy grinned at her.

When Lucy didn't move away from the reception desk it dawned on Amelia that the bride-to-be wanted it sorted then and there. 'Give me a moment,' Amelia said as she darted into the back office to make some calls, starting with Sally.

A few minutes later, Amelia returned and found Lucy, now settled in one of the large comfy sofas in the drawing room, sipping a glass of champagne.

'We have an afternoon's spa booked for you and the other ladies in the party for the twenty-third, followed by an evening of entertainment at the Whistling Haggis.' Sally had instantly reassured Amelia in her lovely West Country buttery tones that she'd plan a great time for them. After Big Davey had guffawed loudly at being in charge of a hen-do, he said he'd get his thinking cap on and come up with a plan but Amelia wasn't to worry as they'd have a night to remember. Amelia was slightly more reassured by Sally's response but being just three days away, she realised she'd have to trust Big Davey too. Clearly she'd need to up the ante with the hen and stag element of the wedding package in the event of other guests leaving it until the last minute!

Lucy jumped up and squealed. 'Thank you so much! I'm going to go and tell Carly the good news.' As Lucy skipped away, Amelia thought it would also be prudent to check in with the groom as soon as possible in case he wanted something more involved than a sedate afternoon drinking whisky in the bar.

As the afternoon crept on, Amelia managed to get through her most urgent jobs despite being held back by James enquiring about an invoice, Toby who wanted to run a menu change by her and then just as she was heading out the door, Craig called her back asking if she could talk him through the amounts of champagne in the cellar so he knew what was allocated specifically for Christmas Day and the wedding.

Finally, at one minute before three, Amelia grabbed her coat to go and meet the mysterious Benedict Geissler. Before leaving she checked the pad with his details on it and keyed his number into her phone just in case he hadn't been able to find the folly.

Despite the intrigue, Amelia knew it could also be slightly unwise to meet a strange man in an out-of-the-way place so she also pocketed a rape alarm and a travel-sized body spray that would certainly halt him if sprayed in his eyes. And, of course she had her trusty penknife in her pocket in case things got really serious. With a quick cheerio to James, she ran out the door and across the gardens to the clump of trees where there lay a rather muddy and steep short cut. Clambering up the incline, Amelia managed to make it to the top for just a few minutes past the arranged meeting time. Catching her breath at the top, she circled the large round tower and saw that he was already sitting on the little stone bench, looking out at the amazing views.

'Hello, I'm so sorry I'm a bit late,' she said as she rounded the bench and sat beside him. 'I'm Ame...' she looked at him and gasped. His face was pale and sweaty, and he was gasping for breath. The takeaway cup of coffee he'd been drinking slipped from his grasp as he clutched at his chest.

'Let me call for help.'

But he shook his head, his face screwing up in pain, his thin little moustache twitching as he struggled to breathe.

He grabbed Amelia's arm with a vice like grip, taking her aback at his strength as he looked a fairly elderly gentleman. He drew Amelia towards him. 'The... girl,' he gasped.

'Wait, please let me get help!' Amelia took her phone out her pocket but Benedict Geissler knocked it out of her hand.

'The girl...' he repeated, staring at her with wide eyes as he clutched his chest and throat.

'The girl? What girl?'

'The...girl...and...I...' he gasped again, then with one last 'ohhhhhhhhhhh', he released the grip on her arm and pushed a piece of paper at her. Amelia recognised it. It was an article that had run a few months previously in a national paper that advertised the hotel. There was a picture of Amelia at the reception desk. She had a copy of the same article framed in the bar area. At the top of the cut-out, someone had written the date *Here! 26th December* and *reunited* in biro. He jabbed a finger at the article and struggled to gasp, 'Miss...*nnnng*...' he gasped. 'Pain...' he gave a strange, strangled noise as the piece of paper fluttered to the ground.

'Mr Geissler?' Amelia said quietly, waiting for another strangled gasp. 'Mr Geissler,' she repeated more loudly with rising panic, then she realised the man on the bench beside her wasn't going to say anything else ever again.

He was dead.

CHAPTER 7

Two hours later, Amelia got back to Stone Manor, numb with cold and from what had just happened. After calling an ambulance Amelia had tried to resuscitate Benedict Geissler but despite her best efforts she soon realised it was a futile exercise

She also called Constable Ray Williams, the local police officer, as she had no idea what else to do. By the time the ambulance, then Ray, reached her, Amelia had moved away from the bench and was standing leaning against the folly, her brief interchange with Benedict Geissler replaying over and over in her head. As the paramedics did their job, Ray kindly put a blanket over her shoulders to stop her shivering.

'And you've never seen him before?'

'Nope. Never.'

'And you have no idea why he wanted to meet you?'

Amelia shook her head again. 'I thought he wanted to book a room but then he said it wasn't about that. He said he needed to talk to me about something else. It was all very mysterious and I haven't a clue what he was trying to tell me. He kept talking about a girl. I think he was trying to tell me her name but didn't get beyond *"Miss"*.'

By the point she'd gone over everything for a third time, Toby had arrived. Constable Williams had thought it prudent Amelia had someone with her and had called him as soon as he'd arrived on the scene.

'This will be transferred over to CID at Inverness to investigate.'

'You think it's suspicious?' Toby asked.

'SOCO will have to process the area and the DI will want to question you again. But considering his age and that he was clutching his chest and struggling to breathe, and he was saying he was in pain, it could very well be a heart attack, especially in this cold weather. Maybe a shock to the system if, as you say, he had an accent and wasn't from these parts. 'You get your sister home now, Toby. I think a large dram is in order to help deal with any shock.'

'Don't worry, I'll look after her.'

'I'm not an invalid, you know,' Amelia had grumbled at her brother as they walked back to Stone Manor.

'I know, but let me at least look after you for the next forty minutes.'

'Half an hour,' Amelia conceded.

Now in the warmth of the kitchen Gideon made her a cup of tea and she felt a lot better.

'You're definitely coming with us to the Whistling Haggis tonight,' Gideon said. 'It'll stop you dwelling.'

'I am okay,' Amelia said for what felt like the hundredth time since getting back to Stone Manor. 'I'd never met the man before, it's just… odd. And sad.' She finished her tea and stood up. 'I'm going to head out front. From Carlo and Lucy's detailed itinerary, I believe that the last of their party will be arriving any minute. And can we keep this death under wraps? I know it'll probably end up going all round the village but I'd like it to stay as secret as possible. I'd rather not put off the guests.'

'Of course. I won't say a word to anyone,' Toby said as Gideon mimed zipping his mouth shut, locking it, then throwing away the key.

Out at the reception desk, James had just welcomed the new guests, Mr and Mrs King, as Carlo and Lucy had appeared out of the bar to welcome them.

'Dan!' Carlo said affectionately and gave the other middle-aged man a fond embrace as Lucy squealed, 'Alice' and enthusiastically hugged the other woman and talked animatedly about the plans for the hen-do.

'Hang on, hang on!' Carlo broke away from Dan King. 'Where's my beautiful goddaughter!'

'India!' Alice King called out.

A second later a rather sulky goth appeared from the drawing room. Wearing pale make-up and with heavily lined eyes, she was all in black, the only colour being her bright turquoise shoulder-length straight hair. Although trying hard to remain cool, she fought to keep a smile from her face as she said, 'Hi, Uncle Carlo.'

Then Amelia gave a little shiver.

Dan and Alice's daughter, although trying to look older than her years was probably only sixteen, which was still just a girl. And with her surname...

Was this who Benedict Geissler wanted to tell Amelia about? He'd said *Miss ...nnnng*. Had he been trying to say Miss *King*?

Was India, Miss King, *the girl*?

Amelia was still mulling this over a couple of hours later when she sank into one of the upholstered booths in the Whistling Haggis and took a grateful sip of the glass of whisky Toby had ordered for her.

'I thought you'd bailed on us!' Gideon complained as he helped himself to a salt and vinegar McCoy from Toby's packet. 'Mind you, no one would blame you after the Mr Geissler episode.'

'I'm okay, really. I just feel so sorry for the poor man and his family. Being out with you guys is a perfect distraction, as is work. I've been busy.'

'Have you seen much more of Lorcan today?' Gideon asked.

'Nope, just when you and I overheard him talking in the bar.'

'Ooh, do you think he'll be back tomorrow?'

Toby frowned in confusion at how excited Gideon seemed by Lorcan's whereabouts.

Amelia cleared her throat and changed the subject. 'We had a couple walk in with no reservation. They're over here from the States. Their accommodation fell through somewhere else and they'd read about Stone Manor and thought they'd see if we had a room free on the off-chance!'

Alaiya and DeShawn Johnson had seemed lovely and there was something about them that made Amelia wonder if they were on their honeymoon. 'I also had Betty to book in,' Amelia added. 'That took quite a while!'

'Ooh, Hamish's infamous great auntie from Skye!' Gideon said.

'The one that no one wanted staying with them. What's she like?' Toby asked.

Amelia laughed. 'She seems lovely. Definitely a little eccentric. I get the impression she was the one wanting to stay here as she finds a lot of her family rather dull! She's *very* chatty and wanted to know everything about the hotel.' Chatty was quite the understatement. The septuagenarian had kept up a non-stop commentary from the moment she walked through the front door. Betty managed to ask a constant stream of questions whilst commenting on the hotel; all without seemingly taking a breath.

She kept up this chatter all the way up to her room, then all the way back downstairs again, until the moment when Amelia's best friend, Sally, and her fiancé, Hamish, turned up to take her back to Hamish's farmhouse for a family dinner with all the other relations.

It was the first time Sally had met this side of Hamish's family and Amelia knew she'd been nervous, although Amelia couldn't for a moment think what the old aunt wouldn't like about Sally Bishop.

Warm and friendly, Sally had the loveliest sing-song West-Country accent and was one of the kindest people Amelia knew. Best friends from their days at boarding school, Amelia and Sally had seen each other through all the good times as well as the bumps from disastrous love lives and career lows.

When Amelia's godmother died, Sally had been there for her. As well as a shoulder to cry on, she'd helped Amelia turn her inherited house into Stone Manor Hotel. It had come at the perfect time for Sally, who had fallen out of love with her career.

Being a make-up artist had always sounded so glamorous to Amelia, especially when Sally flew out for a catalogue shoot in Hawaii or a horror film in Norway, but what first attracted Sally to the job started to put her off, when the excitement waned and the loneliness and transiency of hotel living began to grate.

On arriving in Glencarlach, Sally had segued from falling out of love with her career, to falling into love with Hamish, the burly, shy farmer. Sally had retrained in beauty therapy and now, as well as owning her own hairdressers in the village, was also the in-house Stone Manor beautician for guests wanting anything from seaweed wraps and facials to blow dries and manicures. She was also booked for Lucy's wedding make-up. Now after getting Amelia out of her recent bind, she could also add hen parties to her resumé.

'I'm sure Sally will win the family over with her usual ebullient charm,' Gideon said.

Toby smiled. 'Of course she will.' He sat back in his chair and looked between Amelia and Gideon. 'Right! So, who is going to break first and tell me what you two are up to? Gideon's been sitting like a meerkat, jumping to attention every time the door's opened waiting for you, and I kept catching *you,*' he pointed to Amelia, 'giving *him,*' he pointed to Gideon who looked suitably offended, 'pointed looks all day. Way before the Mr Geissler incident. So, spill.'

'We think something suspicious is going on,' Gideon said, crunching down on another crisp.

Amelia rolled her eyes. He could have held out a little longer, surely!

'It's probably nothing. It's just my imagination,' Amelia cut in, sensing her brother's disapproval.

'It probably is your imagination, Amelia. So, just leave whatever it is you think you've got suspicions about.'

'Will do.' Amelia smiled and took another sip of whisky. 'Now, are we going to have tonight's special on the board? I'm in the mood for one of their burgers!'

Toby, however, was no fool and was instantly suspicious of how quickly she'd agreed to drop the subject. 'At least tell me what it is that's aroused your suspicion,' he said wearily.

Gideon leaned forward against the table conspiratorially, moving his orange juice out of the way. 'It's all to do with Evangelina Wilde and that sly, murderous toad, Ricky Varelli.'

'We don't know for sure Ricky is a sly, murderous toad,' Amelia cautioned Gideon.

'But you practically heard him taking out a hit on someone?'

'What?' Toby said aghast as he looked from Gideon to Amelia. He then shook his head. 'What? Why would you think that? Ames, I love you dearly but you will try and find a drama out of a person washing their hands!'

'Especially if there's blood on them!' Amelia said, warming to her conclusion that what she overheard had sounded off.

Toby glanced over his shoulder but the nearest table was too far away to overhear their hushed tones and the general noise levels of the bar meant no one could easily eavesdrop on their conversation.

Amelia related what she'd heard.

'Now, that's suspicious!' Gideon interjected. He counted points off on his fingers. 'One, he has a plan. Two, it seems to have gone awry. Three, he's going to make sure no one catches him. Four, he's going to remove the problem. Five, it could be *permanent*!'

Toby groaned. 'One,' he held up his finger, 'he might be… might be… I don't know, planning on selling a car! Two, it's gone awry because someone didn't go through with buying it! Three, he's… he's maybe been caught doing something dodgy with road tax. Four, he's going to remove the problem by getting the right road tax. And five, he'll make sure it's permanent so this doesn't happen again.'

Amelia looked at Gideon and they both shook their head at Toby.

'I just get the feeling it wasn't as mundane as selling a motor,' Amelia said. She'd heard his tone and it wasn't the tone of a man obsessed with poor car dealership. 'And, Mr Geissler was clearly trying to tell me about a girl and we've got one staying with us at the moment *and* she's part of the wedding which is on the 26th, the day he had written at the top of the article about Stone Manor! That is *definitely* odd. And what if all these odd things are connected?'

Toby ran his hand through his quiff in despair. 'Oh, Ames, last time you got a feeling something was off and went poking about you were attacked by a psychopath, Gideon got shot and Stone Manor could have burned to the ground.'

'But if I hadn't gone poking about, maybe much worse could have happened,' Amelia said in her defence. It wasn't as if she'd gone looking for trouble. She just seemed to stumble upon it.

'And Lorcan and Evangelina know each other,' Amelia said.

'We overheard them talking,' Gideon added.

Toby gave a mock look of shock. 'Hold the front page. Two people in the same place at the same time talk to one another!' He sighed and gave them a look.

Amelia shook her head. 'They've clearly known each other before and are keen to keep it to themselves.'

'So that's why you were so interested in Lorcan.' Toby sat back in his chair, looking thoughtful. 'Although it is kind of odd that he didn't mention that he knew her when we were talking about Evangelina Wilde staying at the hotel. *And* he did look uncomfortable when Davey brought it up. I just thought it was down to lustful thoughts.' He then banged the table and shook his head. 'No, don't do this! Don't drag me into your conspiracy nonsense. Maybe they do know each other; maybe Ricky *is* up to something, but it doesn't mean you two should turn all Scooby Doo and try and get to the bottom of it.

'You've just been filming a crime drama, Gideon, it's art spilling over into life for you. Amelia, you live with a man who writes thrillers and crime novels and you're always reading that kind of book too, you live and breathe all that stuff. And you've just had the horrible experience of someone dying in front of you. You're bored, Gideon; and Amelia, you're keen to go all rogue sleuth and jump to conclusions. In fact, you're probably just imagining this because you're at a loose end waiting for Jack to come home.'

Amelia sat up straight in her chair as Gideon breathed an 'uh-oh' under his breath.

'I am *not* some little woman sitting at home, putting my life on hold while waiting for a man to come and rescue me from tedium!' Amelia said, hotly, very tempted to throw her whisky over Toby's head. Which she definitely would have done had it not been her favourite whisky and had there not been a massive queue at the bar.

'I'm sorry, I didn't mean it like that.' Toby spread his hands on the table and studied them a moment while he chose his next words. 'You two are the most important people in my life and I love you both dearly. I could have easily lost you both the last time events kicked off. I don't want you to put yourselves in any danger.

'If Ricky is as dodgy as you fear he is, is it wise to dig any further? I love the way you both search for meaning and excitement in the everyday occurrences, but really, Glencarlach is a sleepy little village in the north of Scotland. There's an excited ripple if the café trials a new type of cake. A sheep escaping makes the front page of the *Wester Ross Chronicle.*

'What happened here before, the events that we all unwittingly got mixed up with was a one-off, an aberration to an otherwise normal Scottish village. We have to face up to it, Glencarlach isn't the crime central of the Highlands. It's an ordinary little place. Nothing. Ever. Happens. Here.'

The door suddenly opened, causing an icy blast of air to whirl around the bar. Amelia shivered. Seconds later, Constable Ray Williams walked in, large flakes of snow melting on his shoulders. He was accompanied by the Reverend Roddy McDade who looked very pale.

At the bar, Ray had a quick word with Big Davey who nodded and turned down the music before pouring a large brandy and handing it to the minister.

With the music stopping, the chatter began to cease. Everyone looked at Ray who'd taken off his hat and looked very serious, his big bushy moustache twitching side to side. He cleared his throat.

'Good evening, everyone. If I could just have a few moments of your time? I'm looking for anyone with any information to step forward. You see, I'm sorry to report, but earlier on this evening there was a robbery...'

CHAPTER 8

21ST DECEMBER

The insistent banging on the door eventually penetrated Lorcan's deep sleep. Grabbing his threadbare dressing gown from the back of the bedroom door he stumbled down the stairs to the kitchen in the dark. His first thought was that there was an emergency, but his brain clicked into gear reassuring himself that it couldn't be his parents as they would have telephoned either his landline or his mobile (once he had explained numerous times to his mother that the occasional call wouldn't give him a brain tumour).

Family emergency aside, his next thought was that there was a fire – but he'd switched off all the equipment in the studio and a quick sniff of the air detected no hint of burning.

He squinted at the digital clock on the microwave as he went to open the door. It blinked 06.58. *Not even seven o'clock!* Who the hell would be at his door at that time? A figure stood with their back to the glass. Lorcan fumbled for the kitchen light, snapped it on and the figure turned around.

And Lorcan's chest seemed to constrict as he felt momentarily light-headed and a bit breathless. *It'll be the early hour*, he told himself as Evangelina Wilde smiled at him.

He could see his reflection in the glass; untamed dreadlocks, Star Wars boxers, an ancient Nirvana T-shirt... No doubt he'd have bloodshot eyes to add to the winning combination. He pulled his robe tightly round his body, belting it in a last-ditch attempt to cover himself and opened the door.

'I'm sorry, I didn't mean to wake you, I hadn't thought I would get here this early but I didn't really sleep well last night...'

'Come in, come in,' he said, glancing round to check for festering socks and mugs of forgotten tea. Ruby wasn't the most observant of cleaners and, with her arthritis, tended to avoid anything which needed bending down to or stretching up for, which really only left a two-foot window of cleanable surfaces. He was relieved to see his home was relatively tidy and he didn't even have any of his underwear drying on the radiators.

Evangelina walked in, pulling the heavy hood from her face, and Lorcan could have sworn the bulb wattage went up a few notches as the room seemed to get brighter.

'Can I get you a tea? Coffee?'

'Um, do you have anything...'

'Stronger?'

'I was going to say herbal.'

'Ah, no. Oh, unless you mean *herbal* herbal like grass or hash and, er, that would still be a no...' Oh God! What was happening to him? He was blabbering on like an idiot.

'Oh, I wasn't meaning drugs!' Evangelina looked aghast. 'I meant herbal as in peppermint or chamomile tea or a fruit tea...' she trailed off, glancing uneasily around her as if expecting to see a bong and couple of syringes littering the kitchen tops.

Lorcan filled the kettle. 'Just the hard stuff, I'm afraid. I mean regular tea and filter coffee. There might be some instant decaf somewhere.'

'Tea is fine. I'm so sorry for just turning up unannounced like this. I got your address from James at the hotel. I told him I wanted you to do a painting for me. I don't know what I was thinking. My head's been all over the place since I saw you.' Her eyes were darting all over the kitchen, as if unable to rest on any one object for longer than a couple of seconds. Eventually she looked up at him, her ice-blue eyes almost searing a hole in his. 'I wanted us to talk. I…' She stood there and gave a helpless shrug of her shoulders.

'Talking would be good.'

She sat down heavily on a chair. 'I don't even know what to say or where to start.'

'We can talk about the weather. That's safe.'

She looked round at him and gave a small laugh. 'The weather?'

'Oh yeah, it's a massive topic around these parts. Especially at the moment as there's much debate over how much snow is likely to fall over the next few days and will we all get snowed in.'

The kettle switched off and he made a cup of tea, automatically adding a lot of milk and a sugar.

He handed her the mug, realising what he'd done. 'Sorry, I should have asked how you take it.'

'Exactly the same as I've always done,' she said with a smile, blowing on the top of the mug.

He jerked his thumb over his shoulder, towards the door leading to the rest of the house. 'Can you give me ten minutes while I go and change and possibly blow my brains out over my ineptitude at having a sane and sensible conversation, please? Then we can discuss the last fifteen years. What we've been up to, places we've been, any pets, any kids. We can cover it all. Just let me get out of my night attire and brush my teeth first.'

Lorcan bolted out the room, slamming the door behind him. He had a quick glance around the lounge, scooping up a big pile of music magazines and dropping them down the side of the sofa.

He spied a couple of scented candles on top of the mantelpiece – an as yet unused housewarming gift from one of his first parties. He lit them.

He paused for a second then blew them out.

Then re-lit them but moved them to the small side table beside the lamp.

Then he blew them out again because who in their right mind would light a candle next to a lamp. And scented candles didn't appear very manly.

Then he lit them again because he didn't want to send out the wrong signal by looking overly macho and not in touch with his feminine side.

Then he blew one out because he didn't know what the hell he wanted the room to look like any more.

He took a step back to survey the room and wondered, for the first time in his life, if he should have cushions. He'd never felt the need for an abundance of soft furnishings, figuring sofas were comfortable enough, given they had soft, padded seats, but maybe there was a conspiracy, of which he'd been out the loop, and his home seriously lacked style because of the absence of squashy squares of fabric.

Despairing at himself, he ran up the stairs and had a record-breaking shower, sprayed on half a can of deodorant and brushed his teeth before racing back to his bedroom to look through the pile of clothes on his chair.

Pulling on a pair of newly washed jeans, he picked up his favourite T-shirt, but on closer inspection thought it probably best he swap it for one that didn't have Heinz tomato soup splattered over the chest like an arc of arterial spray. He selected an only slightly crumpled blue shirt instead.

Remembering he had a bottle of aftershave, he hurried back to the bathroom. His sister had given it to him at Christmas; something trendy that was meant to smell like rain. Well, it would be a step up from Imperial Leather and Sure deodorant. He found the sleek black bottle at the back of the cabinet and splashed some on.

It smelt nice, but hardly reminiscent of a cloudburst.

He closed the cabinet door and looked at his reflection in the mirror, turning his head from left to right, running a hand over his stubble, wondering if he should also have a quick shave and tidy up his goatee.

He stopped. What the hell was he doing?

He clutched the sides of the sink, closed his eyes and leant his head against the cabinet. He breathed in and out for a few seconds before looking back up at his reflection, his pale aquamarine eyes taking in how he must look to her.

A bit of an eejit, probably.

This was not a date. It was someone from his past coming over to talk. They'd coincidentally ended up in the same small village and by all accounts a brief chat to cover the intervening years would probably be marginally less awkward than going out of their way to avoid each other for the duration of her stay.

Tying back his hair he went downstairs, noticing the lounge was now a fragrant blend of cinnamon, orange and cloves.

'Right, I'm a bit more presentable now…' he said as he opened the door to the kitchen, but he found himself speaking to an empty room. The mug of tea sat untouched on the table with only the faint smell of gardenias in the air to indicate the one true love of his life had ever been there.

CHAPTER 9

'Yes, it's very unfortunate that the church was broken into but it hardly proves your point.'

'But it also disproves your point that no crime ever happens in Glencarlach,' Amelia riposted at Toby as she helped with breakfast.

Loading her tray with cafetières and teapots, Toby shook his head. 'Stealing some silverware and the pantomime props, whilst horrible, is hardly going to make the perpetrator go on the FBI's most-wanted list, is it? It'll be kids larking about, that's all.'

Amelia said nothing. If it was kids, she could understand they'd possibly take the pantomime props but why the silverware too? And if it wasn't kids, she could understand the silverware going missing, but why then the pantomime props! And the kids in and around the village, whilst getting up to the usual hijinks of underage drinking and camping out in haunted woods to scare one another, didn't usually do anything worse than a bit of graffiti in the bus shelter which could normally be traced back to the guilty party due to everyone knowing everyone's business and all the toings and froings of young love.

But there was something about this robbery which bothered

Amelia. Especially because it had been such a cold night and the village's youth weren't really out and about, far preferring to be at home watching television and on their PlayStations. There was one upside to the robbery being announced so publicly: everyone was talking about it, and as far as Amelia knew there had been no gossip about Benedict Geissler's suspected heart attack on the grounds of Stone Manor. The police had cordoned off the area around the folly but because it was out of the way, no one was likely to be out walking near it.

'Are you still planning to spy on Lorcan and Evangelina?' Toby asked quietly.

'Not at all!' Amelia said as if it had never crossed her mind. She couldn't speak for Gideon though and had a feeling he'd be keeping a close eye on their comings and goings. And then Amelia hoped he'd report everything he'd witnessed back to her!

Amelia carried her tray through to the dining room where Evangelina had just returned from an early morning walk, face still pink from the cold. She and Betty were making polite conversation with each other across their tables about the snow which had started falling again in big flakes. With poor visibility, it didn't look like it would be stopping anytime soon.

'Did you have a nice evening at Hamish's?' Amelia asked as she placed a large pot of tea down on Betty's table. Wearing a floaty dress in emerald and gold with matching headscarf, Betty looked like she'd be more at home in a Noël Coward play. The hair under the scarf was a very bright shade of orange and Amelia wasn't sure if it was a wig or just a lot of henna dye as she was sure she'd never seen such a colour occur naturally in hair before.

'It was lovely. And so nice catching up with all the family. I'm looking forward to Hamish and Sally's wedding later in the year. It's mainly funerals I go to now. Still, there's usually a nice spread at those.' Betty popped a sugar cube in her teacup and stirred it delicately.

'Okay,' Amelia said as brightly as possible. 'I'll give you a moment to look at the menu,' she said as she moved to the next table where DeShawn and Alaiya Johnson were sitting holding hands over the table. Just as Amelia plonked the large cafetière on the table DeShawn stifled a yawn.

'I'm sorry,' he apologised, 'I'm incredibly jet-lagged.'

Alaiya smiled. 'He suffers really badly from it. Coffee will help.'

'When was it you flew in?' Amelia asked.

'We flew into London a couple of days ago, but jet lag can throw me off for days,' DeShawn said. 'We spent the night there and picked up the hire car and took our time travelling north, stopping at sights on the way. We were just north of Oban when our original hotel called to say there was a problem and they couldn't fulfil our booking.'

'We had no idea where else to stay,' Alaiya carried on. 'We pulled into the side of the road and googled accommodation near us and your beautiful hotel popped up. We were so lucky to get something this close to Christmas.'

'And are you over in Scotland for anything special?' Amelia probed.

DeShawn nodded as he stirred milk into his coffee. 'It's actually our honeymoon,' he said, looking up at his wife with a soppy grin.

Amelia mentally gave herself a high five! She'd been right. 'That's lovely! Congratulations!' She'd make sure to send up a chilled bottle of champagne to their room later that afternoon.

At that moment Betty floated into view. 'Oh my,' Betty said, smiling at DeShawn. 'I just overheard you say you were on your honeymoon! How lovely!' Then she whispered something in DeShawn's ear. He laughed good-naturedly as Betty moved back to her seat then grinned at his wife. 'It would seem I'm quite the novelty around these parts!'

Alaiya chuckled and opened up a croissant.

Amelia felt herself go hot then cold. What had Betty said?!

Had she been inappropriate towards the newlyweds but DeShawn was still smiling so it clearly couldn't have been too bad. She hoped.

Amelia moved over to Evangelina's table where Ricky had now joined her.

'Good morning,' Amelia said cheerily as she popped down the herbal tea and coffee Evangelina had requested when she'd returned from her walk.

'Morning, Amelia.' Evangelina smiled.

'Have you anything nice planned for today?' Amelia asked, with a glance at Ricky, who didn't even look up from his phone.

'Ricky's got work to catch up on so I thought I'd pop into the gym and maybe have a browse in your library.'

'Lovely!' Amelia said enthusiastically. 'I hope you wrapped up warmly when you were out earlier, the temperature has really plummeted overnight.'

Evangelina looked slightly flustered at the mention of her walk.

Just then a loud American voice ripped through the dining room. 'Ricky Varelli! I hope you're not working! Not when there's so much scenery!'

Ricky, who'd just taken a sip of coffee, almost spilled it down his front and he hastily put his cup back in its saucer, dabbing at his mouth with his napkin.

Vanessa swanned over to them in garishly clashing velour leisurewear, her long black hair elaborately coiffured and held in place by a headband. Amelia noted that today Vanessa's sunglasses were just as big as the ones she'd worn previously but the shades were much lighter.

'Evangelina! You look so fresh! The country air is clearly agreeing with you,' Vanessa said as she bent over and kissed Evangelina on the cheek. 'You always look so peaky in London. The number of times I thought you must be pregnant before I realised it was just your natural demeanour.'

Evangelina merely smiled back at Vanessa as she skewered a grapefruit segment with her fork.

A moment later Terence bobbed into view. He looked delighted to see Ricky and Evangelina.

'Beautiful part of the world, beautiful, isn't it!' Terence said to Amelia as she stood patiently by, ready to take their breakfast orders. 'It would be nice to have a bolt-hole around here,' Terence carried on, now addressing Ricky. 'Think you'd fancy that, Ricky, once you take early retirement?'

Evangelina smiled. 'I think we're a long way from that.'

'Oh? I thought that was your plan. Get out of the rat race in a couple of years and then move out of London up to Scotland,' Terence said, looking surprised.

'That was always *my* plan,' Evangelina said, taking a sip of her tea.

Ricky gave an expressive shrug. 'I think I may just start reducing my workload in a couple of years and ease into retirement.'

'Bit of a commute though?' Terence said as he popped on a pair of glasses to look at a menu Amelia handed him. 'If you're still set on moving to this neck of the woods.'

Ricky pulled a face. 'No harm in keeping on the place in Mayfair as well as buying up here. Evangelina could always stay up in Scotland and I could visit on weekends and holidays.'

Amelia noticed how Evangelina kept smiling, but also said, 'Well, nothing's set in stone.'

Ricky cleared his throat. 'How's life with you, Terry?' From where Amelia was standing it was very obvious Ricky wanted to end the conversation around retirement.

'Can't grumble!' Terence said affably, then, 'You don't mind us joining you for breakfast, do you?'

'Of course they won't!' Vanessa laughed. 'We have so much to catch up on! It's ridiculous that we never manage to see each other despite us all living in London!' She gave Ricky and

Evangelina a dazzling smile as she sank down gracefully into the seat her husband had pulled out for her.

A second later Carlo entered the dining room with Dan and Alice, with India following a few feet behind them.

There were many 'hellos' and 'mornings' shouted out amongst the party and Amelia saw Betty putting on her glasses and sitting upright in her chair to get a better look at everyone coming in.

Carlo came over to Amelia. 'Can Lucy have her breakfast in our room please?'

'Of course.'

'Great, she'd like a pot of tea and the scrambled eggs and smoked salmon.'

'No problem, I'll get it sent up.'

'Thank–' Carlo stopped mid-sentence. He seemed to pale slightly.

'Mr Todero?'

He stared off into the middle distance for another second then rubbed his eyes, blinking furiously, but then a moment later he shook his head then flashed her a grin. 'You know what, Amelia, can you double the order for room service and I'll head back to the room too.'

'Of course.' Amelia watched him go before turning back to the Kings. 'Would you like me to join all the tables together?' Amelia asked.

'No, please don't go to any bother. We can sit at that one,' Alice said, pointing to another table, and she and Dan walked over to it, with India trailing laconically behind.

Amelia took their order for tea and coffee and turned to go back to see what DeShawn and Alaiya wanted off the cooked menu, but they'd already left the dining room.

CHAPTER 10

'Caught you!' Gideon shouted into Amelia's ear as he snuck up behind her a little later that morning.

'I was just looking at the time!' Amelia explained as she quickly dropped her phone into her pocket.

'Or checking to see if you've had a message from Jack?'

'So?'

'Not too long to wait until you're reunited! Now then,' Gideon lowered his head conspiratorially down to Amelia's, 'has you-know-who appeared?'

'No. And I somehow doubt he will. I can't imagine him wanting to have a heart-to-heart with Evangelina in front of a whole crowd of people.'

'Whatever. It won't do any harm to keep a close eye on Evangelina. Oh, don't worry,' he added, seeing Amelia's panicked look, 'I'll be ever so discreet.'

Just then a slightly out of breath Vanessa rushed up to them. 'Excuse me! Do you have someone free to show my husband the grounds and all your... um... growing things?' she waved a heavily jewelled hand around airily. 'He's very much into horticulture.'

'In this weather?' Amelia asked doubtfully.

'He won't mind a bit of snow!'

'Well...' Amelia ran through who was on today, thinking who'd be the best to give a tour.

'Fabulous! I'll go and tell him the good news!' Vanessa said and quickly ran up the stairs in her pristine white trainers.

Amelia would have bet money on them never having once been worn inside a gym.

At the reception desk Amelia called through to Wee Davey to see if he was free. After arranging for him to take Terence Maxwell on a tour, Amelia hung up and looked out the window at the snow, lost in thought. Since their conversation the night before, she had been mulling over Toby's comments.

When she was renovating the hotel she'd also been trying to solve a centuries old mystery to find hidden treasure, as well as uncover the murderously intentioned saboteur who didn't want her to stay at Stone Manor. Although highly stressful, it had also been exciting and exhilarating! She'd loved solving the mystery, using all the well-honed detective skills she'd accumulated over many years reading mystery novels. Overhearing Ricky acting suspiciously the other night had sparked something inside her. Then with the strange case of the robbery from the church, and Benedict Geissler's last words about a girl, it felt that spark then ignited something deep within her.

Something that excited her.

And it wasn't just because she felt at a loose end. Right now, her instincts tingled invitingly, telling her something, somewhere was amiss.

With James coming out to reception, Amelia hurried off to her little office where she pulled out a brand-new notebook from the top drawer of the desk. If there was one thing Amelia liked almost as much as a mystery, it was an organised list. She opened up the cover and folded it back by running her palm down the spine.

At the top of page one she wrote 'Weird Things Happening.'

And then she started writing.

Amelia was still writing half an hour later when Gideon popped his head round the door of the little office. 'Knock knock! Are you ready for my debrief?' He closed the door behind him and sat on top of a box of printer paper.

'Well?'

'Evangelina spent what seemed like hours in the library picking a book. She was there so long I was convinced she must be there to have a secret assignation but no, nothing! Lorcan never appeared. By the time she finally left I'd looked through practically every book in your library. I managed to get to "W" and felt I had to take one away!' He waved a book at Amelia.

'It's odd,' Amelia said, thinking aloud.

'I've read books before!' he said, offended.

'No, the whole situation. But maybe we should let them be. After all, Lorcan's a friend and he may open up to us, anyway.'

'Oh my God, that's so reasonable of you,' he said in disgust. 'But I want to know! And in other news, India King?'

Amelia sat forward in her chair.

'Possibly the most inactive teenager I've ever come across. She's glued to her phone! I really can't for a moment think why heart attack man would try and tip you the wink about her.'

With everything she'd already observed about the teenager, neither could Amelia.

There was another knock on the door and Toby squeezed into the office. Compact for one, crowded with two, it was like a comedy sketch with the three of them in it.

'I've got some news!' Toby said, his eyes shining brightly.

'You're in the Guinness Book of Records for having the least amount of understanding of what constitutes personal space?' Gideon asked shoving Toby slightly away from him.

'Nope! My mate, Max, you know, the editor of the paper? He just called to give me a heads-up. The *Secret Guest* is coming here!'

Amelia sat bolt upright. 'Seriously? When?'

'I don't know, but the *Secret Guest* messaged the paper to say they'd have their review in for Stone Manor for the edition going to copy the second weekend in January.'

'Wow!' Gideon said.

Amelia echoed his sentiment. The *Secret Guest* had been reviewing hotels all over the world for a few years and their articles held a lot of sway in the industry.

'Did your friend give a clue to their identity?'

Toby shook his head. 'Nope, Max has no idea who they are, if they're male or female, young or old, or if they're even British! All the correspondence is done through an anonymous email.'

'Do you think they're here already?' Amelia mentally ran through the list of current guests.

'I don't know, or they could be about to arrive.'

'Maybe they've already been?'

'No, Max said the article was going to be about spending Christmas in a hotel.'

'Wow! This is exciting! I wish we knew who it was.'

'Oh come on, you're always wonderful to everyone, even the arseholes,' Gideon piped up.

'I know, but it would be useful to know,' Amelia said.

'Why don't the two of you stop worrying about what Ricky Varelli is up to and start sleuthing to see who the Secret Guest is? Just a thought,' Toby said as he struggled to open the door without landing on Amelia's lap.

'Now, THAT is a good idea!' Gideon said.

'And I know just the place to start,' Amelia said opening up the laptop.

'So, what have we got so far…?' Gideon asked an hour later.

Amelia flipped her notebook back over to the first page and skimmed through the notes she'd made as they read through some of the Secret Guest reviews.

'Okay…so there's absolutely no hint about them being male or female. Sometimes they review the hotel as a single person, other times with a companion which has been male and female with no hint as to their relationship to the Secret Guest. A couple of times they've been in a larger group. Whoever it is gives nothing away!' Amelia put her pad down in frustration.

'But we do know the Secret Guest has been to Spain, Greece, Ireland, England, America and Italy in the last couple of years,' Gideon said. 'Any of the wedding group could be moonlighting, I imagine they all have quite jet-setting lifestyles. There's the Johnsons? What about the elusive Mr Griffin who hasn't turned up yet?'

'Good point.'

'Obviously we can't come right out and ask, but there are lots of lovely ways we can slip little leading questions into conversation.'

'Nothing too obvious though, Gideon, please!'

'I will be the epitome of discreet!' he said as he gave her a little wave as he left the room. Amelia powered down the laptop and had a bit of a tidy up before she headed back out to the front where she found Gideon not very discreetly sulking behind the desk.

'I can't find anyone to interrogate. Terence Maxwell is still out exploring the grounds with Wee Davey, I've no idea where Vanessa de Courtney is: probably painting her watercolours. Alaiya and DeShawn are off exploring the village in the hope he can push through his jet lag, and I just saw Evangelina head towards the sauna in her robe and flip-flops. There are many things I'd do in the name of investigative journalism but that kind of dry heat plays havoc with my hair and anyway, I don't have my speedos with me, but,' he said as an aside as he patted his stomach, 'trust me when I say I'd look very good in them at the moment as I've had to buff up for my police drama role. The month of no cake was worth it.'

'Cake!' Amelia suddenly exclaimed. Checking her watch, she

realised there was someplace she needed to be. Calling out to James that she was heading to the village and would be back soon, she left a confused Gideon in her wake as she grabbed the keys to hotel's all-weather, all-terrain Jeep. Her sleuthing nose was tingling and she knew just the person she needed to talk to.

CHAPTER 11

Fridays at 3pm was well known as the time Constable Raymond Williams stopped in at the café for his end-of-the-week treat of hot chocolate and caramel shortcake.

Amelia got to the café just as Ray was asking for whipped cream, marshmallows *and* sprinkles. He turned to her with a sheepish smile. 'It's been a hard week, I thought I'd go for the full works,' he explained as Mary popped the skyscraper of a drink in front of him.

'No one can blame you for needing a little pick-me-up,' Amelia agreed after ordering a latte.

Taking her coffee, along with an empire biscuit, Amelia followed Ray over to his table.

'Would you mind if I joined you?'

'Of course not, Amelia! I'd be delighted to have the company!'

She sat down opposite him as he spooned up some of the whipped cream, leaving a few little sprinkles decorating his bushy moustache. He dabbed at it with his napkin and gave a jovial chuckle. 'Oops, the biggest risk of extra adornments!' Putting his napkin down, he gave Amelia a grave look. 'How are you doing, Amelia? After that unfortunate incident?'

'It was quite a shock but I'm okay now, thank you. Have you found out any more about the man?'

'He had a business card on him: some kind of insurance investigator for the Civil Service it would seem, although he looked past retirement age to me. He had an ID card too, and it seems he's got an address in Berlin. But it's the Inverness lot who have taken over the investigation and they'll be contacting next of kin and all of that. They'll also be carrying out the post-mortem but I don't know when that will be, due to the Christmas holidays. It's a mystery why or how he got here as he wasn't booked into your place or the Whistling Haggis and he had no car keys on him either.'

'Maybe his phone had information?'

Ray sucked on his teeth. 'We didn't find one. Being an older gentleman, he possibly didn't want anything to do with new-fangled technology, although even my old mum who's almost ninety has one, although she does pocket dial me all the time.'

Amelia sat back in her chair and took a bite of her biscuit as she mulled this information over. The number she'd taken down from Mr Geissler was definitely for a mobile. Where could the phone be if it wasn't on his person? She wondered if she should mention it to Ray, or possibly wait to speak to whoever was being sent over from CID at Inverness. But a little part of her wanted to hold back. Clearly Benedict Geissler had wanted to speak to her about something. This fact made it seem very personal to Amelia.

'Now, I don't want you to be dwelling on this, Amelia,' Ray said kindly. 'Luckily the SOCOs finished up quickly because of the weather so the police presence at the folly is away now.'

'Good to know. I'd hate it if my guests were worried, especially after the robbery last night, too,' she said, playing up the worried resident reaction, hoping to fish for more information.

Ray cleared his throat and put down his spoon. 'Now, Amelia, I want you to be assured that we take all crime very seriously and we will leave no stone unturned to find out who did this despicable act so close to Christmas.' He shook his head.

'It's so unusual to have anything like this happen here.'

Ray nodded. 'We pride ourselves on having a very low crime rate in this area.'

'Which is in no small part due to your excellent police presence.'

Ray seemed to puff out his chest a little. 'Even with the financial cuts, we aim to service the area as well as we always have.'

'Is Reverend McDade okay?'

'He had a little bit of a turn to be honest.'

'No wonder, especially with the pantomime props being taken. They've been working so hard on it.'

'All on the pantomime committee are disgusted by it,' Ray agreed.

'Will it still go ahead?'

Ray gave an emphatic nod. 'Our production of *Aladdin* won't be beaten by a bit of petty theft. We can rally around the village and get replacements for the bits and pieces that were taken.'

'Was it much?'

'An entire box of costumes plus some fake pieces of treasure. It was all plastic, but maybe in the dark it looked like bejewelled crowns. The coins were all either chocolate or made from the silver tops from milk bottles. It's not the expense so much as the inconvenience and the upset.' Ray sighed. 'It was the last thing Roddy needed.' He paused to spoon up some of the whipped cream and Amelia let him take his time before he carried on. 'He'd been told earlier the church needs a new roof, which is in addition to all the other repair works the building needs.'

'Are there church funds to cover it?'

Ray sighed again. 'Not if they've to cover substantial repairs in another four nearby parishes. There's talk of joining up a couple of churches in neighbouring villages and closing the redundant one.'

'That's just awful!' Amelia said.

'It is, Amelia, it is. It would rip the heart out of the community.'

Amelia didn't want to say she thought there would be slightly more outrage if something ever happened to the Whistling Haggis.

They sat in contemplative silence for a few moments until Amelia probed a little deeper into the robbery.

'But what about the more valuable goods? You mentioned some other things had been taken as well as the pantomime props.'

'Yes. Ornate silver lanterns. We always use them to lead the procession for the Christmas Eve service. Luckily they're insured but they've been used for many years and there's the sentimental value of them. It's a sorry state of affairs when items like that are stolen.'

'Was it just the lanterns?'

'Well…' Ray took a gulp of his hot chocolate, leaving a creamy line on his moustache.

'I'm only asking, because, well, as a local business owner I'd like to know if we're a likely target…'

'We are being more vigilant in this area. I would hope that this is a one-off. Some drunken tomfoolery or such like. There was another thing stolen…' He left Amelia poised for information as he took a bite of his caramel shortbread and chewed it thoughtfully for a moment. Eventually he swallowed. 'I can't think for the life of me why someone would want to take these though… the thief also took a big bunch of lilies from the pulpit.'

Amelia's drive back to Stone Manor was a little more treacherous than the drive out. In even just the short time she'd been in the café, there had been another dumping of heavy snow. Thankful for the Jeep's ability to get through pretty much every terrain, Amelia parked it in Stone Manor's car park.

She turned off the engine but instead of heading back into the hotel she sat a moment mulling over her conversation with the constable.

Reaching over the passenger seat, Amelia opened the glove compartment and had a quick rummage before unearthing a torch. After checking to make sure it worked she locked up the Jeep, but instead of returning to the warmth of the Stone Manor kitchens she cut across the gardens to the path that led up to the folly.

Although the snow had stopped, the sky still had an eerie orange glow and Amelia didn't think the snow would stay away for long. It would have been far more sensible to wait until daylight to conduct her search but she was also aware she couldn't waste any time. She scrambled up the path which was tougher going than the last time. The fresh falling of snow had settled on the branches of the overhanging trees and every time Amelia disturbed one, she got a cold dump of snow land on her and by the time she'd reached the top of the path and burst out from the shelter of the trees, she was soaking and even colder.

She paused to catch her breath and brush snow from her hat and shoulders then slowly and rather sombrely walked forward. Staring at the stone bench, a chill crept through her body which was nothing to do with the weather. She remembered the wide-eyed stare of Benedict Geissler as he tried to speak to her with his dying breath. She swept the torch over the bench and checked underneath it too but there was nothing but snow. She stood with the bench behind her and looked out into the darkness.

'What did you do with your phone, Mr Geissler?' she said softly under her breath. He had wanted to see her about something important that he felt unable to share unless in person. And he wanted to do it in a private, quiet setting. Was there someone he didn't want seeing him? He'd clearly had a mobile at some point when he'd been in contact with her. He had no known relatives in Glencarlach, and no room booked anywhere to Amelia's knowledge. So where was his car? She knew just how tricky it was to get to Glencarlach on public transport and there had been a sense of urgency to Benedict Geissler, one she felt would be at odds with him taking hours to get to her via the Wee Local Happy Bus. Something didn't add up.

But first his phone. If he'd dropped it, it would have been beside the bench and the police would have already found it. Had he dropped it further away? Or had someone taken it? She took out her own mobile and found the number that he'd given her and that she had keyed into her phone. She pressed the green button and, holding the phone away from her, listened.

There was not much wind and no other noises nearby but Amelia still couldn't hear a ringtone. She walked around the area, shining the torch around her as the number rang out. Eventually it cut onto his clipped tones instructing her to 'leave a message.' She waited a moment then dialled his number again, this time walking down the east path that led to the folly, it was steep but wide and even underfoot, and the most common route used. It was also fairly exposed. Twenty minutes later, after as thorough a search as she could manage Amelia conceded the phone wasn't there, and if it was it was buried too deeply in snow for her to find. And she had to face it, if the scenes of crime officers had swept the area, they would not have missed a mobile phone a few feet away from the body.

Returning to the bench she walked forward a few steps towards the edge of the hill and looked down. But maybe they missed something if it was off the beaten track. It was a far steeper drop than the tourist route or the way she'd come up. She was staring down into the darkness contemplating her next move when she felt a snowflake land on her cheek, closely followed by another one. It was now or never she thought as she redialled the number.

Because it was so dark she instantly saw the phone light up with her call. It was quite far down but, from what Amelia could see from her torchlight the phone seemed to be sitting on a natural ledge made by some rocks jutting out. There were also handy looking tree roots sticking out the earth at convenient intervals, but even so, she couldn't see any way of getting to it that didn't involve her scrabbling around dangerously in the dark. Well, she hadn't got this far to turn back now, she thought as she started the slippery descent.

Thankful she'd worn her hiking boots with the good grips, she half slid, half scrabbled down the side of the hill, clinging onto whatever natural hold she could find. It was slow progress, hampered by the slippiness of the snow. Every so often she had to redial the number to show her how far she still had to go.

In one heart-stopping moment when her foot slipped, Amelia managed to descend ten feet in one go. Terrifying though it was to drop so quickly, it did mean she was only inches away from the phone when she managed to stop. Snatching it off the rock she tucked it into her pocket and paused a moment to ease the burning in her arm muscles. Amelia shone the torch above her to see how far she had to climb back up.

And for a split second she could have sworn she saw a face peering at her before it melted back into the shadows.

CHAPTER 12

Sheer determination got Amelia back up that hillside – that and wanting to know who else was up there, and also her desire to get back to help with the dinner service and the fact she was desperate for the loo.

She made a mental note to only attempt derring-do activities after emptying her bladder in future.

Finally getting to the top of the hill, she crawled away from the edge for a moment, lying in the snow, before standing up, on slightly shaky legs. Shining the torch around her, she saw there was nobody else there. Had it been a trick of the light?

But a quick shine of the torchlight onto the ground showed that as well as her own footprints by the edge of the hill, there was another set. This was very puzzling. Why did the person not call down to see if she needed help? Perhaps they didn't want to draw attention to themselves. Had they been looking for the phone too? Well, whoever it had been was long gone now.

Amelia checked her watch and saw it was half past five. She needed to get back to Stone Manor, but first she'd need to change. Slithering down the shortcut path to the grounds of

Stone Manor, Amelia kept a reassuring hand on her pocket to feel the outline of Benedict Geissler's phone.

Bypassing the hotel, Amelia jogged to the Gatehouse and let herself in, hurrying through to the bathroom. She did a double-take when she saw her reflection in the mirror; there were pieces of tree bark caught in her hat, and her clothes and skin were filthy from the dirt and rubble of the hillside. She even had a cut along her cheek that she hadn't felt at the time. Now in the warmth of the Gatehouse, it was stinging.

After the quickest shower possible she threw on clean clothes and, leaving her short hair to dry naturally, dabbed some concealer on over the cut before hightailing it back to the hotel. Door to door she'd been less than twenty minutes. She went in through the front entrance to avoid Toby's questions about where she'd been and, bundling her coat away, slipped behind the reception desk.

It was perfect timing as seconds later she heard, 'Psst! Ames!' Toby was calling her from the staff door.

Normally Toby would just come out into reception if he wanted to speak to her but instead he beckoned her to come over. When she got to him, Amelia wrinkled her nose when she saw the state of his apron: it was smeared with what looked like blood.

'I've been gutting fish. I didn't want come out front, not when the Secret Guest could be floating about.'

'Good point.' Amelia looked over her shoulder but there was no one in sight. 'So, what's up?'

'I'm in a bit of a bind for service tonight. There's another person down with this cold and I'm short staffed because of all the extra bookings.'

'Don't worry, I'll step in.'

Toby gave a relieved smile. 'And, I've also…'

'Sent for the cavalry!' Gideon announced as he appeared behind Toby. He was already dressed in the black trousers and shirt all those front-of-house wore. Gideon pushed the door slightly further open and Amelia noticed he also had a wheelie case.

'I'll just take this up and get settled and be down in five minutes.'

'Has someone else booked in?' Amelia asked in confusion.

'Yes! Me!'

'But...' Amelia started to say.

'You're short staffed,' Gideon pointed out, 'and quite busy with high-maintenance guests. If I move in here, I can be on hand any time, night or day.' He frowned, then backtracked slightly. 'Well, day. Let's just stick to me helping during the day and early evening. It makes perfect sense. Toby's here all the time anyway so if we're upstairs he'll be even closer! And I'm at such a loose end at the cottage by myself. You've still got rooms free if you get any last-minute walk-ins. I thought I'd take the Nesbo room for Toby and me. I love its Scandi-vibed décor.'

Amelia jumped back quick to avoid getting her toes run over by the case wheels as Gideon pushed on through. As he got the key and carried the case up the stairs Amelia turned back to Toby who was smiling apologetically and still trying to remain hidden behind the door.

'I wonder if his altruistic generosity would be so forthcoming had we not got a reclusive film icon, an agent, a producer and a viscount staying with us,' Amelia mused.

Toby grinned. 'Must go, I've still got a salmon to fillet.'

Despite Gideon often being nothing but a nuisance when she was trying to work, Amelia had to admit he did know his way around formal service. Before he made it as an actor, Gideon had spent the 'in between-jobs' time working in restaurants. Being strikingly good looking, with a quick mind and plenty of charm, he'd managed to bag positions in some high-profile London establishments.

Surveying the tables, he darted about, repositioning cutlery by just millimetres, his golden eyes scanning the tables critically for anything he deemed out of place.

Grabbing a handful of menus, he disappeared into the bar to distribute them to those having pre-dinner cocktails.

Just then there were loud voices as Dan, Alice and India came down the stairs. India, who was trailing at the back, intent on scrolling through her phone practically careered into Amelia. The girl looked up at the last minute and did a comedy double-take and went bright red under her white foundation when she saw Amelia. She quickly put her phone behind her back and for a second Amelia thought she was going to speak but then the teenager ducked her head back down and scuttled off after her parents. Amelia stared after her, thinking back to Benedict Geissler's words about 'a girl'. India did seem to be acting oddly, but then again, it was her observation that most teenagers often displayed strange behaviour.

Amelia watched as the wedding party mingled with each other in the bar and she was quite intrigued to see how they would all interact with each other. There were some big characters already and Amelia wondered how the group dynamic worked. She was still observing from afar when Evangelina arrived down at reception.

She looked stunning in simple black skinny jeans that elongated her long slim legs even further, especially paired with the high-heeled boots. A simple, wide-necked cashmere top finished off the look. Wearing a little more make-up than usual, the effect of dark eyeliner emphasised her eyes behind a heavy side fringe of her blonde hair. She gave Amelia a smile in greeting just as Ricky hurried down after her, hastily tucking in his shirt front.

'Is that my favourite cousin?' Carlo appeared out of the bar and hugged Ricky then greeted Evangelina with a 'Ciao, bella!' and a kiss on both cheeks.

Evangelina hung back slightly as the two men entered the bar and just as she got to the doorway she paused and, taking a deep breath, straightened her spine and thrust her shoulders back, before following. For all the world, it looked to Amelia that Evangelina had to brace herself before she went in.

'Well, their little party has about as much life as Harvey Weinstein's career!' Gideon whispered into Amelia's ear an hour or so later, as he hurried out to see her in reception after he'd distributed the dessert.

Amelia couldn't help but agree. During the time she'd been in the dining room with the guests she'd been aware of Vanessa holding court with stories from her acting days. Terence spent most of the meal nodding in agreement with his wife. Lucy and Carlo were too busy whispering to each other to notice anyone else. Alice kept darting anxious looks at her husband with Dan returning smiles of encouragement. Ricky was jumpy, almost too quick to laugh and insisted on keeping everyone's drinks topped up, much to Craig's displeasure as he saw that as his job and at one point they both reached for the bottle of Rioja on the table at the same time, almost knocking it over. Throughout all of this, Evangelina looked lost in another world and barely picked at her food and only when Amelia asked if everything was okay with her meal, did Evangelina look flustered and said it was delicious then ate a couple of mouthfuls. India looked half asleep, slumped in her chair until Amelia realised she was watching TikTok videos under the table.

'If I hear another of Vanessa's anecdotes on her time doing Chekov, I may just go and find my own Cherry Orchard and hang myself from the nearest tree,' Gideon said with a sigh. 'I've had more fun evenings lancing a boil.'

'This wasn't actually about you,' Amelia pointed out. 'You were helping out Toby with his staff shortages, remember?'

Gideon raised an eyebrow. 'Darling, please! You've known me long enough to know I only helped out because I thought tonight would be fun and full of insider gossip, not a one-woman retrospective.' He craned his neck to see inside the dining room. 'What happened to the honeymooners? Too busy bonking to eat?'

'They're eating at the Whistling Haggis tonight.'

'Maybe they'd seen Vanessa perform on Broadway already.'

'Shhh, Gideon.' Every so often Amelia had to remind Gideon that his Rada-trained, well-modulated voice had a habit of carrying.

'But, tonight wasn't a complete waste of time,' Gideon said in a teasing tone. 'I found out a little bit of background on some of our guests.'

He leant forward, over the reception desk and this time lowered his voice. 'Carlo, Terence and Dan are old friends, they met at school, some posh boarding one. They jokily refer to themselves as the three Musketeers!

'Ricky was clearly the poorer, younger cousin and went to a normal London state school. It's obvious he still has a bit of a chip on his shoulder about it too, despite being successful now. He's the D'Artagnan character!

'Dan is a lawyer and frequently does bits and bobs of work for both Terence and Carlo. Sounds like quite the old boys club; you scratch my back, I'll scratch yours, that kind of thing.

'Carlo inherited the family import and export business and then made an even bigger fortune by getting into property during the eighties and nineties.'

Amelia couldn't help but be impressed with Gideon's sleuthing.

Gideon looked behind him before carrying on. 'Dan and Alice are stressed about something and weren't entirely looking forward to this time away. Ricky and Evangelina aren't happy, not sure why, some kind of grown-up shit...'

Amelia raised an eyebrow.

'...A lot of people think Lucy's a gold digger, Dan tried to get him to use the same lawyer for a prenup that Ricky used but Carlo refused because they're *totes* in love, even if it is cringe to watch them sometimes. And Lucy has cool make-up and clothes and doesn't mind people borrowing them sometimes...'

Amelia put a hand up to stop him. 'Wait, you gleaned all that from eavesdropping?'

Gideon pulled a face. 'Not quite. I know you were wanting to keep an eye on India even though the only thing she's done since she got here is sit, fixated on her phone! So, when she slipped out the side door I followed her into the bar and caught her sneaking a vodka into her glass of Coke and I promised I'd not say a word if she gave me some goss.'

'Gideon!'

'What! Come on, you can take the hit of a vodka for some proper insider information.'

Amelia had a feeling condoning underage drinking wasn't an entirely healthy or ethical payoff, but let it go.

'Now, I'm guessing they're about to finish dessert. I'll go through and help Craig in the bar, let him off early. There's no point in us both suffering.'

As Gideon swanned off, Amelia smiled; although he'd deny it, Gideon really wasn't always as selfish as he liked to make out.

After dinner, once the guests had all left the table, Amelia helped clear the dining room and discovered the chiffon scarf Alice had been wearing had fallen under a chair. She took it through to the bar but couldn't see Mrs King. Amelia popped through to the drawing room in case she'd gone there. As she approached the door Amelia could hear voices. Neither belonged to Alice. It was Ricky and Evangelina and it sounded as if they were having an argument.

'...and you know I don't like it when you wear high heels. It makes me look short when I stand next to you,' Ricky said petulantly.

'I wouldn't have thought it would have made a difference tonight seeing as you didn't come near me,' Evangelina replied. Although her voice was light, Amelia could detect a flinty edge.

'Well, you hardly give me any encouragement to.'

'Unlike some.'

'What! Don't be ridiculous!' Ricky spluttered. 'I don't know what you mean!'

'You *really* want to play this game?'

'I don't…' Ricky spluttered. 'You have nothing…'

'I'm going for a drink,' Evangelina said wearily, and as footsteps approached the door, Amelia quickly hurried to the bar to leave Alice's scarf on one of the chairs.

Vanessa was standing looking at the framed article about the hotel. The same one Benedict Geissler had a copy of. 'What a darling little article!' Vanessa exclaimed as she saw Amelia.

'What's this?' Terence came up behind her.

'Oh, that's a magazine article one of the national papers ran when we opened,' Amelia said. 'My brother, Toby, has a friend who's an editor at the paper and thought it would be an interesting story.'

'Of course it is,' Vanessa gushed. 'Inheriting a house with a torrid past and a hidden ruby. It sounds like something that handsome boyfriend of yours would conjure up.'

By now Lucy and Dan had also come over to look at the article. 'Ooh, what a history to this place!' Lucy said in wonder. 'Is it an old building?'

Amelia caught Vanessa turning away and rolling her eyes.

'It's 1700s, with little bits added on since then.'

'Are there ghosts?' Lucy asked.

'There are stories, mainly about the grounds but I've never seen anything,' Amelia said.

'I think I'd faint outright if I saw a ghost,' Lucy said as Terence gave her shoulder a reassuring squeeze.

Vanessa leant in closer to the article as she swapped her sunglasses for a pair of reading ones.

'What is that behind you?'

Amelia laughed slightly. 'It's a painting.'

'Is it a cat depicted as Hercule Poirot?'

'It is!'

'Where did you manage to find such a… quaint piece?'

'It was my godmother, Dotty, she discovered it in a charity shop.'

Amelia remembered how Dotty had found it hilarious to see such an ornate gold frame surrounding such an absurd subject. She'd given it to Amelia as she knew how amusing she'd find it with her love of Agatha Christie and detective fiction. It had been amongst the few items Amelia had kept from her flat when she'd packed up and moved to Glencarlach for good.

Vanessa craned her neck to look out to the reception desk where the photo for the article had been taken. 'The painting's not there anymore!'

'No, we regularly move the paintings around,' Amelia said. She'd actually removed it not long after the article for fear Gideon would throw it out one day such was his disgust for it. It had been one of the paintings she'd submitted for the art fair, carefully marking it as not for sale in case it accidentally ended up in the charity auction. Although artistically awful, it held a lot of sentimental charm for Amelia.

Gideon came up behind them. 'Oh God, that atrocious thing! I hope it was in the pile of frames you gave away to Lorcan. What an affront to art!'

'Anyone fancy a game of gin rummy?' Terence asked the group. 'Come on, old girl, if you like that painting so much I'll commission one for you,' he winked at his wife.

Vanessa stood back from the painting. 'Well, darling, it would certainly be an improvement on all those paintings of horses you insist on having. Disgusting smelly things.'

'The paintings are disgusting smelly things?' Lucy asked innocently.

'The paintings are the closest I get to the real thing unfortunately,' Terence said, darting a look at his wife and Amelia could see he was clearly put out by his wife's dismissiveness of all things equine.

Leaving the guests, Amelia headed back to the dining room to finish clearing the tables. Pulling off the cloths she threw them on the floor behind her, and almost covered Vanessa who'd followed her through.

'Oh sorry!' Amelia said, picking up a bundle of tablecloths.

'I've got a question,' Vanessa said. 'Do you know when your godmother bought that painting from a charity shop and where she could have got it?'

Amelia paused a moment. 'It would have been one of the charity shops near Chelsea, she haunted those places and... um... it must have been... ten or twelve years ago she gave it to me but I remember she'd had it for a few years before then.' Amelia remembered when Dotty had given it to her, she'd left school and was sharing a flat and Amelia had found the large frame to be very practical in covering up the massive cracks on the wall.

Vanessa smiled and turned on her heel, leaving a cloud of Coco Chanel in her wake.

Finally, after another hour of helping the waiting staff clear the room, Amelia was ready to head home to flop onto the sofa with a nightcap to watch some mind-numbing television programme before bed.

In the kitchen, she caught Gideon taking a selfie with one of the leftover langoustines from dinner. On seeing her he quickly dropped the seafood and hurried over, blocking her exit. 'You heading home?' he asked.

'Yes, thanks for your help tonight.'

'No problem, poppet. Would you be able to do me a little favour in return?'

'Sure, if I can.'

'Oh, you definitely can!' he said, then reached out and holding her chin, gently turned her face up to the light to inspect her cheek. 'I didn't want to bring it up earlier but now it's just you and me, you can tell me where you disappeared to before dinner, and why I saw you running full pelt towards the Gatehouse with half the forest attached to you. *And* how you got this wicked cut? Concealer can only hide so much.'

Amelia batted his hand away. 'I'm fine. It's far more interesting a story when I tell you the *outcome* rather than the *reason* I was a bit reckless.'

Gideon folded his arms and raised an eyebrow.

'Well, not exactly reckless.'

'Foolhardy? Dangerous? Stupid?' Toby said, appearing behind her and leaning against one of the worktables. 'Would one of those adjectives serve better?'

Amelia sighed. She'd hoped her brother wouldn't need to know about her rock-climbing antics. It was the sort of thing he got annoyed about.

She dug deep into her coat pocket and pulled out the phone. 'I found this.'

'And what is *this*?' Toby asked, coming over to take a closer look.

'I'm pretty sure it's Benedict Geissler's phone. I found it down the steep embankment in front of the bench.'

'The bench by the folly that he died on?' Gideon clarified.

'Yes.'

'You went back up there?'

Amelia nodded.

'Ooh, morbid much!' Gideon shuddered.

'It's not as if his rotting corpse is still there!' Amelia said with an eye-roll, not wanting to admit she'd felt a little chilled at returning to the scene of his death.

'Hang on, that's a pretty sheer drop,' Toby said, staring at her.

'It's not too bad as there are tree roots to grip and rocks jutting out to get a bit of a foothold on.'

Toby ran his hand through his hair and gave her a despairing look.

'But now I just have to work out how to open it.' Amelia had tried a few four-number codes, including the classic *1234* but nothing had been successful.

'Shouldn't you hand it into the police?' Toby said.

'They don't think he had a phone; they're not looking for one.'

'I don't think the law works like that, sis!' Toby said in exasperation.

Gideon tapped his index finger on his lips, as he thought. 'So, how did the phone get from the bench to over the brow of the hill?'

'Exactly!' Amelia said, glad someone in the room was on her wavelength. 'It's too far for him to have accidentally dropped it, and even if he'd dropped it then accidentally kicked it, it still wouldn't have reached the edge.'

'So, he either threw it away himself...' Gideon started to say.

'Or someone threw it for him,' Amelia finished.

And then they said in unison, 'But why?'

CHAPTER 13

22ND DECEMBER

Despite her argument with Ricky the previous evening, Evangelina arrived for breakfast the next morning bright-eyed and full of smiles.

'It will just be me this morning. Ricky has other plans today,' she said, sitting down at a table.

'Chamomile tea?' Amelia asked.

'Please... actually, can I have a regular tea instead please. And the full Scottish.'

'Of course.'

Amelia was heading back to the kitchen when she almost bumped into Lorcan who was standing fiddling with his phone. 'Hi, I left my ladders and my bag with all the picture hooks and wall mounts in it the other day, when I was getting those high-up paintings,' he said, dropping the phone into his pocket.

'No problem. Make sure you get some breakfast. Do you want to go sit down?'

'That would be great.' He peered into the dining room. 'Ahh, um, actually, I think it's probably better if I go and find my things, then get out your hair.'

Amelia followed his gaze, to where Evangelina was helping

herself to fruit from the buffet table while Lucy stood beside her, chatting animatedly. Though she seemed preoccupied with some melon slices, Evangelina's gaze kept sliding over to the door, and to Lorcan.

'Why don't you head back through to the kitchen after you collect your ladders?' Amelia said. 'You can grab a bite there?'

'Thanks, that would be great.' He headed down the corridor to the library then stopped. 'Oh, and Amelia,' he called out to her, 'I ended up taking all those paintings in frames home with me. Hope that's okay. It'll give me more time to look through them if they're in the studio.'

Amelia gave him a thumbs-up sign and smiled as that reminded her about getting Jack's book tour poster framed, and that he'd be back home in just a few hours.

'You look like the cat who's got the cream,' Gideon remarked when he saw her, moments later in the kitchen. 'Oh, of course! Jack's back today!' He made kissing noises as Toby slid a tray with a breakfast order on it towards him. 'Whose is this?'

'Carlo Todero's.'

'Have we had any more thoughts on the identity of the Secret Guest?' Gideon asked.

'I honestly don't know. It could be anyone,' Toby said with a helpless shrug.

Gideon studied the tray. 'Should we put something else on it to pretty it up, just in case it's him?'

'Like what?'

'I don't know, a flower?'

Amelia looked out the window. 'Good luck finding a flower under all that snow.' Although no more had fallen overnight, there were still a couple of inches lying. Amelia took a moment to enjoy the view as it looked set to be a beautiful day. That morning's sunrise had been a riot of cerise and magenta streaks and the sky had now settled into a bright blue with not a cloud in sight. But despite this and the sun shining valiantly through, the temperature was still in the minuses.

Gideon peeked under the silver cloche to inspect Carlo's order. 'Toast and boiled eggs?' he said wrinkling his nose. 'That's hardly going to show off your culinary expertise.'

'Maybe it's what he wants for breakfast?' Amelia suggested as she gently propelled Gideon towards the door. 'And he probably won't like it if it's cold by the time he gets it.'

By mid-morning, with nothing overly pressing to get done, Amelia ducked out and drove to the village to pick up some treats to stock up the fridge in the Gatehouse. By the time she'd parked on Main Street, the beautiful turquoise sky was darkening over.

'Snow's coming,' Big Davey said sagely from the doorway of the Whistling Haggis when he saw her.

Amelia looked out over the murky grey water, which had become very choppy, causing the small boats in the harbour to bob dramatically.

'Will you be coming in for the Christmas cake competition?' Big Davey asked.

'Yes! I'm looking forward to it,' Amelia called out as she locked the Jeep and ran over the well-gritted pavement to the shop entrance, where Jean had positioned a selection of snow shovels and sledges.

'You'll be looking forward to seeing Jack tonight,' Jean said as she rang through Amelia's purchases, which included a far healthier selection of food than she'd been surviving on for the previous couple of weeks. 'Will he make it along to the Christmas cake competition?'

'I'm not sure; it will depend when he gets in.'

'He'd best not leave it too late, in case the roads have to shut.'

'Do you think it'll come to that?' Amelia asked, with a glance out the window, where the sky had closed in even more.

'Oh yes, we're due for a right dumping over the next couple of days. We're quite far from the A-road so we'll be cut off fairly quickly when it gets bad, if the gritters don't make it in time. Oh, don't worry,' she added, seeing Amelia's face. 'I'm sure Jack will be fine.'

Getting back to the Jeep, Amelia checked her phone. No messages. She knew Jack's flight to Inverness was mid-afternoon, so he probably wouldn't have checked in yet. He'd then have to pick up his car from the airport and drive to Glencarlach which would take about an hour and a half. Chucking her shopping bags into the boot, Amelia drove back to the Gatehouse, confident that Jack and she would be tucking into Christmas cake together in the Whistling Haggis in a few short hours.

After stocking up the fridge and giving the Gatehouse a quick tidy Amelia parked the Jeep back at the hotel and was about to go inside when she saw a figure in the distance, about to head up to folly through the shortcut. There was no mistaking the flash of turquoise hair. India King. Amelia thought it good that the young girl was finally going out as a dose of fresh air would be a healthy break from being glued to her phone. But as Amelia watched her she thought there was something slightly suspicious about the teenager's demeanour as when she got to the entrance to the shortcut she had a look behind her then darted quickly out of sight.

Without a second thought, Amelia followed, hurrying over the snow to catch up with the girl. She slowed down as she reached the top of the incline and walked slowly so as not to draw attention to herself. But nonetheless the snow crunched under her boots. Then Amelia saw India just a few feet away, phone in hand, looking under the stone bench.

Was India looking for Geissler's phone too?

She saw India look at her phone again then slowly turn round, searching the area, then she walked carefully over to the steep edge Amelia had been clambering about on the previous day and peered down momentarily before turning away and looking back along the ground to the bench. Heart hammering, Amelia pressed herself up against the cold, damp wall of the folly, suddenly sure that the face which she'd thought had peered over at her in the dark belonged to India.

Not waiting another moment, Amelia hurried down the path, back to Stone Manor. What had Benedict Geissler been trying to tell her about India King?

'I think we need to keep a closer eye on India King,' Amelia said a short time later.

Gideon, who'd been pressed against the entrance door looking up at the snow fall, which had returned with a vengeance, turned to Amelia. 'Is she after more illicit vodka? The minx!'

'No, because I followed her up to the folly and she was searching for something, focusing mainly around the bench.'

'Looking for the phone?' Gideon suggested in a low voice.

'Possibly. And, I think she'd been up there the night I found the phone.'

Gideon gave her a questioning look.

'I didn't say anything, but just as I was climbing back up, I shone my torch up and I swear there was a pale face staring down at me. I'm now pretty certain it was India. Especially as last night, when she was going in to dinner she acted strangely when she saw me. I didn't think much of it at the time but with hindsight it could have been guilt.'

'Because she didn't hang around to see if you were in trouble and needed help.'

Amelia hushed him as his voice got a little louder with incredulity.

'Possibly, but I want to find out a little more about the girl.'

'Do you still think she's who the dead guy was talking about? Was he warning you about her? Does she have Psycho Emo tendencies? Did he even die of natural causes or do you think she could possibly have killed him?'

Amelia shrugged. 'Ray said because it's over Christmas, a post-mortem could take longer than usual. And I don't even know how long one would normally take! I'll ask Ray when I see him next.'

'And we're still no closer to working out who the Secret Guest is,' Gideon said with a dejected sigh.

'Hmm. At least these things can help take my mind off worrying about Jack.' Amelia cast a glance at the snowflakes, now as big as saucers, that were still falling. She turned away.

'Still no word?' Gideon asked.

Amelia checked her phone again but there was nothing new since Jack's last message telling her his flight to Inverness had been cancelled and that he was trying to get another flight and would let her know when he'd organised it.

'Oh, darling, don't worry, he'll be here. His sheer doggedness is part of his annoying charm,' Gideon said, turning his attention to the Christmas tree.

Amelia smiled and read through some emails, one of which was from Big Davey letting her know he had everything organised for the hen-do.

The only noise was the deep sonorous tick of the grandfather clock. Gideon played with the tinsel for a moment or two before sighing dramatically. 'I'm bored.'

'I've got some bed linen that needs to be sorted.'

He gave Amelia a look. 'Not that bored.' He wandered over to the drawing room, had a look inside and then returned to the desk. 'Where *is* everyone?' He leant over it to read Amelia's computer screen as she opened another email.

'I'm not sure, Gideon. We've discovered our guests prefer not to be fitted with tracking devices.'

'But how can we keep tabs on people and work out who the Secret Guest is if no one is about!' He drummed his fingers on the desk. 'Betty's with Hamish and Sally; the honeymooners are in their room, "getting over their jet lag",' he made air quotes. 'All the wedding party have gone out to visit a local castle. Together. Maybe the elusive Mr Griffith will turn up today.'

'You could always go and check on Toby?'

'He had his headphones in while he was making the fondant potato things. I suppose I could go and... Ooh, hang on!' He perked up as he heard a door close on the first floor and seconds later DeShawn and Alaiya walked slowly down the stairs dressed for the outdoors. They looked very serious and were deep in conversation. At the same time the front door opened and Vanessa walked in with Terence. Both couples converged at the bottom of the stairs at the same time.

'Hello there!' Terence said in his usual affable way when he saw the Johnsons.

Alaiya rested her hand on her husband's arm in an almost restraining way.

Vanessa peered at DeShawn over her glasses, then with a dismissive toss of her head, completely blanked the newlyweds and sailed on past into the bar where she could be heard calling out to Craig for her usual; a Campari and orange.

Terence made an innocuous remark about the weather then followed his wife into the bar.

Amelia saw Alaiya whisper something to DeShawn and he nodded. Amelia couldn't hear what was said, but she knew Gideon had, as being barely two feet away, picking some imaginary fluff from the bottom stair, his eyes widened.

'Would you like a dinner reservation for tonight?' Amelia asked them.

'No, thank you. We'll be eating out again tonight,' Alaiya said as they left.

Amelia smiled. 'Have a lovely afternoon.'

The second the door shut behind them, Gideon hurried over. 'Did you see that?'

'I did! What did Mrs Johnson say to her husband?'

'She said, "Don't rise to it, she's not worth it." *Some*thing has clearly happened!'

Amelia watched as the Johnsons walked away from the hotel, arm in arm, shoulders hunched against the falling snow. 'But the question is, did that something occur since they've been here? Or before?'

'Exactly!' Gideon agreed. 'You know, I'm sure Craig mentioned earlier he could do with a hand. I'll start with dusting off that bottle of Campari. I'm surprised the seventies haven't called yet asking for their drink back!'

Amelia laughed. Until Vanessa had shown up the Campari had sat untouched on the shelf and Amelia was pretty certain it would remain untouched unless Vanessa ever returned to Stone Manor.

And with boredom forgotten, Amelia watched as Gideon marched towards the bar, homing in on potential gossip like a heat-seeking missile.

CHAPTER 14

Lorcan hadn't expected to speak to Evangelina again. He thought the way she'd run away the previous morning was a fairly strong indication that she'd changed her mind about wanting to talk. He'd planned on avoiding Stone Manor at all costs until he was sure the wedding party had left and Evangelina was ensconced back in London. With her husband.

Lorcan had had some strong words to say to himself after the giddy excitement he'd felt when she'd turned up at his house. He felt like a teenager with his first crush. Or more accurately, he felt like the twenty-year-old Lorcan who'd fallen completely and utterly head over heels for Evangelina all those years ago. He'd spent the intervening hours wondering if he'd actually ever fallen out of love with her. But she was married! And he knew that! But yet, he'd still felt that kick of excitement and the intervening years had fallen away instantly when he'd seen her again.

Yes, it was far better he completely avoid her.

Until he realised, he'd left his ladders in the very place he was trying to avoid…

Although he'd scuttled past the dining room that morning, he knew she'd spotted him. He'd quickly collected everything he needed and had been on his way out, when he turned to see her standing in the doorway. He'd been so surprised he'd nearly dropped his ladders on his foot.

'I'm so sorry for leaving the way I did,' Evangelina said, quickly, a little breathlessly. 'I want to explain. Can we try again?'

Lorcan knew this was the point he should have looked past her, into the middle distance and said 'No,' with the perfect balance of hurt and regret. And she'd know his affections weren't to be trifled with.

And then she might have said something like, 'What about us?'

And that's when Lorcan would have said, 'We'll always have Glasgow.' And then he'd have hoisted up his ladders, his bag of tools over his other shoulder and looked at her sadly, possibly a little wistfully and said, 'Where I'm going, you can't follow. Someday you'll understand that. Not now. Here's looking at you, kid.' And channelling his best cool and detached Rick Blaine from *Casablanca*, he'd have walked away. And not looked back. And in this fantasy, his ladders didn't clunk, he didn't struggle to carry them and he managed to fit through all the doors with his cumbersome bag smoothly and in one go without knocking chunks out the wall or swearing as he bashed his knuckles against the doorframe.

But of course, it didn't play out like that. He looked at her like a startled deer in headlights, croaked an 'okay' and then they'd stared at each other for a long moment until he said, 'I'll come by later, about five. I'll see you in the drawing room. If it's too busy we can find somewhere quieter.' He figured a public place would be better and the drawing room would be relatively quiet. He visited Stone Manor a lot and it wouldn't look strange if he turned up. It also meant that, with her husband being close it was less likely he'd make an absolute fool of himself by declaring his undying love and suggesting they run away together. Less likely, but not completely outwith the realms of possibility he acknowledged hopelessly.

She'd nodded in agreement then turned and left in a floral wave of gardenias that brought back so many memories. Couldn't she at least have had the decency to change her perfume in the intervening years?

And since their encounter that morning, Lorcan had been holed up in his studio, looking through his old photos and paintings, living in his memories and torturing himself by checking his phone every few minutes, counting down the hours.

Would he never learn?

He checked his watch; it was almost 2pm. At least he had something to take his mind off Evangelina for the next wee while. He had another rendezvous. And Lorcan trusted *this* meeting wouldn't make his heart race to the point he thought he needed medical assistance and leave him stuttering.

Since the phone call a few weeks previously and the mysterious commission, Lorcan had waited patiently and asked no probing questions.

He'd been promised answers and an explanation today and was looking forward to finding out the reason for all the secrecy. Then he could throw all his efforts into the Glencarlach art exhibition.

And try to avoid having his heart broken. Again.

CHAPTER 15

The rest of the afternoon passed uneventfully for Amelia. Jack had managed to send her a quick update on his travel plans; Toby was hidden away in the kitchen; and Gideon hadn't resurfaced from lending a hand in the bar from where Amelia frequently heard Vanessa's loud laugh ringing out. Carlo and Lucy returned from the castle explorations, giggling conspiratorially together as they ran upstairs, followed a few minutes later by the Kings.

'Fancy a drink, darling?' Dan asked, shaking snow off his hood and stuffing his gloves back into his pocket. At that moment Vanessa laughed uproariously from the bar.

With a brief glance at her husband Alice shook her head, making the pompom on top of her woolly hat dance about. 'Maybe we should pop to our rooms first and freshen up.'

'Good idea,' Dan said as he followed his wife and daughter up the stairs.

Evangelina briefly poked her head out the drawing room door, saw the Kings going upstairs then went back inside the room, picking up that day's *Guardian* and sitting down beside the fire.

Amelia wondered if it was just a coincidence that Alice and Dan didn't want to go for a drink because they knew Vanessa was there. Amelia guessed the American agent could possibly be a little overbearing.

Just as the grandfather clock struck five a car pulled up at the bottom of the front steps. Someone engulfed in a massive parka with a furry hood got out the passenger seat, opened up the back door and helped Betty out. As they made their way up the steps, the parka hood slipped down to reveal the masses of reddish golden tresses of Sally.

'Oh my goodness, this weather!' Sally exclaimed as Amelia opened the door for her and Betty. Hamish was just behind them.

'What a great day!' Betty declared. 'I'm going to go and visit that nice young man, Craig, to see if he can make me a little aperitif before dinner.' She gave Sally a hug before heading towards the bar.

Once out of earshot, Sally turned and gave Amelia a fixed grin. 'I'm exhausted! We thought we'd lost her at one point but she'd run off to make snow angels with some kids!'

'Aye, she kept us on our toes, right enough!' Hamish agreed.

'That's us officially finished entertaining Betty duty. It's on to Hamish's mum and dad now.'

'They've got her for the tricky bit – Christmas lunch!' Hamish said.

'And I thought I talked a lot!' Sally said, stifling a yawn. 'Although I hope to have half her energy at her age!' She turned to Hamish. 'Are all her stories true?'

'Oh aye,' Hamish nodded. 'She was, still is, quite the character. Travelled the world, had multiple affairs, a couple of notable actors, artists and politicians. Had a right old party time in London when she was younger. Got in with a bohemian crowd, was even an artist's muse for a while. It was all drugs and orgies as I understand.'

119

'Wow, I feel really dull now,' Amelia said slightly wistfully, loving the fact Betty had led such a colourful life.

'Some of the family still regard her with suspicion,' Hamish said with a sad little shrug.

'Are you still up for the Christmas cake competition in the Whistling Haggis?' Sally asked.

'Definitely!' Amelia said, dropping her pen down on the desk and closing over her notebook.

'You ladies have fun; I'm going to give it a miss as I've got an early start tomorrow morning!' Hamish said as he put his hood back up and hurried down the steps to his car.

'Is Betty really that exhausting? She seems so sweet?' Amelia said as Sally waved goodbye to her fiancé.

'Yes! She has so much energy and always on the go and expects us to keep up. Her stories are wild. Did you know she was at Woodstock?' Sally said, clearly in awe. 'Anyway, how are you? When's Jack due home?'

'I don't know. He managed to get booked on a later flight to Aberdeen, which took off half an hour ago. It means a much longer drive but at least he's heading in the right direction.' Automatically, Amelia looked out at the snow, where it was still layering up on the ornamental fountain on the driveway, giving everything an amorphous white shape. And then, looming out the snow, stomping up the steps came Lorcan, wrapped up like he was about to scale Mount Everest.

'Hiya, thought I'd have a couple of drinks if that's okay. Maybe the drawing room?'

'Of course,' Amelia said and couldn't help but wonder if he knew Evangelina would be there.

'Lorcan!' Sally called out as he was unzipping his jacket to hang up on the coat stand by the front door. 'You up for the Whistling Haggis Christmas cake competition tonight? I want this one to stop worrying about Jack,' Sally said, with a nod to

Amelia. 'And what better way to do it than by demolishing tons of fruit cake and marzipan.'

'Sounds good,' Lorcan said, unhooking the ice grips from his boots. He pointed out towards the end of the drive. 'Looks like you've got someone coming.'

Amelia turned to see two yellow orbs of car headlights appear from the blizzard. The little car crept slowly along towards Stone Manor, skidding slightly as it circled round the fountain.

'It'll no doubt be Evangelina's friend, or possibly the elusive Mr Griffin,' Amelia said as the car came to a careful stop. Evangelina also came to the door of the drawing room.

Moments later the main door opened and two people walked in.

'Nisha!' Evangelina cried in delight at the same time Sally exclaimed, 'Kit?!'

The woman, Nisha, smiled at her friend then noticed the others in reception. Her eyes widened slightly before she said, 'Lorcan?'

CHAPTER 16

I t was like a Western standoff with everyone staring at each other.

'Hiya, Nisha,' Lorcan said eventually, looking a little like a rabbit caught in headlights.

Nisha slowly took off her hat, shaking out shoulder length black hair as her dark brown eyes swept over the scene. Her lips parted to say something but that was when Evangelina ran over and hugged her, saying, 'It's so good to see you!'

Taking this as a cue, Sally also launched herself at the other guest, who, on closer inspection, Amelia realised was familiar.

'Ames! Do you remember my cousin, Kit?'

Now it was Amelia's turn to do a double-take. Sally's cousin, Kit, was a couple of years older than them. Amelia remembered him as a bit of an awkward, scrawny teenager deeply into prog rock and the Dungeons and Dragons role-playing game. He'd certainly changed a lot! Gone were the thick glasses and teenage acne, and his long lank ponytail had been cut off to reveal dark wavy hair that he brushed away from his thick eyebrows revealing deep blue eyes.

'Long time no see, Amelia,' he said, his accent only showing a slight hint of the soft West Country lilt of his cousin's. Grinning at her, he shook snow from his mop of hair.

'What are you doing here?' Sally asked, giving him another gigantic hug, almost squeezing the life out of him.

'I couldn't let my favourite little cousin be all alone up here in the wilds without at least one family member on side at Christmas.'

Sally hugged him again.

'Just as I couldn't abandon my best friend at Christmas either,' Nisha said archly to Evangelina.

'Do you two know each other?' Sally asked her cousin, pointing to Nisha.

Kit shook his head. 'No, it was a highly serendipitous meeting at the hire car point at Edinburgh airport.'

Nisha laughed as she unbuttoned her coat. 'We both got talking while we were waiting for the guy in front of us to finish and realised that we were heading to the same place. It saved on money and gave us company.'

'You didn't happen to book under a pseudonym, did you?' Amelia asked Kit, wondering if he could be 'Mr Griffin' wanting to surprise Sally.

'No, although that does sound very cloak and dagger!' he said with a vulpine smile. 'I'm afraid I don't have any reservation at all. If there's no room, could I kip on your sofa, Sals?'

'Don't worry!' Amelia said. 'We've got rooms!' And she went to book them in. As she did so she glanced up at Lorcan who was scuffing one Doc Martened toe against the other, looking very uncomfortable.

'Have you two…' Nisha started to ask but before she could finish the sentence Evangelina quickly linked her arm through Nisha's. 'Let's wait and have a proper catch-up once you settle in, yeah?'

The look shared between them wasn't lost on Amelia as she handed Nisha the key to the Highsmith Room.

'I'm so glad we made it,' Nisha said. 'The roads are getting really bad, especially the last few miles leading to the village. There were a couple of highway maintenance vans that had stopped and were unloading traffic cones as we were passing. It looked like they were going to shut the road.'

Amelia looked worriedly out the window. She turned back to Nisha, a smile on her face to mask her concern that Jack might not get back home.

'Come on, I'll help you get unpacked,' Evangelina said as Nisha walked up the stairs, giving Lorcan an apologetic look as she followed her friend.

Sally's cousin sauntered over to the reception desk as Amelia typed in the name *Kit Trelawney*.

'You are looking very well, Amelia.' He winked. 'Sally's kept me up to date on everything up here. What a great place you have! I'm looking forward to a few days' rest and recuperation!'

Sally beamed up at her cousin. 'We were just about to head to the Whistling Haggis to watch the judging of the Christmas cake competition. Want to come with us?'

'Definitely. Let me go stick on a fresh shirt first.'

'There you go, the Cleeves Room.'

'Ah, great!' He winked again at Amelia before turning and bounding up the stairs.

Sally hugged herself and squealed in happiness. 'I'm so happy he's here! I've not seen him properly in so long! He always seems to be working abroad now. Our parents had all booked a Caribbean cruise together over Christmas so it's lovely we'll be spending Christmas together too!'

Amelia turned to Lorcan who was still standing hesitantly.

'Why don't you skip the drink here, Lorcan, and we can head to the Whistling Haggis together? We're meeting Gideon there too.'

He reached to get his padded parka. 'That sounds a great idea,' he said with a brief glance up the stairs.

Amelia grinned. She was also very much in the mood for some Christmas cake. With a side order of finding out just how well Lorcan and Evangelina knew each other and just how Nisha Khatri and Ricky Varelli fitted into the picture.

Gideon had already reserved a table by the time they piled into the Whistling Haggis. The snowfall didn't look like it was going to let up any time soon. Even just walking had proved a challenge and Amelia was thankful for the tyre marks on the drive which had compacted the snow, allowing them to walk more easily, otherwise they'd have been tramping through almost foot-high drifts.

Amelia introduced Gideon to Sally's cousin.

'Do all men down your neck of the woods look like Ross Poldark?' Gideon asked Sally as Kit went up to the bar to get a round in.

Sally laughed. 'He's got to keep me sweet as I have plenty of photographic proof that he hasn't always looked like that! He was no oil painting as a teenager, trust me.'

Amelia turned to Lorcan and segued smoothly in with, 'Speaking of paintings, how's work for the exhibition getting on?'

'It's going well, everyone has been so generous with items for the auction,' he said as he chipped away absent-mindedly at a rough bit of wood on the table.

'I wondered if you and Evangelina had had time to catch up with each other. You know each other from before, yes?'

Lorcan looked back at Amelia sharply.

'I kind of overheard you talking. And you know her friend, Nisha, too?' Amelia asked in a friendly conversational way.

Lorcan sighed and made a half-hearted attempt at his usual easy grin. A crowded pub wasn't the most private place to be digging a little deeper into his relationship with Evangelina but with everyone else chatting with each other, no one noticed Amelia leaning in a little further to him as he spoke.

'Yeah, I knew Evangelina. Years ago, when we were both in

Glasgow. I was at the Art School and Evangelina was at the RSAMD, as the Royal Conservatoire was known back then. We had a lot of friends in common and hung about in a group together, living the typical student life.'

'Nisha too?'

He shook his head. 'She wasn't studying there; she was an old school friend of Evangelina's. The place she was studying didn't have the same nightlife as Glasgow so she came up for regular weekends.'

'You never let on you knew Evangelina!'

He puffed out his cheeks. 'To be honest I didn't know if she'd remember me.' He laughed as he smoothed down his goatee. 'I'd look a right eejit if I made a big play of us being friends and then she didn't know me from Adam. My student days feel like a lifetime ago.'

Amelia nodded. She could see how that would be quite a blow to anyone's ego.

'I just wanted to play it on the down-low.'

'Maybe she felt the same.'

'Maybe.'

Just then Kit came back with a tray groaning under the weight of multiple drinks.

'I already love it here! Everyone is so friendly. And everyone seems to know you and your fiancé, cuz.'

'Everyone knowing everyone else's business can be both a blessing and a curse,' Sally said as she plucked a large glass of red wine from the tray.

Kit took a deep swallow of his pint and smacked his lips in approval, then sat back in his chair. 'The guy behind the bar said there was a robbery the other night?'

Sally gave her cousin a playful swipe on the arm. 'No work!'

'Work?' Gideon asked, his interest clearly piqued.

'He's a journalist,' Sally said.

'Oh!' Amelia said with an intake of breath as she felt a foot whack against her shin. She rubbed her leg as Gideon leant back in his chair, frantically pointing at Kit and mouthing '*Secret Guest.*'

Kit clearly mistook Amelia's gasp as being one of horror as he quickly clarified, 'I'm not tabloid paparazzi or anything like that. I'm investigative journalism. And I'm looking forward to a relaxing few days when I don't have to even think about work,' Kit said cheerily as he picked up the menu and turned it over to read that day's specials. 'Although with all these Winter Festival events the guys were telling me about at the bar, it sounds like it's going to be busy around here. Not quite such a sleepy little place, after all, eh?'

'So, do you travel a lot with your work?' Gideon asked.

Kit nodded. 'Yes, at times.'

'Been anywhere exciting lately?'

'It depends what you define as exciting?' Kit said with a wry smile. 'Unless covering political unrest in Cuba, government corruption in Caracas or eating disorders in models in the Berlin fashion world floats your boat.'

'What about Italy? Venice to be precise. Or San Sebastian?'

Kit gave him a strange look and it was Amelia's turn to do the kicking as she gave Gideon a warning shake of the head. His line of inquiry was hardly covert!

But before anyone else could talk any further Big Davey rang the bell that normally meant last orders.

'Okay, ladies and gentleman and everyone else in between. It's time for the highlight of our day. It's the Christmas cake competition!'

There was a rowdy cheer from the bar. Being towards the back, Amelia stood up to get a better look. Just then the pub door opened and Toby came in, slightly out of breath and shaking snow off his hat.

'Have I missed anything?' he asked as he craned his neck to get a better look towards Davey.

'Just Gideon's woeful lack of subtlety,' Amelia said, realising her brother looked a little flustered. She grabbed hold of his arm and pulled him back. 'Have you entered a cake into the competition?'

He turned and grinned at her as Big Davey continued to bellow to the pub. 'Now then, tonight's very special guest judge is none other than our doyen of groceries... The. Divine. Jean. Maddox.'

There was a chorus of cheers and wolf whistles as a rather gin-flushed Jean stood up.

'Now, I hope you've all been careful with the amount of brandy you've been adding as we don't want Jean getting too merry. She's got a piece of mistletoe with her and she's not afraid to use it!'

'Well, you won't be first in my sights, if that's the case, Davey,' Jean fired back to the approval of the pub and Davey played up to the cheering as he clutched his hand to his heart and staggered back, pretending to be wounded.

'I do have a very strict criteria to meet,' Jean said. 'I'm looking for moistness...'

Some wag in the bar shouted out 'oo-errrr'.

Jean cast them a withering look and carried on. 'Plenty of fruit. Excellent flavour. I like a generous amount of marzipan! And of course, it willnae have hurt if someone slipped me a tenner before we started.'

Another cheer went up.

'Obviously I'm joking. Davey has kindly been collecting all the cakes. He's cut them up and placed them on plates with the baker's name stuck to the bottom so I've no idea who made the cake.'

'And with that, let the tasting commence.' Davey rang the bell again.

As most of the pub pushed forward to get a better look, engrossed in Jean's comments Gideon took Amelia to the side.

'What do you think of Kit being the Secret Guest?'

Amelia looked over to where Kit and Sally were chatting happily to each other and laughing. 'I'm not convinced. He wasn't even sure there would be a room for him?'

Gideon looked over at them, his eyes narrowing thoughtfully. 'I'm sure Sally could have easily let slip something about you having bookings but not being fully booked.'

'True. But let's not put all our eggs in the one basket. We need to be on guard for everyone.'

'And to keep a close eye on India King,' Gideon reminded her.

'As well as putting on an absolute kick-ass wedding that could put our name on the map of venues.'

'Just another normal week then!' Gideon said with a laugh.

Toby sidled up to them both. 'What are you two whispering about?'

'Just wondering which one's your cake,' Gideon said smoothly. 'Can you tell?'

Toby shook his head.

'Fancy your chances?' Amelia asked.

'Evidently the same lady has won it the last three years in a row.'

Amelia watched as her brother looked on, chewing his lip. 'Oh my God, are you nervous?'

'No!' he scoffed. There was a pause. 'Well, maybe a bit. I just realised I've totally put my name on the line with this! What if I'm last? How will that look for the hotel?'

'Don't worry, they only read out the top three.'

'I'm getting a drink in. Fancy another?' Toby said.

'Yes please.' Amelia nodded.

'A Coke, please. Full sugar,' Gideon added. 'I feel like living dangerously!'

Gideon waited until Toby was out of earshot before asking, 'Anything more about Lorcan and Evangelina?'

Amelia brought him up to speed, telling him about Nisha too.

Gideon frowned. 'It does sound a plausible enough reason to not immediately announce they know each other, but why all the secret conversations behind closed doors?'

'That's what I thought. There's definitely more to it than Lorcan's letting on.'

A hushed air of expectancy fell on the bar as Davey rang the bell again.

'Okay, after much deliberation, Jean has her top three. Drum roll, please!'

People started banging on the tables.

'In third place it's... Roddy McDade!'

A cheer went up.

'In second place it's... Toby Adams!'

'Woooooooo!' Amelia cheered as her brother grinned at the applause he received.

'And in first place, winning this very highly coveted wooden spoon...'

'Oh!' Gideon gasped as he saw the prize given out. 'It *is* an actual wooden spoon with a ribbon tied round it!'

'Is... Annie Campbell! Her fourth year in a row!'

A cheer went up as a very delighted lady went up to claim her prize.

'Phew! I live to bake another day,' Toby said in relief. 'Who's that with Sally?'

'Do you remember Kit?'

'Her cousin?'

'Yup.'

'Bloody hell!' Toby said as he turned and looked again.

'And we have him as a potential suspect as the Secret Guest,' Gideon added as they sat back down at their table with Toby drawing up another stool.

As they drank and chatted and reminisced, plates of the Christmas cakes were plonked on each table and the bar got steadily rowdier with pre-Christmas bonhomie. Amelia snuck a glance at her phone. It was half past eleven and there was still no update from Jack. She sat back for a moment letting all the voices wash over her as a little knot of anxiety niggled at her stomach as she tried not to think of cars skidding on icy roads and ending up in deep snow drifts. Much as the evening had been fun, she now just wanted to get home.

'I'm going to call it a night, guys,' she said, standing up and getting her belongings together.

There was a chorus of disappointed 'ohs' but Amelia blew them all a kiss and made her way outside. The door closed behind her and the warmth and noise from inside the pub was a memory as she was immediately catapulted into a silent, snow-muffled winter wonderland. She looked up at the old-fashioned street lamp and the flakes of snow falling, landing on her cheeks. Jamming her hands into her pockets she started back to the Gatehouse. She'd just got to the corner and was about to turn up the lane when she heard Gideon calling after her.

'Wait up!' he shouted, his breath clouding in the cold.

'Not fancy staying?'

He shook his head. 'Not tonight.'

They linked arms cosily together as they made their very slow way through the deep snow.

'It's a bit of a workout, isn't it!' Amelia said, slightly out of breath from the exertion.

'Good for the calf muscles, I imagine,' Gideon said before pausing briefly to light up a cigarette.

'I thought you'd stopped.'

'I can't be too virtuous all the time, darling! I still need some sort of vice.' Gideon flashed her a grin, but despite his smile, he looked tired and a little drawn, the angular planes of his face looking bonier than usual.

'Are you okay?' Amelia asked.

He nodded as he exhaled the cigarette smoke. 'I'll be fine, I just needed to get out of the pub, have some fresh air.' He looked at the end of his cigarette and laughed at the irony. 'You know what I mean.'

Amelia sometimes forgot how successfully Gideon had managed to turn his life around. When she'd first met him, he was never far from a drink, but his glib party-like persona hid far deeper issues of depression, repression and alcoholism. He'd managed to stop drinking, never complaining if anyone drank beside him, still liking the social aspects of popping into the Whistling Haggis.

'Was it tough being in the pub tonight?'

He squeezed her arm a little as they continued to walk. 'It wasn't so much the pub. You see, I'm so glad I gave up alcohol; it really was the best thing I ever did and I genuinely don't miss it. I tend to not even think about it. By not drinking I managed to stop that incessant chatter in my head which was always either goading me to drink or berating me for drinking.

'But tonight, it was the Christmas cake being passed around that made me feel... odd. I had this horrible moment when I looked at everyone else eating the cake, eating *Toby's* cake, and for one tiny split second I just wanted to be like everybody else and eat the damn cake and I just thought how bloody unfair it is that I can't eat even a tiny piece.

'But I know they'll be laced with booze and I don't want to risk getting a taste for the brandy or whisky or whatever that's in it in case I spiral. And that sent me into a tailspin of how easily I could lose everything, that it's all so tragically fragile and how I could so easily fuck everything right up in a thoughtless moment of self-destruction. So, I thought I'd better leave.' He gave a dry laugh. 'And the bloody stupid thing is I don't even like fruit cake.'

Amelia squeezed Gideon's arm.

They walked a little in silence.

'I also know that Jack is horribly late,' Gideon blurted out. 'I know you must be worried and I don't want you to think I'm not mentioning it because I don't care. I just didn't want you to start getting maudlin.'

'That's okay. I know he'll get here when he can.'

An owl hooted and Gideon jumped then stumbled. He would have fallen headfirst into the snow had Amelia not grabbed hold of him to keep him upright.

'I don't care how long we've been living in the countryside, but I will *never* get used to the damn hoots, wails, yowls and rustlings of the night. Traffic and busy streets hide a lot of unsavoury spooky noises I'd rather not know about,' Gideon said, repositioning his hat that had fallen down over his eyes. 'How do you manage to live in the Gatehouse without practically dying of fright every night? It's bad enough living in the village with people all around me!'

'I like it!' Amelia said.

'What about sharing a wood with the headless horseman?'

'That's all made-up nonsense.'

'I don't know. There's a lot of ghost stories connected with this place. Too many for my liking.' They stopped for a moment. 'Oh my God, I've now convinced myself I can hear horse hooves,' Gideon said.

Amelia gave a little shiver as she, too, fancied she could hear a far-off rhythmic pounding.

They both stood completely still. They heard a neigh in the distance.

'Fuck!' Gideon wailed, looking at Amelia in terror. 'It *is* a horse. The headless horseman is coming to get us!'

CHAPTER 17

'I t...' Amelia tried to think of an alternative explanation of the noise but now, getting closer, it was definitely that of a horse.

'Oh my God, he's going to kill us!'

'We don't know that! He's just meant to haunt the wood,' Amelia said in a voice that came out far braver than she felt.

'Didn't he off one of your godmother's ancestors?'

Amelia realised she and Gideon were now hugging each other tightly.

'He's coming,' Gideon said in a very small voice, then screwed his eyes tight shut, blindly awaiting his fate.

The whiteness of the snow on the ground and in the trees, and the lights along the drive gave enough illumination for Amelia to make out a horse and rider looming from the way they'd come... and it looked like the horseman was raising an arm in greeting. The folklore had certainly missed out the detail that the headless horseman gave a friendly wave as he cantered past. And Amelia wasn't even sure the figure was headless. She was sure she could see a bobble hat. It also looked very much as if it was wearing a sky-blue North Face-style padded jacket. And it was definitely calling out her name.

Gideon gave a wail as Amelia frantically waved back.

Seconds later the horse pulled up beside them, steam pluming from its nostrils as Jack slid down from the horse's back. Amelia let go of Gideon's hand and rushed towards Jack who immediately pulled her off her feet and gave her such a knee-trembler of a kiss that it knocked the breath from her.

Amelia only reluctantly untangled herself from Jack when she heard Gideon shout out, 'Get a room, you horny buggers!'

'I told you I'd make it back on the twenty-second.' Jack checked his watch. 'And by my calculations I've got about three minutes to spare.'

'I'm sure you could use that time wisely by giving some other poor person a heart attack!' Gideon said haughtily.

'Good to see you too, Gideon.' Jack grinned, his green eyes crinkling at the corners.

'But… but…' Amelia said, gesturing to the horse.

'The road's closed. I drove as near as I could but couldn't get closer than a couple of miles away when the hire car got stuck in a drift. I was trying to push it out when the farmer came by. It was Gary McDougall. He let me take one of his horses. It's unshod so can go over snow.'

Amelia didn't know who to embrace next; Jack again, the horse, or Gary McDougall!

'But how are we going to get it back to him?'

'Don't worry, he's following with his son on a tractor. They're trying to clear some of the minor roads leading to the farther out farms. One of them will take it back.'

'Could you not just have come on the tractor?' Gideon asked, rubbing the horse's nose.

'I wouldn't have got here in time and it would have kind of ruined my dashing hero plan. I figured a horse was sexier.'

Amelia couldn't have agreed more judging by the way her libido was leaping about and her overwhelming desire to drag Jack into the Gatehouse.

'It wouldn't have shaved a couple of years off my life,' Gideon grumbled. 'Well, you two love birds clearly have some catching up to do so I shall head back to the hotel.'

'Will you be okay?' Amelia called out.

Gideon took a deep breath, looked back along the drive as if weighing up his answer. He eventually smiled and gave her a wink. 'You should know by now, poppet, I'm always absolutely splendid.'

23 December

Amelia rolled over in bed, her nostrils twitching at the welcome smell of coffee. Opening one eye she saw the outline of Jack at the bottom of the bed, carrying her favourite mug with steam billowing up from it.

'Morning!' Amelia stretched contentedly as Jack placed the mug on the bedside table beside her and bounced back into bed.

'I am so glad to be back!' Jack said with a happy sigh as he reached over and began kissing Amelia's neck, sending little shivers of delight through her body.

'Me too!' Amelia said, idly tracing a finger across his taut abdomen. He made to move on top of her but accidentally knocked the bedside table lamp onto the floor which made the coffee splosh out the mug and onto a pile of books waiting to be read.

'This must seem really pokey and small, compared to your sprawling Upper East side apartment,' Amelia teased as Jack righted the lamp, amorous intentions dampened as he mopped up the spilled coffee.

A few months previously they'd gone over to New York so Jack could show her around his old haunts and she'd been blown sideways by his stunningly beautiful converted warehouse apartment in one of the most coveted parts of the city.

Jack lay back on the pillow and gave a slight chuckle. 'I'm afraid it'll be getting even more squashed than we first thought. Turns out I had a lot more stuff than I'd realised and I ended up not getting rid of quite as much as I'd planned.'

Amelia rolled over to look at him, wondering if his massive corner sofa was one of the items he didn't get rid of. There was no way it would fit in their cosy and cramped little Gatehouse.

'Don't worry, most of the furniture is away,' he said as if reading her mind, 'but I have kept my bookshelves and most of my books, and lamps. And the odd chair or two. And hat stand. Then there are the paintings. There's also my antique cocktail bar.' He looked at her sheepishly. 'Turns out I'm no Marie Kondo when it comes to ruthlessly decluttering.'

'I love all those things but...' She sat up and looked around their bedroom, where the small double bed, slim wardrobe and bedside tables took up all the room. 'When's it coming?'

'Bulky stuff coming on container ships in about a month. I have some smaller things coming express air freight which will be here sooner. I'll organise a storage unit.'

'That'll give us some time to think of what to do.' She drew her knees up to her chest. 'We're going to have to move, aren't we?'

Jack also sat up and kissed her shoulder. 'Probably. I mean, having a bed where my feet don't hang out the end would be nice.' To illustrate, he wiggled his toes.

'As would having an actual study where you can write rather than commandeering the kitchen table.'

'Hey, there's no rush. I know how much this place means to you. And me.'

'True, but it will be fun house hunting together.'

'We could maybe get somewhere like Lorcan's, with amazing views...'

'That would be lovely,' Amelia thought wistfully.

'So, what's the plan for today? Can we spend all day in bed

together?' Jack asked hopefully, kissing her neck. 'If so, you'll have to be gentle with me.'

'Is that so?'

'I'm still bruised from the other night,' he said checking his arms.

'Bruised?'

'Yes, when that jogger ran into me and knocked me over.' He moved on to his other arm. 'See, there!'

Amelia peered at a very small, bluish pigmentation of the skin above his elbow.

'Oh dear, poor baby!'

'Well, it was a big bruise right after and... and now you're just mocking me.'

'Only a little bit,' Amelia said as she gave the mark a kiss.

'It was really annoying though. I hadn't realised that my hotel key must have fallen out my pocket on impact and straight after talking to you I went for a drink–'

'Knew it!' Amelia said with great satisfaction.

'–and when I got back to the hotel it was late, and the night porter was very suspicious of me, especially as I'd had a couple of beers. You know, he said I didn't look like a writer! What the hell is that meant to mean?'

'Are you more upset he didn't recognise you?' Amelia teased.

'Hey! I'm secure in my anonymity. I'm no Gideon! But of course, I had no picture ID on me as I'd left my driver's licence here and my passport was in my room, which he wasn't willing to let me into the room to get! Luckily I had one of my author flyers with me and I showed him that and he reluctantly let me into my room.'

'Phew!'

'And that is why I won't be in a hurry to go back to... busy,' he kissed her shoulder, 'jostling,' he kissed the hollow of her collarbone, 'suspicious,' he kissed her neck, 'London,' he kissed her a little further up her neck, just below the earlobe, which he knew made her melt, 'anytime soon.' He went to kiss her on the mouth but Amelia very reluctantly put her finger to his lips.

'I really wish we could do this all day, but I can't,' she said and gave a frustrated groan. 'I need to work. It's all hands on deck as we're short staffed due to a cold bug and we've now got more people staying. Although Gideon has moved into the hotel to be on hand to help.'

After they'd both stopped laughing Jack gave a stretch and yawned. 'Well, if I can't tempt you to a day of wanton debauchery I should probably go and grab my bags from the hire car I abandoned last night. I didn't think I'd look quite so heroic with my wheeled suitcase and duty-free bags in tow. The snow seems to have stopped for now, but I don't know if I'll be able to dig the car out. Then I guess I'll spend some time reacquainting myself with Glencarlach.'

'You mean going for a drink in the Whistling Haggis?'

Jack nodded. 'Then I'll make us a nice dinner for your return home as I know you'll have eaten crap for the last couple of weeks.'

'You have no faith!' Amelia said in mock outrage.

'I saw all the empty Pot Noodle containers in the bin.'

'Ah… well, I'm going for a bath,' Amelia said before he could bring up any more junk food wrappers he'd discovered.

A few minutes later, Amelia sank happily back into her bath, going over what needed to be done that day. Her phone ringing jolted her out of her reverie. Still lying back, luxuriating in the hot water, she answered.

'Sorry, say that again?' Amelia said into her mobile seconds later. Sitting bolt upright, she ignored the sandalwood and rose scented bubbles cascading over the top of the tub and splashing onto the floor.

James carefully repeated what he'd just told her. 'Mr Todero is reporting a theft. Betty woke up in the middle of the night to see someone standing in her room. And the boiler light is flashing and it's making a funny noise.'

CHAPTER 18

23RD DECEMBER

Arriving ten minutes later with her hair damp and cheeks still pink from the hot water, Amelia went to see Betty, who James had sat in the drawing room with a cup of tea. Fully expecting to find the elderly lady shaken by her ordeal, she was taken aback to find Betty holding court with some of the other guests, clearly revelling in retelling her story.

'I definitely thought my time was up!'

Alaiya, who was sitting next to her, patted her hand. 'You must have been terrified?'

'Well, dear, I did have a moment when my life flashed before my eyes, and do you know what I thought? I thought, I really should have taken more lovers.'

Alaiya burst out laughing as DeShawn topped up Betty's teacup from the pot on the table beside her.

Amelia went over to Betty. 'Are you okay?'

'Oh yes, dear, I'm fine. When you get to my age, you don't really think anything can surprise you anymore.'

'Can you tell me what happened? Did you recognise the person, Betty?'

'No, I didn't have my glasses on. I just saw the shape, I don't even know if it was a man or a woman, dear.'

'I wish you'd called out. I could have come through,' DeShawn said.

'But I didn't have my lipstick on,' Betty said with a laugh. 'Don't worry, I told the person to get out and that I had a gun.'

'What!' everyone said at the same time.

Betty calmly went into her bag and pulled out a tiny, mother-of-pearl handled pistol. Alaiya, DeShawn and Amelia all moved back.

'This was given to me by a rather famous actor in the early sixties when we travelled through South America together surviving on not much more than Mezcal and LSD.'

'Betty, do you have a licence for that?' Amelia asked.

'Oh, but I've never used it.'

'I...um, I don't think that's the point.'

Vanessa, wearing another gaudy leisure suit, chose this moment to rush into the drawing room. 'I heard we've got an intruder.' She clasped her hand to the chunky diamond necklace around her neck.

'We don't know if that's the case,' Amelia said quickly, not wanting to cause any panic. 'It may have been someone sleepwalking or someone having a little too much to drink and getting the wrong room.'

'Had you locked your room?' Vanessa said.

'Well, I *think* I locked it, but I'd had such a lovely time catching up with family and I'd had a couple of martinis, so I may have forgotten,' Betty said.

'So, it could be more of an opportunistic thief then?' Vanessa said. She then noticed Betty's gun. 'Wow, I like your style, Betty. Maybe we should all be armed.'

DeShawn glared at Vanessa. 'Wouldn't a knife in the back be more your weapon of choice.'

'Shawny,' Alaiya said in a warning tone.

DeShawn hunkered down by Betty. 'You take care, let me know if you need anything, I'll see you later.'

'Thank you, dear.'

Amelia watched as the Johnsons left, with DeShawn turning and glowering at Vanessa as he did. Before Amelia could ask any more questions about what had happened Hamish and Sally appeared. Betty, clearly loving the drama, retold the story while James brought her another pot of tea, this time with a small measure of brandy 'for her nerves' which, to Amelia, seemed far steelier than her own, especially as Betty still had the little pistol on her lap. Eventually Hamish managed to take hold of the weapon and gingerly carried it over to Amelia.

'Is there somewhere I can store this?'

'We've got the safe.'

'Is it okay there or should it be handed in at a police station?'

'I'm sure it will be fine in the safe for now. I'll have to ask Ray what we do with it, though.'

'Will Betty be in trouble for having it?'

Amelia shrugged. 'I don't know, but I'll be discreet.'

'Thanks, Amelia. My parents will be taking Calamity Jane here for the day, if we can get her to leave,' Hamish said, looking back over his shoulder at his old great aunt who'd now been joined by Alice and Dan King who cast worried glances at each other as they heard about Betty's ordeal. In fact, Alice had paled significantly and Amelia feared she would have an uphill struggle in allaying people's concerns over an intruder.

But first she had an illegal firearm to contend with. Popping a napkin over the gun so as not to alarm any more guests, Amelia let herself into her office and opened the safe. Apart from the usual documents lying on the bottom, a bulky envelope had appeared. Opening it up and taking a peep, Amelia found it contained a wad of cash. Returning it beside the gun, Amelia made sure the safe was locked.

Turning to leave she noticed an envelope addressed to her

sitting on top of the closed laptop. It was marked 'PERSONAL'. Sticking it in her pocket to read later she closed the office door behind her and went off to see Carlo Todero and find out what had been stolen.

'My wallet and car keys. I just know someone has been going through my things. I'm very particular about where I place my belongings.'

Carlo was pacing the room of his suite as Lucy sat on the edge of the bed looking very glamorous in a silk negligee and matching peignoir. And full make-up.

'We'll check all the rooms downstairs in case you dropped–' Amelia started to say.

'They were both on my bedside table last night,' he cut in. 'When I came up after breakfast they'd gone.'

'What were your movements this morning?' Amelia asked, just in case he suddenly remembered he'd gone to check something from his car.

'I got up just at five and went out for a walk.'

'He gets as many of his ten thousand steps in first thing, in all weather!' Lucy added.

'Then I went to the library to do my meditation,' Carlo said.

'Every morning without fail,' Lucy said, squeezing Carlo's arm.

'I then spent half an hour or so checking my emails then went for breakfast, probably just after 7.30.'

Amelia looked at Lucy who gave a delicate shrug of her shoulders. 'I'm dead to the world when I take my little blue pills. A brass band could have paraded through the room and I wouldn't have noticed, but Carly is such a creature of habit, I wouldn't doubt him for a moment.'

'Is your car still in the car park?' Amelia asked.

'Yes,' Carlo said.

'I don't suppose you've been checking in unlikely places?' Amelia asked.

Carlo looked at her.

'I mean, did you start checking the other guests' rooms yourself.'

'No, I did not. Why?'

Amelia paused, then realised it wouldn't take long for Carlo to find out about Betty's encounter. 'There was someone in Betty's room last night.'

'There's a thief in the hotel!' Carlo said hotly as Lucy gave a little gasp. 'Lucy, darling,' he said, 'what jewellery did you bring?'

Lucy held up her hand and flashed a massive square cut diamond engagement ring. 'There's this, but I never take it off. And the tennis bracelet you got me for our six-month anniversary.'

'What about your silver pendant?' Carlo said in concern.

Lucy shook her head, her hand flying to clutch at the ornate and chunky pendant around her neck. 'I don't think it's valuable.'

'But it's sentimental. Your father gave it to you.' He turned to Amelia. 'Is there a safe we could put our items in.'

'No,' Lucy said forcefully. Then she gave an apologetic smile. 'Sorry, but I always have them with me and I feel safer wearing them rather than have everything out of sight.'

'Well, let me know if you change your mind. We have a safe,' Amelia said.

'Are you going to phone the police?' Carlo asked.

'Yes, I'll go and contact Constable Williams. In the meantime, we'll search the hotel thoroughly.' Letting herself back out of Carlo's suite she saw James waving up at her. Amelia hurried down to meet him.

'I managed to get hold of the plumber, Tom Hastie. He said he'll come right over to check the boiler.'

'Great! Thanks, James. Oh, and why is there an envelope of money in the safe?'

'Ah, yes! Wee Davey was on night duty and said Mr Griffin turned up just after one in the morning. Paid in cash.'

'Thanks, James!' This new information just added more intrigue to the guest, Amelia thought. 'When you swapped over your shift with Wee Davey, did he mention anything odd about last night?'

'Just about the boiler. Betty clearly didn't raise any alarm. The first we knew of it was when she came down for breakfast.'

'Right. I'll speak to Davey once he's caught up on his sleep and see if he remembers anything or anyone strange,' she said and then went back to check on Betty.

'I hear it's all going down now! That Carlo had his wallet stolen!' Betty said, looking excited at the prospect. 'I wonder if it's connected to all the toing and froing last night, along with the lights.'

'The what?' Amelia asked. She looked to James who was by the door. He shrugged and shook his head.

'Floorboards creaking, doors opening and closing and hushed whispers. I couldn't sleep very well so heard all of it. All through the night and into the morning too. Then later, when I was looking out the window I'm sure I saw a faint light in the grounds.'

'I didn't hear anything,' Alice said.

'Neither did I,' Alaiya agreed.

'We did have another guest check in last night. Mr Griffin arrived about one in the morning,' Amelia said.

'Oh yes, I heard that too, but all the other noises were separate to his arrival,' Betty said.

Amelia was stumped. Could Betty have been imagining things? And could she have imagined the intruder?

'It wasn't terribly loud noises. But trust me, I've been around enough to know all the signs of secret assignations.' Betty smiled knowingly.

❄

'It's a funny one,' Tom Hastie said, scratching his head as he stared at the boiler. 'I fitted this and know it's a great boiler. I can't understand why it's low pressure already.'

'Can you fix it?'

'Of course. I've topped up the pressure but I'll go grab my toolkit from the van and give it a once-over. You don't want it to be packing in with this cold weather.'

Amelia couldn't agree more.

As she came out of the boiler room, Toby beckoned her over. 'I don't want you to panic…'

'That's *not* the best thing to say if you want me not to panic.'

'Good point. Okay. We've got mice.'

'What?'

'I just found one, dead in the storage room.'

'It was dead?'

Toby nodded.

'Well, maybe it was one mouse, singular, and now it's dead there aren't any more?' Amelia said hopefully.

'Mice don't tend to be loners but maybe this one had gone rogue. We can only hope. But meantime we have to take action.'

'Oh God!'

'Don't panic, I've put traps down and I've sent Gideon out to see if he can get anything locally to help with extermination. All the storage areas are well sealed and no food is left lying around. Our hygiene levels are excellent. We're also doing a deep clean of the kitchen at the moment. It's just not the best thing to have going on when we've got the Secret Guest.'

'Argh! If only we knew who it is. Okay, thanks, Toby.' Amelia was about to leave when a thought struck her.

'Do you remember Lorcan saying he had a mouse issue in his studio a while back. I'll go see if he still has anything we can use.'

'I can get Gideon to swing by?'

'No, it's okay.' Amelia could also see how Lorcan was getting on framing Jack's tour poster. And she wanted to check he was okay with the Evangelina situation too. She hated seeing her friend unhappy.

By the time Amelia had returned to the reception area Vanessa and Terence had joined the melee in the drawing room surrounding Betty.

'We have an intruder!' Vanessa said, rounding on Amelia. 'What are you going to do about it?'

'Well, first work out if there's an actual intruder or if it's been an error.'

'Could it have been you, old girl? Taking a wrong turn last night?' Terence asked.

All eyes turned to Vanessa. 'I moved to our other room. I couldn't sleep...' she said.

'I was snoring again,' Terence interjected apologetically.

'...but I certainly didn't get lost on my way to the room next door,' Vanessa continued.

'There was a lot of other banging though,' Betty added. 'Definitely more than just one person.' She took another sip of tea and a bite of the shortbread that had now appeared beside her on a little plate.

There was a murmur of discussion.

'Well, I definitely didn't see anyone else when I moved to the room next door,' Vanessa said.

'We should ask the new guest if they saw anything,' Terence said.

'The new guest in the Simenon Room? I'd noticed he's put his Do Not Disturb sign out,' Vanessa said.

'We could try and corner him later?' Terence suggested.

'No one will be cornering anyone!' Amelia said firmly before backing away, hoping no one would follow her.

Leaving everyone talking in the drawing room, Amelia headed to the kitchens and as she walked past the bar, saw a figure hunched over a table with a towel over their head.

'Is everything okay?' Amelia tentatively asked, pausing in the doorway.

Evangelina emerged from under the towel, releasing a cloud of steam and the aroma of eucalyptus. 'Oh! Morning.'

'Are you okay?' Amelia asked.

'I've got a dreadful cold,' Evangelina said. 'It started last night.' Right enough, her eyes were puffed up and her throat was croaky.

'Can I get you anything?'

She shook her head and gave an enormous sneeze. 'Ricky got me some cold and flu remedy after dinner.'

'Did you manage to sleep okay?' Amelia asked, wondering if she'd had a restless night and had taken to pacing the floor of the hotel, she may have seen someone entering Betty or Carlo's room.

'He got me the one that knocks you out so I slept very soundly.'

Bang goes that idea, Amelia thought.

Evangelina gave another sneeze and, with a rueful look, put the towel over her head again.

Leaving Evangelina to her steam inhalations Amelia grabbed the keys to the Jeep and headed to Lorcan's.

Progress on the road was slow and despite the great traction on the Jeep, Amelia spent most of the journey white knuckling the steering wheel as she drove at a snail's pace.

She parked as close to Lorcan's as she could then walked the last few hundred yards up the dirt track that led to his house. She rang the bell and waited, looking out over the land, taking in the views. It was a beautiful day, with the sun bright in the perfectly clear turquoise sky and the snow sparkling as if someone had sprinkled glitter over the fields. Amelia had to squint slightly to shield her eyes from the glare of the snow. Despite the sun it was still baltic and she stamped her feet as she waited for Lorcan to come to the door.

She rang the bell again. He could be sleeping off a heavy night from the Whistling Haggis but she doubted it, as when she'd left the pub, he'd been sitting staring thoughtfully into his barely touched pint.

She went round the back of the house in case he was listening to loud music, completely oblivious to the doorbell but, looking in through the large plate windows, Amelia could see the kitchen was empty. She spied a half-drunk mug of tea on the table, so he couldn't be far away. She got out her mobile to phone him to let him know she was outside.

She stood for a moment as the call registered then a couple of seconds later heard a faint ringtone. She paused and listened then followed the noise to his studio. If he was in a creative mood he may have forgotten all about time she guessed as she cancelled the call then banged on the heavy wooden door. No answer.

'Lorcan!' Still no reply. He could have his headphones in, she thought as she tentatively touched the door. It gave easily, and she pushed it open all the way.

The studio was completely silent; no muffled bass of music coming from a set of headphones and more importantly, no sign of Lorcan. His phone was on one of the workbenches and Amelia could see from the screen there were three missed calls and a couple of text messages he hadn't picked up.

She looked round, half expecting him to pop up from behind a table and shout 'surprise' at her. His phone beeped again. Without thinking Amelia looked at the screen. It was a message from Evangelina saying 'can we talk?' Clearly Lorcan wasn't with Evangelina.

Amelia stood for a moment, wondering what to do when she heard a noise.

She held her breath, senses alert.

Seconds later, she heard it again; a croaky groan. She moved slowly to the back of the studio, where she could see propped against the wall the stack of the frames she'd given him from Stone Manor.

Continuing along the length of the workbench she saw one of Lorcan's Doc Marten boots sticking out. Moving around a little more she realised it was still attached to the rest of Lorcan, who was lying out cold on the floor.

CHAPTER 19

With great effort Amelia roused Lorcan and with him leaning heavily on her, they stumbled out of the studio and into his kitchen. He sat in one of the chairs as he tentatively touched the back of his head and winced. A quick search of the freezer unearthed a packet of peas and Amelia pressed it to the egg-sized lump.

'What happened?' she asked as she got him a glass of water.

'I don't know.' He tried to shake his head but then thought better of it. 'I didn't sleep very well last night so I got up really early, must have been before six. I made some tea and then I popped into the studio to get a couple of things. That's when someone came up behind me and hit me on the back of the head. Next thing I knew you were here helping me up.'

'Did you see who did this?'

'No, I was just aware of someone rushing at me. I barely had time to register it happening when I was knocked out.'

'We need to call Ray.' Amelia took her mobile from her pocket.

'No.' Lorcan covered her phone with his hand.

'But someone attacked you! You could have died!'

'But I didn't. I'm not getting the police involved. Ray's got enough on his plate with the road being closed off and the church robbery business. In fact, it's probably the same kids.' He removed the bag of peas, placing it on the table and gingerly touched his head.

'You seriously think local kids would do something like this?'

'Well, I can't think who else it would be. I'm quite an affable person and don't tend to make enemies, especially not ones who want to hurt me,' he said it lightly but wouldn't meet Amelia's gaze.

'But… you at least need to get yourself checked out by a GP.'

'If I survived a few hours on my studio floor in these harsh temperatures I think I'll be okay.' He gave Amelia a rueful smile. 'I'm sure I'll be fine after a cuppa.' He made to stand up but Amelia gently shoved him back down in his seat as she went and made tea.

She splashed some milk in his mug then added a few spoonfuls of sugar in case he was in shock then plonked it down beside him on the table.

'Drink it up and you might see sense and report this,' she said with an exasperated sigh.

He took a deep swallow of his tea. 'Jesus, that's sweet! Well, if the concussion doesn't get me, you're making sure the diabetes will!' He gave a feeble laugh.

'Can you remember anything else?' Amelia asked, leaning a little closer.

Lorcan screwed up his eyes as he tried to recall… 'I think whoever did this may have already been in the studio, as I didn't hear the door open behind me. It's my fault as I never keep the doors locked. They probably went in to see if there was anything to steal, I disturbed them and they panicked.'

'They may have stolen something,' Amelia said glancing out at the barn.

'There's isn't anything valuable to take, well, nothing that isn't a massive heavy piece of unmovable machinery.' He sighed and prodded the defrosting bag of peas with his index finger. 'I should probably go and have a look; in case something is missing.'

Lorcan stood up and held on to the table for a second. 'Don't worry,' he said to Amelia who stared at him in concern, 'I'll just wait until the room goes still. Hell, I normally feel like this after a few Jamesons!'

Amelia followed Lorcan out to the studio and they went to the back where she'd found him.

Lorcan studied the area thoughtfully. 'My pile of canvases has definitely been moved, and so have the ones in the frames you gave me and… these boxes.' He had a look inside. 'But everything's there that should be.'

He moved back to the canvases and stared at them for a moment, before saying, 'Someone's looked through these as I'd put Jack's book tour poster at the front.'

Instead, the painting at the front was of a massive deer in death throes, from an arrow protruding from its flank, which had been one of the first paintings Amelia had removed from the walls of Stone Manor as it was so grotesque and bloody.

Lorcan continued to look through the frames.

'You don't think someone stole the signed book tour poster do you?' Amelia asked worriedly.

'Well, no offence to Jack, but I can't really imagine it would be a hot item for the black market… aha! Don't worry, here it is!' And with a flourish, Lorcan turned a frame round to show Amelia.

'Wow! It looks amazing. I hadn't realised it would be that big though!' Amelia knew Jack was going to love it. Although looking at the size of it they would definitely have to move house as Amelia wasn't sure there was a wall big enough to hang such a large frame in the Gatehouse.

'You could always submit it for the Glencarlach Winter Festival Art Exhibition while you find a place to hang it,' Lorcan said, then laughed as he saw the scepticism on Amelia's face. 'Art is totally subjective. I'm sure there'll be other people in the village who'll appreciate it. Just make sure you put a little red dot on it so people know it's not for sale.'

'I've submitted a landscape of Glencarlach from 1840, which is going into the auction too. I've also handed in that cat dressed as Poirot but I won't let it go in the auction afterwards though. Although hideous it is of sentimental value to me.'

Lorcan gave a chuckle. 'Yes, I saw that down at the village hall. It's certainly a talking point!'

'What about you?' Amelia asked.

'Yeah, I'll pop something in. That's why I had these canvases out as I was looking through some old paintings. And that box of photographs too.' He pointed to the cardboard box on the workbench.

Amelia started going through the propped-up paintings.

'Oh, um, do you mind not looking through those. They're not my best work,' Lorcan said but too late as Amelia had already paused on a painting that had caught her eye.

'Oh my! This is beautiful,' she gasped as she lifted it out. 'Lorcan…?'

Lorcan was looking down at his feet sheepishly. Amelia held it up to the light. It was an oil painting of Evangelina.

'Oh yeah, I painted that years ago when we were friends,' he said, in an offhand manner.

Amelia looked back at the painting. Evangelina was sitting on a chair in a messy kitchen, sun streaming in from the window beside her. Wearing an oversized man's stripey shirt, she was bare-legged. One foot was up on the chair seat and she was hugging that knee. The painting itself was astonishingly beautiful, but it wasn't the skill of the brushwork that held Amelia entranced. It was the expression on Evangelina's face. Lorcan had caught her carefree and natural, the curve of her mouth the split second before she laughed, her eyes twinkling with merriment, as if she was sharing a joke with the only other person in the world that mattered to her. The expression on her face was that of unconcealed adoration for the artist, which he'd mutually reciprocated in the delicateness of the painting itself.

Lorcan and Evangelina hadn't just been friends.

They had obviously been very much in love.

Amelia slowly put the painting down as her brain ticked over. If Ricky knew about Evangelina's relationship with Lorcan, despite it being in the past, could he be jealous? Then, with a horrible chill settling on her skin Amelia remembered the phone conversation she'd overheard him make, which Gideon thought had sounded like he was taking a hit out on someone.

Had Ricky been taking a hit out on Lorcan?

CHAPTER 20

'I honestly don't know what all the fuss is about,' Lorcan grumbled as he followed Amelia down the track to where she'd left the Jeep.

'I just think it's better for you to be with company. If you're adamant you're not seeing a doctor for your head injury, I don't want you being all alone up here in case you get concussion or delayed brain damage,' Amelia said lightly. 'You either stay at Stone Manor for Christmas or I phone Dr Kaur, who will no doubt have to call Ray because of the suspicious circumstances. And obviously, because you don't have any say in this, your stay is a freebie.' Although potential concussion was a concern, Amelia was far more worried about Lorcan being attacked again.

With Amelia batting away all his protestations and offers to pay, Lorcan resignedly got into the passenger seat with his large rucksack as Amelia carefully positioned a blanket over the framed book tour poster in the boot so Jack wouldn't accidentally see it.

Closing over the boot Amelia got into the Jeep. 'So,' she said, putting on her seat belt, 'you and Evangelina were more than friends?'

Lorcan looked straight out the windscreen for a moment before answering with a quiet, 'Yeah.'

Amelia started up the engine and began the careful drive back to Stone Manor. 'What happened?' she asked.

Lorcan puffed out his cheeks and exhaled as he seemed to pick his words carefully. 'We were young and went out for a bit and then… you could say it was a case of bad timing. My work was getting a bit of notice and Evangelina was making waves in the film industry and was on the brink of greatness. We had a long talk one night and bared our souls and Evangelina decided we should focus on our careers. Cherish what we had, etc., etc.'

Amelia glanced over at him. Although he was acting fairly blasé, there was definitely pain etched behind his eyes, which wasn't just down to the crack on the head.

'And that's what we did, we both wished each other well and… and got on with our lives…'

'And here you are, thrown together again! Fate is funny, isn't it?' Amelia sighed.

'Some might say fate, I just say coincidence,' Lorcan said lightly.

Amelia took a deep breath. 'Do you think Ricky could have done this?'

Lorcan again touched the back of his head. 'It did cross my mind. That's why I didn't want to involve the police, in case it's a warning. But,' he shook his head, 'he doesn't know about Evangelina and me. Evangelina didn't want him to find out and I certainly didn't say anything. And even if he did somehow find out about us, it all happened so long ago. It just doesn't make sense for him to do this.'

Amelia focused on the road in front as her brain ticked over.

If, and it was a *big* if, Ricky knew about Lorcan and Evangelina and felt threatened and had been behind the warning attack on Lorcan, she felt it was much better that Lorcan stayed in a busy hotel rather than on his own in the back of beyond.

Amelia knew there was a risk by having Evangelina, Lorcan and Ricky near each other but at least this way, Lorcan had a host of other people looking out for him. And Amelia was interested to see how Ricky reacted to Lorcan; if he'd act guilty around him, or have a tell which let on he was jealous.

Then there was also the romantic part of Amelia that wondered if Lorcan and Evangelina were meant to be reunited. Besides, from what she'd seen of Ricky and Evangelina, they weren't exactly love's young dream.

'Amelia, do you mind not telling anyone about the attack?' Lorcan said as they parked up at Stone Manor. 'I just don't want to make a fuss about it.'

Taking the key out the ignition Amelia turned and looked at him. 'Okay, if you're sure.'

'Yeah, I just feel a bit odd about it all, to be perfectly honest.'

'Not a problem,' Amelia agreed as they got out the car. They headed into the hotel where Toby, Gideon and a couple of other staff were crowded round the reception desk. On hearing them come in, Toby whirled round.

'Ames! Lorcan!'

'Hiya! Look who has decided to stay with us for Christmas!' Amelia announced cheerily. She stopped, realising everyone was acting rather strangely. Toby was looking at her with a fixed grin on his face.

'What's going on? Oh God, you've found more mice haven't you?'

'Au contraire, my darling,' Gideon piped up. 'We have solved the mice…'

'… mouse,' Toby corrected.

'…mouse problem,' Gideon said. 'I managed to gather together a few traps, but, as you know, prevention is always better than cure, and I've got the best mouse prevention solution going!'

Toby and Gideon parted to reveal a large fluffy ginger cat sitting beside the computer screen.

'Isn't he lovely! Can we keep him? Please?' Gideon gushed, lifting the cat up and cuddling him. The cat closed its eyes and purred. Amelia looked at the reception desk and saw there was a plate with some ham and what looked like some chicken liver parfait.

Following her gaze, Toby cleared his throat. 'We had a lot of extra food and I thought he might like it.'

Gideon still held the cat close and Amelia went and scratched the cat under his chin. The cat purred more loudly and rubbed its cheek against her hand.

'What's his name?'

'The farmer called it Cat Seven as they've already a few mousers on the farm so could spare this one.' As Amelia hadn't immediately said 'no' to keeping it, Gideon risked putting the big ball of fluff back on the desk where it started to lick its paw.

It was very cute, Amelia had to admit, although it didn't look very much like a killer mouse catcher.

'Well, I think it's a very sound investment but he needs a name as we can't just call it Cat Seven,' Amelia said, her heart melting as the cat came over and rubbed its head against her hand.

'How about Ginger?' Toby suggested.

'Something more festive,' Amelia suggested just as one of the sous chefs came out from the kitchens whistling 'Jingle Bells'.

'Let's call him Jingles,' Amelia said as the cat yawned and flicked an ear.

'Jingles,' Gideon repeated. 'A name that will surely put an icy shard of fear into any mouses heart!'

Jingles was very quick to make himself at home in Stone Manor. As Amelia got Lorcan the key to the PD James Room, Jingles jumped down and sashayed on through to the drawing room where he immediately curled up into a ball in front of the fire and went to sleep. He probably needed a snooze after his rich lunch of pâté and ham, Amelia figured, hoping that once his energy was restored, he'd be up and prowling around for mice.

After Lorcan was settled into his room and with nothing else immediately needing attention, Amelia knew she'd have to give Constable Williams a call about the intruder, Carlo Todero's missing belongings and Betty's gun. Taking a deep breath, she lifted the phone…

…just as Toby appeared from the bar. 'I've found the wallet and keys!' he called over with a grin.

Dropping the phone, Amelia hurried into the bar to see her brother.

'I was just getting some brandy to add to a sauce,' Toby said as she followed him round behind the bar, 'when I saw a key sticking out from under the dishtowel.'

Amelia lifted up the dishtowel he was pointing to and there indeed sat a wallet and set of car keys. She checked the inside of the wallet to confirm they belonged to Carlo Todero.

'I guess he left them on the bar and they got knocked down and ended up getting pushed to the side and accidentally covered.'

'Looks like it,' Toby agreed.

Amelia felt great relief when she knocked on Carlo's door a moment later. Lucy opened it and when she saw what Amelia was carrying, gave a little clap of delight.

'Carly! Look what Amelia's got.'

Carlo came to the door. 'Where did you find them?' he asked, looking inside his wallet.

'They were in the bar.'

Carlo studied the wallet, turning the soft brown leather in his hands for a moment, then glanced behind him to the bedside table. 'I could have sworn…'

Lucy gave his arm a squeeze. 'You've got them back, that's the main thing,' she said gently.

'I…uh. Yes.' He looked up at Amelia and she thought he looked a little more tired and drawn than before. 'Thank you for finding them. Excuse me, I need to get on.' As he walked back over to his laptop Lucy slipped out into the corridor, gently closing the door behind her.

'I'm so relieved you managed to find them. I worry he works too hard. We were meant to be having a work-free few days around the wedding but with this bad weather all our sightseeing plans have gone awry which has meant he's back to business.' She gave a delicate little shrug of her shoulders, 'I suppose once a workaholic, always a workaholic!' She gave a sad little smile. 'Oh, did your boyfriend manage to get back okay last night? Your friend Gideon was telling me he'd been struggling to get home because of the weather.'

'Yes, he did, late last night.'

'That's such a relief.' She tilted her head to the side and gave a little smile. 'I wonder! Is there a chance he'd be around the hotel tonight, while I'm at the hen party, and if he is, would he be able to chat to Carly? It could be like his stag-do, and talking to his favourite crime author would be one sure way of getting him to turn off his laptop. I often think Carly should take early retirement and write crime novels. He's very clever and his mind just seems to work things out so quickly! I suppose that's why he's been so successful in business!'

She laughed then pulled a face. 'Although, I've never been entirely sure what he does to be honest. That sounds so dim of me, doesn't it!'

'You don't know anything about his work?' Amelia said, a little surprised.

Lucy laughed again. 'I know he owns a lot of property that he rents. And imports and exports things. He once told me he finds things people are looking for and they pay him lots of money for the privilege. Now, I'm glad I caught you because I wanted to ask if you'd be able to come to my hen-do tonight.'

'Well, I…' Amelia was taken aback by the invitation.

'You see, I don't have any of my friends at the wedding and it seems a little one sided. Don't get me wrong, Carly's friends are lovely but I don't really know them very well.'

Amelia didn't like to say that at least Lucy knew them a little. She'd only just met Amelia!

Sensing Amelia's hesitancy, Lucy put her hand on Amelia's arm. 'Even if you don't make the spa treatments but come to the Whistling Haggis later, that would be lovely. Sally will be joining us for that bit too after she does our pampering session. Betty's having dinner with her family and Alaiya made some excuses about wanting to spend the evening with her husband. India doesn't want to socialise with her mother as that's lame, evidently!' Lucy gave a sigh. 'There won't be that many people at it.'

'Well…'

'It would really mean a lot to me. And if your lovely boyfriend is busy talking crime with Carlo…'

Amelia was very aware that keeping this bride and groom happy could end up in great reviews and placing Stone Manor on the map for destination wedding venues and she knew she needed some brownie points as they currently thought there was a thief in the hotel. And Amelia had to admit, she was more than a little intrigued to see what Big Davey had organised for the hen-do.

Amelia smiled. 'That would be lovely, thank you.'

'Super!' Lucy exclaimed with another little hand clap. 'I'll go and let Carly know he has a date with his favourite author. Shall we say about eight?'

'Yes, I'm sure that will be fine,' Amelia said, hoping Jack wouldn't mind.

'Wonderful!' Lucy said effusively. 'He really does obsessively follow his blog,' she laughed. She looked at her watch and gave a little gasp. 'Oh my, speaking of my hen-do, we're all due to meet in the spa in five minutes! I'd better get a move on,' she said slipping back into her room.

Amelia went back down the stairs wondering how she was going to break the news to Jack that he had a little bit of networking to do tonight.

Back at the reception desk Amelia looked through the pile of that day's mail. There was also a package for the attention of Ricky Varelli, no doubt the one he'd been eager to receive. Then Amelia remembered the note that had been left for her on her laptop. Taking it out of her pocket she opened it. On a rich cream velum, there was written in very neat block capitals;

NOT ALL YOUR GUESTS ARE AS THEY SEEM. BE CAREFUL

Amelia turned the letter over but there were no other markings on the paper and checking inside the envelope showed it to be completely empty. It was postmarked as being local. Who on earth had sent it? And what guest, or guests, were they alluding to? And why did she have to be careful?

Just at that moment Ricky came in from the front door, stomping snow onto the welcome mat. Amelia hastily put the letter back in her pocket and retrieved his parcel from under the desk.

'Mr Varelli, this arrived for you.'

He came over and took it from her, staring at it for a moment. 'It's a bit bloody late now!' he said gruffly before he turned on his heel and walked up the stairs to his room.

For someone who'd been so eager to get the package he suddenly appeared quite unconcerned about it.

Before she could think any more of Ricky Varelli's strange behaviour, Jack walked in, whistling 'Walking in a Winter Wonderland'.

'You look very cheerful,' Amelia said, making the decision not to tell Jack about the note. Well, not just yet as he'd only been home a few hours and she didn't want him worrying about her.

'I'm feeling very cheerful,' he said, waggling a big poster tube at her.

'What have you got there?'

'Something I picked up on my travels. But I think it will look better with a frame. I messaged Lorcan and he said he'd help me out and that he was staying here now?'

'Yup, long story. He's just settling into his room, the PD James one. Just head up. Are you going to give me a peek?' Amelia nodded at the tube but Jack held it out of reach.

'Not yet, I want it to be a surprise, once it's framed in all its glory.' Jack glanced around him. 'It's so quiet, where is everyone?'

'Ah, getting ready for the first part of the hen party. Sally is doing her mani-pedi, facial pamper package special in the spa.' Amelia checked her watch. 'I'm going to join them at the Whistling Haggis for the evening entertainment but I'll get there a bit early to try and speak to Wee Davey. And would you be able to meet Carlo in the bar at eight to schmooze our groom and regale him with entertaining anecdotes about your writing.'

Jack groaned. 'I don't have any entertaining anecdotes about my writing! I spend most of my day sitting, staring at my computer in frustration before bashing out three thousand words, two thousand of which I delete the next day because I don't like them.'

'You'll maybe want to romanticise all of that a little.'

'I'll try. I'll talk about characterisation.'

'And there's that great story of when you almost got in the same lift as Stephen King!' Amelia reminded him, trying to get him a little more enthusiastic.

'Oh yes!' Jack exclaimed, clearly warming to his task at hand. 'I'll go give this to Lorcan and then take notes in the bar. I may just be able to come up with some stories.'

'Well, you are a writer after all!'

CHAPTER 21

Lorcan sat on the edge of the bed in the lovely PD James Room and took two paracetamol in the hope it would stop the throbbing of his head. He tentatively felt the place he'd been struck by something very heavy, but even the light pressure from his fingertips hurt.

He played over in his mind the moments leading up to his being knocked unconscious to see if he could remember anything about the incident. But there was nothing. There was no handy reflection that allowed him to see who was behind him. No strong aftershave or perfume to give his assailant's identity away. No indication of height or build. He just had a very sore head.

He knew Amelia suspected Ricky, but Lorcan wasn't so sure. It had been one of the reasons he'd agreed to stay in Stone Manor. He was worried whoever had attacked him had done it for reasons other than him having lustful thoughts about a married woman.

He had a sneaky suspicion his attack had to do with his latest secret commission. Especially as his rendezvous yesterday afternoon didn't pan out the way he'd planned.

Lorcan had waited over two hours at the designated meeting

spot. Luckily he'd taken his Jeep otherwise he'd have risked hypothermia. He'd called the number he had but it went to voicemail. Not knowing what else to do he hid the commission under the back seat and waited.

There was nothing. And then next morning when he went into his studio he was knocked unconscious and then whoever had done it went through all his paintings. It was far too coincidental to not think the events were somehow linked.

When Amelia was waiting for him to pack his bag he went to his Jeep to retrieve his commission, not knowing what else to do with it. And when he got to his room, he rolled it up and hid it inside a tall ornamental vase. Hardly a long-term solution but he hoped he'd get a call soon and could hand it over.

Having it in his possession for this long made him feel distinctly uneasy.

There was a knock on the door. When Lorcan opened it he found Jack, standing grinning at him. He let him in his room.

'How was your book tour?'

'It was good,' Jack said. 'Tiring though. I'm glad to be back in all honesty.' Jack held up the poster tube. 'Are you sure you don't mind framing this?'

'Of course not.'

'Something simple.'

'White frame or black?'

'A white frame, please.'

'No problem. Is it okay if I look at doing it after the exhibition?'

'Take all the time you need. The poster's actually quite big and I doubt it'll fit in the Gatehouse, anyway.'

'Ah, Amelia mentioned you might be looking to move.'

'Yeah, and I'm hoping when we do, Amelia will love American football as much as I do and then she'll be as excited as I am to have this vintage New York Giants poster signed by some of their greatest players of all time; Carl Banks, Justin Tuck, Osi

Umenyiora, Lawrence Taylor and Michael Strahan. A couple of them even played on the team that got them their first Super Bowl win in 1987!'

Jack looked so happy with his poster that Lorcan hoped Amelia did end up embracing the sport as much as Jack.

'Well, I shall keep this safe here until I get around to framing it for you.'

'Thanks, mate!' Jack said with gratitude. 'Now I'd better go as I'm helping with dinner and then doing an anecdotal talk about my time as a writer as a kind of stag-do for Carlo Todero.'

'Wow, good luck. Oh, and be sure to tell that story about when you nearly got in the lift with Stephen King,' Lorcan said as Jack left his room.

Lorcan sat back down on the edge of the bed and looked at his phone again, just in case he had a message.

CHAPTER 22

The Whistling Haggis was unsurprisingly mobbed when Amelia arrived a couple of hours later. Squeezing in through the door, she made her way up to the bar, careful not to disturb the loops of tinsel that had been hung along the edge.

'We've almost finished setting up in the back room,' Big Davey said when he saw Amelia.

'I know, I'm early, I was hoping to catch Wee Davey for a moment.'

'Aye, I'll go get him.'

A moment later Big Davey's son appeared from the back of the pub.

'Can I have a quick word?' Amelia said.

'Of course, boss,' Wee Davey smiled.

'Last night, did you notice anything strange about your shift?'

He sucked his teeth as he had a think. 'It *was* an odd night, actually. Everyone seemed to be restless, if you know what I mean. There were quite a lot of doors banging and I'm sure I heard a couple of mobile phones ringing in the early hours. I wasn't at the front desk all the time though, as I was setting up the dining room and had some things to sort out in the leisure area.'

'Of course.'

'Mrs King popped down to reception, must have been about two in the morning.'

'Really?'

He nodded. 'She said she couldn't sleep and asked if she could have some tea. She'd gone through all the bags in their room.'

No wonder she couldn't sleep if she'd gone through the supply that had been refreshed that morning. She'd no doubt have been wired from too much caffeine, Amelia thought.

'She also asked for some toast. I know we're not meant to do food after eleven, but she seems nice and what with the Secret Guest being here I thought it best to be as helpful as possible. Was that okay?'

'That was great customer service,' Amelia said to Davey's obvious relief. 'Anything else when you took it up to her?'

'Well, she actually followed me into the kitchen, chatted away to me while I was making it and then I took it upstairs for her. I didn't see anyone else moving about up there. I took it into her room and laid it on her table and she pointed at her husband in bed and made a comment about him being able to sleep through anything. Then I went back downstairs to the desk. And then of course there was the boiler.'

'Of course. How did you know it wasn't working properly?'

'Because Mr Todero called down to tell me his shower wasn't running warm. That was really early in the morning, not long after five. There was quite a to-do about that because he thought it was just his room and went into the Vine room they've also got, for Lucy's bridal room because of all that wedding superstition. But then he found that wasn't working either but by then he'd managed to lock himself out of his own room and because Lucy takes sleeping pills and wears earplugs she didn't hear him knocking and he didn't want to be too loud to wake everyone else up. So, he came down dripping wet – don't worry he'd taken clothes in to change into, he wasn't like, naked and being inappropriate,' Wee Davey clarified, 'and we went to see if we could work out the boiler but it's so fancy neither of us had a clue so he said he'd just leave his shower until later and head out for his early morning walk.'

'Right. And Mrs Maxwell?'

'Oh yes, that was earlier on. I saw her leave her room and slip into the other one that they've booked. But that was all. And, of course, Mr Griffin arrived just after one. He was right wrapped up he was, so it must have been freezing. He just handed me the envelope of cash, said it would cover everything and then he went up to his room.' Davey shook his head, frowning.

'What is it?' Amelia asked.

'Dad!' Wee Davey hollered across the bar. 'Was there anyone in here last night that was a bit *weird*.'

Big Davey came over, chuckling. 'You've seen my clientele, son, you have to be a bit more specific.'

'I mean someone you didn't recognise? When he checked in, Mr Griffin was all wrapped up, massive hat, scarf, the works but you could see he had longish dark hair, a beard and moustache and big bushy eyebrows. And glasses. Anyone here like that last night?'

Big Davey shook his head. 'No, most left after the Christmas cake competition and it was just a few regulars and I knew everyone.'

Wee Davey's frown deepened as he turned back to Amelia. 'That *is* odd then. Because Mr Griffin didn't have a car and even if he did, with all the roads closed, how did he manage to get here? He didn't look like he'd been walking for miles, and if he wasnae here in the pub before, just where had he been before turning up at Stone Manor?'

CHAPTER 23

Amelia was left mulling over this bombshell as Wee Davey went to serve another couple of people at the bar. Where indeed had Mr Griffin come from? Was it the strange parallel universe that had popped out Benedict Geissler too? Then Amelia's reverie was broken by someone shouting her name. She turned to see Evangelina and Nisha sitting together at the end of the bar. They waved her over.

'Sally finished with us first so we thought we'd come and get a head start on the celebrations,' Evangelina said showing off her beautifully painted nails to Amelia.

'How are you feeling now?' Amelia asked.

'I'm a lot better, thanks,' Evangelina said, 'I really thought I was in for the 'flu when I came downstairs this morning, but apart from a bit of a sniffle, I seem to be fine, now!'

'That's great news.' Amelia smiled.

'Yes, and I hear you're joining us this evening, too?' Evangelina said to Amelia.

'Yes, it was very kind of Lucy to invite me along, I mean, I don't know her at all,' Amelia said, still finding it a little strange to be included.

'Oh, don't worry!' Nisha laughed. 'You've known her longer than I have and I've been invited too!' She took a sip from her bottle of beer. 'Do you not think it slightly odd that it's her wedding and there's absolutely no one here on her side?'

This thought had crossed Amelia's mind too.

'She's never really shared information about her family,' Evangelina said diplomatically, keeping her voice low. 'I get the impression she was raised by her dad, and that they were close, but he's not here anymore. I think he must have died when she was quite young. Possibly an older brother cared for her after that. I'm not sure. She doesn't talk about any family, but then, she's never opened up to me, this is all what I've gleaned from comments she's made. I've never met any of her friends.'

'Gold digger?' Nisha asked with an arched eyebrow.

Evangelina frowned then shrugged. 'I know Dan suggested the same family lawyer who did mine and Ricky's rigorous prenup but Carlo wasn't interested. They're besotted with each other and she does seem to care very much for him. Some women just want to find security and quite often that's through a husband, I suppose.'

'Looking for a father figure if she lost hers at an early age?' Nisha suggested.

'Possibly. I'd like to think it was genuine. Let's face it, it's mutually beneficial. Carlo always likes to be surrounded by beautiful things, from cars, to art, to home décor. He's always been a bit of a magpie. And Lucy is very beautiful.' Evangelina gave a sigh. 'And let's face it, how often do true love matches last?'

Nisha went to speak then closed her mouth and patted her friend's hand.

'You're very lucky living in such a beautiful part of the world,' Evangelina said to Amelia after taking a sip from her glass of wine.

'I know, I love it here.' Amelia smiled. It was something she'd never take for granted.

'This is your dream too, Evie,' Nisha said in a matter-of-fact way.

Evangelina sighed. 'It is. I'd love to move back to Scotland. My happiest time was when I was studying here.'

Amelia had to bite her tongue to stop asking if Lorcan had been a contributing factor to this happiest time. Even though Evangelina was the one to have broken up with him, the wistful way she talked about the past made Amelia wonder if a little of her regretted leaving him to follow her acting career.

'I would heartily recommend Glencarlach as a place to live,' Amelia said. 'Do you think you and Ricky would move here?' she added, hoping to fish for a little information.

'I'd jump at the chance! But Ricky…?' Evangelina pulled a face.

'I'm sure I read somewhere you can sometimes buy properties that have laird titles attached. I can see Ricky go for that,' Nisha said. 'And a title would be another way he could pit himself against Terence. Oh God, imagine Ricky as a laird, walking through the heather, organising shooting parties, wearing tartan trews…'

Amelia got the distinct impression Nisha wasn't a fan of Evangelina's husband.

Evangelina gave a wry smile. 'I don't think he could cope with bitter winds, patchy broadband and delayed post, though. He was practically going crazy waiting for an Amazon Prime package. He couldn't believe he wasn't able to get it the same day.' She paused to take another sip of her drink. 'But I know I could definitely live here. It's so beautiful. Life doesn't seem so hectic, either.'

'But you never went out anywhere in London to *have* a hectic life!' Nisha exclaimed.

'I know. Because I felt so claustrophobic there. I started to become almost agoraphobic as I didn't even want to leave the house. But here, I feel free.'

'Just please don't forget you're still in demand. *Doctor Who* called again. *Emmerdale* are interested. There was even a rumour that Richard Curtis is keen for his next romcom.'

'I think my acting days are over,' Evangelina said. 'But if I do change my mind I will let you know, Nish.'

'Oh, are you an agent too?' Amelia asked.

Nisha nodded and took another swig of beer. 'Although I'm not sure how long I can carry on after that bitch Vanessa poached half my clients,' she said bitterly.

Amelia's eyes widened. 'Vanessa de Courtney?'

'Yes, the obnoxious Wicked Witch of the West End herself.'

Evangelina turned and patted Nisha's hand. 'You're doing very well and haven't risen to any of her barbed comments.'

'Just because I haven't killed her yet, doesn't mean I'm not planning to!' Nisha said. 'Although having to be nice to her is slowly killing *me*!'

'How did she manage to steal your clients?' Amelia asked.

'By whispering poison in their ears and manipulating like the evil bitch she is. It wouldn't surprise me if she's holding some clients to ransom and blackmailing them. She's renowned for her underhand tactics. And we all know she doesn't stop at stealing clients…'

Evangelina sighed as she twirled the base of her wine glass on the bar top.

Nisha flicked her dark hair over her shoulder as she sat up slightly on her barstool. 'Oh, look who's just come in!'

Amelia turned to see Lorcan heading up to the other end of the bar. As if sensing an audience, he glanced over at them, gave a bit of a start, then a little wave just as he tripped and stumbled into the bar, dislodging a big swathe of tinsel, which he unsuccessfully tried to latch back onto the antique brass hooks that ran around the edge of the bar. Amelia could see him reddening under his woolly hat.

'Clearly as suave and sophisticated as always!' Nisha said with a gentle laugh. 'I have to say, it was quite a shock seeing Lorcan

Flynn after all these years. Such a coincidence to end up in the same little village. I suppose that's another reason you wouldn't mind moving here, is it?'

'Nish,' Evangelina said wearily.

'What's Lorcan like?' Nisha asked Amelia. 'I mean, I remember him from way back in the day. Did you know we all knew each other in Glasgow?'

'Lorcan mentioned it, yes.'

'I was very fond of him. He was always lovely,' Nisha said.

'He still is very lovely,' Amelia agreed.

'Is he with someone?'

'No, he's single.'

'Nisha, I don't know where you're going with this but please stop,' Evangelina said, firmly. 'It's all in the past, now. We went out briefly and then we stopped.'

'I remember how miserable you were when you split up. I could quite happily have wrung his neck,' Nisha said.

Amelia watched Evangelina closely before saying, 'Um, did you split up with Lorcan?'

Evangelina shook her head. 'No, Lorcan thought it best we concentrated on our careers. And that's what we did. We *were* very young.'

Amelia was speechless. That wasn't what Lorcan had thought! He'd said it had been Evangelina's decision. Was one of them lying? Or had they split up with each other due to a misunderstanding? And what did that mean for them now?

'And then, on my next film I met Ricky and...' Evangelina gave a small shrug then took a sip of wine. Setting the glass back on the bar the actress gave a sigh. 'He wasn't always like he is now. When I met him he was vibrant and excited about life. We had adventures.' She smiled at the memories. 'But people change. Over the years he's become more insular...'

'...cantankerous. Controlling,' Nisha added.

'I feel we're like strangers now. And he always gets worse

when it's this group together. I think he still feels he has to prove something with Carlo and Carlo's friends.'

Just then Big Davey came over. 'That's the rest of your party here, ladies.'

Amelia turned to see a giggling Lucy, resplendent in 'L' plates, tutu and fairy wings coming through the door with Sally, Alice and Vanessa.

'Oh God, the things I do for our friendship!' Nisha said under her breath.

'Please play nice,' Evangelina said to her friend as all of Lucy's hen party headed through to the back room.

Sally had done an expert job in getting the hen party relaxed after her various spa treatments as there was definitely a chilled vibe as the hens gathered round the table. Despite a little trepidation about Davey's plans, Amelia was delighted to see that he'd decorated the room tastefully. Amelia knew the food would be great. She was just a little sceptical on what the 'special party games' would consist of!

They'd already eaten and the first of the party games was well under way, courtesy of the Glencarlach Knitting and Crocheting group when Amelia's phone rang. It was Gideon. Excusing herself from the shrieks of hilarity around the table as the hens all attempted to crochet life size penises, Amelia let herself out the back room and into the main pub.

'Hey, Gideon!' Amelia said, 'everything okay?' She tried not to imagine any disastrous scenarios, especially involving a pied piper-esque attack of mice swarming through the hotel.

'The eagle has flown the building,' Gideon whispered into the phone.

'What! There's an eagle? In the hotel?' She briefly wondered if they could catch mice.

'No! Actually, I suppose it's more a case of the dopiaza has left the Taj Mahal!'

'What? Gideon, is everything okay?'

'Oh my God! Have you never seen a spy film?' he said in exasperation. 'I'm trying to talk in code. Our person of interest, you know, *the girl*, has gone and buggered off.'

'India!'

'Congratulations! I'm hot on her tail. I have been keeping an eye out but so far she's just been glued to her phone. Tonight, though, with Alice away to the Whistling Haggis and Dan sitting enraptured by your raconteur boyfriend, young India decided to minesweep the booze from the men's dinner, grabbed a hip flask and headed off rather unsteadily into the night.'

'We need to keep an eye on her!'

'Yes, darling,' Gideon drawled, 'which is what I'm doing.'

'Where did she go?'

'She's currently pacing around the war memorial at the harbour.'

That was just along from the Whistling Haggis. Amelia headed over to one of the small windows that were set deeply into the thick walls of the pub. She wiped the condensation to peer along Main Street but visibility was too poor.

'Do you think she's arranged to meet someone?' Amelia asked, cupping her hands over the glass to stop the light from the pub reflecting back at her.

'I couldn't say. She's been walking around it, as if trying to find something. She's still glued to her phone.'

'Where are you?'

'Opposite side of the road.'

'Give me a minute, I'll come and join you. Should I get Alice?'

'Getting her mother involved may make the situation worse.'

Hanging up the phone, Amelia hurried to the back room to grab her coat and almost bumped into Evangelina who was coming out the ladies.

'Is everything okay?'

'I don't know! Yes, probably! I'm not sure.'

'Can I help?' Evangelina asked, her hand hovering over her coat on the hooks.

Amelia was worried in case India would be freaked out by her and Gideon trying to help. A friendly face of someone she knew would probably be better. She also didn't immediately want to involve Alice as Gideon had a point.

'That would be good,' Amelia said as she turned to leave, squeezing past all the pub goers on her way to the door.

She paused briefly to put on her hat and gloves and then pushed open the door and almost tripped over Lorcan who was standing outside smoking a cigarette. Amelia's sudden stop caused Evangelina to career into the back of her.

'Amelia... Evangelina...' Lorcan started to say then clearly didn't know what to add and just stood looking perplexed.

'Hi, sorry but I'm in a bit of a hurry,' Amelia said as she made to push past him.

'Is everything okay?' Lorcan asked.

Just then Gideon appeared, slightly out of breath from running. 'She may have had more to drink than I realised,' Gideon said. 'She's now sitting at the foot of the war memorial sobbing her heart out.'

'Who?' Evangelina asked as Amelia and Gideon hurried along the pavement.

'India,' Amelia called behind her, as Lorcan and Evangelina followed.

Right enough, a couple of minutes later and they discovered India King, slumped in the snow, crying. She cried even harder when she saw she'd been discovered.

'India, love, what's wrong?' Evangelina asked, sitting down beside her.

'You're going to tell Mum and Dad I've been drinking. They'll kill me and I'll never be allowed out again.'

'No, no. Let's get you back and you can sleep this off,' Evangelina said, brushing the turquoise hair from the teenager's face, revealing large streaks of eyeliner and mascara down her pale face.

'What are you doing out here, India?' Amelia asked her.

'Trying to find it.'

'Trying to find what?'

'That's the point, I don't know. And it could be anywhere. And I couldn't find the one at the folly either,' India wailed, before leaning over and being sick.

Amelia and Gideon looked at each other across India's head to the sound of her retching into the snow.

'I think we need to get India back into the warmth, and plenty of fluids,' Amelia said to the agreement of the others as Gideon handed India a handkerchief. Sheepishly, India stood up and together they all walked back to Stone Manor.

Back in the warmth of the kitchens, pint of water in hand, India seemed far calmer and a lot more sober. And horrified her parents would be told of her antics.

Lorcan went to get a blanket for the teenager as Amelia, Evangelina and Gideon sat around her.

'I'm sorry I was sick.'

'Better to get it out your system,' Evangelina said.

Gideon dismissed India's apologies with a wave of his hand. 'One day, when I publish my memoirs, you'll read stories about my behaviour which will pale your little adventure into insignificance, my love. Now, what was it you were trying to find by the war memorial?'

'A geocache.'

'A what now?'

'A geocache,' India repeated. 'Geocaching, you know? When people hide little things like notes and whatever in tins or Tupperware boxes and you have to find them from co-ordinates and then log the find online. There is one at the folly too but I couldn't find it.' India looked up at Amelia. 'I saw you up there that night. I was worried in case you recognised me and would tell Mum and Dad; they're so overprotective. I'm glad you got back up that hill okay. It looked really steep and dangerous. Wasn't it really stupid to be climbing up it in the dark?'

'That's a discussion topic for another time,' Gideon said with a pointed look towards Amelia.

'And this geocaching was the reason you were at the war memorial tonight too?' Amelia asked India, ignoring Gideon.

India nodded. 'There's nothing else to do. It's so boring here.'

'Is that why you drained all the glasses after dinner?' Gideon asked.

India nodded again.

'India, have you ever heard of a man called Benedict Geissler?' Amelia asked.

India thought a moment before shaking her head.

'And you hadn't arranged to meet anyone at the folly or anywhere else?'

'Like who? I don't *know* anyone here; everyone's really old and boring,' she said sulkily. 'I'm going up to bed now,' she handed the empty glass to Amelia and headed out the kitchen just as Lorcan returned with the blanket. He gave it to her as she left.

'Do you think she'll be okay?' Amelia said to the group once the door had closed behind India.

'Probably in about five years' time when the arrogance and rudeness fade,' Gideon said.

'I mean in the short term. Will she be okay through the night?'

'At her age, she'll have the constitution of an ox,' Gideon said, wistfully. 'And did you see how much she vommed back up? All that alcohol will be out her system by now, she'll no doubt sleep like a baby and be up at the crack of dawn, bright-eyed and bushy-tailed. Although I'm slightly more concerned about her woeful choice in hobbies. Geocaching!'

'She should maybe take up crochet,' Evangelina said with a laugh and Amelia joined in, much to the puzzlement of Lorcan and Gideon.

'What happens at a hen party, stays at a hen party!' Amelia said firmly, refusing to divulge any more.

Amelia didn't have the energy to go back to the Whistling Haggis and hoped Lucy and the others wouldn't be too offended by her abrupt disappearance. Evangelina had also shown no inclination to return either. After another couple of minutes' chat, Evangelina announced she was heading up to her room. As Evangelina went out the door, Jingles came in and went over to Gideon, meowing plaintively.

'Have you not been fed?' Gideon said as he picked up the large ginger furball and carried him back out into the main hotel, chatting to him as he went. Much as she loved having Jingles about, Amelia again wondered just how efficient a mouser he would be as he looked far keener to sneak into the kitchen to scrounge for food than prowl round the boundaries of the hotel.

'Amelia, can I have a quick word?' Lorcan said quietly to Amelia.

Amelia had never seen Lorcan look as unhappy or stressed before. And it had only been a few hours since she'd discovered him knocked unconscious on his studio floor. 'Why don't we go get a nightcap and we can have a *long* chat?'

He gave her a tired smile and nodded as they went through to the main part of the hotel.

Amelia could see Jack was still in the drawing room, clearly holding court with the other guests of the hotel, noticing that DeShawn and Alaiya had also joined them. As Amelia and Lorcan walked into the deserted bar, there was a burst of raucous laughter and Amelia was pleased that Jack's evening seemed to be going well.

With it being Craig's evening off, the bar was unmanned and

Amelia poured Lorcan and herself a whisky and they sat up on the stools.

Lorcan gave a massive sigh and rubbed his eyes before eventually saying, 'It's so strange seeing her after all this time. It's like nothing's changed but everything's changed at the same time. We realise we need to talk but that's easier said than done in a small hotel in a small village. And even then, I'm not even sure where to begin.'

Amelia merely nodded in what she hoped was a supportive way.

Lorcan took a sip of his whisky. 'And that's not all. There's something else that's happened and I really don't know what to do. A few weeks ago, I … Evangelina!' Lorcan's head darted round to the doorway. Amelia turned to see Evangelina standing there for a moment before she doubled over with two gigantic sneezes.

She blew her nose. 'I'm sorry to interrupt but could I get a whisky or a brandy, my cold seems to be back with a vengeance!'

'Of course,' Amelia said, sliding off the barstool. 'Why don't I make you a hot toddy; warm whisky with some ginger, honey and lemon in it?'

Evangelina nodded and sneezed again. 'That sounds wonderful, thank you,' she said with a grateful smile.

As Amelia got to work making up the drink the silence hung heavy and awkward in the air between everyone.

Amelia handed over the medicinal drink to Evangelina, and with another thank you and goodnight, the actress left to go back to her room.

Lorcan drained his whisky. 'I'm going to head up now, too. I'm done in. It's been quite a day.'

'Are you sure?' It seemed as if Lorcan was going to divulge something else, something that was clearly upsetting him, but it looked like the moment had passed.

'I am, Amelia, thank you.'

'You know I'm here if you need a chat?'

Amelia watched Lorcan leave as she nursed her own whisky for another few moments, lost in thought.

An hour later, with Jack's soiree ended, the hens having returned and the night shift in place, Amelia and Jack headed back to the Gatehouse. Yawning noisily, Amelia linked her arm through Jack's and leant against him as they continued in companionable silence.

Jack paused at the back door as Amelia nearly walked into the back of him.

'Don't tell me you've forgotten your keys,' she said when he still didn't move.

'Uh, no. I don't think we're going to need keys.'

'What...?' Amelia took a step to the side and looked at the back door. It had clearly been kicked in, with splinters of wood sticking proud of the door frame where the lock had once been.

CHAPTER 24

CHRISTMAS EVE

W ord of the break-in travelled fast in Glencarlach. Early next morning, stopping in at Jean Maddox's shop for some milk and bread, Amelia was met with equal amounts of sympathy and questions from the shop owner.

'I don't know what's happened to this village!' Jean said, pursing her lips into a small hard line. 'First the church, now your home,' she shook her head. 'Was there much stolen?'

'No, nothing we could see.' That had been the strange thing. Despite going through their upturned house, neither Amelia nor Jack could identify anything that had been taken. All the small valuable items like jewellery and watches were still in their place despite the ease with which they could have been stuffed into a pocket. There was even a twenty-pound note and some loose change on the kitchen counter that had been ignored, though the cupboards below had been opened and emptied.

'Just wanton vandalism, then!' Jean Maddox said in disgust.

It had been what Jack and Amelia had wondered as they sat up until the small hours in the kitchen in Stone Manor telling Toby and Gideon what had happened. With no way of securing the door, Jack and Amelia had grabbed a bag of essentials and taken one of the last free rooms in the hotel.

But although the Gatehouse had been left in a mess, it wasn't pointless vandalism. It looked very much like the perpetrator had been looking for something. But what that something was neither of them could fathom. Cupboards had been rifled; drawers pulled out; even Jack's still unpacked case and duty-free bags had been emptied onto the bed. Jack had seemed very concerned at that, but had sighed in great relief when he saw that whatever it was he was looking for was still there.

Interest piqued, Amelia had tried to see what Jack had in his hands but he'd kept it behind his back muttering about spoiling her Christmas present surprise.

Leaving Jean's shop, Amelia crossed the road and immediately got waylaid by Reverend McDade. 'Amelia, I heard what happened. What a dreadful business! Are you and Jack okay?'

'We are, thank you.'

'Thank goodness neither of you were in when it happened. That just doesn't bear thinking about.'

'I know, we were lucky.'

'Has Constable Williams been informed?'

'I'm just about to go and see him.' She now had quite the list of things to offload to Ray; her break-in; Betty's gun; the possible intruder at Stone Manor; and finding Benedict Gessler's mobile phone, which she'd decided to hand over to the authorities, mainly because she'd not been able to get past the four-digit security password.

And also, because Amelia had had a horrible thought as she lay in bed unable to sleep. What if it had been Benedict Geissler's mobile phone that the person who broke into her home had been looking for, not knowing it had been sitting at the bottom of Amelia's bag since she'd found it. But if it was the reason for the break-in, why?

'I hope to see you at tonight's Christmas candle walk,' Rev

McDade carried on cheerfully. 'It's times like this it is important to remember we are all part of the caring community of Glencarlach.'

'Thank you. Yes, we're all looking forward to it. I've mentioned it to all the guests and I hope we'll get some of them coming along too.'

The minister beamed. 'Wonderful. It's one of the highlights of my year. I will see you later, Amelia.' And with that he hurried off.

Amelia looked along the pavement, wondering how far she would get before bumping into another concerned villager. Then her phone rang. Cutting off the *Tales of the Unexpected* ringtone she saw it was Jack calling.

'Hey! I'm at the Gatehouse and I've managed to get hold of Angus and he's meeting me here with a new lock.'

Angus owned the local hardware shop and was the village handyman. He seemed to be able to fix anything and clearly didn't mind coming out on Christmas Eve.

'The mess isn't too bad. It seems it was a thoughtful burglar, if there's such a thing! I've tidied up the kitchen and bedroom already and I'll square away the rest soon.'

'Are you sure you don't want a hand?'

'I'm fine really, just go and speak to Ray and I'll see you later.'

'Okay.' Hanging up she continued along Main Street as Craig came towards her, clearly heading towards the hotel to start his shift. Hands stuffed deep in his pockets he looked quite miserable.

'Morning!' she said cheerily.

He looked up, distractedly, giving Amelia a faint smile.

'Good day off yesterday?' she asked.

'Yeah, it was fine, thanks.'

Amelia supposed there wasn't much to do in a little camper van on the edge of the land of Stone Manor when the entire village had been snowed in.

He glanced at his watch and with an apologetic shrug said,

'I'm cutting it fine, sorry! The boss is a tyrant if I'm late!' He winked at her before continuing along Main Street. At the corner of the Whistling Haggis, he turned and made his way up the lane which led to Stone Manor.

Amelia ploughed on. A few shops up ahead she could see Lucy looking through the display of sledges outside the outdoors shop. Amelia didn't fancy getting stopped by her, just in case something else was added to her ever-increasing wedding wish list. Amelia had no idea how the outstanding items still to be delivered would get to them in time for Boxing Day, despite the assurances from the sellers that they would move heaven and earth. And with the cold weather, Amelia was now concerned about releasing doves into the open in case the poor things froze to death.

As Lucy picked up one of the sledges to check it over, Amelia realised she was at the door of the café. She'd not had any kind of caffeine injection that morning and her nostrils twitched expectantly as she caught a whiff of their dark Columbian roast. Slipping inside would be a convenient way to avoid Ms Carvalho for a few minutes. Amelia had had quite a restless night and she knew a coffee would definitely help perk her up, along with a slice of their baked apple and cinnamon cake. With cream.

Not needing any more convincing, Amelia darted inside the café and joined the queue waiting to be served. As usual, the café was busy but there were a couple of free tables Amelia noted as she looked round.

In fact, Sally's cousin, Kit, was sitting at a table, sipping coffee and scrolling through his phone. She'd see if he fancied company as she'd barely spoken two words to him since he'd rolled up in the snow storm the night before last and it would be nice to catch up with him, especially if she could also subtly ask if his work as an investigative journalist ever extended to hotel reviews. Amelia was now at the top of the queue and she could check out the cake selection, nestled in the glass display cabinet. Weighing up her options, she was aware of someone's mobile phone ringing beside her. The carrot cake looked lovely and moist, as did the chocolate fudge, but considering the apple cinnamon cake was a festive special, Amelia decided to go with that.

The woman in front turned to Amelia. 'Your phone's ringing, love,' she said.

Amelia could still hear a phone but it definitely wasn't her ringtone. This one was a strange piece of music that sounded like a harpsichord plonking away.

But it did sound very near.

And then she remembered she had another phone in her bag.

Benedict Geissler's.

She dug deep into her oversize tote amongst the notebooks, pens and random snacks and pulled it out. Right enough, the phone was lit up. She pulled it out and held it for a moment, noticing the caller ID said 'KT'.

She tentatively answered it. 'Hello?' And suddenly the noise in the café seemed amplified, the volume of chatter doubled and she could hear George Michael singing 'Last Christmas' play in real time, and then a nano-second later, in her ear.

There was an inhalation of breath in her ear and then a very tentative, 'Amelia?'

Amelia slowly turned and looked at the table Kit was sitting at.

Kit Trelawney.

KT.

Their eyes met, as they still held their respective phones up at their ears.

Still not breaking eye contact, Amelia said, 'I think we need to talk.'

'I think you're right,' Kit agreed.

CHAPTER 25

Amelia waited until she'd had a sip of her fortifying flat white with an extra shot before asking, 'Why are you phoning this number?'

'Shouldn't I be asking: how did you get hold of Benedict Geissler's phone?' Kit riposted. They both glanced down at the table where Amelia had placed Benedict's phone. Neither of them made a move to touch it.

'Oh, so how... um... how–' Amelia hedged around how to put her next question when Kit interrupted.

'I arranged to meet him by the memorial but he didn't show yesterday. So I tried again today, still nothing, but I realised, if I sat in here, I've got the memorial in my sights. It's far warmer. I hate the cold.'

'–did you know him?'

Kit sat up slightly, senses alert. 'Past tense?'

Amelia nodded and listlessly stabbed her pastry fork into her cake, losing a little of her appetite.

Kit sat back in his chair and exhaled. 'Shit.' He looked out the window for a moment, lost in thought before turning back to

Amelia. 'What happened? And how did you know him? And, how the hell did you end up with his phone?'

'Well, I didn't know him. He called the hotel and said he wanted to meet me, but not at the hotel. We arranged to meet at the folly and when I got there he was having a heart attack and he died before I could do anything. And then I found his phone the next day.'

'Found it?' he asked sceptically.

'Yes. Near where he died. And I'm about to take it to our local constable and tell him. And to tell him about Betty's illegal gun, a possible intruder at Stone Manor and then the break-in at our house last night.' Amelia paused for a moment before adding, 'I'm sorry about your friend.'

'He wasn't really a friend, but thank you.' Kit ran a hand through his black hair distractedly. 'Hang on, you said you were broken into last night? And there was an intruder in the hotel?'

Amelia nodded. 'Betty came across them in her room. Which is how we found out about her illegal weapon.'

'Did she see who it was?' Kit asked.

Amelia shook her head, slightly surprised that out of all those revelations, Kit hadn't focused on Betty having a gun as Amelia personally found that to be the most completely absurd concept to get on board with.

'And your break-in, what was stolen? Did you see anything?' Kit asked intently.

'Nothing was stolen and no, both Jack and I were out all night.'

'I have to think.' Kit rubbed his temples.

'Kit? What are you doing here? You're not just here to visit Sally at Christmas, are you?'

Kit sighed. 'Trust me when I say it was an additional bonus. I adore her. And, I'm asking, *please* don't tell her anything that's going on.'

'That won't be difficult, because at the moment I don't have a clue what's going on either!' Amelia said. 'What have you got yourself wrapped up in?'

'I don't know exactly!' Kit said. 'That's what I need to figure out!' He drummed his fingers on the table. 'Benedict Geissler called me a few weeks ago, about uncovering a story. I'd worked with him previously. He was a good contact. He was very cagey this time though and didn't want to give much away. But he was following a lead. Said it would be a huge career-making story for me and would settle a decades-old mystery. But it looks as if he could have taken all other information to the grave with him.'

'But didn't he work in insurance?' Amelia was sure that's what Ray had told her.

'There's a bit more to it than that.'

'But clearly, it was something to do with Glencarlach. He had a newspaper cutting with an article on Stone Manor with him.'

Just then, Amelia saw Constable Williams walking past the window. Kit turned and looked too as the constable opened the door of the café and stepped inside.

'Does he know you're on your way to see him?' Kit whispered across the table.

'Yes.'

'Does he know you've found Benedict's phone?'

'No.'

'Right. Can you keep it safe for a little longer?' he said, sliding it towards her. 'You can hand it in shortly, but just not yet.'

'Okay.'

'I need to go and make a couple of calls. I'll meet you back at the hotel as soon as I can. Please, just keep this under your hat for now?'

Still not sure what 'this' all was, Amelia nodded. Kit got up from the table and hurried out the door, slamming it closed behind him, which elicited a few looks of disapproval from the customers. She watched him get out his phone and call someone as he paced up and down the pavement.

Constable Williams headed over towards Amelia. 'Your friend seemed in a hurry,' he said amicably.

'Oh, that's Sally's cousin.'

'Oh, that's nice, is he visiting her for Christmas?'

'Yes,' Amelia confirmed, although it would seem that was now up for debate. She wished Kit hadn't run off as she had so much more to ask him. 'I was on my way to see you about last night, and a couple of other things too but thought I'd have a quick coffee.'

'Ah, I know only too well the allure of the delights of this café.' He gave a little chuckle as he patted his stomach. 'I'm awfully sorry about your break-in last night, Amelia. You say nothing was taken though?'

'Yes, everything was turned out of the cupboards and drawers though, as if whoever did it was looking for something.'

'Like what?'

Amelia shrugged. 'That's the thing, Jack and I have no idea. We had some money lying around but that was left, as was my jewellery and Jack's watches.'

'Were your passports and birth certificates and any other documents like that left? Identity theft is on the rise you know.'

'They're all kept in an envelope in a drawer and it hadn't been touched.'

'How curious. Is the lock fixed now?'

'In the process of.'

'Angus?'

'Yes.'

Ray nodded in approval. 'Now, you said on the phone there were other issues you wanted to talk to me about?'

'Yes,' Amelia said. 'It turns out Betty–'

'Ah, hold on,' he said as his phone began to ring. 'This is Constable Williams,' he answered in a very officious voice. He looked very grave as he listened to the other end of the conversation and Amelia took the time to have a couple of forkfuls of her cake.

Ray ended the call. 'Well, that was an interesting conversation.' He looked gravely at Amelia. 'That was the DI from Inverness. They ran the post-mortem on Benedict Geissler. He didn't die of a heart attack as first suspected.'

Amelia paused, forkful of cake midway to her mouth.

Ray took a deep breath. 'It wasn't a natural death at all. Benedict Geissler was poisoned.'

CHAPTER 26

'Poisoned!' Gideon exclaimed.

Amelia tried to hush him, but it was just the two of them along with Jack and Toby standing in the kitchen at Stone Manor a couple of hours later.

'But how?' Toby said.

'And why?' Jack asked.

'It's the *what with* that interests me!' Amelia said. 'Potassium cyanide.'

'Potassium cyanide?' Gideon echoed.

'Wow!' Jack said. 'That's very old school. Very Agatha Christie, isn't it?'

'It is!' Amelia said. 'It was evidently a massive dose and would have been very fast acting. I must have *just* missed the murderer!' she added, failing to keep the excitement out of her voice.

'For which we are all thankful! If you hadn't, you could have been the next victim, Ames!' Toby said in horror.

'But if I'd managed to catch just a glimpse I could help solve it,' Amelia pointed out.

Toby shook his head in despair.

'So, how did they poison him?' Gideon asked. 'Was it in the coffee he was drinking, the one you said he spilled?'

'No, it was by injection! There was a little puncture mark at the side of his neck.'

'So, the murderer snuck up behind him and did the deed?' Gideon said.

'It would seem so,' Amelia agreed.

'But why was he here and why did he want to speak to you?' Jack said. 'And more pertinently, should we be worried if the murderer hasn't finished yet?'

Amelia shrugged. That was why she was desperate to speak to Kit. She'd not told the others about his involvement but as the day wore on and he still hadn't got in touch with her, Amelia was getting worried. Although he didn't know why Benedict Geissler was here he clearly knew *something* more than Amelia did.

'I feel very uneasy about all this,' Jack said.

'You're not the only one,' Toby agreed.

'Well, it's not as if I've gone looking for this. Mr Geissler came looking for me!' Amelia pointed out, not liking the worried glances between Jack and her brother. It was time to deflect the attention away from her connection to the murder. 'But on a lighter note, what do you make of Evangelina and Lorcan?' Amelia said, hoping to change the subject.

Luckily, Gideon took the bait. 'It's just like *Loveboat*!' he exclaimed. 'Remember that really cheesy eighties American drama! The captain always got guests together! You're that captain,' Gideon said excitedly, pointing at Amelia. 'Except we're not on a boat!'

'And we're not in a cheesy eighties American drama,' Jack pointed out.

'You could be with that accent,' Gideon fired back. '*And* your awful dress sense.'

'Come on, guys,' Toby interjected. 'You're meant to be helping me at the moment, remember?' He handed Jack a peeler and pushed a box of vegetables towards him. They were meant to be organising that night's dinner service as another of the casual staff couldn't manage to get in from a nearby village due to the road being closed. But every time they started talking about service, Amelia couldn't help but think aloud and they would all veer off topic to discuss Benedict. Or Lorcan. Or Evangelina. Or Betty…

'They just have this look in their eye when they talk about each other,' Amelia said, referring to Lorcan and Evangelina.

'And where are we standing on Ricky being the one to knock Lorcan on the head?' Gideon asked.

'I'm not sure,' Amelia said. It had seemed a nice fit originally but the more she thought about it, the more difficulty Amelia had thinking Ricky had been behind the attack on Lorcan.

Jack nodded, looking very serious as he listened.

'He may have wanted to look through Lorcan's paintings,' Gideon piped up, 'looking for evidence of their romance?'

'It's a bit of a long shot though, don't you think?' Amelia said thoughtfully. 'That Lorcan was going to have a painting sitting there of his ex-girlfriend.'

'Yes,' Gideon said, narrowing his eyes and pointing the knife he'd been using to cut up orange slices, 'apart from the fact that's *exactly* what happened!'

'Maybe he'd been lying in wait for Lorcan, was bored then idly looked through the paintings, saw the one of his wife, worked himself up into a ball of incandescent rage and threw himself upon Lorcan when he entered the studio,' Amelia said, smacking the pestle she'd been using to crush fennel seeds into the palm of her hand for emphasis.

'Or, it could have been the same kids who broke into the church,' Jack pointed out as he picked up a potato.

Amelia felt deflated and looked over to Gideon for support.

'But Glencarlach isn't really known for its delinquent youth problem!' Gideon said, popping an orange segment into his mouth.

'I hear all sorts of troublemakers are moving to the village now! Actors and everything!' Jack said, raising an eyebrow at Gideon, clearly trying to wind him up. Gideon, rather than rising to it, threw a balled-up dishcloth at Jack's head. It wasn't that long ago that Gideon would have flounced off in a diva fit at Jack's remark. Now, although both of them still bickered away at each other it had morphed into good-natured sparring and Amelia had a sneaky suspicion they were actually very fond of each other, though neither would readily admit it.

Amelia glanced at the clock on the wall. 'We should leave for the Christmas Nativity walk.'

'God-botherers usually give me the heebie-jeebies,' Gideon grumbled.

'You don't have to come,' Amelia pointed out.

'I don't want to stay here in case Toby ropes me into doing any more.'

'The chance would be a fine thing.' Toby sighed as he plucked the peeler out of Jack's hand and prepared the vegetable himself. 'Just go! I'll be quicker doing it all myself.'

'Isn't that why you moved into the hotel?' Amelia said to Gideon as she gave the fennel seeds a final pummelling. 'So you could be close to hand to help out while we're short staffed?'

Gideon chuckled in delight. 'I do so love your naivety, my darling!'

Donning their coats, gloves and hats, they made their way into reception. Amelia had mentioned to everyone about the Glencarlach Christmas Eve tradition but hadn't thought many would be bothered with it. Clearly she'd misread her audience as most of the guests had congregated in the reception area, all bar Mr Griffin, Kit and Evangelina.

Feeling a little like a tour guide, Amelia uttered the words,

'Follow me!' and they all made their way down the drive towards the village.

Although not even five o'clock it was already completely dark and Amelia felt a little thrill of Christmas anticipation as she linked her arm through Jack's as they meandered down the driveway as fresh flakes of snow began to fall.

'Wow! Is that DeShawn Johnson? Is he staying here!?' Jack asked, glancing behind.

'Yes! How do you know him?'

'He used to be a running back for the Dallas Cowboys,' he said, keeping his voice low. 'Got a horrific injury in a game and tore three ligaments in his knee. He had months of physio but he was never the same. It ended his career.'

'That's awful!'

'Well, it worked out all right for him in the end,' a voice said beside them. Amelia hadn't noticed Betty stride up beside them wearing a patchwork velvet cloak and matching cloche hat. 'He turned to music,' Betty said, a twinkle in her eye. 'I do love a bit of drum and bass. I was delighted to see him here with his lovely wife. I'm guessing you don't get many Grammy and MOBO award-winning music artists around here.'

Amelia had a flashback to the first morning when she caught Betty whispering into DeShawn's ear. She'd been worried the older lady had been inappropriate, but she had clearly been letting him know she was a fan. Hamish's relative was a constant surprise!

'And of course, that opened doors in Hollywood,' Betty continued. 'He's still very fit and was touted for a main role in one of those superhero films.'

'I read about that!' Jack said.

Amelia had been too busy trying to set up her hotel to be reading gossip columns.

'What happened?' Jack asked Betty, who was clearly a walking combination of *Grazia*, *Hello!* and *Empire* magazines.

'Some scandal involving his agent. He had fired them over some unethical shenanigans and then all these rumours went round about him and no one wanted to go near him. It all turned out to be false but by that point the damage had been done and the role had gone to someone else and filming had started.' Betty pulled her hat a little lower onto her ears. 'Luckily, he's now back on track and has signed up for the lead in a new sci-fi detective series on HBO which promises lots of sex and violence!' she added gleefully.

Amelia looked back to where Vanessa, head to foot in her white fur coat, complete with Cossack-style furry hat, was walking with Terence and Dan, her voice carrying in the night air, and Amelia felt she didn't have far to look to discover who the unethical agent was.

They continued on to the church where Rev McDade was waiting outside to welcome them along with a large proportion of the village.

'I'm afraid that due to the robbery we can't use our traditional lanterns but we've managed to cobble together a few nice pieces to help light the way,' he said holding up a novelty garden sunflower mosaic tea light holder. One by one, the rest of the crowd got out torches, turned on the flashlights on their phones and held up an assortment of candle holders. As they all slowly walked along Main Street, Rev McDade retold the story of the nativity.

At the far end of the harbour, they stood around the minister as he finished telling the story and then everyone sang 'Away in a Manger'. Jack pulled Amelia close and kissed the top of her head as the snow continued to fall. Amelia snuck a glance at Gideon, who despite his dislike of religion was heartily singing along. To keep a fine balance everyone then sang 'Santa Claus is Coming to Town' and then Rev McDade waited until everyone had quietened down before announcing, 'We've got some cups of mulled wine and hot chocolate courtesy of the Whistling Haggis.'

As everyone moved towards the refreshments, Amelia untucked her arm from Jack's. 'I'll go grab us some wine,' Amelia said as she went over to the stall, fruitlessly scanning the crowd for a glimpse of Kit.

As she joined the queue she noticed Ricky breaking away from the crowd. There was something furtive about the way he hurried over the snow to one of the big rubbish bins, looking behind him as he went. He stood by the bin for a moment or two before he unfastened the top couple of buttons of his coat and Amelia could see him remove a bulky package. It looked very like the one she'd handed him earlier that day. The one he suddenly had lost all interest in receiving.

He crammed it into the bin then, quickly refastening his coat, crossed back over to the crowd and rejoined the group with Carlo and Vanessa.

CHAPTER 27

It was far too tempting to leave without rescuing the package from the bin. Amelia sensed something very fishy going on and she was determined to get to the bottom of it. Sipping at the mulled wine and letting Gideon and Jack's chatter wash over her, Amelia kept a close eye on the bin. No one went near it apart from those wanting to use it as a rubbish receptacle.

'We should head back now,' Jack said, checking his watch as much of the crowd dispersed.

'Yes, Toby will have a plethora of tasks for us by now, I'm sure,' Gideon agreed. 'Come on, Amelia, no shirkers!'

But Amelia continued to hold back, keen for the area to clear. 'You guys carry on and I'll catch you up, I just wanted to catch Davey for a quick word.'

'Well, don't blame me if you get all the potatoes to peel. Last one in gets the worst kitchen job.'

'I'll cope,' Amelia said as she made a shooing action. Jack looked thoughtfully at her but turned towards Stone Manor, cajoling Gideon along with him.

When most of the villagers had moved on, Amelia went over

to the bin and peered inside. The top layer was mainly the disposable paper cups from the mulled wine, but as she delved a little deeper she found the square box she'd seen Ricky dump. Pulling it out and shaking off the dregs of drinks and a couple of pieces of discarded chewing gum, Amelia saw it was definitely the package she'd handed him the day before, still unopened.

It was a very light box and as there were no markings to warn her that it was fragile, she gave it a little shake. Something rattled inside.

Despite her curiosity she wanted to wait until she was alone back at the hotel before she opened it. Making sure to hang back from the others, she walked along the drive to Stone Manor, ducking in through the back door. Managing to avoid everyone she headed towards the little office where she ripped off the parcel tape. Inside was a torch – which was clearly what had been rattling around – a black beanie hat, fake glasses, wig and a selection pack of different styles of stick-on facial hair. Amelia sat back in her chair, looking at the items for a few minutes as she contemplated what to do until she realised she'd be needed in the kitchen. She put them all into the top drawer of her desk and went to see what she could do to help Toby.

Everyone was bustling about, apart from Gideon who was leaning against the wall with a mug of tea. As soon as he saw her he drained the contents of his mug, banged it on the table and grabbed Amelia by the hand.

'Let's go through to the bar and help out. I've a feeling it'll be busy in there tonight. We'll only get in the way in here,' he said as he led her through the doors.

'I should at least check–' Amelia glanced over her shoulder but Gideon's grip was firm.

'It's like feeding time at the zoo!' Gideon whispered to Amelia as they rounded the corner of the bar to see the guests congregated round Craig who was making a dry martini.

Lorcan was sitting at a table in the corner with a pint of Guinness in front of him, trying to look inconspicuous as he read a book.

'The cavalry's here!' Gideon announced as he slipped behind the bar to help Craig.

Taking a step back, Amelia watched all the guests interact. Betty, now clutching her martini, walked jauntily over to Lorcan and sat down beside him, clearly not picking up on the 'leave me alone' hints he exuded by having his head buried in a book.

Alaiya was sitting at one of the tables talking earnestly to her husband. DeShawn kept glancing up at the group around the bar, his jaw clenching rhythmically. He tried to stand up but Alaiya grabbed hold of his hand and whispered something to him as he reluctantly sat back down.

Dan and Alice King were chatting with Lucy and Carlo, Alice admiring the ornate chunky pendant Lucy was wearing – the silver one she hadn't wanted to put into the safe. She seemed to be wearing all her jewellery tonight, clearly not wanting to leave any piece out of her sight. Vanessa swooped in on them, Campari and orange in hand, keen to join in admiring the necklace and even more eager to show off her own rather impressive diamond choker.

Evangelina, who had made it downstairs but looked quite unwell, with her red nose and puffy eyes, was standing with Nisha. Although they were in conversation, Amelia noticed how Evangelina's eyes kept sliding over to where Lorcan sat.

Betty took a large swallow of her martini and smacked her rouged lips as she stood up, then leant across the table and surreptitiously slid a little piece of paper to Lorcan. He looked up questioningly then hastily tucked it into the cover of his book. Because of where Betty had positioned herself Amelia was the only one who could have seen her. The older woman made her way up to the bar, giving Evangelina the ghost of a wink as she passed her and made her way into the dining room.

One by one the guests followed with their pre-prandial drinks and sat down at the large table set out festively for the Christmas Eve dinner.

Having the wedding party at one large table and all other guests at their own, smaller tables would have been a little off balance, Amelia had felt. So she had put the rectangular tables together to make one long table in the middle of the room to seat all sixteen guests. She was also interested to see who sat next to each other.

Dan and Alice did; Vanessa sat as diagonally opposite Terence as possible. Ricky and Evangelina sat seats apart from one another and Lorcan, who clearly didn't know where to go, eventually opted to sit opposite Evangelina, next to India. If sitting on Carlo's lap had been an option, Lucy would have done so but in the end sat as close beside him as she could. Nisha plonked herself down next to Lorcan giving one of his dreadlock's a playful tweak as she did. DeShawn sat next to Evangelina, with Alaiya sitting next to her husband. Terence seemed delighted to be sitting in between Nisha and Betty. There were two unclaimed seats; one beside Dan and the other beside Alaiya, at the diagonally opposite ends of the table. Of the two guests who were still to appear, Amelia was curious about Mr Griffin's non-attendance but was far more concerned by Kit's no show.

As if reading her mind, Vanessa said, 'I wonder if our elusive guest from the Simenon Room will make an appearance tonight?'

'Maybe he'd prefer some peace and quiet?' DeShawn said archly from the other end of the table.

Terence guffawed then said, 'Well, he'll be plum out of luck with that if he sits opposite you, old girl!' he indicated the empty seat opposite his wife. 'Be a good man, Ricky, keep an eye on her, eh?' he said, raising his glass to Ricky who was sitting to the right of Vanessa.

Toby took that moment to appear with a couple of large trays of seafood appetisers to the delight of the diners.

'Isn't this marvellous!' Vanessa announced as she pounced on the food. 'Oysters remind me of the last time I was in Italy.' She sighed happily. 'I love Venice! So romantic! Remember that wonderful time we had in the Danieli, Terence?' she hollered down the table to her husband who had tucked a napkin into his collar and was poised to swallow an oyster. He shook his head. 'Sorry, old girl, that wasn't me. I've never been to that city. Isn't it meant to smell something awful in the summer?'

'Oh!' Momentarily flustered, Vanessa looked down at her plate for a moment then looked up and smiled. 'It's so easy to forget when one travels so extensively! I remember now, it was with a group of my girlfriends! We'd all met treading the boards in our youth and we were having a reunion.'

'Your youth? Would that be your carefully managed fictitious youth or your actual youth; when Adam was a boy?' Carlo said teasingly, which elicited a hearty laugh from the table and although Vanessa laughed along, Amelia clocked the dagger of a look she gave Carlo.

Amelia was aware of Gideon sidling up to her. 'Vanessa's been to the Danieli. That was one of the places on the Secret Guest's list!' he whispered.

'Oh! Although, the Danieli is very well known. Even I've been there for cocktails!' Amelia said, remembering the fantastically romantic and decadent long weekend she and Jack had spent in the beautiful city a few months previously.

'Well, I'm going to do a bit of snooping and find out if she's been to any of the other places on the Secret Guest list.'

Amelia watched as Gideon made his way back to the table on a mission. He bent down and whispered something in Vanessa's ear. What he lacked in diplomacy he made up for in directness, Amelia mused as she watched Vanessa's eyes widen and her face paled slightly. Amelia wondered how important the secrecy was for her to have such a reaction to Gideon's questioning.

Amelia watched as she turned and pulled Gideon's shirt front down and whispered in his ear. They had a brief exchange before Gideon patted her hand to release it, smoothed down his shirt front and continued to circulate round the table, but not before giving Amelia a knowing nod.

The rest of the meal passed in a blur for Amelia as she scuttled back and forth to the kitchen then to the bar to collect yet more wine and cocktails. There were going to be a few sore heads the next morning she thought as she and Craig went round the table time and time again, refilling everyone's glass. Carlo had given instructions for free-flowing drinks, and to include all the guests, not just his party, and it seemed everyone was happy to take him up on his generosity.

Just after the main course had been cleared, Carlo stood up and cleared his throat and as he caught everyone's attention a hush descended on the room.

'Now, before you all start to panic at the thought of a speech, I want to reassure you I'll be keeping it brief. As you know, in less than forty-eight hours this beautiful woman to my left is going to make an honest man of me,' Carlo reached out and held on to Lucy's hand.

'It's about time *someone* did!' Terence called out to a few laughs of agreement from the wedding party.

'As one of my oldest friends has pointed out, it has been a lengthy process to find the right one, but just like a pure diamond, perfection can take time. And it has been very much worth the wait.'

Alice let out an appreciative sigh as Lucy beamed up at Carlo.

'I know some of you have thought I've rushed into this but I can assure you, the moment I met Lucy Carvalho seven months and four days ago, I knew she was going to be the future Mrs Todero, so for me, our engagement has felt like an eternity.'

'How did the two of you meet?' Betty asked.

Carlo pulled Lucy to her feet. 'We met at an art auction, didn't we?'

'Yes,' continued Lucy. 'I don't really know much about art,' she demurred, 'but I'd pass the same auction house every day and there was this darling little watercolour that had caught my eye and so I thought I'd see if I could bid for it. The guide price was quite low, unlike some of the other pieces there.'

'The main lots were Italian Renaissance pieces, which is my favourite era, which is why I was there,' Carlo explained and Amelia could see Lorcan staring intently at the groom-to-be.

'Well, it soon became obvious, I was going to be outbid,' Lucy said. 'I got up to my limit, I was bidding against a man near the front and I couldn't compete any longer and then suddenly this voice from behind me joined in with a ridiculous amount for this tiny watercolour and the other man immediately backed down.' She looked at Carlo with tenderness. 'Anyway, I thought nothing more of it and I sat through to end of the auction, which was very exciting, although I had to sit on my hands in case someone thought I was bidding!' She gave a laugh.

'And then, as she got up to leave I signalled for one of the staff to bring her over the painting…'

'…Who told me it was mine and I obviously thought there was a mistake…'

'…And that was when I introduced myself and confessed all.' He raised her hand to his lips and lightly kissed her fingers. 'That I'd won the bid for you. It was the disappointed sigh I'd heard when you backed down from bidding. The sadness emanating from you broke my heart and I decided you needed to be the owner of that little watercolour of foxgloves.'

'And I offered to pay what my bid limit was…'

'And I said I wouldn't dream of taking your money,' Carlo said softly, looking at her adoringly.

'So, I offered to buy him a drink as a very small token of my appreciation.'

'And obviously I said yes as I'd already decided I was going to marry you. I knew I couldn't let this beautiful creature who had an artistic soul similar to mine disappear from my life.'

'Wow!' Vanessa said drily. 'That was some day's shopping trip. Art *and* a wife!'

'Stop putting a dampener on romance,' Carlo said good humouredly as he raised his glass. 'So, please join me in a toast…' He paused and blinked. 'Uh… sorry, um…' He looked around him in momentary confusion then rubbed his hand across his forehead. Lucy whispered something to him, her face etched with worry, as Carlo screwed up his eyes. He then nodded slightly and there were a few long seconds of silence before his usual easy smile was back. 'Apologies. I seemed to have been a little overcome with emotion there. And possibly a little too much wine.' Carlo gave a slight chuckle and everyone else laughed along.

But Amelia clocked the questioning glance Dan shared with Alice and that Vanessa leaned in to whisper something to Ricky who frowned and nodded.

'Anyway,' Carlo continued, 'a toast; to love, and romance. And foxgloves,' he said as he chinked his glass against Lucy's.

'I couldn't have said it better, myself,' Lucy said, smiling at Carlo.

Everyone else around the table raised their own glasses and took a drink, and normal chatter resumed. With everyone seemingly moved on from the strange little scene, Amelia brought out the desserts.

'Well, that was quite odd, wasn't it?' Gideon said, sidling up to her. 'Do you think Carlo's all right?'

'It did seem as if he'd suddenly forgotten where he was.'

'A little bit of early-onset dementia?'

'Well, it would explain him mislaying his car keys and

thinking they'd been stolen,' Amelia said in hushed tones. *And maybe he* had *been the one to turn up in Betty's room in the middle of the night if he'd been disorientated*, she thought, *but then either not remembered or was too embarrassed to admit to it.*

Amelia remembered an old neighbour of hers, Mr Duncan, who used to insist that people would break into his flat and hide his belongings. Mr Duncan had also tried to get into Amelia's flat a couple of times, using his key, convinced that she was squatting in his home and had changed the locks. He'd caused his son and daughter no end of worry and after a couple of incidents where he'd been found wandering some miles from home with no idea where he was, it had been decided he was better off in a home with round-the-clock care.

Amelia watched Carlo, who was once again acting as the life and soul of the party and felt a wave of sorrow. He seemed so full of life and vitality; it would be so sad if he was struggling with dementia.

'Judging by the knowing glances from the other's reactions, I'd wager that kind of episode had happened before,' Gideon said as he polished a champagne cooler with a napkin then studied his reflection in it.

Craig arrived with fresh bottles of wine, giving the red to Amelia, as he went round the room with the bottle of white.

Amelia shot Gideon a warning glance to lower his voice but no one seemed to have heard as Vanessa was calling out Betty's name across the table. 'Betty!' Vanessa boomed. 'I bet you were a good-time girl in your youth! I overheard you say you used to live in London in the seventies and eighties.'

'Yes, I did!' The older lady said, smiling in nostalgia as Amelia headed over to go round the table to fill up their glasses. 'I was an artist's muse you know. I ran with such a bohemian crowd back then.'

'What does an artist's muse do?' India asked.

'We inspire,' Betty said with a dramatic sweep of her arm, as Amelia deftly moved her full glass of wine out of reach.

Nisha smiled. 'I don't think you get jobs like that anymore, unfortunately.'

'Oh, I saw it as more of a vocation,' Betty said with a wink as she took a hearty swallow of wine.

Vanessa sat back in her chair. 'I can imagine it being quite the time of hedonism then; there was so much money in the city in the eighties. Endless parties full of booze and drugs! *Obviously* the eighties were a little before my time.'

'Not by much,' Amelia heard Nisha say not too quietly and Alice had to quickly turn a laugh into a cough.

'I was there in the early noughties,' Vanessa said. 'And oh my, they really were naughty! Coming to London's West End and knowing no one was fairly daunting as you can all imagine and I realised very early on I had to be sociable if I wanted to make any friends in the city.'

'Just how sociable are we talking?' Carlo asked in amusement.

'Well, I befriended my own group of artistes, you know; actors, poets, dancers, painters. In fact, there was even a little scandal involving one of my amours at the time. He was an artist, into quite awful abstract things as I recall. Well, one of his friends whom he shared a house with was embroiled in some very illegal pastimes!' She paused as she looked around the table making sure she had everyone's attention. 'Only international art theft!'

Amelia, who was now nearer Vanessa's end of the table looked up and it was clear Vanessa had everyone's attention, even Craig had stopped pouring and was watching her.

'You may remember the story in the press. He was known as the Romeo Robber!' Vanessa's voice register had lowered as she really embraced taking on the storyteller's role. 'Now, what was his name? We were never properly introduced but I passed him on the stairs once…Oh well, I'm sure his name will come to me eventually. Anyway, the Romeo Robber – as the press called him

– would ingratiate himself with lonely and very rich wives and start clandestine affairs.'

Terence snorted into his glass of wine. 'We've all met cads like that!' he said, then took a large swig.

Vanessa cleared her throat and continued, 'After inveigling himself into his victim's life he would quickly become acquainted with all the artwork around the home. He would get to know the alarm codes and was quite often given a spare key to enable the nocturnal visits. And of course, he would learn the rhythm of the household; when staff came and went, when the house was busy and quiet, when the husband and wife were away for a weekend or a holiday. Then he would break in and steal whatever took his fancy!'

There were a couple of exclamations around the table.

'The couple or housekeeper or whoever, would return and notice the theft,' Vanessa said. 'Under police questioning no one would have a clue how it could have happened and of course the wife wouldn't be able to say anything as she would be in danger of losing everything if the scandal of the affair was to become known. The Romeo Robber was very careful in choosing his victims for that very reason.'

Vanessa sat back in her chair, letting everyone take on board her story. 'He got away with it for a long time until he came up against a husband who suspected his wife was having an affair and had hired a private detective to follow her.'

'Ah, yes!' Betty interjected. 'Sometimes a good old gumshoe gets far better results than the police.'

'The usual scenario happened,' Vanessa carried on, looking around the table as she spoke, 'he and his wife went away, there was a robbery – but this time the cuckolded husband had a suspect. The wife called her lover and warned him the police were on their way, which gave him just enough time to run. The police only managed to recover a couple of the stolen pieces and no one knows where the rest of them ended up. The only other paintings they found were his own rather uninspiring pieces he'd painted. Some of them were really rather odd, not to my taste at all. It must have been quite galling for the man, being a rather talentless artist surrounded by the stolen masterpieces.'

Carlo nodded solemnly in agreement. 'Maybe it was jealousy which led him into his life of crime to steal them,' he said.

'What happened?' Betty asked.

Vanessa shrugged. 'The police could link him to many crimes but it seemed he just disappeared. It turned out his name and persona were completely fictitious and the police had no lead on him. It felt like the entire force was camped out on my lover's doorstep for days! And the press! And various other interested parties. The events drew quite an international crowd as I recall, with people from America, Japan, France, even Germany trying to get interviews. Of course I happily chatted to them all. I remember it all so clearly! I probably still have some of their business cards.'

'You must have a great memory!' Lucy said in admiration.

'Oh, I certainly do. I never forgot any of my lines. Or a face! You know, I've often wondered where that art thief ended up. My lover was taken in and questioned but of course he knew nothing and hadn't been involved, just shared the house with the art fraudster. I bet he wished he had been involved though considering the huge amounts of money involved! Would you ever be tempted to do that, Lorcan?'

Lorcan, who'd just taken a drink, gave a spluttering cough and turned quite red. 'Eh, excuse me, what now…?'

'To steal art?' Vanessa said with a slight smile. 'I'm sure someone as connected as you would know what to steal and where to pass it on to.'

Lorcan cleared his throat. 'Well, you may be surprised to hear this, but no, I wouldn't have the first clue. I just like to focus on *creating* pieces of art. I don't think my Catholic guilt would allow me to do anything so criminally minded.'

'Really? Now that *is* an interesting take. Catholic guilt! Yes, you Catholics do seem to have the monopoly on that. No sex before marriage, but if you do and you have a little accident, definitely don't make it worse by having an abortion! You know, I'm sure there's a little part in all of us that could easily turn to the dark side of the law if pushed. Even upstanding pillars of the community like Dan here! I bet he has something illegal or dodgy he's done in his career he'd rather remained hidden despite coming across as a dull shit most of the time.'

Dan's jaw almost hit the floor as Alice looked at Vanessa with unconcealed rage.

Carlo stared levelly at Vanessa, the little muscle in his jaw clenching and unclenching rhythmically as he tapped the base of his wine glass with his middle finger until he said in a jovial tone, 'Do you really think this is the time and place for one of your little games?'

'Grr!' Vanessa growled playfully. 'How noble coming to dear Dan's rescue. Or maybe I got a little close to home, there, Carlo! You yourself are such a man of mystery! Have you really achieved all you've achieved in life by being completely law abiding?' Vanessa continued, turning to look down the table to where he sat. 'I just think there's sometimes a fine line and an even finer reason to turn to criminal ways. We'd all like to think we wouldn't, but... How much would it take to give just that little push–'

'Lay off Carlo, Vanessa. We're here as his guests,' Ricky said quietly.

'Oh, I might have known you'd stick up for him!' Vanessa turned to Ricky, her eyes flashing. 'We all know how much you idolise him, darling. It's so pathetic. Would you rather I start on you? Or maybe your wife? I'm sure even the angelic Evangelina can't have led as blameless a life as she's letting on. She must at least have some sordid little secrets hiding away.'

Amelia saw that Evangelina's hands were shaking slightly, despite her unruffled demeanour.

Nisha cleared her throat and said, 'Maybe you're tarring everyone with your own moral brush, Vanessa, but I'd wager most of us round this table lead quiet, law-abiding, even rather humdrum lives.'

'Well, you're very trusting, aren't you!' Vanessa mocked patronisingly. 'I wouldn't be surprised if someone round this table had done something *very* wicked, indeed. I know we've got at least two blackmailers!' Her voice had risen sharply as she dropped this bombshell. A hush descended on the table as she delivered her killer line. 'And possibly even a *murderer!*'

The silence was shattered unnervingly by Terence who accidentally knocked over his glass.

Vanessa sat back in her chair, a smug little smile on her face, clearly relishing the disquiet she'd caused as Craig hurried over to mop up the wine spillage as Terence offered effusive apologies.

'A murderer!' India said as she momentarily looked up from her phone.

'I would say there's quite a big chance of that around a table like this,' Vanessa said.

DeShawn took that moment to stand up, so forcefully, it knocked his chair over. 'You are some piece of work,' he said, his voice shaking with anger. 'You,' he stabbed a finger in Vanessa's direction, 'going on about *other* people being easily led into being corrupt.' He gave a sharp bark of laughter. 'Look in the mirror! You are a poisonous, bitter woman, hell-bent on ruining people's lives. God knows what has happened in your life to make you like this. These people are meant to be your friends? I wouldn't be surprised if one of these *friends* stabbed you in the back one day the way you have done to so many. *Then* you'll know how all your victims feel.' Throwing his balled-up napkin onto his plate he strode out the room.

Alaiya hurried after him, but paused at Carlo and Lucy. 'I'm so sorry. You make a lovely couple,' she said.

'Thank you,' Carlo said, standing up as Alaiya ran out of the room.

'Well, that was a review!' Vanessa said with a laugh once Alaiya had gone. 'Some people just can't deal with being dumped by their agent.'

'Oh, shut up, Vanny, and down another Campari,' Carlo said, contemptuously.

Vanessa didn't appear bothered by the strong reaction from DeShawn and Carlo. She simply threw her head back and laughed.

'Oh, honestly! When will you guys lighten up!' she said when she'd stopped laughing. 'You know how much I love my little dramatic games. Will you ever learn?' She blew a kiss over to Dan who didn't look in the least bit mollified by her words, which didn't come anywhere close to an apology in Amelia's opinion.

Craig took this opportunity to make an announcement, 'Would everyone like to head through to the bar for an after-dinner drink?' His words broke the heavy atmosphere but there was an air of slightly forced jollity as people pushed their chairs back and headed away from the dining room.

Evangelina hung back to speak to Amelia. 'It was a lovely meal, please pass on my compliments to your brother.'

'And from me,' Nisha said, patting her stomach contentedly.

'Thank you, I will,' Amelia said, delighted on Toby's behalf.

'I'm heading up to bed, I just can't seem to shake this cold,' Evangelina said.

'Can I get you anything?' Amelia asked as Nisha gave her friend a disappointed look.

Evangelina smiled but shook her head. 'I've still got some of the cold remedy Ricky got me, thank you.'

'I, however, will be staying up until the small hours of the morning,' Nisha said. 'I've got a very wealthy landowning viscount to flirt with.'

'Neeeesh!' Evangelina said, warningly.

But Nisha simply smiled. 'Let me have my fun. I genuinely like Terence. He loves horses as much as I do. And anyway, that old bitch doesn't deserve him.' The ladies all said their goodnights and left the dining room.

Amelia watched them go, unable to shake the feeling of unease that had settled over her like a veil.

CHAPTER 28

A while later Amelia sank into one of the chairs in the kitchen yawning widely. 'That's the dining room cleared and set up for breakfast.'

'The snow's getting heavy again,' Jack said coming in from the outside recycling bins.

'Don't worry,' Toby said untying his durag and opening the top couple of buttons of his whites, 'we won't run out of supplies even if we get snowed in for a fortnight!'

The kitchen lights flickered slightly as Gideon came in.

'I'm afraid I've left Craig to deal with the masses while I get more oranges and limes. They've gone feral in there. I fear we're only another Campari and dry martini away from Vanessa doing a musical medley on the grand piano and Betty doing a burlesque number alongside and I don't know which one scares me more.'

Amelia stood back up as Toby lobbed citrus fruit at Gideon, which he caught expertly then did a very impressive impromptu juggling act with.

'I'm just going to double check the leisure area is locked up. I don't want anyone deciding a late-night sauna is a good idea,'

Amelia said to Gideon as they headed out through the kitchen door.

'They seem to have recovered from Vanessa's strange party game,' Amelia remarked as they heard gales of laughter and animated chatter coming from the bar.

'Yes, and I've been itching to talk to you since I asked Vanessa about being the Secret Guest,' Gideon said as they walked down the corridor, past the library, towards the small gym.

'Did you ask her outright!' Amelia asked as she tried the handle and ascertained it was locked.

'Darling, subterfuge is my middle name!' Gideon said, offended. 'I bent down and said she clearly had wonderful taste in hotels, almost as good as her taste in men, I thought I'd butter her up a bit. I then asked if she'd ever been to the Triple Creek Ranch in Montana. To be honest, her reaction was a little full-on!'

'I saw her grab your shirt!'

'I know! She whispered something like "How did you find out?" and I said that you and I had been discussing it together and it made perfect sense. She gave me such a strange look and I swear her eyebrows would have jumped up into her hairline were it not for all her facial features being frozen with Botox. She asked me how I'd found out and I said you and I were excellent at deduction and it was our job to find these kinds of things out especially if it was about a Secret Guest. She asked me if I'd told anyone else and I said of course not, because we were also very good at discretion. And I gave her one of my good winks. You know the one I used in the espionage thriller? That one.' He did his wink for Amelia's benefit. She had to agree, it was very effective.

'She didn't deny it?'

'Not at all.'

Well, it certainly did fit. Vanessa had a jet-setting lifestyle and was continually name dropping. She'd be in the perfect position to visit hotels and write reviews on them. She and Gideon meandered their way back to the reception and Gideon gave her a slight nudge.

'Speak of the devil!' he said under his breath and nodded over to where Vanessa stood watching them.

She looked furious and Amelia wondered if they were the first to uncover her identity as the Secret Guest. Amelia was just weighing up if she should say something when the American agent made a beeline for them.

'So, you like finding out your guest's secrets, do you!' she said. 'How did you work it out?' she hissed.

'Well, you were at the Danieli–' Amelia began, but Vanessa interjected.

'Were you there?'

'Um… yes,' Amelia answered not really sure how her afternoon cocktails with Jack were that relevant.

'And in Montana?' Vanessa fired back.

'No, I've never–'

'So how did you know?'

'Um, lucky guess?' Amelia hazarded.

'What are you wanting?'

Amelia looked blankly at her.

'Don't play dumb with me. What do you want to keep this hushed up?'

'We don't want anything,' Amelia said in puzzlement.

'Yes, we just want to make sure you have a lovely time with us,' Gideon agreed, as he bounced the orange he carried off his forearm and caught it.

Vanessa's lip curled. 'Don't try and take me on at a game I'm a master of! I know your kind. You pretend to be so understanding and nice, that butter wouldn't melt, but I can see through all that.' She took a step back and looked at them smugly. 'Just remember, I know a few secrets of my own and I know what *you're* hiding.' And with that she turned on her heel and headed back into the bar as the lights gave another little flicker.

Amelia turned to Gideon, puzzled by Vanessa's rather cryptic departing words. 'She knows what we're hiding? Oh bugger!' she said as realisation dawned. 'Do you think she's found out about the mouse?'

'Oh God, darling, she may well have! And I'm sorry, but I may have accidentally let Jingles follow me into the kitchen a couple of times, which I know is *probably* against health and safety. But nobody saw him and I carried him straight back out again, hidden up my jumper.'

Amelia rolled her eyes. 'Gideon! I just hope she doesn't give us a bad review. Or worse, gets us shut down!'

'Oh, please don't worry. We'll butter her up tomorrow and give her a Christmas Day she'll never forget!' Gideon said as he took his citrus fruit into the bar to adorn more cocktails.

With Vanessa's words still playing round in her head, Amelia went through the storage rooms to check on the mouse traps. They were all empty and Amelia wasn't sure if she should see it as a positive or negative.

'Or have you been doing your job and catching mice?' she asked Jingles who was prowling around the reception desk. She bent down and scratched him behind his ear to his obvious enjoyment. He gave a meow and looked at her hopefully.

'No more food for you tonight!' She'd put food out for him already, before realising Gideon, Toby and James had also fed him. Jingles gave a mournful meow in reply but walked off towards the drawing room, with a swish of his fluffy tail.

The bar was positively jumping and Amelia hurried through in case Craig needed a hand just as the lights gave another flicker and then went out completely.

CHAPTER 29

There were a few gasps and a couple of little cries of surprise as well as a rather dramatic shriek from Gideon. Amelia waited for a couple of moments before realising the lights weren't flickering back on again.

'Darling, unless you've not been paying your electricity bills I do believe we've got a power cut,' Gideon said as he hesitantly walked over, guided only by the faint glow given off by the little tea lights nestled in the glass holders on each table.

'Don't worry, there are plenty more candles,' Craig announced.

Picking up on the current vibe, Amelia realised no one seemed put out, in fact there was definitely a slight frisson of excitement from the half-drunk guests.

Jack and Toby appeared a couple of minutes later with more candles.

'They still all seem in high spirits,' Jack remarked. Amelia agreed, it actually looked quite magical in the bar as the battery-operated fairy lights which were strung up still twinkled invitingly along with the extra candles Craig was lighting, helped by Lorcan and Lucy.

'Oh God, here we go!' Gideon said under his breath as Vanessa went over to the piano and warmed up with a few arpeggios.

Just then James came up to them, his phone in his hand. 'The whole village is down. Must be heavy snow on a pylon. Don't worry, my dad's on the council and he said someone will be out to fix it asap.'

'On Christmas Eve?' Amelia asked dubiously.

'Oy aye, they'll be on double, triple, quadruple pay and then some, for something like this!'

'I'll need to make sure we keep the fires going as the temperature will drop quite quickly if the electricity keeps the boiler off.'

'I'll get the extra blankets out for the bedrooms,' Jack said as he headed to the laundry store.

'The fridges have an inbuilt reserve of power so don't worry about that,' Toby said.

Amelia checked that Craig had everything under control then went to retrieve the heavy duty, high-beam torch she'd bought a while ago in case of this very eventuality. She headed out to the reception area just as Alaiya and DeShawn were coming out of the drawing room. They said goodnight and headed up the stairs to their room.

Taking some of the candles with her, Amelia followed them up the stairs to check on Mr Griffin who still had his Do Not Disturb sign on the door of the Simenon Room. She knocked loudly and called his name. There was no answer.

She tried again but heard nothing.

Looking behind her to make sure no one could see her, she slipped into the Simenon Room. Flicking on the flashlight she swept it around the room.

The bright light of the beam revealed numerous champagne bottles scattered around the floor. Amelia knew there had been no calls made from the Simenon Room requesting refreshments. There were also glasses, which looked very like they'd come from the bar. Around one glass was a smear of vermilion lipstick.

There were some gent's toiletries in the en suite along with some more feminine ones. The bed was unmade and there were some random items of clothes discarded on the floor. On the bedside table there were some little deposits of white powder.

One thing was very apparent: there was definitely no sign of Mr Griffin.

Stepping over the clothes, heart beating quickly with an ear cocked to listen for anyone coming, Amelia moved to the fireplace, running her fingers along the underside of the mantelpiece, knowing exactly where to press to release the secret passage door. Just inside, she saw what she was looking for. Closing the door behind her, she made her way down the secret steps that led to the cellar to confirm what else she thought she'd find.

Five minutes later, checking the coast was clear, Amelia let herself out of the Simenon Room and walked along to the room to the right; Kit's room. She knocked, hoping Sally's cousin would open the door. But again, there was no answer.

Amelia had contemplated calling Sally a few times to ask where her cousin was but she didn't want to worry her best friend needlessly. And Kit had been adamant that Amelia shouldn't say anything to Sally. She left a couple of the candles outside the Cleeves Room then turned and headed back downstairs.

There was now a crowd round the piano as Vanessa played 'Have Yourself a Merry Little Christmas' to a rapt audience, as the tea lights flickered cosily all around. It really was quite a beautiful and Christmassy scene.

Over at the bar Amelia could make out Craig talking to someone sitting on a barstool in front of one of the pillars. It looked like a very intense conversation and Craig was wide eyed with a slightly panicked expression.

Only when she got closer did Amelia realise it was Lucy on the barstool. Craig looked up to see Amelia, and Amelia could have sworn he looked relieved at her interrupting them.

'Hi, Lucy. I'm so sorry about the electricity going off. I want to reassure you that everything is being done to get it back on. It's throughout the village. We will strive to make sure your wedding won't be affected in any adverse way.' Amelia looked at Craig for some backup but he still looked a little shell-shocked.

'Is everything okay?' Amelia asked.

Lucy, who was turned slightly away from Amelia, plucked a cocktail napkin up off the bar and dabbed it to her face with a loud sniff before swivelling back round to look at Amelia.

'I'm so sorry, I seem to find myself pouring out my troubles to your lovely barman.'

Craig gave an awkward shrug.

'Is everything okay?' Amelia asked feeling a cold pit of dread in her stomach, wondering if the power cut had been one step too far and had caused the bride-to-be to spiral.

'I just heard that our wedding photographer might not be able to make it if the roads aren't cleared in time.'

'Oh, um, well, I'm sure we could get someone local,' Amelia said. She glanced up to see if she could see Lorcan, wondering if he'd be keen to take on a last-minute commission if needed.

'And it's not just that... I'm just so worried about my Carly,' Lucy said, and then sobbed into her napkin.

'Carlo? Has something happened?'

'You saw him at dinner, when he was making a speech? This keeps happening. He seems to... to... drift. It's like he leaves the room for a moment. He's been getting more forgetful too, like with the wallet and keys. He misplaces things all the time. And sometimes he forgets where he's been, or where he's going. Sometimes I can't find him.' She gave a very big sigh. 'We've only been together a short while so I don't know how long he's been like this. He's such a proud man he'd never admit to having any

225

weakness but... I can't help but worry about the future. *Our* future... together.'

Amelia quickly ran through all the arrangements for the wedding and what could easily be cancelled. 'Are you possibly having reservations going ahead with the wedding?' she asked as delicately as she could.

Lucy turned to her; eyes huge with fear. 'NO!' she gripped Amelia's arm. '*Nothing* could stop me going ahead with the wedding! But it doesn't stop me being fearful for the future. Especially as he's in an unfamiliar place, and the weather is so bad, and now we have the power cut. I'm just worried for him; in case I can't keep him safe. And after the things Vanessa said at dinner... and the way she was speaking, I can't help but feel worried...'

'Worried?'

'In case it made Carly angry and he...' She shook her head. 'I'm sorry, I don't even know what *I'm* saying any more. And this has all come out because I've had a glass of wine too many and your poor barman has borne the brunt of my ramblings. Oh, and now I need to go and repair my mascara. I must look a fright,' Lucy said and slid elegantly off the barstool.

Lucy looked as perfectly presentable as always, Amelia thought as she watched the other woman walk away. She turned to Craig who was also watching Lucy, a troubled expression on his face.

'It seems you're a good listener,' Amelia said as he cleaned the bar.

'It often goes with the territory.'

'Why don't you head home; we've got this covered here.'

Craig hesitated. 'I don't mind staying. To be honest, I'll be on my own in the van and it's nicer here. Oh, and it seems I've got another customer.'

Betty sashayed up to the bar, empty martini glass held loosely between her fingers. 'I think I'll have another one of these for the road!' she said, swallowing down a hiccup.

Behind her, Amelia could see Jack was still busy lighting more candles and had managed to unearth an antique upright candelabra. The visibility was definitely improving, although the risk of a fire hazard was also increasing Amelia thought, worriedly.

The fires!

Amelia had become so engrossed on a little bit of sleuthing in the Simenon Room she'd completely forgotten to check the fires were still going strong. She chided herself for her lack of focus as she hurried into the drawing room.

She'd got there just in time as the fire was down to its embers.

Amelia added a couple more logs and gave the hearth a quick sweep, removing the items which had been thrown on but hadn't fully burnt. Joined by Jingles on the rug who quietly surveyed her as she worked, Amelia swept out the ash along with numerous scrunched up tissues, a discarded Winter Festival leaflet, empty crisp packet and half a charred, handwritten letter. Brushing them up into the little brass dustpan, Amelia paused as a word on the letter caught her eye as the fire took and blazed brightly once again.

The brush clattered to the hearth, causing Jingles to scarper. Amelia carefully lifted the remains of the letter, gently easing it open. She switched her torch back on so she could read it properly. Most of the letter was completely burnt away but of the bit that was left, the word '… Murderer…' could clearly be made out.

'What do you think?' Gideon asked as he opened the door to his room and did a 360-degree twirl before striking a pose.

'What?' Amelia was thrown slightly, keen to share her find with Gideon.

'My new scarf! Feel how soft it is!'

Amelia made the right appreciative noises as ochre and teal striped cashmere was rubbed against her cheek.

'Toby and I agreed to do one present each before midnight because he needs to be up early and then we plan on sneaking away throughout the...' He stopped talking, suddenly aware of Amelia's slightly out of breath and flushed appearance. 'What's happened?'

Amelia took this as her cue to step further into Gideon's room, closing the door behind her. 'I just found this in the drawing room,' Amelia held out the half-charred letter and the torch.

Gideon took them from her and scanned the contents. Although a large proportion of the note had been burned clean away there was still a fragment of the letter left.

.........o you are! My silence can be bought. I recognised your .... ler! Meet me in ....
......or......ll everyone you are a murderer.

'But where's the rest of it!' Gideon said, turning the charred remains in his hands.

'That's all that was salvaged from the fire. Whoever the recipient was had clearly tried to burn the note.'

'Luckily for us, not that well.'

'It's especially odd when you pair it with this letter I received.' Amelia pulled the other letter out of her pocket that had warned her about not trusting a guest.

Gideon read it and looked up at her in shock.

'And that's not all. When I was in the café yesterday, on my way to see Constable Williams, I–'

A loud knock on the door prevented Amelia from explaining Kit's link to Benedict Geissler.

Gideon opened the door of his room to reveal an agitated Lorcan standing there. 'I'm worried something's wrong,' the Irishman said.

'So are we!' Gideon said. 'Have you had a letter too?'

'A… what?' Lorcan looked from Gideon to Amelia in confusion.

'Ignore him, what's wrong?' Amelia asked, tucking both notes into the back pocket of her trousers.

'It's Evangelina. I'm worried something's wrong.'

'Why?'

'She arranged for us to meet, but she never showed up.'

'You'd arranged to meet?' Gideon said in incredulity. 'Right, call the rozzers, Ames,' he said, swishing one end of his new scarf over his shoulder as he took a step in between Lorcan and Amelia. He looked at Lorcan imperiously. 'And until they get here consider yourself under citizen's arrest. For murder!'

'For goodness' sake, Gideon, don't be ridiculous!' Amelia said, shoving Gideon out of her way so she could see Lorcan. 'What's wrong?'

'Wait...what? *Murder?*'

'But the note, Amelia!' Gideon hissed in her ear. 'Whoever wrote it wanted to meet a suspected murderer!'

'And you seriously think it's Lorcan?'

'Well...' Gideon puffed out his cheeks.

Lorcan continued to look at Amelia in consternation. He'd paled quite considerably at the mention of murder. 'I hope to God it's not murder, but I'm worried about Evangelina. Can you come and help? Do you have a pass key on you to get into her room to check?'

The three of them went along to Evangelina's room and Amelia knocked loudly on the door.

'If Evangelina arranged to meet Lorcan, she could have thought Lorcan was a murderer?' Gideon pointed out to Amelia as she knocked again.

'Just, hang on a minute!' Lorcan said, from Amelia's other side. 'Who am I meant to have murdered. And why!?'

'That's something the police can ask you!' Gideon said.

'Shhhhhh!' Amelia said as she got out the master key from her pocket. 'I don't think either of them had murder on their mind when they arranged to meet up. I saw Betty slip Lorcan a note in the bar and she was clearly doing it on behalf of Evangelina. It didn't look like a threatening one! I'm guessing you've probably still got the note,' Amelia added, turning to Lorcan.

'Uh, yeah, it's here,' Lorcan took it out of this jeans pocket and unfolded it to reveal some delicate handwriting, which was nothing like the bold slanted scrawl on the letter she'd found in the remains of the fire.

'She said she was going up to bed as her cold was making her feel worse.'

Lorcan nodded. 'That was a ruse so we could meet up and talk in peace.'

With a satisfying click, the door to the Chandler Suite unlocked and Amelia hurried in, closely followed by Lorcan and Gideon. The room was in darkness as there were no candles lit. A sweep of the torch revealed Evangelina lying on top of the bed. She was still fully clothed.

Gideon hurried over and prodded the sleeping woman.

'Careful,' Lorcan said. 'Evangelina?' he stroked the hair from her forehead.

Amelia closed the door.

'Evangelina, come on, darling, let's sit you up,' Gideon was saying, trying to rouse the woman.

'Something's wrong,' Lorcan said worriedly.

'I know, it's as if…' Gideon paused to let out a huge sneeze. 'Excuse me. Has she taken anything?' He paused and sneezed twice.

Amelia looked at the side table where there was a bottle of

cold and flu remedy. She read the back label where it stated it may cause drowsiness. It was certainly living up to its claim. But it was a regular, over-the-counter brand, and although almost half the bottle was gone, Amelia doubted that alone was causing Evangelina inability to rouse herself.

There was a groan from the bed as Evangelina finally stirred.

'Thank God!' Lorcan said with obvious relief as he sat on the edge of her bed and began rubbing her hands.

'It looks like she's ODed,' Gideon said to Amelia. He saw the cold remedy on the table and came over. 'That amount would not have caused that reaction!' There was an empty glass beside it. He sniffed it. 'Whisky.'

Amelia shone the torch into the bin and she picked out two whisky miniatures from the minibar. Even with the cold and flu remedy, Amelia doubted it would have caused such a severe reaction.

Evangelina was now sitting up, her legs over the side of the bed. Lorcan talked to her as he smoothed her hair behind her ears.

Amelia poured the remains of the cold remedy into the empty tumbler then held it up and shone the torch onto it. In amongst the pale green liquid, she could see little grainy particles floating around in it. Amelia carefully poured the liquid into the bottle and screwed the lid back on securely before slipping it into her pocket just as Gideon gave another huge sneeze.

Blowing his nose on a handkerchief he pulled out from his pocket, Gideon walked back over to Evangelina. 'Come on, poppet, let's get you a cold shower. And coffee. Strong and lots of it,' he added over his shoulder. 'Not those sachets beside the kettle, filter stuff from the kitchen. We can boil the water on the gas hob.'

'I'll get it,' Lorcan said as he hurried out the room as Amelia heard the shower turn on.

A few minutes later and Evangelina was wide awake and

gasping under the full cold blast of the shower. Shivering in her underwear, palms resting against the tiled wall, she endured the icy water as long as she could until she called out to stop.

'Oh, my God!' she said as soon as Amelia turned off the shower. 'That was horrendous!'

Amelia handed her a towel. 'We'll be out here, waiting, when you're ready.' She lit a couple of tea lights so as she wouldn't leave Evangelina in the dark.

Closing the en suite door behind her, she found Gideon and Lorcan sitting on the bed in silence. They too had lit a few of the candles and the room had a lovely romantic feel.

'She's okay; the water seemed to do the trick,' Amelia said.

'It's brutal, but it works,' Gideon said. He gestured to the table. 'There's the coffee. Evidently Ricky is well ensconced in the bar. He's been dragged into singing the harmonies on 'White Christmas' and it looks like he'll be there awhile. James said he'll give us the heads-up if he leaves.'

Lorcan was still sitting looking at the floor.

'Are you okay, Lorcan?' Amelia asked tentatively.

He looked up and nodded distractedly.

'Why would you th– A-CHOOOOOOO!' Gideon sneezed. 'Oh, I hope I'm not in for this blasted cold that's doing the rounds.'

Amelia went and opened up the window, letting a blast of fresh and freezing Highland air in along with a flurry of snow.

'That's really not going to help my immune system fight off a bug, Amelia!' Gideon pouted as he secured his new scarf more tightly around his neck.

Amelia went over to the bed and inspected the sheets and pillows. She wiped her fingers along the velvet headboard of the bed, just above where the pillows lay. She rubbed the tips of her fingers together and shone the torch on them, looking thoughtfully at the slight yellow residue.

She called Gideon over. 'You get hay fever, don't you?'

'I certainly do, I'm a slave to the summer syndrome.'

Just at that moment the en suite door opened and Evangelina stood in the doorway, a fluffy Stone Manor robe belted tightly around her slender waist.

'Oh, hot coffee!' she said appreciatively padding over to the table and pouring herself a cup. 'Anybody else want some?' she asked, waving the cafetière in the air.

There was a chorus of 'no thank yous'.

'Did you take a little bit more of the cold remedy tonight?' Amelia asked.

'Yes, I did. I was feeling so awful I took an extra dose when I came up after dinner.'

'And, do you suffer from hay fever?' Amelia asked.

Evangelina nodded. 'Horribly so.'

'Is it common knowledge?' Amelia asked.

'To anyone who clicks on my IMDB page or Wikipedia. I've even had to get an injection before. The pollution in London definitely makes it worse; it's one of the many reasons why I'd love to move up to the Highlands.'

'I um, I think maybe we've been using a new cleaning product, one of those natural ones, you know that's environmentally friendly and you may have taken a reaction. Would it be okay if we gave all your clothes a bit of an airing?'

'My clothes?'

'Yes, we always thoroughly clean the inside of the wardrobes too, some of the cleaning product may have inadvertently got onto your clothes.'

Evangelina would need clothes to wear until her own were dried as she couldn't very well float about in the Stone Manor robe for the foreseeable. Seeing as there were quite a few inches of height difference between her and Evangelina, all Amelia's clothes were out. Amelia also didn't want to alert any of the other guests that Evangelina would need extra clothes. She turned to look at Gideon and Lorcan, thought for a moment, then focused on Gideon. 'Have you got some comfortable loungewear Evangelina can borrow while her clothes get laundered? You're quite close in height, both slim. It'll be baggy but something that won't look out of place, that she'd possibly wear. If that's okay with you both?'

Evangelina nodded.

Gideon narrowed his eyes at Amelia for a moment before turning to scrutinise Evangelina. 'I've a pair of the softest slate grey Ralph Lauren track suit bottoms and a darling Bottega Veneta ribbed jumper, in turquoise; it'll really bring out your eyes.'

'Great! We'll get that organised. And then would it be okay if you stayed in another part of the hotel until we clean your room? The Sayers Room is free if you want to go there?'

Amelia and Gideon let themselves out of Evangelina's room just as James was walking past with some more candles.

'James, would you be able to stay a little later tonight and get Wee Davey in early. We need to do a deep clean of the Chandler Suite immediately, we can't wait for Bob and Reena to come in tomorrow. We'll need to wipe down the walls and the headboard too as well as the normal change of sheets. Oh, and best do the insides of the wardrobe too, please.'

'Yes, sure.'

Gideon blew his nose again. 'Right, now you can tell me what that was all about in there! New environmental cleaning products that induce hay fever?' He folded his arms and leant against the wall, waiting for an explanation.

'I think someone has been drugging Evangelina.'

'What?'

'There was some powdery substance mixed in with her cold remedy. Taken alongside the wine she'd had with dinner and then the whiskies from the minibar caused her to pass out.'

'Oh my God!'

'The fact both you and Evangelina were sneezing in that room made me think hay fever. You've been fine up until now and Evangelina seems okay when she's away from her room. I also found some pollen on the headboard.'

'But why would someone want to slip her a Micky Finn?'

'That, Gideon, is the sixty-four-million-dollar question!'

CHAPTER 31

L eaving Evangelina to get changed, Lorcan slowly made his way downstairs. The electricity was still off but there were so many candles lit that all the rooms gave off a welcome glow.

He had no desire to head into the melee of the bar area, especially when he heard Vanessa call out that there would be a five-minute intermission so everyone could get a refill before she started the next round of songs. He slipped into the drawing room and sat down in one of the wing-back chairs by the fire.

In a series of very strange days, today was possibly the strangest, he mused as he watched the flames dance in the grate. First there was the note from Evangelina, courtesy of Betty, asking for them to try and talk, yet again, but then the conversation at dinner had sent him into a real tailspin. Vanessa's comments seemed too specific to be a coincidence.

Did Vanessa know what he'd done? And if so, *how*?

Lorcan was getting a bad feeling that he'd *still* not had any word from his contact. He'd phoned numerous times but his calls always went to voicemail. And he really didn't know what else to do!

A soft footstep in the doorway brought him out his reverie

and he turned to see Evangelina in the doorway, looking unsure whether to come in or not.

'I saved you a seat,' Lorcan said, then gave a little chuckle as he indicated the chair on the other side of the fire in the completely empty room. He waited until she'd sat down to ask, 'How are you?'

'I'm okay. Still needing to warm up after that brutally cold shower. Apart from that, I'm fine.'

The fire gave a loud pop and Evangelina turned to look at it, the flickering colours lighting up her face in an array of yellow, golds and orange.

'Is this when we finally get a chance to talk?' Lorcan asked softly.

Evangelina wiped under her eye and he could have sworn it was to get rid of a tear.

'I'm so sorry for running out on you the other morning, but when you asked me all those questions about what we'd missed in each other's lives and you mentioned children, I–'

'Oh goody! I'd hate to think I'd miss the great revelations of Evangelina Wilde!'

Vanessa strutted slightly unsteadily into the drawing room and stood between Lorcan and Evangelina, with her back to the fire. 'I did wonder if you'd tell him. Oh Ricky! Ricky! Come into the drawing room, there's something you'll want to hear.'

Ricky followed a moment later, looking at Lorcan in surprise. Evangelina looked round at Vanessa with unconcealed hatred.

'What's all this?' Ricky asked gruffly.

'Oh, didn't you realise, honey? They go *way* back. They have quite the history together.'

'We knew each other many years ago, when we were barely out our teens,' Lorcan said for clarification.

'I have a feeling Lorcan doesn't know all the facts of your past,' Vanessa said with a poisonous smile.

Lorcan turned to look at Evangelina who'd started to breathe more rapidly.

'You see, I like to make sure I know all about everyone's past. Call it insurance,' Vanessa gave an expressive shrug. 'It's been amazingly useful to me in the past, you know.'

'Blackmail,' Evangelina said in disgust.

'It's not always been about the money, though, darling. Knowledge is power. I'm not alone in realising that, am I, Amelia?' Vanessa said with a condescending smile.

Lorcan whipped round in his chair to see Amelia, Gideon and Nisha standing in the doorway, all watching Vanessa's little show. He'd definitely picked the wrong room for a quiet tête-à-tête with Evangelina.

'I have no idea how you worked out about me at the Danieli, and Montana,' said Vanessa. 'No doubt you know about my little bolt-hole in Soho too. I guess we all have our ways and means.'

Lorcan looked back at Amelia but she and Gideon were exchanging looks of confusion.

'You see, I'm always amazed at what golden nuggets of information can come up with just the tiniest little amount of digging,' Vanessa carried on coolly. 'GP appointments, trips to abortion clinics, you name it, someone is sure to find out about it!'

Lorcan looked at Evangelina but she was staring up at Vanessa, shaking her head, tears glistening in the light of the fire.

'You are a vile and monstrous bitch!' Nisha said hotly, taking a couple of steps into the room.

'And you are a pathetic excuse for an agent,' Vanessa spat back. 'You have no fight and no killer instinct. It's no wonder so many of your clients jumped ship to me.'

Lorcan sat forward in his chair, willing Evangelina to look at him, which she eventually did. 'Evie, what's going on?'

Evangelina wiped away her tears and took a seep shaky breath. 'I hadn't planned on telling you this in front of an audience but seeing you again, after all this time, all these memories... I needed to tell you. And after the not-so-subtle hints from Vanessa I wasn't sure how long it would stay private and I wanted you to hear it from me, not something cobbled together from a sordid imagination. It's why I arranged to meet you tonight...' Evangelina had started talking in a rush but now seemed to have dried up.

She looked towards Nisha who gave a nod of encouragement. 'It was just after we'd split up,' Evangelina carried on, 'days really. I found out I was pregnant. I didn't know what to do. I was so confused and I know you didn't want to be with me and–'

'What?' Lorcan exclaimed. He didn't understand. Evangelina had been pregnant? So many thoughts filled his head at once, then for her to think he didn't want *her*...

'I needed to work out what to do. I made an appointment at an abortion clinic and an adoption agency, but I couldn't go through with either. I realised, despite how utterly foolish and difficult it would be to be a single parent, I wanted to keep the baby. I was going to let you know. I thought it only fair you knew you'd have a baby out there in the world. I didn't expect anything from you, I just thought it was the right thing to do. I kept chickening out of telling you and then, before I could let you know, I miscarried.' She gave a little shrug. 'It's very common in the first trimester of pregnancy. So, I didn't need to tell you or see though an appointment with any agency or clinic. I just got on with my grief. With Nisha's help.'

'But why didn't you tell me?' Lorcan said, trying very hard to let the words sink in. 'Either of you,' he looked from Evangelina to Nisha.

'I–' Nisha started to explain but Evangelina interrupted.

'Nisha wanted to but I told her I'd never speak to her again if she let you know. I'm sorry. I honestly thought I was doing the right thing. For both of us.'

'But you went through all that on your own?' Lorcan said.

'I had to.'

'No, you didn't,' Lorcan said in anguish.

Evangelina got up from her chair and hurried from the room. Vanessa sashayed away; her evil work done. Ricky stood looking unsure what to say or do. Nisha made to say something but Lorcan shook his head, running after Evangelina.

He found her in the library, in the beautiful bay window. She was standing shivering and crying as she looked out at the snow.

'Evie.' He came up behind her and wrapped his arms around her, wanting to keep her warm and safe and to never leave her side. She turned and hid her face in his jumper. Eventually the sobbing and shivering stopped.

'I'm so sorry you went through all of that. I wish I could have been there.' He had so many emotions flying around, vying with each other. Almost being a father, losing the baby…

'I didn't want you to think I was using it as a reason to get back together, that I was using it for pity,' she said, her voice muffled by wool. 'I knew that when you ended our relationship I–'

'Wait, wait a minute. You broke up with me.' He was so confused.

Evangelina took a step back and looked up at him. 'No, you broke up with me. The night we talked about our future, you thought it best we went our own separate ways to not hold each other back.'

'No! You thought that!'

Evangelina stared at him, her eyes flickering over his.

'Oh my God, we split up over a misunderstanding,' Lorcan said. His legs suddenly felt shaky.

'But how could we both have got it so wrong?'

'Because we're both colossal eejits!' Lorcan said in despair.

Evangelina looked up and he followed her gaze. They were standing under a piece of mistletoe. Lorcan had noticed it had been hung throughout Stone Manor, in strategic spots.

His breath caught in his throat as Evangelina stretched up a little and very gently brushed her lips against his. His arms automatically slid further round her as her hands moved up his back.

Then suddenly she broke away.

'I'm sorry, I can't… I need a little time. Is that okay?'

Breaking away, he watched her run out of the library.

Well, he'd waited fifteen years already; he'd be willing to wait fifteen more.

CHAPTER 32

'Well, that was all very dramatic!' Gideon said after everyone had left the drawing room. 'And what on earth was Vanessa talking about with her "bolt-hole" in Soho?'

'I don't know!' Amelia said, which made her wonder if they'd been talking at cross-purposes and Vanessa had nothing to do with the Secret Guest. So then what had she meant when she said she knew what Amelia was hiding, if it hadn't been the mouse incident...

They got to the reception area when they heard Vanessa calling everyone to give her requests.

Gideon rolled his eyes heavenwards then stopped as he looked up at the bedrooms. 'Did you see Mr Griffin at all?'

'No. There was no one there when I knocked earlier.'

'Oh, he really is the Invisible Man then!' he remarked. 'That book I took out the library when I was spying on Evangelina. It's *The Invisible Man* by H.G. Wells. The main character is called Griffin. Isn't that funny!'

Amelia looked up at the room. 'It is indeed,' she said quietly as Gideon headed into the bar.

Amelia looked along one room to Cleeves. Kit still hadn't

appeared back at the hotel and she was getting worried. Despite her promising Kit she wouldn't say anything to Sally, she couldn't resist texting her.

How are you? Is Kit with you?

Her phoned beeped a reply within a few seconds with a smiley face emoji and:

Kit messaged around lunchtime to say he's met someone and will be away for a bit – I'm taking it to mean he's shagging someone he met in the pub.

Sally then sent a laughing face emoji followed by aubergine and peach emojis.

Amelia couldn't help but smile. Here she was worrying about her best friend's cousin and he was probably having a great time with a hook-up. With his dark Ross Poldark-style good looks he'd definitely be a hit in the Whistling Haggis. She pocketed her phone and went back into the bar where Gideon was helping Craig. He slid a glass of whisky over to her just as Vanessa started back up playing the piano, clearly unperturbed by the events that had just unfolded in the drawing room.

'Double Macallan, no ice,' Ricky barked at Craig, who nodded and flashed him a courteous smile before turning to get the drink. Seeing the expression on the producer's face, Amelia thought better than to try and make any conversation with him.

Grabbing the drink from the bar top as soon as Craig placed it down in front of him, Ricky swallowed it down and asked for another before turning and glowering at the group round the piano where Vanessa was still holding court and was now belting out 'Jingle Bells' with the others joining in, enthusiastically, if not melodiously.

Terence broke free from the crowd and headed over to the

table next to the bar and began to look for something around the chairs and the floor. He then pulled up a bag, a black feather and diamanté drawstring purse style that Amelia recognised as belonging to Vanessa as he rummaged around inside it.

Terence looked up to see Amelia watching him. He held up a little pill bottle and rattled it. 'Angina pills. This amount of partying doesn't end well for her. Never learns though, the old girl. Still likes to think she's in the first flush of youth. Someone's got to look out for her though, don't they, Ricky old boy?' Terence said jovially, patting Ricky on the shoulder. 'And experience has shown it's usually me left to pick up the pieces.'

Ricky just stared at Terence as Craig put down his next double Macallan.

'Craig, would you do me a favour,' Terence said, turning his attention to the barman. 'Can you give Vanessa a glass of water when she gets her next Campari?'

'Of course,' Craig said.

'I know the signs when she's on a bender and I'd wager she's not going to slow down for quite some time. I'll just go pop these beside her in easy reach,' Terence said dropping the pills back in the bag and pulling it closed.

'I daren't suggest she takes one; she'd just laugh and ignore me. That's the trouble when you're that familiar with someone. It's like your favourite pair of battered old slippers. You'd never dream of taking them out on the town but they're what you need when you get home. Fancy high heels are all well and good but can cause all sorts of pain and bunions, whereas the slippers never hurt.'

Terence gave Amelia a wink and headed back over to the piano, dropping the bag down beside his wife and Amelia had the distinct impression all the talk of footwear hadn't been for her benefit. Nor had it really been about footwear.

Jack who had just returned to the bar with yet another lit candelabra, caught Amelia's eye and did a thumbs-up gesture before taking a step back to admire his handiwork. He almost backed into Lucy who was returning to the bar.

Just at that moment there was a smash from beside Amelia; she turned to see Craig backing away from a broken bottle of Campari, the orange bitters covering the floor of the bar.

'I'm so sorry!' Craig said, 'I thought I'd have it to hand after Mr Maxwell said his wife would no doubt be having more and in the gloom of the candlelight I missed the bar and it hit the floor.'

'Don't worry, just be careful you don't cut yourself. I'll grab the cleaning stuff.' Amelia turned to see Lucy watching them, wide-eyed.

Craig caught the look. 'It slipped,' he explained.

Lucy looked at Craig intensely for a second. 'Uh-oh! I don't fancy being the one to tell Vanessa she's been cut off from her favourite drink. She's lovely but she can sometimes get a little mean when she's not happy.'

Amelia thought Lucy's insight was clearly an understatement but as it turned out Vanessa didn't care a jot that she couldn't access her favourite drink; she was having too much of a good time to give it any thought and simply swapped her tipple to champagne and carried on with her Vaudeville-inspired entertainment.

She was the last woman standing: everyone had left the bar. Amelia wondered if she'd have to physically remove her from the piano stool to be able to get to bed. Finally, at just before 2am, Vanessa did one last rendition of 'Silent Night' before standing up and closing the piano lid. She looked around, slightly surprised at seeing it was just Craig, Gideon, Wee Davey and Amelia left.

'Where's everyone gone?'

'They've all retired to their rooms. Terence was the last to go up, about twenty minutes ago,' Amelia said, hoping Vanessa would take the hint and go and join him.

Vanessa checked her watch by the light of the candle. 'Ah,

almost time! Goodnight, everyone!' and with an expressive sweep of her arm, bid everyone a goodnight and sashayed out of the bar.

'Almost time!' Gideon yawned. 'What's she on about? It became Christmas Day almost two hours ago.'

'Probably too drunk to see her watch properly,' Wee Davey said. 'That's the Chandler Suite all cleaned down now. Evangelina's just popped in. I don't know where her husband is though.'

'Do you think he's shocked by the pregnancy information?' Gideon said.

'Who knows,' Amelia said with a shrug. 'Thank you, Davey. Right, come on, Craig, it's time we left. When are you due in tomorrow?' she asked the barman as they made their way through to the back of the hotel to get their coats.

'Ten,' Craig said, winding his scarf around his neck.

'Don't start until midday. We can manage here. You've stayed well over your clocking off time tonight.'

He shook his head, looking serious. 'It's fine, I really don't mind coming in earlier. I figure you need all the help you can get at the moment and I'm happy to work longer hours. I can keep an eye on things.'

'Thank you, but see how you feel in the morning.'

After Amelia checked Wee Davey had everything he needed for his night porter duties, including a couple of extra woollen layers and some torches, Amelia let herself and Craig out and they both gave an involuntary gasp when they saw how heavy the snow had become.

'It's going to be a busy couple of days, with Christmas and the wedding. Do you have an early start tomorrow?' Craig asked as they made their slow progress along the driveway.

'Yeah, although it's really Toby's show tomorrow. I'll be there to help with breakfast and I'm hoping to do the scavenger hunt.'

'Oh yeah, I heard Davey talking about it. It sounds good fun.'

Amelia was looking forward to it and hoped she'd be able to

get away from Stone Manor to meet at the Whistling Haggis for the 11am start time.

At the Gatehouse, Amelia said goodbye to Craig as he continued onwards, hands in pockets, a hunched figure walking slowly through the snow. Letting herself in Amelia was delighted to find the Gatehouse still toasty warm due to the thick walls retaining the heat of the log burner.

After changing into pyjamas and a quick brush of her teeth, Amelia got into bed.

'Merry Christmas,' she whispered as she snuggled up against Jack's warm body.

'Merry Christmas, beautiful,' Jack murmured back sleepily as he wrapped his arm around her, pulling her close.

CHAPTER 33

CHRISTMAS DAY

'That's a request for another four Mimosas!' Jack said as he hurried into the kitchen the next morning at breakfast.

'Either everyone is starting the day as they mean to go on or it's hair of the dog all round this morning,' Toby said as he grabbed another bottle of champagne from the wine fridge.

'I'd say a bit of both,' Amelia said, as she passed Jack, blowing him a kiss as she took the plate of smoked salmon bagels through to the dining room to add to the buffet table where Gideon was filling a tray with ingredients for guests to make their own Bloody Mary cocktails.

Despite a few sore heads, everyone seemed in good spirits. Amelia was over the moon that the electricity had been turned back on through the night and the boiler was belting out glorious heat once again.

'A Bloody Mary always helped me get going in my drinking days,' Gideon said as he popped some celery stalks into a highball tumbler.

'Are you okay being around so much alcohol?' Amelia asked Gideon in a low voice. She often worried about him when he was so close to temptation, especially when he helped out behind the bar.

Gideon smiled. 'Don't you worry about me. I find I'm lucky enough to be able to detach myself from this stuff,' he said, clanking a spoon against the bottle of Grey Goose vodka.

He looked behind him at the table where Nisha sat looking suspiciously at a slice of toast. 'And seeing those poor sods holding their heads in their hands while they wait for the room to stop spinning is enough to remind me how better I am never drinking.' He leant in closer to Amelia. 'Are you all set for later?' he asked quietly.

Yes, it's just the one sitting at five and...'

'No! I don't mean hotel stuff!' Gideon scoffed. 'The scavenger hunt!'

'I, um, yes?' Amelia said, wondering what, if anything, she needed to be 'set' for.

'I've already messaged Sally and she's raring to go. I'm assuming Captain America will be suitably focused too? Let's get to the rendezvous point fifteen minutes early.'

'Rendezvous point? You mean the Whistling Haggis?'

'Yes! We can formulate a game plan.'

'Okay,' Amelia said, wondering how on earth a scavenger hunt could warrant a game plan. She'd thought her and Jack joining up with Gideon and Sally to make a foursome would be good fun, she'd never thought it would bring out a competitive side to Gideon!

Just then Terence sidled up to peruse the Bloody Mary ingredients. 'Morning, Amelia, this is a good shout!' he said taking a couple of glasses and pouring in rather hefty amounts of vodka in each.

'Can I get you and Mrs Maxwell some tea or coffee?'

'Oh, this will do us just fine, my dear,' he said as he topped up the glass with tomato juice. 'Mrs Maxwell has yet to surface. She slept in the other room last night; I must have been snoring again,' he said as he shook liberal amounts of Tabasco sauce into the glass. He turned and looked over at Nisha sitting on her own, still staring listlessly at the toast. 'Although I'll maybe wait a little longer before disturbing Vanny. I could hear her using the big white telephone earlier on, if you catch my drift. It sounded grim. I can see someone else in need of one of these little pick-me-ups,' he said taking the drinks over and handing one to Nisha before pulling out a chair for himself at her table.

Betty came into view at that moment, her eyes lighting up at the sight of the Bloody Marys and Amelia left her to it as she went back into the kitchen.

Passing through the reception hall she saw Lorcan come in the front door, blowing into his ungloved hands.

'You're brave,' she called out.

He looked up, clearly startled to have his thoughts intruded on.

'You're brave; going out without gloves on!' Amelia clarified.

'Oh right!' He looked down at his hands as if he'd not even noticed. He stomped snow off his boots. After hours of more relentless snowfall during the night all the carefully dug out paths had filled right back up again. Even the bottom of his long woollen coat had a couple of inches of snow caked around its hem.

'Are you going to get some breakfast?'

'Um, sure, in a bit. Is everyone downstairs?'

'Mostly.' Amelia had no idea how to delicately put her next point so she just blurted out, 'Did you and Evangelina manage to talk last night?'

Lorcan shook his head. 'Sort of. I hope we'll speak later.'

'Are you okay?'

He puffed out his cheeks. 'I think so.'

'And are you okay still staying here?' He and Evangelina obviously had history and a lot to work through, but she didn't want his stay at Stone Manor to cause him distress.

As if picking up on her inner turmoil, Lorcan gave her a reassuring smile. 'I want to be here, Amelia. I think it's where I need to be at the moment.'

'You know I'm here if you want to talk.'

He gave her an appreciative grin, a little of the Lorcan-sparkle returning. 'Just as long as Gideon doesn't accuse me of trying to murder someone!'

'Ah, well, no guarantee of that but I think we've had enough drama for one Christmas, don't you?'

Lorcan nodded and started back up the stairs to his room just as Ricky hurried down. Amelia wished him a cheery 'Good Morning,' but Ricky just gave an inarticulate grunt and kept his head low.

He had a quick look in the drawing room then hurried through to the dining room. Amelia thought he seemed quite agitated but didn't think he'd welcome a polite enquiry into his well-being.

Amelia watched as Lorcan made his way slowly up the stairs. He looked so dejected and sad as he trudged along to his room. She would definitely try and have a chat with him later. 'Lorcan!' she called out just as he reached the top of the stairs. He looked at her over the banister. 'Fancy a dram with Jack and me at the Gatehouse after dinner?'

He smiled and nodded. 'That would be really good, Amelia, thank you.' He gave her a little salute before carrying on to his room.

Most of the other scavenger participants had had the same idea as Gideon and were congregated in the Whistling Haggis well before the start time. Armed with a plastic bag to collect things in, a notepad and pen, plus phones for taking photographs, the teams were looking serious, despite the number of Santa hats, reindeer antler headbands and stick-on elves' ears worn by the inhabitants of Glencarlach. And many of the hotel's guests, Amelia noted as she waved over at Alaiya and DeShawn. A little farther away stood the King family with Lucy and Carlo. Then the door opened and Terence and Nisha walked in.

'We haven't missed anything have we?' Terence asked, coming up to Amelia. 'Vanessa's bloody well ignoring my knocks despite her knowing I was keen to take part. Luckily, Nisha here was happy to step in to be my partner.'

Amelia remembered Nisha's comment the night before and wondered how much she was joking when she said she wanted to flirt with Terence. And did 'stepping in' to be Terence's partner only extend to the scavenger hunt?

'All these Christmas activities are making me feel young again!' Terence said and gave a laugh. 'I don't suppose anyone would be up for a bit of sledging later?'

Carlo gave a guffaw. 'I'd be up for that. Lucy?'

'I don't think I've brought any waterproofs with me.'

'We just get wet and cold! That's half the fun!' Terence said.

Lucy didn't look convinced.

'Good excuse for a hot chocolate laced with brandy and a soak in the tub afterwards,' Carlo said and gave Lucy a kiss.

'Oh my God!' Gideon said under his breath. 'Do they never stop with the PDAs?'

Big Davey rang the last orders bell and a hush descended.

'Righty-ho, everyone. I'm going to do a quick rundown of the basic rules. Groups can be a minimum of two, maximum of six. You only successfully complete the hunt if you return in the same group with the same number of team players that you started with. In other words, no leaving a man behind and no acquiring extra team members along the way. The hunt will finish when we declare a winning team has returned with a fully completed checklist. Or 1pm, as some of us have got other things to do this afternoon than wait for a bunch of slowcoaches. If no participating team has secured all the items on the list, I will adjudicate to decide a winner and I also have the final say on whether or not I think a task has been completed properly. I will also give extra points for creativity and ingenuity. Photos from magazines, etc. will not earn as many points as those from real life.'

'Have we all got fully charged phones?' Gideon asked as Big Davey handed out the envelopes.

They all nodded. Gideon had sent them all texts reminding them to do this and Amelia had made sure to get hers up to full as her battery life was often only at twenty per cent and she really feared he'd check and throw her off the team for lack of commitment.

'I will now hand out the envelopes which contains the list of items required for the hunt. You must not open this list until it is eleven o'clock,' Davey said.

As all the envelopes were passed around the teams, all eyes stayed on the clock above the bar. The second it clicked on to eleven, Big Davey rang the bell and people streamed out.

Amelia, Jack and Sally clustered around Gideon who ripped open the envelope and scanned the list.

'Okay, this all seems doable. Picture of a castle, something minty, picture of a sheep, a team selfie with Rev McDade, a pine cone, a football, build a snowman, picture of a camper van, piece of mistletoe... yadda yadda yadda... Right, we need a strategy! Let's get to the farthest point we'll need to get to the items and work our way back here.'

'Are we allowed to split up or must we stick together?' Sally asked, bouncing up and down on the spot, clearly enthused to get going.

'We have to stick together!' Gideon said, looking at the instructions. 'Right, I know there are definitely sheep out on the top field of the Grant farm.'

'We can access a shortcut through our grounds,' Amelia said.

Jack looked over Gideon's shoulder as he also scanned the list, 'I've got a football at the Gatehouse so we can pick that up on the way past.'

'And this can start us off!' Sally said triumphantly, pulling out half a packet of polo mints from her pocket and dropping it into the carrier bag Gideon held out. He looked towards Jean's shop which she'd opened up specially for the hunt. People were queued up clearly waiting to buy mints.

Standing outside was Rev McDade, smiling widely. He waved at Amelia and came over. 'Merry Christmas! Do you need to take a selfie with me?' he said jovially.

'Yes we do! And merry Christmas,' Amelia said as they got into position with Gideon holding the camera.

Taking the photo then pocketing his phone, Gideon strode off in the direction of Stone Manor, Sally trying to keep up with his pace.

'Is there a scavenger hunt bootcamp Gideon went to that he forgot to tell us about?' Amelia grumbled as she and Jack followed at a much more leisurely pace.

'I'd hoped we could split up so you and I could go to the Gatehouse and play hunt the football for a bit,' Jack said.

'If only! The next couple of days are going to be hectic. We've not even opened Christmas presents yet!' Amelia said in disappointment. They'd been at the hotel first thing to help Toby with the Christmas Day food prep.

Jack stopped and pulled Amelia back. They stood together in the middle of Main Street holding hands. Amelia looked up into his eyes, which crinkled as he smiled down at her as he said, 'I know the next couple of days are crucial for Stone Manor and you and Toby, and we're all going to work our asses off to make it the best Christmas and wedding your guests have ever been to. We can have our own little Christmas whenever we choose. A bottle of something nice in front of the fire, eating nothing but chocolate and watching boxed sets of whatever Nordic crime series takes our fancy. Presents can wait. As long as I'm with you it doesn't matter what day it is.'

Amelia went up on her tiptoes and was about to kiss Jack

when Gideon completely ruined their romantic moment by hollering at them to get a move on.

'What on *earth* is that!?' Gideon said accusingly as Jack hurried out the Gatehouse a few minutes later, pulling the door closed behind him.

'A football!' Jack said as he dropped it into the bag of scavenger loot.

'I know I'm about as far from a footy-loving lager lout as it gets and I don't know the difference between Arsenal and my elbow, but even I know what a football looks like. FootBALL. *That,*' he pointed to the bag, 'is oblong! The list doesn't say rugby balls!' Gideon said, looking like he was about to start hyperventilating.

'It's an American football,' Amelia said, gently pushing Gideon onwards. 'The list says a football, it doesn't say which country it has to come from! Think of it as one of the bits of creativity and ingenuity. I bet there aren't any other teams with a genuine American football!'

'And probably for good reason,' Gideon huffed as they carried on through the woods towards the Grant farm. The hike was onerous through all the snow-covered branches and despite it being a shortcut, Amelia thought it may have been more prudent to have gone to one of the other farms. They were slightly farther out but at least they were on a road that some of the local farmers had made a gallant effort to clear.

'Here we are,' Gideon said cheerily as he vaulted over the drystone wall much to the interest of a flock of sheep clustered around a food trough. 'Come on, Sally, give us a pose!'

The others clambered over the wall and Sally walked very slowly near the sheep, careful not to spook them. She bent over sideways with her thumbs up as Gideon took a photo of her with a half dozen or so of the sheep in the background.

'Smashing,' he said, returning his phone to his pocket. 'Now for the camper van.'

'Are we going to get a snap of Craig's camper van?' Amelia asked, thinking they should have started at that point as it was a mile or so in another direction.

'No need, there's one down here,' Gideon said as he walked off, further into the field.

'A camper van?' Amelia asked as she hurried on to keep stride with Gideon.

'Yup, it looks like a pristine original model. I came across it a couple of days ago when I was out walking. Here we go!'

They got to the top of the field and right enough, at the bottom end, tucked away from the road and in the shelter of a large tree was a cherry red and cream two-toned vintage Volkswagen camper van.

As they approached it, Amelia's heart beat a little faster as she could see from the licence plates that it wasn't a British van.

'Oh, she's gorgeous!' Sally enthused as Gideon took a photo of it on his phone. 'I'd love one of these for Hamish and me! Imagine bumping about the country, setting down wherever you fancy, a bit of barbeque on the beach, a night in a forest. It's the dream, isn't it.'

'Those plates,' Amelia said to Jack, 'the D means it's German, doesn't it?'

Jack nodded. 'And the first letter of the registration number is B, which is...'

'Berlin,' Amelia said as she went up to the driver's side and scraped away the snow and ice so she could take a look inside, but there was nothing other than a bottle of water and an AA road map on the front passenger seat.

Amelia got out her phone and took photos; focusing in on the registration plates.

'We don't need loads of photos, I'm sure one would do,' Gideon said, 'and we should probably try and keep the photos on one phone to make it easier for judging.'

But Amelia wasn't taking them for the scavenger hunt.

'I wonder who it belongs to!' Sally mused as she circled round it.

Amelia had a very good idea. She would put money on it being the vehicle Benedict Geissler travelled to Glencarlach in.

CHAPTER 34

'Right! Onwards we go!' Gideon called out and headed back up the hill again.

'Are you okay?' Jack asked as he fell into step with Amelia.

'I have a feeling this van belongs – *belonged*,' she corrected herself, 'to Benedict Geissler.'

'Oh shit! Of course, that makes sense!' Jack agreed. 'No one knew how he got here or where he was staying. You want to call Ray?'

'Hmm,' Amelia said as vaguely as possible. What she really wanted to do was have a look inside it first.

'Hang on,' Jack said, clearly having tuned in his mind-reading powers, 'it could be a murder clue and you don't want to be going putting your fingerprints all over it!'

Amelia waggled her gloved hands at him.

'Or your DNA for that matter! You could be facing jail time for tampering with evidence!'

'But we don't know it *is* evidence or that it definitely belongs to Benedict Geissler in the first place,' she said looking as wide-eyed and innocent as possible.

'You can get away with many things, Amelia Adams, but playing dumb isn't one of them.'

'It would just be a quick peek! But not now, we don't have time, especially as Gideon is on his mission. Later.'

'What about present opening and chocolate eating by the fire?' Jack said hopefully.

'As you said, we can have Christmas any day!'

'Come on! Stop dilly-dallying!' Gideon shouted over his shoulder as he continued to march up the hill.

Breaking into a slight run, Amelia and Jack caught up.

'If we head towards the hotel we can get hold of a piece of tinsel, mistletoe…?' Gideon asked Amelia.

'Yes, we've got bunches of it, everywhere. Wee Davey went a bit mad with it, like he's trying to start an orgy!' Amelia said.

'Some fresh sage?'

Amelia shrugged. 'I'm sure Toby will have some.'

On entering the hotel, they each darted off to get the next few items on the scavenger list. Amelia hurried into the drawing room to get a sprig of the bunched-up mistletoe adorning the fireplace and discovered Lorcan and Evangelina sitting either end of the large sofa. They'd clearly been deep in conversation and looked up guiltily at the intrusion.

'How are you feeling?' Amelia asked her.

'I feel fine now, thank you. My room has had a deep clean and I've got my clothes back. I'd also like to stay on in the Sayers Room, by myself, if it's available for the next few days. I think I need a little space.'

'Of course,' Amelia said, keeping her face as neutral as possible. 'I'm so pleased you're okay. Right, I'd best be off! Later!' Amelia added, waving the piece of mistletoe at the pair, then realised her faux pas. 'Oh, I don't mean for you guys to kiss later… or well… unless you want to… um. I'm just going to leave now!' With a wave, Amelia hurried through to reception where

Jack was standing with a piece of tinsel and Sally was holding a carrot.

'For the snowman's nose!' she said by way of an explanation.

They popped their haul into the bag just as Craig walked out of the kitchen with a couple of bottles of champagne.

'How are we doing for supplies?' Amelia asked him, tallying up just how many bottles they'd gone through that day.

'I'm just popping these into the smaller fridge in the bar,' Craig said. 'We've still got all the bottles put aside for the wedding. We have the bottles for New Year but we may have to dip into that depending how tonight goes. This group like their fizz.'

'We can put in another order before New Year's Eve, we just don't know if it'll get through in this weather.' Amelia stopped talking as she suddenly noticed bruising down the side of Craig's head and face and a split lip.

'Oh my goodness, what happened?' He hadn't had the injury that morning. Craig had appeared for his shift just after nine, despite Amelia proposing he start a little later.

Craig looked sheepish. 'I slipped on the steps out by the bins and bashed my head against the door.'

'Are you okay?' Amelia asked in concern. She'd thought Wee Davey had gritted the whole area overnight. She'd certainly asked him to.

'I did see stars for a moment,' he said with a rueful look. 'Toby gave me an ice pack and I feel fine now.'

'Are you sure you're fit for work?'

'Oh yes! And you need me here.'

'We do, but only if you're okay. Make sure you take plenty of breaks and if you feel at all dizzy or anything, let us know.'

'Okay, boss. Um, Amelia…?'

Just then Gideon barged out of the kitchen, the swing door hitting off the wall. 'Let's go!' he called out waving sage leaves above his head.

Amelia ignored Gideon tugging at her coat sleeve for her to follow him. 'Yes, Craig?'

'I… I was just going to wish you luck.'

'Thanks!'

'He could only spare us two leaves,' Gideon moaned as they headed out the front door and down the gritted steps. 'It turns out other competitors turned up asking for some too! What's more, he gave them some! Can you believe it! He should be sabotaging the other teams, not helping them! Where's the loyalty?'

'Oh be quiet, Gideon!' Amelia said cajoling him along.

They walked briskly back along the drive and just before the large wrought-iron gates at the very end, which led to the lane towards the village, Gideon stopped abruptly and pointed to a large tree set back slightly from the perimeter wall. 'Pine cones!'

'Shall we stop here and make the snowman too?' Sally suggested.

'Good idea,' Amelia said.

Gideon picked up a pine cone and popped it into the bag while Amelia rolled some snow to make a body.

'I'll do the head,' Sally said, following suit.

'It needs to be bigger!' Gideon said to Sally a few moments later.

'It doesn't say anywhere about being anatomically accurate,' Sally grumbled. 'We can stick it on top and then pack on more and add definition if you don't think it looks right.' She turned and rolled her eyes at Amelia, clearly having lost much of her enthusiasm for the scavenger hunt.

Sticking in a couple of twigs for arms, Sally stuck some dark stones into the snow for the eyes and smile, which Amelia thought looked rather sinister. She then placed the carrot in place for the nose.

With a ceremonious 'tadaaaaa' Jack put a Santa hat on the snowman's head.

They all stood back to observe their work.

'It needs something else,' Gideon said, critically.

'A scarf?' Sally suggested.

'Yeah, that would finish it off,' Amelia agreed. They all looked at each other. The only person wearing a scarf was Gideon.

'No!' he said, clutching his neck protectively. 'You're not getting the one hundred per cent cashmere gift Toby got me!'

'Well...' Sally gave a shrug.

Gideon looked around the ground. 'There must be something else we can use, like a leaf garland or something! Look!' He pointed to a mound of snow about thirty feet away with the edge of a piece of wool sticking out of it. 'Looks like someone's chucked their scarf over the wall. We can use that,' he said hurrying over.

'He's so competitive!' Sally moaned quietly to Amelia. 'I wish I'd stayed at Hamish's mum and dad's now. Peeling sprouts would have been preferable to him barking orders at me.'

'Don't worry. We're nearly done. We still need a picture of a castle though...' Amelia said as she watched Gideon tugging at the piece of wool.

'Hang on!' he shouted over his shoulder, 'it seems to be attached to something.'

'The Whistling Haggis has the painting of Urquhart Castle in the main bar!' Amelia said with a flash of inspiration. 'We can go and get a photo of–'

Gideon's blood curdling shriek ripped into the air as he stumbled backwards into the snow.

Amelia, Jack and Sally ran over to him.

'Are you okay?' Amelia asked him as he scrambled backwards, feet kicking into the snow as went. He stopped and jumped to his feet, looking deathly pale.

'The scarf IS attached to something,' Gideon said shakily. 'Oh God, Sally, it's Kit!'

CHAPTER 35

Against the odds, Kit was alive. As Jack called emergency services, the others dug the journalist out of the snow, piling their warm coats on top of him. His lips had a dreadful blue tinge but he had a pulse, albeit a weak one.

'What were you doing out here?' Sally berated her cousin through sobs as Gideon put his arms around her.

'His body and his hands still feel quite warm,' Amelia noted in what she hoped was a positive voice as she tucked her jacket around his torso.

'He must have been wearing his self-heating gilet and gloves!' Sally said. 'He told me he'd bought them to come up here with as he hates being cold! Oh, thank goodness! But what was he doing out here?'

'He may have fallen and hit his head,' Amelia said to Sally as she pointed out the pinkish tinge to the snow under Kit's woolly hatted head. 'We shouldn't move him in case we make any injury worse.'

'But was the snow really that deep to cover his body entirely?' Sally said.

To Amelia's eye it looked as if nature had had a helping hand, as the snow seemed to have been banked up around his body to shield him from the drive.

Gideon and Amelia shared a look over Sally's head. Gideon clearly had the same thought as Amelia: this was no accident.

As Sally continued to talk to Kit, Amelia glanced over to Jack who was still on the phone. She shivered.

'Right,' Jack said, coming over. 'They're sending an air ambulance because the roads are still impassable. Luckily we're at the very edge of the woods and there's enough open space in the field beside us for them to land. You'll be able to go with him, Sally.'

She nodded. 'Oh, but Christmas Day! Hamish's mum and dad…'

'I'll call Hamish. They'll all understand, Sally. You need to be with Kit,' Amelia said giving her friend a hug.

Then they huddled around Kit and waited for help to arrive.

It was a very sombre group of three that walked back to Stone Manor once Kit and Sally were safely on their way to hospital. Amelia felt quite numb with shock, although she could have wept with relief when Kit had regained consciousness and had tried to talk just as the air ambulance had landed a couple of hundred yards away.

They trooped into the kitchen which was bustling with activity. Toby glanced up from basting the turkey. 'Hey, guys, how did you do? Did you win?'

'If finding a half-dead body was on the list we would have romped home,' Gideon said wearily as he slowly unwound the scarf from his neck.

'What?' Toby said, baster poised mid-air.

'We found Kit, buried in the snow, just inside the Stone Manor gates,' Amelia informed her brother as she sat on one of the kitchen chairs. 'Don't worry, he's still alive,' she added when she saw her brother's shock. 'I don't know how long he'd been there but it looked like he could have been there overnight.'

'What happened?' Craig asked, looking up from decanting port.

'We don't know for sure. Looks like he could have sustained a head injury.'

'Sally?' Toby asked.

'Shaken. She went with him in the air ambulance.'

'Oh, I thought I heard a helicopter. This is awful.'

Amelia nodded. 'We now just have to wait. Sally said she'd phone as soon as she has news. I think keeping busy is the best plan.'

The others murmured their agreement.

'I've prepped the glasses for the champagne cocktails and we just need to add the champagne at the last minute,' Craig said. 'The reds are decanted and in the dining room and the white wine chilling in the ice buckets.'

'And I locked the bar over,' Toby said. 'I did a quick inventory of the cellar earlier and we seem to be missing a few bottles, mainly champagne. I think us being short staffed has maybe given some guests the idea they can help themselves.'

Amelia thought back to the floor of the Simenon Room scattered with illicitly purloined bottles.

'Good thinking, but don't worry, I'm sure everything will be amazing!' Amelia said appreciatively as she checked out the bruising on Craig's face. It had darkened considerably in the intervening hours. He saw her looking and touched his injury self-consciously.

'How's your head?' Amelia asked.

'I don't even notice it,' the barman said, obviously lying but clearly not wanting to make a fuss.

Amelia looked at her watch. She and Jack just had enough

time to go back to the Gatehouse and get changed in time for that evening's extravaganza.

Just as they'd finished getting ready and Amelia applied the final slick of her red lipstick, Sally phoned.

'He's going to be okay!' Sally said, her voice shaking with emotion.

Amelia put the phone on to speaker so Jack could hear too.

'He's suffered a concussion,' Sally continued, 'he's got a touch of hypothermia, but other than that he's fine. He'll need careful watch, intravenous fluids and rest but doctors are delighted he's responded so well. His heated gilet and gloves helped save his life. Turns out he was also wearing heated socks! Thank goodness he's a Southerner wuss afraid of a bit of cold!' Sally added and then gave a shaky laugh.

'Did he say what happened?' Amelia asked.

'After seeing you in the café he left and made a couple of phone calls about someone called Benedict. He then headed back to Stone Manor and that's when someone ambushed him from behind. He didn't see or hear a thing and has no idea who it was who did it.'

'So, he didn't hook up with someone in the Whistling Haggis then.'

'Nope. Whoever did this to Kit, sent that text so no one would worry and we wouldn't be out looking for him, then they turned off his phone and put it back in his pocket.'

'Has he spoken to the police?'

'Not yet, although he's saying he's not sure he's even going to tell them about it in case it causes more problems!' Sally's voice rose an octave, clearly upset about her cousin's attitude. 'Why would he do that? We can't allow someone to be going around knocking people unconscious!'

Amelia silently agreed with her friend. First Lorcan, now Kit!

'He even said it might be best that people don't know he's regained consciousness in case it puts others at risk?' Sally continued. 'What risks, Amelia? And what did you and Kit talk about in the café? Is it something to do with this Benedict person? Kit was talking about him in the air ambulance too, but he wasn't making much sense.'

Amelia's stomach twisted uncomfortably, aware that Sally could very easily blame her for her cousin's injury. Despite Kit not wanting Sally involved, Amelia couldn't lie to her best friend. 'It turns out Kit knew Benedict Geissler a man who'd arranged to meet me at the folly a few days ago. Mr Geissler died before I could speak to him and Kit wanted to find out more.'

'Ugh! Honestly! He was meant to be on holiday, not chasing some story... oh...' There was a moment's silence and then Sally asked, 'Is that why Kit came up to Glencarlach? Was he meeting him?'

Amelia took a deep breath. 'You're his main reason but...'

Sally laughed. 'Oh, don't worry, I know what he's like. He's a workaholic and it's why he has no friends.'

Amelia could hear a faint cry of protest in the background and guessed Kit was within earshot.

'I'll phone you later. He's just been wheeled back in from getting tests. I'll go and question him further. In fact, I plan on interrogating him so much he'll be begging for the police to take over,' Sally said grimly before hanging up.

'I just knew it wasn't an accident,' Amelia said to Jack as she pulled her boots on. 'Clearly, whoever did it, dragged Kit's body to where they thought he'd go undiscovered until a thaw, not realising his hatred of the cold and love of a gadget meant he was protected from the worst of the elements. And to drag Kit any distance, the person must be quite strong.'

'He had a lucky escape,' Jack agreed as he shrugged on his bulky outdoor coat. He glanced over to the pile of presents nestled beside the hearth. 'Later?'

'Definitely!' Amelia agreed, aching to be sitting beside their fire, ripping open the wrapping paper and scoffing multiple selection boxes. But first she had to pull off a successful Christmas at Stone Manor.

And break into Benedict Geissler's camper van to find out just what he'd been doing in Glencarlach, she mentally added to her to-do list.

Back at Stone Manor, Amelia and Jack arrived just as Hamish had come to pick up Betty. With all the drama over Kit, and with Sally away, Hamish confided in Amelia that a big family Christmas gathering was the last thing he wanted once he'd escorted Betty down the front steps and to his car.

Amelia understood but, as she waved them off she knew she also had to put on her best professional host persona and welcome Stone Manor's guests as they descended the stairs for their Christmas dinner.

The Johnsons looked splendid as they stood by the fire in the drawing room, with DeShawn in a tux and his beautiful wife in a figure-hugging, full-length black sparkly cocktail dress with a split up to the thigh. Craig went round the room with a tray of champagne glasses. Dan and Alice sat on the sofa, chatting to the Johnsons; Dan also in a tuxedo and Alice in a demure navy-blue velvet dress with long sleeves and buttons right up to the neck. India stood looking out the window in a long black dress that wouldn't have looked out of place in Morticia Addams's wardrobe.

Ricky was sitting on his own in a chair, looking uncomfortable in a three-piece suit and he kept running his index finger under the collar. He took a proffered glass of champagne from Craig and practically downed it in one.

Then Evangelina appeared at the top of the stairs wearing a beautiful red silk blouse and black satin cigarette trousers, with very high stilettos. When she got to the bottom of the stairs Amelia found herself engulfed in a fragrant hug by the actress.

'Thank you,' Evangelina whispered in her ear, then glancing at the top of the stairs, she gave a shy grin to Lorcan who stood there beaming down at them for a moment before heading down to join them. Amelia noticed Evangelina was holding a manilla envelope.

'Merry Christmas, Lorcan,' Amelia said as Lorcan gave her a kiss on the cheek. 'You scrub up well,' she added taking in his very cool 1970s-style drainpipe suit.

'Ach, I couldn't go letting the side down now, could I,' he said with a wink as he smiled at Evangelina.

Gideon came up behind Amelia, looking every inch the dashing heart-throb actor in a tuxedo. 'They seem very blasé about their friendship now, don't they!' he remarked, watching as Evangelina and Lorcan walked into the drawing room. 'Did you know she moved into the Sayers Room? I had money on her just bunking in with Lorcan but maybe they want to play it down.'

'How's Toby?' Amelia asked.

'Cool as a cucumber. Nothing flaps that brother of yours. I left him doing fancy little patisserie tuille things: I was getting stressed watching him.'

Nisha was next to arrive down, also looking stunning in a pale pink and gold sari. She went straight up to Evangelina and gave her a hug and then they shared a nod of understanding as Evangelina went over to Ricky and handed him the envelope.

'Uh, what have we here!' Gideon said as he also clocked what was going on.

Amelia could see Ricky redden. 'What's this?' he asked.

'You know what it is, just a few years too late. I want out this sham of a marriage. I was going to wait until after the wedding but I just can't bear to be married to you any longer.'

Gideon grabbed Amelia's arm. 'Omigod! It's just like the Christmas episode of *Eastenders* when Dirty Den presents Angie with the divorce papers! But it's actual *real life*!' he hissed excitedly as Nisha went to stand next to her friend.

'Ah,' said Ricky, 'I did wonder why Nisha wanted to come on

this trip. Clearly it was to gloat over this little thing you had planned.'

'No, Ricky,' Nisha said calmly. 'It was to offer support and friendship.'

Lorcan, judging by his shocked expression, clearly hadn't a clue what Evangelina had planned.

With everyone unsure how to react to the drama unfolding in the drawing room, the next couple's arrival was a welcome distraction as Carlo, in a very expensive suit, and Lucy in a strapless black dress, looking incredibly glamorous, walked in. Her diamond ring flashed on her beautifully manicured hand as she gave everyone a little wave.

On the top landing, Amelia could hear knocking and Terence calling his wife's name as he stood outside the Vargas Room. A moment later, he came down the stairs looking dashing in a kilt; he'd mentioned to Amelia earlier that he had a little Scottish heritage and was clearly cashing in on it for the fashion-stakes. He was unaccompanied.

'The old girl still seems to be avoiding me,' Terence said with a mixture of annoyance and worry. 'She's had hangovers before but never one to last this long. No doubt she's planning on making a show-stopping entrance as soon as we've sat down for dinner. Always one to steal the limelight, is Vanny!'

Amelia smiled at Terence but said nothing. She saw that Craig was opening another bottle of champagne. Not wanting to run out she went to get the key for the bar to get another bottle from the fridge.

'Oh, Amelia!' Alice called out as she came up behind Amelia. 'Is it possible we could have some more towels as ours seem to have gone from our room…'

'Of course,' Amelia said as she turned the key in the lock.

'It was the strangest thing,' Alice continued. 'It was after the scavenger hunt. We'd come back to have a warming drink before we went out sledging. Dan didn't think he'd locked the door but why on earth would someone take towels?'

'It's not a problem. I'll take some right up.' Amelia unlocked the door to the bar and opened it wide, switching on the light as she did so.

And with a gasp Amelia stopped in the doorway as she took in the scene before her.

Alice, who was standing right behind Amelia, let out a scream.

Vanessa was sitting at the grand piano, her body slumped over the keys, but there was no way she was about to serenade the guests with Christmas classics. Her eyes stared wide and lifelessly; an unopened bottle of champagne clutched in her stiffened hand.

CHAPTER 36

'Well, Amelia, you do have an uncanny knack for finding bodies,' Constable Williams said, not unkindly, as he stood in front of the closed door to the bar.

'To find one body is unfortunate; two is carelessness,' Gideon ad-libbed as he gave a little shudder.

A moment later, the local GP Dr Kaur came out from the bar, closing the door behind her.

'I can definitely confirm life extinct,' she said grimly.

Terence, looking very shaken, stepped out from the dining room where all the other guests had congregated. He held up a little bag containing numerous bottles of pills. 'This is all the medication she was on. She had a bit of a dicky ticker, you see.'

'I can't make a call on cause of death,' said the doctor. 'That will be handed over to the police and a post-mortem will be carried out. It could be natural. Do you have her physician's details?'

Terence nodded and began to scroll through his phone then turned to show Dr Kaur.

Thanking him, Dr Kaur took the bag and noted down the

number, then returned to the bar to make the call. Terence turned and in a trance walked back into the dining room.

'What will happen now?' Amelia asked Constable Williams.

'I've called it in to CID.'

'Do you think it's likely to be a natural death?'

The constable puffed out his cheeks as he rocked back on his heels. 'I wouldn't like to comment on that. It's over to Inverness and their DI now. Although with the storm tonight there won't be any chance of anything getting through, neither by road nor helicopter.'

Automatically, Amelia looked through the window on the door at the snow swirling manically. She gave a little shiver.

'I'm going to take a belts and braces approach,' Constable Williams said decisively. 'I think enough has gone on around here lately to arouse suspicion. It won't hurt if I take some initial statements. I may as well start with the two of you,' he said as he ushered Amelia and Gideon into the drawing room.

'Did you pick up on there being anyone with bad feeling towards the deceased?'

'To be honest, I don't really know anyone who liked her,' Gideon said as he and Amelia sat on the sofa.

Once Amelia, then Gideon, had given Ray a detailed account of their day and recounted the last time they'd seen Vanessa, Ray closed his notebook. 'I'll need to speak to all the other guests and everyone who has been working here today. No one will be allowed to leave until I've recorded their statement. Not that they'd get very far!' He gave a little chuckle. 'Although I'm fairly certain we'll be bumped up the priority list for getting the road cleared.'

'I'll let everyone know they'll be questioned,' Amelia said as she stood up.

'Shall I contact Hamish and get him to bring Betty back?' Gideon asked.

'Please,' Constable Williams said. 'Would you be able to send in Toby next, seeing as he was the one who'd locked the bar door?'

Amelia and Gideon left and Toby was already waiting outside, along with Jack.

'My turn,' Toby said as he went into the room, closing the door.

Amelia had a quick glance into the dining room where the guests were congregated in little groups, talking in hushed tones.

'Make sure no one follows me,' Amelia said to Jack before hurrying along to the billiards room and slipping inside. At the large, ornately carved fireplace, Amelia felt along the underside of the mantelpiece until her fingers found a little ridge. She pushed it up and a section of oak panelling popped outwards a few feet away.

The hidden corridor between the billiards room and the drawing room was narrow. With a mustiness filling her nostrils, Amelia willed herself not to sneeze as she felt her way along carefully, knowing the stairs jutted in sharply about halfway along. She didn't fancy giving herself concussion on top of everything else. She also didn't want to risk lighting up her phone in case she drew attention to her hiding place. She inched along until she came to the end of the little passageway where the exit to the drawing room was situated. Having no intention of bursting into the room she did however hunker down until she could peer through the ventilation grate and see Toby sitting on the sofa with Ray standing taking notes a couple of feet away.

'…and what time was that?' she heard Ray ask.

'It must have been around two in the afternoon.'

'And you didn't return to the bar area?'

'No, I spent the rest of the afternoon in the kitchens.'

'And when you left the bar and locked it, do you recall seeing Mrs Maxwell?'

'No.'

Amelia presumed her brother would have noticed if he'd had to circumnavigate a dead woman.

'Would you normally lock the bar during the day?'

'Not normally, no, but we've noticed a few bottles going missing. With the wedding tomorrow and the roads being the way they are, we didn't want to risk running out.'

'You suspected someone was stealing booze?'

'Yes.'

'Who else has a key to the bar?'

Amelia heard Toby sigh. 'That's the thing. I hung the key back up on the board behind the reception desk and anyone could have had access to it. Everyone was back from the scavenger hunt by then. I'd laid out a light buffet in the dining room. There was talk of people going sledging and guests and staff were milling about.'

'But you don't recall Mrs Maxwell being one of them?'

'No, I'm sorry, I was too preoccupied with the Christmas dinner and tomorrow's wedding buffet.'

Amelia thought about the key. It had been particularly easy for *anyone* to get access to it as it had a little brass tag attached which helpfully had 'bar' printed on it.

Ray scribbled down some more notes, thanked Toby then asked him to send in Jack.

Amelia took her phone out of her pocket, delighted to see it was still almost at full charge from earlier. Making sure it was on mute, she hit 'record' and placed the phone on the little ledge by the grate. Moving silently, she crept back along the passageway and out into the billiards room again.

Amelia had been thinking about Geissler's camper van since they'd stumbled across it that morning, and she was itching to get a look inside, certain Vanessa's death was linked.

With everyone waiting in the dining room, Amelia knew she

only had a small window to get to search the camper van and get back. Hurrying through to the staff area, she rammed on her snow boots and grabbing her outdoor clothes headed out into the snow, still winding her scarf around her neck as she ran over the Stone Manor grounds.

CHAPTER 37

Lorcan stood looking out his bedroom window at the storm, his own mood matching the turbulent sky.

He'd been absolutely floored when Evangelina had handed Ricky the divorce papers. He didn't flatter himself to think he was the reason, as Evangelina obviously hadn't just drawn them up that afternoon in her room. She'd clearly been planning it, but he couldn't help but wonder what this meant for them. Would there even be a *them*?

But before he had a chance to speak to her, Vanessa's body had been found and that's when the shit *really* hit the fan. It was a shock, yes, but what was more of a shock was when he overheard Amelia and Gideon discussing the other body Amelia had discovered a few days before.

Benedict Geissler's!

Well, it certainly went a long way to explain why Benedict had never turned up for their prearranged rendezvous. Lorcan had been too shocked to ask Amelia any details, but hanging back to listen in to their conversation, he'd gleaned it had been murder.

Lorcan couldn't believe he'd missed this piece of news within

Glencarlach. He had a sudden flashback to when he'd first moved to the village and he'd been the 'stranger'. The Irish stranger from Glasgow.

Even worse, he'd been an Irish stranger with dreadlocks, beard and 'artistic ways'.

It hadn't been easy fitting in, but he'd persevered; turning up at the Whistling Haggis, buying people rounds of drinks and being his naturally self-effacing, charming self. He'd won over the ladies of a certain age first, after all, he could talk himself out a whole heap of trouble with his mother – and she was a tough one to crack. Then he'd worked on the person who seemed to hold the most sway in the village – Big Davey the barman. After many long chats stretching into the lock-in hours of the morning, word gradually spread from Big Davey that the new lad wasn't a bad sort, and so people started passing the time of day with him in the pub. It was a real coup when the farmers began to accept him; they were the hardcore villagers, with generations of standing in the community.

And now he was one of them, Lorcan reminded himself. Despite being slightly unnerved he reminded himself that this was not some conspiracy to keep Geissler's death from him.

To be fair, he'd had a lot on his mind. There had very possibly been talk of a person dying up at the folly, but between people gossiping about the break-in at the church, the Glencarlach Winter Festival, and being knocked unconscious, Lorcan could have easily missed something like the death of a stranger. And then he'd been totally consumed with Evangelina coming back into his life.

Something caught his eye and he peered out the window, trying to make it out in the blizzard. It looked like two figures hurrying over the grounds. Funny, he could have sworn he'd seen someone else do the same a few minutes earlier. It looked as if they'd been wearing a long red coat, one very much like the one

Amelia wore. He came away from the window, drawing the curtains to keep the heat in and the snowy vista out.

Something strange was going on. He'd never had any contact with a dead body before and he wondered if it was usual procedure for people being questioned for a heart attack.

Unless it wasn't a heart attack.

But Terence had been adamant it was. He'd felt for the man as they'd all sat in the dining room, numb with shock over the events, with Terence repeatedly saying Vanessa shouldn't have been partying so much. He clearly blamed himself for not intervening, although Lorcan doubted anyone could have made Vanessa do anything she didn't want to do.

It was more the looks that Amelia shared with Gideon that alerted Lorcan to something being amiss. He wasn't blind to the not-so-subtle remarks made by Gideon. The fact that Sally's cousin, Kit, had disappeared as mysteriously as he'd appeared was also deeply troubling.

He paced the floor of his room, panic rising again.

Lorcan knew there was slim chance he was being paranoid, but he doubted it. It was too much a coincidence that, having done the commission for Benedict Geissler, Benedict Geissler was murdered, then Lorcan's studio was broken into and he was then knocked unconscious.

And it made his suspicions about the village hall all the more credible.

He turned up the day before to hang a few more paintings for the exhibition and he'd been certain someone had been in. His cleaner, Ruby, also cleaned the hall and he knew she only went in once a week and she'd already been and, true to form, had missed all the high-up bits. He was wiping down the higher up windowsills when he'd noticed the broken catch on the window. He'd gone back out and skirted round to the back of the hall and found one of the wheelie bins had been strategically placed directly underneath the broken window.

Coincidence?

Possibly. But there were an awful lot of coincidences piling up.

Naturally, he'd gone back inside to check out the paintings. He'd carefully listed all those that had been submitted for the exhibition and the auction.

None were missing. He checked the list again. It was fine and he'd berated himself for being jumpy and pushed it to the back of his mind.

But now, it was forefront and ringing alarm bells.

He stopped pacing as it wasn't doing him or the carpet any good.

He wondered about seeing Evangelina but knew now wasn't the time as he'd feel he was intruding. Although he doubted Evangelina was a fan of Vanessa's, they'd been a group of friends for many years and needed to be together in grief.

He picked up his book but after attempting a couple of chapters he realised he wasn't concentrating on what he was reading as his eyes were jumping all over the paragraphs, unable to settle.

He threw the book down and looked around his room. He didn't have the heart to put on the television as the only thing worth watching was the *Doctor Who* Christmas special but it was almost finished, and he'd already recorded it anyway.

With nothing else to do, Lorcan picked up the tube Jack had given him containing the prized signed New York Giants poster that he'd agreed to frame. Jack had been so excited about it he thought he'd take a look, despite not really knowing a huge amount about NFL.

Popping off the top of the tube he peered inside. He could see the bright colours of the poster, but… there was something else in there too.

He reached inside and could feel something rough, like canvas. Intrigued, he pulled it out.

And stared.

Then he sat down heavily on the edge of the bed, feeling quite faint.

This wasn't good. This wasn't good at all.

CHAPTER 38

It was hard work making it through the blizzard. Amelia had to keep her head down as she stumbled along to protect her skin from the bitingly cold wind, snow and hail stinging her face. Despite the harsh conditions, Amelia went as fast as she could knowing she didn't have the luxury of time. It was with great relief she got to the farmland where they'd taken photos of the sheep just that morning. She slithered her way down the field until she got to the camper van, which was camouflaged with all the snow.

Amelia went round to the driver's door and, crossing her fingers that it was open, tried the handle. Locked. A quick scout around the other doors proved them all to be locked, too. That left the windows. Scraping away the hardened snow and ice from the side windows, Amelia tugged hard. She felt it give a little but clearly the weather had frozen the window shut.

Taking out her trusty Swiss Army knife, she ran the blade around the window seal and this time when she tugged, the window gave a little more and slid open. Standing on the van's runner, Amelia reached into the van to try and prise open the door's lock. Frustratingly, she just couldn't reach it.

'You might need someone with slightly longer arms,' a voice shouted at her over the wind.

Amelia gave a little shriek at being caught, lost her footing and slipped. She ended up dangling half-in and half-out the camper van window, her feet flailing to catch a grip again.

Two familiar strong arms helped pull her back down to the ground.

'What are you doing here?' she said turning round to Jack.

'We could ask the same of you!' Gideon said as he appeared from the other side of the van.

'But...'

'Oh, come on!' Jack said with an exaggerated eye-roll. 'I've known you long enough to know you'd be back down here the second you could get away.'

'And with a murderer on the loose, call us old fashioned–'

'I prefer gallant,' Jack corrected.

'–yes, gallant!' Gideon agreed. 'We thought a bit of having your back wouldn't go amiss. We also saw you leave; you were hardly incognito with your scarlet jacket against the snow! And clearly, you need my assistance.' He lifted his hand and dangled a set of keys at her. 'Now, before you do any more damage to this vintage beauty, why don't you try these.' Gideon threw them to Amelia.

'But how...' Amelia said, lost for words.

'They were sitting on top of the front passenger side wheel. Got the idea from a film I was in a while back where the hero hid his keys in a similar place. Easiest way to have your car stolen, I would have thought, but it worked in our favour tonight!'

Amelia unlocked the door and with a metallic grating noise she slid the van door open. They climbed inside and found a brief respite from the weather and having their voices being whipped away by the wind.

'Ooh, this is nice,' Gideon said appreciatively as he eyed up the dinky little kitchenette and seating area.

A quick look around made Amelia realise Benedict's van was as sparse and minimal as his conversation had been.

She checked in the cupboards, the overhead shelves and in the glove compartment but found nothing other than some basic food supplies, a couple of beers and a holdall containing some clothes and a washbag. There was a well-thumbed Harlan Coben thriller and a booklet, which on closer inspection turned out to be a gallery guide of an art exhibition currently running at The National Gallery in London. Stuffing them inside the holdall, along with the AA road map from the front seat and the contents of the glove compartment, Amelia slung the holdall over her shoulder.

Just then Gideon's phone pinged. 'It's Toby,' he said reading his message. 'Dr Kaur has called the undertakers to remove the body until the police can get out. Ray's sealed off the scene and he's going to make some turkey sandwiches for later if the guests are hungry. I mean Toby is, not the constable. He thinks constantly about food, that brother of yours,' he said, pocketing his phone, 'although I have to admit I'm quite ravenous and could *murder* a chipolata!' He pulled a face. 'That's maybe the wrong choice of wording for this evening.'

'Let's go,' Amelia said as she, Jack and Gideon jumped down from the van, closing the window then sliding the door shut and locking it. Amelia replaced the keys where Gideon had found them.

'Obviously we'll hand this bag over to Ray and tell him about the van, but probably best to wait for the morning,' Amelia shouted to the other two as they battled their way back up the hill.

'Yes,' agreed Jack. 'We can keep it safe until then.'

'And we'll make sure no one can go through his belongings as there's a high probability the murderer may want to get their hands on these.'

'Wait!' Gideon hollered and stopped. Amelia turned to look at him, wiping snow from rim of her woolly hat. 'You... I mean... you *are* going to look through all his things, aren't you? Not just hand them straight over.'

Amelia gave him a look. 'What do you think?'

'Well, thank God for that!' he said as they continued their way through the snow.

Back at Stone Manor, Amelia stood with Constable Williams and watched as the local undertakers took Vanessa, zipped up in a body bag, out the front door on a stretcher.

Ray nodded at them then went off towards the dining room, no doubt to update the guests.

'Come on, let's go up to my room,' Gideon said. 'Jack's already there with the bag.'

Upstairs in the Nesbo Room, Amelia carefully emptied the contents of Benedict Geissler's holdall onto the bed.

'He seems to have bought into the capsule wardrobe idea,' Gideon remarked as he inspected four pairs of black socks, four pairs of black underpants, two pairs of black trousers and two red checked shirts. His washbag contained only toothpaste and toothbrush, small travel soap in a dish, a comb, pair of nail scissors, a deodorant and an electric razor. From the glove compartment there was an assortment of classical CDs, the soundtrack of *West Side Story* and a Barbara Streisand greatest hits compilation. Amelia had checked the food containers whilst in the van in case something had been stuffed inside the jar of coffee or cornflake packet but there was nothing; no second phones, no coded letters, no plug-in drive, not even a microfiche-style implant à la Jason Bourne.

Amelia sat back on her heels in disappointment.

Jack flicked through the novel, removing the leaflet.

'Oh, this was the exhibition I tried to go and see.'

Gideon plucked it from Jack's hand. 'Renaissance art! You and Carlo can start your own club!'

Just then there was a knock on the door.

'Shit! Quick, hide it,' Gideon said, flinging a dressing gown over the purloined personal effects.

Amelia opened the door to find Lorcan standing there. He was holding a poster tube and Amelia thought he looked a little shaken.

'Merry Christmas,' Amelia said, somewhat ironically. 'Come on in. How are you?'

Lorcan came inside the room although he didn't answer her question.

'How's Terence?' she asked.

'Numb with shock still, I think,' Lorcan replied faintly. From the look on Lorcan's face, Amelia didn't think Terence was the only one in shock in Stone Manor.

'I should really get back downstairs,' Amelia said.

'There's plenty of time to do that,' Gideon said. 'And, we do have things to get on with here,' he added archly with a raise of his eyebrow and a nod towards the mound of belongings under the dressing gown.

'I suppose,' Amelia said reluctantly, hating to think it looked as if she was avoiding her guests and staff, whom she also considered friends.

'I think you'd better stay for a little bit longer, Amelia,' Lorcan said. He looked quite agitated as he pulled on his goatee.

'Are you okay?' Amelia asked, gently.

'You know, it's been a very strange time, of late,' Lorcan said. 'These last few days have been quite, um... odd. Unexpectedly odd in so many ways. Um... so, after Ray questioned me, I didn't know what to do so I came up to my room, and, I uh, I thought I'd look at the poster you gave me, Jack. The one you wanted me to frame.' Lorcan held aloft the poster tube he'd come in with.

'Fantastic!' Jack said and Amelia could see an excited twinkle in his eye.

'I picked up something very special while I was away,' Jack explained. 'I gave it to Lorcan and asked if he could frame it. What do you think of it, Lorcan?'

The Irishman nodded. 'Oh, it's special, all right.'

'Something, *very* special!' Jack said. 'As soon as I saw it, I knew I had to have it!'

Amelia was intrigued. Lorcan had opened the top of the tube and was carefully pulling something out of it.

'I know it's maybe a little bit of a statement piece, but when we get a new house, I'll find the perfect spot for it,' Jack said gleefully. 'I can't believe I managed to get my hands on it!'

Lorcan looked up briefly. 'In all honestly, neither can I!'

'Do you know how rare this is?' Jack said.

'Yes, I really do,' Lorcan said in a measured tone.

'I know not everyone will appreciate it, but to me, it's a piece of priceless art.'

'I, um… I think most people would see it as a priceless piece of art,' Lorcan said quietly. He finished taking the item out of the tube and held it up. It was a rough-edged canvas; the subject matter was a three-quarter portrait of a long-faced young man with a beard and moustache. To Amelia's untrained eye, the painting looked old.

'But…' Jack stepped back in confusion.

'Because it *is* a piece of priceless art,' Lorcan said. 'A priceless Renaissance painting that was stolen a few days ago from The National Gallery in London.'

CHAPTER 39

'No!' Jack looked round the room in confusion. 'It's meant to be a vintage New York Giants poster, signed by some of their greatest players.'

'Don't worry,' Lorcan said as he peered into the tube again, 'it's still there. I'm guessing by your reaction you didn't realise this had joined it.'

'No!'

'Phew, I'm rather relieved about that. I didn't have you down as an international art thief, but as I said, it's been a strange time lately. Now we just need to work out why you've got it and who could have given it to you. And to confuse matters even more, Benedict Geissler contacted me a few weeks ago to get me to paint a copy of it,' Lorcan added as he pulled out another painting from the poster tube; an exact replica of the first one.

'What?' Amelia looked up at Lorcan. 'You knew Benedict Geissler?'

'Yes, I knew him from time I spent in Berlin. I'd copied a painting for him a few years ago. He and the police were using it to try and catch an art thief. It worked. I'm guessing this was for a similar sort of sting operation but I'll never know for sure as he never showed up for our meeting. Then I overheard you and Gideon talking tonight about his death, and that he had been murdered.'

Amelia took a closer look at the paintings. They were pretty much identical. 'What even is this painting? Do you know it?' She really had no clue about art. She could recognise the Mona Lisa and would be able to pick a Van Gogh out in a line-up, but that was really the extent of her art knowledge.

Lorcan held it out at arm's length and gave a faint smile. 'I do. It's a portrait of Cesare Borgia and was part of the Renaissance exhibition in London, before it was stolen a few days ago.'

'I tried to get in to see that,' Jack said faintly. 'But the gallery was shut because of the theft.'

'If only you'd known you had part of it!' Gideon said, scrutinising the original and copy.

'It had been missing for centuries and most in the art world thought it had been destroyed but then it recently turned up in someone's attic in Rome and after being authenticated it was credited to the Florentine artist Domenico Ghirlandaio, in a similar way his *Salvator Mundi* painting was discovered in a private family collection and attributed to him.'

'Sorry, say that again?' Amelia said looking away from the painting sharply.

'A private family had discovered the...'

'No, the artist's name.'

'Domenico Ghirlandaio.'

'Ghirlandaio,' she repeated out loud. 'The Ghirlandaio. The. Girl. And. I. Ohhhhhhhhhh.' Amelia took a deep breath. 'Benedict Geissler wasn't trying to tell me about a girl! He was trying to tell me about the painting. *This* painting! Or should I say *these* paintings!'

They all stood around the bed where Lorcan had carefully placed the paintings. They stared at them for a few moments.

'How *on earth* did you end up with it?' Lorcan asked again, incredulously.

'When you were knocked into and sent flying in London,' Amelia said, unable to drag her eyes away from the portrait. 'You thought you'd dropped your room key but you must have been pickpocketed. Then they let themselves into your room and hid the painting in your poster tube.'

'But why? And why me?' Jack said, clearly mystified.

'I somehow doubt you were the intended final recipient, just the mule to take the stolen goods out of London. Remember we were broken into? It wasn't like a normal robbery; nothing was stolen. Whoever did it had clearly been looking for something. Obviously to get this back.'

'Whereas I'd had it in my room,' Lorcan said with a grin. 'Sorry, I know it's a bit inappropriate, but I can't get my head around the fact I had an original Ghirlandaio at the side of my bed!' He shook his head in astonishment.

'Obviously, it was someone coming up here from London,' Amelia said, thinking out loud. 'Which accounts for all the guests, well, apart from Betty. The guests all either already lived there or came through there from a flight, like the Johnsons did.'

'But why bring it here?' Gideon said as he leant forward to inspect the original more closely.

'I guess there would be too much heat staying in London. Obviously Benedict was onto the thief. Maybe there's a fence up here to take it off their hands?' Amelia hazarded a guess.

'There's Dougal, the antiques guy who has a shop in Ullapool,' Jack said. 'He comes into the Whistling Haggis every couple of weeks or so, but he's only ever been interested in war memorabilia and carriage clocks as far as I know.'

'No, this wouldn't get flogged openly in a shop,' Lorcan said. 'It'll be handed on to very specialised people on the black market for a private sale. In fact, it's most likely been stolen to order. Obviously Benedict knew something; unfortunately he never had the chance to pass the information on to me.'

'Or Kit. He'd asked Kit to come here too, for an inside, career-making scoop, but clearly he liked to keep his cards close to his chest as Kit's none the wiser either. He tried to make some calls...'

'And we all know how that ended up,' Gideon said.

'So, is the person buying it here, in Stone Manor?' Amelia said. 'And is this where it's meant to have ended up all along? When Benedict Geissler tried to talk to me he said what I thought was "Miss King" and then said he was in pain, but he must have been trying to tell me about the missing painting.' Amelia rubbed her eyes as she delved into her memory to bring up their encounter. Although brief, it had made an impression. 'He showed me the newspaper article about Stone Manor. At the top were the words "Here", "26th December", and "reunited".'

'Oh, wait a minute,' Lorcan said as he scratched his head. 'There's something I remember reading... ah, now what was it. Something about there being a partner to this painting...'

'Hang on,' Amelia said and lifted up the dressing gown from Benedict Geissler's belongings and picked up the gallery guide. She checked the index and then flicked to the page dedicated to Ghirlandaio. She scanned the information until she found what she needed. 'Listen to this. "It is believed that the rediscovered portrait of Cesare Borgia was part of a pair, the other being of his sister Lucrezia Borgia, both commissioned by their father, Pope Alexander VI, also known as Rodrigo Borgia.

'The paintings were completed shortly before Ghirlandaio's death in 1494. The infamous and powerful Borgia family regularly courted scandal and were rumoured to be responsible for the deaths of many of their enemies, often, it was suggested, by the means of an untraceable poison. Cesare and Lucrezia were in particular very close, but despite rumours of incest, nothing was ever proven. A letter dated from the late fifteenth century indicates the paintings were intended to be kept together, to mirror the closeness of the siblings, but despite the wishes of Pope Alexander VI, over the centuries the painting of Cesare was lost and that of Lucrezia Borgia was sold numerous times and ended up as part of a private collection until it was stolen in 2004. It has never been recovered.'

There were photos of the two paintings and Amelia was in no doubt that the painting lying on Gideon's bed was the stolen Cesare Borgia.

Amelia closed the booklet over and looked up at the others. 'Could the painting of Lucrezia Borgia have been one of the paintings stolen by the Romeo Robber? And he wanted to reunite it with its partner of Cesare?'

'Remember Vanessa's little performance on Christmas Eve, talking about the Romeo Robber?' Gideon said.

'Yes, she was letting someone in the room know she knew their real identity. I'm even more convinced that Vanessa's death was not natural. It's why she was killed. She'd obviously worked out the Benedict Geissler connection and that he'd been murdered. Then maybe she got greedy and tried to blackmail the murderer. She must have been the one to send this blackmail note to the murderer who then tried to burn it in the fire,' Amelia said as she retrieved the note from her pocket and placed it on top of Geissler's belongings for the others to see. 'But why go to all the trouble of bringing the stolen painting up here? That's what I don't understand,' Amelia said as she sat down heavily on a chair, feeling confused.

'To reunite it with the other one?'

'But why here? Why bring one painting all the way up here before passing it on to pair up with the other one?'

'Unless the other one is up here?'

They all looked at the photograph of the Lucrezia Borgia painting in the gallery catalogue.

'I can honestly say I've never seen that painting before. Who here would have that sort of thing, anyway? I can't imagine Big

Davey has it as the reveal picture behind a display of KP nuts,' Gideon said.

'Your studio was broken into and you were knocked unconscious. Maybe someone thought you had it,' Gideon said to Lorcan.

'I just assumed it was the copy of Cesare they were looking for. But it was under the back seat of my Jeep all along in the hope Benedict would call again,' Lorcan said. 'There's something else, I can't prove it, but I think the village hall was also broken into.' Lorcan gave everyone a rundown of what he'd discovered.

'And Lucrezia isn't one of the pieces you'd catalogued?' Amelia said.

'No, a Florentine portrait would have definitely stood out amongst the still lives, landscapes and harbour views.'

They sat for another hour going round in circles with various theories but getting no further forward.

Eventually, just after nine, Toby let himself into the room. If he was slightly surprised at the impromptu gathering, he didn't show it.

'That's pretty much everyone cleared out now,' Toby said, emitting a yawn. 'Ray's still about but most of the guests have gone to bed. There's tons of food in the kitchen. I'm going to have a shower as I've been running around all day in that hot kitchen.' Toby headed into the en suite and a moment later the shower was switched on.

'I'm going to go and check downstairs,' Amelia said.

'Just one thing,' Lorcan said. 'What do we do with these?' he pointed at the paintings.

There was a moment's silence as everyone contemplated the art before them.

'I'd be in favour of rolling them up and putting them back in the poster tube while we figure out what's going on,' Amelia said.

'I feel very uncomfortable about all this,' Jack said.

'No one would think for a moment you'd steal this.'

'Apart from the fact I was in London at the time of the crime and oh look, I have it in my possession!' Jack said sarcastically, running his hand through his sandy hair.

'You're not the one who also has a copy of the painting,' Lorcan pointed out.

'And it doesn't look good that I've been right in the middle of finding the dead bodies,' Amelia said. 'Ray knows us and would never think we'd be involved but if this case is taken over by some detective inspector from the Inverness Police force who doesn't know the first thing about us, coupled with the fact you unwittingly carried that back from London and I have Benedict Geissler's phone and personal effects in my possession and we've got a replica kicking about too... well, there's even more reason for us to try and find out the identity of the murderer and thief, *and* their motive before we hand anything over,' Amelia said grimly. 'What do you think, Lorcan?'

'Why don't you want my opinion?' Gideon said huffily.

'Gideon, you love being involved in this kind of thing,' Amelia pointed out.

Gideon gave a slight sigh. 'Okay, you've got me on that.'

'I'm absolutely fine with not letting on to anyone yet,' Lorcan said. 'I trust Ray but someone else being brought in may be more interested in making arrest quotas than finding out the truth. You're right, Amelia, if we rock up with this little lot and no real explanation... well, it doesn't look good for any of us and he could very easily lock us all up and throw away the key. I vote we try and get to the bottom of this and go in armed with proof.'

Jack gave a solemn sigh. 'But we need to be very careful. There are already two dead bodies and Kit is in hospital and only just missed being number three. We can't underestimate whoever is after the painting. Any of us could be a target if we get too close to the truth.'

And with Jack's words resonating, Amelia let herself out of the Nesbo Room and headed downstairs.

CHAPTER 40

James and Wee Davey were behind the reception desk, talking in hushed voices as Amelia came back out the billiards room, her phone, which mercifully hadn't run out of charge, safely retrieved from the secret passage and in her pocket.

'Do you want to get off home? I've got here covered,' Amelia said.

The other two exchanged a glance. 'We don't mind staying for a while longer,' James said, and then in a slightly quieter voice said, '*Do* you think she was murdered?'

'I don't know.'

'She wasn't a very nice woman, but no one deserves that,' James said.

'She was actually quite nice to me,' Davey piped up. 'She would talk to me when she was up late in the bar. She seemed really interested in all the art in the hotel. Although I don't know how much of an expert she was as she seemed to like that odd painting, you know, the one of the cat dressed as the French detective.'

'Belgian,' Amelia corrected automatically.

'Yeah, she seemed kind of fascinated by it. Maybe she's an Agatha Christie fan too.'

'Maybe,' Amelia said. 'Thank you for staying a bit longer. Have you eaten? Can I get you some food or tea or a beer or something?'

'I wouldn't mind some of that buffet stuff Toby did. Not many of the guests ate it,' Davey said, looking enthusiastic.

'I'll bring some out.' In the kitchen Amelia could see a silhouette of someone standing outside the back door. By the stature, Amelia guessed it was Ray. 'Hello, Constable Williams,' she said opening the door. The blizzard had subsided a little, but it was still snowing quite heavily.

Ray turned and smiled. 'Evening, Amelia.'

'Are you going to be here all night?'

'Yes, I'll be in and around the property until someone comes to take over.'

'Can I get you some food?'

'Oh no, I'm still absolutely stuffed after my Christmas lunch. Luckily, I'd finished eating by the time I got your call and Mrs Williams has promised me leftover Christmas pudding whenever I come off my shift. Although, I wouldn't say no to a cup of tea.'

'Of course, I'll bring it right out.'

Amelia busied herself in the kitchen. Toby had really outdone himself with the food. After taking out a groaning tray with a couple of bottles of beer for James and Wee Davey, Amelia returned to the kitchen to make Ray his tea, popping a mince pie on a plate just in case he did find himself to be a little peckish after a little longer waiting in the cold.

Handing over the tea to Ray, Amelia saw Jingles wander round the side of the building, giving them a cursory glance as he walked past.

'Are you not worried that poor moggie will freeze unless you get it back in,' Ray said before blowing onto his steaming tea.

He had a point; it was very cold. Calling out the cat's name, Amelia heard Jingles emit a pitiful meow. But didn't return.

Amelia headed out after it. 'Jingles,' she called out, following the little paw prints in the snow. 'Come on, Jingles! Let's get back inside,' she called, coming up to the cat who was busy pawing at something behind one of the bins just as the security lights switched on. 'What have you got there? A mouse?' Amelia said as she bent down to pick him up. She paused when she saw Jingles was scratching at something that looked very much like a bunched-up Stone Manor towel.

'Why on earth would someone put that in here?' she said aloud to the cat who stopped pawing at the towel and began weaving between her legs.

Amelia lifted the towel, realising there were two of the big bath towels. They were sopping wet and quite rigid due to the low temperatures. Amelia could see they were dirty too. Stained with a reddish-pink tinge. By now Ray had wandered over.

'What have you got there, Amelia?'

'I just found these?'

He looked closely at the towels. 'Unless I'm very much mistaken, I do believe that's blood.'

'I think you're right.'

Ray cleared his throat. 'I'm going to have to call this in. Christmas night or no Christmas night, Detective Inspector McGregor will want to know about this.'

And he'd no doubt want to talk to the person who'd stumbled across it, Amelia thought with a sinking feeling.

Leaving Ray to secure the evidence and call this latest development in, Amelia carried Jingles into the drawing room then settled into her little office with a flask of filter coffee, mound of pigs in blankets, two mince pies and a slice of fruit cake. Plugging in her earbuds Amelia opened up her notebook and pressed play on the recording on her phone.

26th December

Amelia woke when Jack placed a mug of fresh hot coffee on her desk early the next morning. Stretching out her stiff back and neck, Amelia yawned widely and checked the clock to see it was just after five.

Jack sat on the edge of the desk and turned her notebook towards him, scanning her notes. Clearly not able to decipher any of her handwriting along with numerous scribbles and arrows, he quickly turned it back round.

'Did you find out anything?'

'DeShawn is certain he's going to be arrested,' Amelia said. After Ray had questioned him he'd left the room and DeShawn expressed his worries to Alaiya, saying it didn't look good for him, being a non-British black man who had a history with the victim and clearly held a grudge as she'd almost ruined his life. And if that hadn't been enough, he'd threatened her in public at the Christmas Eve dinner.

'Ray also spent a lot of time questioning Terence. Especially as he had all her heart medication.

'The Christmas Eve dinner was brought up, about Vanessa being bitchy to everyone and when Ray questioned Carlo, he suggested there was ill-will between him and the deceased, with Carlo worrying she'd ruin the wedding.'

Jack nodded thoughtfully.

Amelia sighed and took a big swallow of the coffee. 'My only issue with those scenarios though is that, if it is another poisoning, and it probably is, one of the other guests being angry with Vanessa would lend itself to a crime of passion, something like a stabbing, or a strangling.'

Jack nodded in agreement. 'You're right, a poisoning is clearly meditated and planned.'

Everyone on the recording had expressed shock at Vanessa's

death. But although shocked, no one seemed particularly sorrowful. Ricky was the most shaken, Amelia had noted, but it could be down to the shock of being issued divorce papers by his wife.

'Obviously Constable Williams was concentrating on purely the murder angle as he clearly doesn't know anything about the stolen art.' Amelia had listened through the recording hoping that someone would have mentioned the Romeo Robber, but no one did.

'And going by the Romeo Robber angle, it's obvious there are only a few male suspects that could be responsible for the theft of the Lucrezia Borgia painting in 2004.'

'Carlo, Terence, Ricky and Dan,' Jack counted them off on his fingers. 'DeShawn is only thirty, which would mean he'd have to have started his robbing spree not long out of nursery!'

'But, what doesn't make sense is that Vanessa knew all these people. She was even married to one. Why would she only realise the identity of the Romeo Robber now?'

'Maybe she *chose* only to remember it now, or that something triggered a memory,' Jack mused.

'To be honest there is one person that fits more than the others as a suspect. Carlo Todero. He said himself, he loves Renaissance art. It has been alleged that he's made his money from dubious means. Even Lucy said that he'd once told her that he managed to acquire things for people who wanted them. Lorcan said often art is stolen to order. Carlo is an avid fan of yours and reads your blog so knew your whereabouts and could easily have followed you in London. He's also clearly very fit and probably wouldn't have had too much trouble moving Kit's unconscious body from the main road. And finally, it's his wedding everyone has gathered here for. He's been the organiser of this event since day one. He planned to have it here in Glencarlach.'

Jack nodded solemnly. 'There's only one problem. The night

we were broken into, Carlo was with me the whole time, when I was talking about my books in the drawing room. He only ever left for a few moments to get another drink, certainly not giving him enough time to run along the driveway in full view, break into the Gatehouse then conduct a thorough search of the property before returning with another single malt.'

'Ugh!' Amelia put her head in her hands. 'I know, it's not perfect.'

'Unless he had an accomplice?'

'But who? Everyone was either listening to you or at Lucy's hen-do. It was the night we found India drunk but although I left early with Gideon, Lorcan and Evangelina, I'm pretty sure everyone else stayed together and are accounted for.'

Jack shook his head. 'Maybe we *should* take everything we know to the police.'

'I just need a little more time to figure it out,' Amelia said. Throughout the night as she listened to the statements and went through her notes, it felt like she'd been trying to work out the hardest jigsaw puzzle without knowing the picture on the box. But despite the magnitude of the task, she felt at times the answer was in her grasp, only for it to suddenly dissipate like a wisp of smoke. She *knew* she was close to working it out, she just needed to engage those little grey cells a bit longer…

Just then her phone rang. It was Kit.

'How are you?'

'I'm fine, feeling better,' he said. 'I really just want to get out of here now. You're up early; I thought I'd just be leaving a message on your answerphone.'

'Well, I've got a lot to do.'

'I heard there was another victim.'

'Vanessa. Yes. It looked like it *could* have been by natural causes but I think it's far more likely it's another poisoning, especially after Geissler and what happened to you.'

There was a heavy pause. Both knew Kit had had a lucky escape.

'Well, it's about Geissler I'm calling. Just after I left you at the café I spoke to an old colleague of his. They'd worked together in the insurance and reclamation of the thefts of arts and artefacts. The spate of robberies of rich families went back to the late eighties and continued through the nineties and into the two-thousands and it really hammered the company in payouts. Evidently Geissler didn't think the police were doing a good job and decided to start his own investigating. After retirement he didn't really stay in touch with his old colleagues but my contact did remember the name Geissler was certain was a top suspect–'

Amelia held her breath. Would it be Carlo? Dan? Terence? Ricky? She had her money on Carlo…

'It's a Mr Sebastian Calver.'

'Calver?' Amelia repeated in disappointment.

'Yeah. He's going to see if he can find anything else and I'll immediately forward it on to you. I said it was urgent. Oh, I've gotta go. The doctor's doing his rounds and I need to convince him I'm fine to discharge.'

She hung up. 'He might have more information soon. Now I need to go home and have a shower; it's going to be another busy day, with the wedding,' she said, draining her coffee and standing up.

'There's no way they'll go through with the wedding now,' Jack said. 'Not with everything that's happened.'

CHAPTER 41

'Of *course* we're still going through with the wedding!' Lucy's shrill voice rang out through Stone Manor. A moment later there was the sound of something smashing against a wall.

Amelia heard this eruption just as she'd been leaving and hurried up the stairs. Dan's face appeared briefly, looking at her with wide eyes for a split second before he drew back into his room, quickly shutting the door.

Amelia knocked tentatively on the door of the Christie Suite and Carlo opened it immediately.

'I'm so sorry about the vase, I'll obviously pay for all the damages,' he said apologetically as he saw Amelia look at the pieces of shattered porcelain lying by the door.

'We are not cancelling the wedding,' Lucy said again. She was standing in the middle of the room, breathing heavily, two angry red dots on her cheeks. Amelia hadn't put Lucy down as an angry or violent bridezilla, but then again, weddings could do funny things to people.

'No, *mia cara*, not cancelling, merely postponing for a very short while, just out of respect,' Carlo said in a soothing voice.

Lucy shook her head, her long dark hair snaking over her pale shoulders. 'This wedding is going ahead as planned. It *has* to be today!'

'But I don't see what a couple of day's difference would make, my love.'

To Amelia's surprise, Lucy burst into tears.

'I'll leave you two to discuss this in private,' Amelia said, backing away from the door.

'No!' Lucy said vehemently, and looking up at Amelia fiercely. 'There is nothing to discuss. The wedding will go ahead as planned.' She thrust her chin up challengingly at Carlo who looked helplessly between his future wife and Amelia.

He went to speak but no words came. Eventually he spread his hands out and gave a little shrug. 'The wedding shall go ahead as planned,' he said with weary resignation.

'Of course,' Amelia said and she closed the door over, leaving them together to carry on further discussions, hopefully without any more breakages.

As she was passing the rooms to go back downstairs a thought struck her. Moments earlier, when Dan had looked out the door, it hadn't been his room he'd been looking out of. His was at the very far end of the corridor. The room he'd been in was the Vargas room. Vanessa's 'painting' room.

She knocked on the door of the Vargas room. No reply. She was unlocking it with her key when the handle started to turn. Opening the door a crack, Dan stood there in stripey pyjamas and a navy terry-towelling dressing gown, looking miserable.

'Mr King...'

'I know this looks bad... well, I suppose it is bad.' He hung his head.

A throat cleared behind her and Amelia turned to see Alice, also looking rather abashed.

'We can explain,' she said, and beckoned Amelia to go inside.

As soon as they were all in the Vargas Room, Amelia closed the door and Alice began to talk in a rush.

'Before you think the worst of us, we didn't have anything to do with Vanessa's death. She was a nasty piece of work but you have to believe us when we say we're totally innocent of her murder. We were however, trying to get some papers back. Some rather damaging papers.'

'That she was blackmailing you over?'

Alice paused for a moment, then nodded.

'A few years ago, I rushed through two property deals, for houses in London and France,' Dan said. 'I knew it would all be passed eventually but I forged the sign-off signatures. I wasn't personally gaining anything from it, but my client would have had to pay a hefty fine if there was a delay. Once I got the real signatures I swapped the documents and I thought it would all be fine. I don't know how Vanessa found out about it but she did and she had a copy of the original papers I'd forged and threatened to use it against me unless I agreed to her terms. I feared I would have been ruined.'

'What did she want?'

'A property in London. A bolt-hole, she said, one that I'd pay for. The rent was extortionate. She could easily have afforded it herself but she obviously didn't want it in her name. I'm pretty sure it was so that she could conduct affairs without Terence finding out.'

'But I found the deeds to this bolt-hole,' Alice said. 'I confronted Dan and he had to tell me the truth.'

'I didn't want you to think I'd been using it to meet her!' Dan said, clearly unsettled at this notion.

'Oh, darling, I found it hard enough to believe you could have done something dodgy! I knew you would never have started up an affair with that frightful woman!' Alice turned to Amelia. 'She was draining us. All the money we'd put aside for our retirement was disappearing fast. We're not rich like Carlo or Terence or

Ricky. We have a very nice life but a lawyer and a maths teacher don't pay enough to keep her sordid little secrets afloat. I said to Dan we'd have to either get it back or come clean and face the consequences.'

'When we arrived here, she teased me, telling me she had the documents with her as something else had come to light about them,' Dan explained. 'She said that she'd be open to discussing a final payment that would get her off my back as she said she now had bigger fish to fry.'

'Did you manage to find the documents now?'

'Yes,' Dan said, 'they were in the bottom of her paint box.'

'And this client you forged a signature for, did it happen to be Carlo Todero?'

Dan looked blankly at Amelia for a moment, then laughed. '*My* Carlo? No! No way. He'd never be party to anything even remotely shady. All my dealings with him over the years have always been legit. He's old school, believes in handshakes, word is honour type of thing. No, one of the reasons I wanted to keep it quiet was so that he didn't find out about it. He'd be so disappointed.'

Amelia was slightly surprised to hear this. From what she'd been led to believe, she'd been under the assumption Carlo used slightly underhand business techniques. 'So, who was this client? Was it a close friend?'

'No.' Dan looked slightly abashed. 'It was someone I'd never had any dealings with before. I just felt a bit sorry for him. He was about to spend time in the big house. Wanted to do the property deals before he went away so he could make sure his children were secure and had family homes to go back to, here and abroad. He had two kids, a son and a daughter, and it was all for them.'

'Do you know what crime he'd done?'

Dan shook his head. 'I didn't like to ask, but reading between the lines, he insinuated it was a white-collar crime, nothing violent or anything like that. He seemed very well to do and nicely spoken.'

'And Vanessa was interested in it?'

'Yes, she referred to it as the deal that kept on giving.'

Dan and Alice stood there for a moment looking at Amelia before Alice said, 'Are you going to tell the police about this?'

'I very much doubt your forged signature on an old property deal is directly linked to Vanessa's death but…'

'Well, hold on to this for now,' Dan said, handing Amelia an envelope. 'Obviously I'd rather this didn't come to light, but if the police ask, give them it. And if Carlo finds out… well, I'm done with secrets,' he said and ran his hand over the stubble on his chin.

'Right!' Alice said, taking charge. 'We're going to shower and get ourselves ready for a lovely wedding and hope we can put all this behind us. First though, we are going to wipe down everything we touched inside Vanessa's room,' she said as she pulled out a cloth from her dressing gown pocket. 'It's all very well being done with secrets, but we don't have to draw attention to us going through Vanessa's room.'

'Yes, dear,' Dan said appreciatively.

'Oh, did you get the extra towels?' Amelia asked.

'We did, thank you. So strange! It had just been a couple of hours earlier we'd heard Carlo say *he* was missing towels! He was quite agitated about it. We heard him say they'd been in the bathroom and then they'd suddenly gone! We thought there was a serial towel thief, but, a little later on, when we mentioned ours had disappeared too he told us he'd actually found them again! He looked a bit embarrassed about it,' Alice said, biting her lip.

'Has Carlo been forgetful lately?' Amelia asked.

'Yes. Oh, it's just awful to see,' Alice said, looking at her husband. 'It's just been in the last four, five months?'

'That sounds about right,' Dan said. 'Although it's maybe been going on a lot longer and we've just noticed it now.'

'That poor girl, Lucy. She's meant to be starting out on a new life as a married woman and I worry it may not be long until she has to be a carer for him. And how long will she even get with him if he's deteriorating as quickly as we fear?'

'Yes, quite so,' Amelia murmured. Suddenly, Carlo didn't really seem such a good fit for the Romeo Robber, either from the nineties or from stealing the Ghirlandaio a few days ago. But to be honest, Dan seemed even less likely, as Amelia doubted he'd really be able to manage anything without the help of his resourceful and practical wife who wouldn't for a minute court art theft as a suitable endeavour.

That left Terence and Ricky. But all the facts kept coming back to Carlo. Maybe he was struggling with a bit of dementia, but it didn't mean he *hadn't* committed crimes. And he possibly had thought pretending to have a deteriorating memory could excuse him if he didn't have a solid alibi.

Amelia's head was throbbing. She needed to go home, take a couple of paracetamol and have a hot bath. 'Just out of interest,' Amelia said as she was turning to leave, 'what was the name of the client?'

'It was a Mr Calver, Mr Sebastian Calver. I never heard from him again, I guess he must have gone to prison.'

Amelia stared.

Just half an hour ago, Amelia had never heard of Sebastian Calver but now, his name had been mentioned twice. And of the other people linked with the man, two of them were dead.

CHAPTER 42

After a hot soak, a quick power nap and sustenance courtesy of a spicy Pot Noodle followed by a Snickers bar, Amelia felt she could take on the world once again.

Opening her laptop, Amelia felt her pulse quicken when she realised Kit had forwarded on the information from Benedict Geissler's old work colleague. She opened up the file and read the information, which did not disappoint. Sebastian Calver was currently in prison, serving an eight-year sentence.

For stealing a painting from a gallery.

Amelia read that he was due to be released after serving half his sentence. Which would make him free at the end of January; just a few weeks away!

There was a load of very dense information about Calver's background in art and his obsession with the Renaissance period and in particular the life and work of Domenico Ghirlandaio. As Amelia read on she couldn't help but wonder at Sebastian Calver's state of mind. It sounded like he was delusional; he felt he had a connection with the late artist, especially the paintings of Cesare and Lucrezia Borgia. In one particular disturbing passage, Amelia read that he'd even wanted to call his children after the Italian family, but luckily his wife had put a stop to it. There was only a brief passage about the collapse of his marriage. It mentioned that his late wife took full custody of the children when they were still very young and wouldn't let her ex have access to them until she sadly passed away from cancer a couple of years later. He must have been back in touch with them at some point Amelia realised, if he'd contacted Dan to organise the property for them. She also read he'd spent years in France and Italy, as well as the UK. Then there were pages of the pieces of art Geissler had suspected were stolen by Calver along with dates and times and police records detailing the events around the thefts.

With great interest, Amelia then followed the links on YouTube to the press coverage and news reports. Benedict Geissler was being interviewed from outside the court the trial had been held in. The little bar at the bottom of the screen had his name and occupation as 'art insurance recovery expert'.

Amelia turned up the volume on her laptop to hear the report better.

'Although we welcome the court's decision we are also disappointed that there will be no further investigation into similar art thefts throughout the eighties and nineties,' Benedict Geissler said into the camera. The shot cut to Sabastian Calver being jostled into the back of a police transport vehicle.

Then it cut back to the reporter describing the frustration of the previous victims of art theft and the cuts being made to the Metropolitan Police, which many said was the real reason no manpower could be spared to open the cases once again.

Amelia watched the article again and sat back in her chair.

There was nothing in Benedict Geissler's report to indicate Sebastian Calver had been given an early release date and she searched the internet to see if anything popped up but everything she read had his release date as the end of January at the earliest. If that was true, and Sebastian Calver was the Romeo

Robber, he couldn't have stolen the Ghirlandaio from The National Gallery.

But then, who had?

Amelia did another search for the two Ghirlandaio paintings. It felt strange to look at the portrait of Cesare Borgia, knowing it was currently languishing in a poster tube in Stone Manor.

Then she brought up the painting of Lucrezia Borgia, along with some interesting facts about her life, including information of her penchant for dispatching her enemies with the poison, cantarella, which she'd kept in a silver ring she wore and sprinkled over her unsuspecting victim's food.

'I would not have liked to have gotten on the wrong side of you,' Amelia muttered as she stared at the painting of the infamous Italian noblewoman.

There was something incredibly familiar about it, though, she thought. She stared at the picture a while longer, unable to shake the nagging feeling.

She checked her watch and reluctantly shut down her laptop as she realised she'd need to get back to the hotel to help with the preparations for the wedding.

As Constable Williams had predicted, because the Detective Inspector had to get to Glencarlach from Inverness, the local area had jumped up in priority for getting the roads cleared. As Amelia and Jack walked up to Stone Manor, they saw that the front of the hotel was cluttered with police cars as well as the local florist's van.

On entering Stone Manor, a tall, grey man in his late fifties came over and introduced himself as Detective Inspector McGregor. He did not seem happy. 'I'll be leaving some officers in the hotel to ensure the guests and staff can't leave until we get further statements.'

'Oh, the irony!' Gideon remarked. He was leaning over the reception desk. 'Snowed in for days and now the roads *are* cleared, we're not allowed to leave at all!'

The DI gave him a long look before turning back to Amelia. 'I understand you and Mr Temple live on the grounds?'

'Yes, the Gatehouse.'

'Do you now think it's definitely another homicide?' Jack asked.

McGregor gave him a cool look. 'We call it murder over here. And to be honest, given Mrs Maxwell's history of heart problems going by the medication she takes, coupled with the amount of partying she's been doing, I fully expect her demise to be a natural death, despite what your village constable thinks. Clearly erring on the side of caution, he's taken it to the top brass, whilst doing a very thorough job of questioning the guests.'

The way he said 'very thorough' suggested to Amelia the detective inspector wasn't meaning it as a compliment.

'Obviously we'll know more after the post-mortem, or *autopsy*, if you're more comfortable with that term,' McGregor said giving Jack a cool look. 'Although I wasn't keen to disturb even more of the force on Boxing Day for something that is most probably an outcome of poor health and lifestyle choices, I was persuaded that I had to leave no stone unturned. I also believe that you, Ms Adams, discovered Mrs Maxwell?'

'Well, I opened the door to the bar and there she was, if that means discovering...'

'Hmm. And you were also the only witness to the death of Mr Benedict Geissler at the folly in the grounds of Stone Manor?'

'Yes. Yes I was.'

'And you were part of the party who stumbled across Kit Trelawny, also on your property, and he is currently in hospital recovering from a suspicious head injury.'

'Yes,' Amelia said faintly. The way Detective Inspector McGregor put it, her involvement at best sounded ludicrously coincidental and at worst, rather incriminating.

'Well, rest assured, if this does turn out to be foul play, I'll be starting my inquiries with you,' he said with a wintry smile. 'Oh, and one more thing, Constable Williams took statements from everyone apart from…' He flicked open his notebook and scanned the page. 'Mr Griffin in the Simenon Room.'

'Yes, no one has had any contact with him after he checked in.'

'We'll need access to his room.'

'Of course.' Amelia led them up the stairs and got out the pass key. She opened it up wondering what mess she'd find this time and how many more bottles would be littered across the floor. But when she opened the door she couldn't believe the scene before her.

Everything was gone; the bed was made; and the side table had been cleaned so none of the white powder remained. A quick glance into the en suite showed it to be completely empty also.

There was no indication that anyone had ever been there.

Mr Griffin had seemingly vanished into thin air.

CHAPTER 43

Over the next three hours, along with a huge number of police, the wedding photographer arrived, as did all the other Stone Manor staff and it was all hands on deck as word got out the roads were cleared. Even Sally had managed to get back and immediately became ensconced with Lucy, getting her ready.

The massive ice sculpture of two swans had been delivered, placed on a silver plinth in the middle of the dining room. Amelia was greatly relieved at this as she'd been worried she'd have to drag in a lump of ice from the garden and get creative with a chisel and bread knife.

The forensics team had dusted the bar for prints and had photographed every inch of the room. They did this with the Simenon Room as well as the Vargas Room. As soon as they left, James and Craig went in armed with J-cloths and Mr Muscle.

Gideon had arranged the roses beautifully, which were still blooming and fresh, thanks to the cool temperatures of the storage rooms, and the local florist had excelled themself with the arrangements, which included the bride's bouquet and the buttonholes and corsages.

Doves cooed gently in ornate golden cages and Lucy had

agreed to keep them as a decorative feature rather than setting them into the wild to fend for themselves in the cold temperatures. Toby put the finishing touches to the wedding buffet Carlo and Lucy had requested instead of a formal sit-down meal, and in the spirit of generosity, Carlo had invited the other guests of the hotel to the wedding and buffet. The invitation had been readily accepted by Betty, the Johnsons and Nisha. Despite the death and possible murder of Vanessa hanging over Stone Manor, the atmosphere was surprisingly upbeat.

As the photographer mingled with the guests, taking snaps, Lorcan came over to Amelia. 'I'm going to head off to the village hall to get everything ready for the art exhibition and tomorrow's auction.'

'I hope you make it back in time for the buffet.'

'I should. I've been cataloguing all the pieces as they've been coming in.'

Amelia stood back a little and watched the guests milling about. Rev McDade chatted to Carlo and Terence in front of the mantelpiece where the ceremony was going to be conducted. The Kings stood with Ricky, making light conversation. Another little group had formed with Nisha, Evangelina, Betty and the Johnsons. Although the scene was set for a happy occasion, Amelia couldn't help but look at everyone with suspicion. One of the guests at Stone Manor was a cold-blooded killer. Her attention focused on Carlo who was still Amelia's number-one suspect.

Carlo looked very relaxed in a navy-blue suit and dark tan shoes. But then, why would a killer with no conscience look stressed or guilty.

There was a sudden hush and a moment later, the string quartet which was nestled into the reception area began to play. Amelia turned. Standing at the top of the stairs was Lucy Carvalho, looking beautiful in her wedding dress, which hung from her delicate frame like a waterfall of satin. Sally, a little behind the bride, had transformed an already beautiful woman into an absolutely stunning one. Lucy's make-up was flawless and understated and her long dark hair was half caught up in a tiara, with the rest hanging in shiny ripples down her back.

Sally waved down at Amelia and Amelia gave her a thumbs-up of approval in reply.

Pausing at the top, for maximum impact and for the photographer to get a few more shots, Lucy waited a moment before gliding down the stairs. Everyone's eyes were on her, even some of the waiting staff had paused to get a look of the bride. Amelia was rather amused to see James had a huge soppy grin on his face.

Craig stood a little behind James, leaning against the door jamb of the bar, and Amelia thought he looked sad. He self-consciously touched the cut on his head and frowned, then slipped away, back into the bar, shoulders hunched. Amelia supposed not everyone loved weddings, depending on their own personal history and it struck Amelia how little she knew about Craig Cameron, the nomadic, mixologist. Had he started his camper van cocktail work as a result of a broken heart?

As Lucy walked slowly by, beaming with joy, and possibly just a little bit of smug satisfaction, Amelia could see the glorious dress up close. It had a beautifully scalloped neckline which showed off Lucy's chunky silver pendant perfectly.

As the bride joined her groom in front of the minister and all the guests took their seats, Amelia once again had the sensation of trying to grasp at smoke as something began to bother her. But this time, instead of it fading wispily into the ether, the thought took on a form. Something nagged at her as she looked at all the Stone Manor residents before her.

Amelia's stomach knotted apprehensively as she went over to the framed newspaper cutting all about Stone Manor, with the controversial Poirot cat painting in the background.

Amelia reread it, despite having almost dedicated the article to memory. Then she peered a little closer.

And she finally understood why Vanessa had been so fascinated by it.

Suddenly the jigsaw was taking shape for Amelia. She looked over at Carlo who stared adoringly at his wife-to-be.

Yes, all the pieces were coming together perfectly.

CHAPTER 44

It was a beautiful ceremony. The guests all watched as Lucy Carvalho married Carlo Todero, exchanging personal vows with such a heartfelt sincerity there was barely a dry eye in the house. Amelia watched it all with an emotional detachment and wished they'd hurry up and get on with it so she could escape; Amelia desperately needed to speak to Lorcan!

Finally, as the service ended and the string quartet played something classical and tasteful that Amelia vaguely recognised from a television advert, the register was signed. Passing on a rather garbled message to Gideon, Amelia made her escape, taking the Jeep for speed.

Thankfully Lorcan was still in the village hall. He was surrounded by large felt screens, on which some paintings were already hanging. He was looking down at a table that was covered in spreadsheets and pages of adhesive red dots.

'Hey, Amelia,' he said, glancing up as she hurried over.

'Where's my painting? Is it still here?'

'Uh, yes, it's over...' He stood up and looked around, tugging thoughtfully on his goatee.

The knot in Amelia's stomach intensified as Lorcan was

clearly struggling to remember where he'd put it. Then he went over to a pile of stacked up canvases and pulled out the gaudy and quite ridiculous painting of the cat dressed as Poirot.

'Here we go! But... hang on.'

It was just as Amelia suspected.

'I'm sorry, that should have a red dot on it to indicate it's not for the auction!' Lorcan said, looking puzzled as he picked at the green dot on the top right of the painting.

'I know, but the person who broke in here wasn't looking to steal the painting. They were looking to get it into the auction to make a bid for it.'

'But why?'

'How easy is it to paint over an existing painting?' Amelia asked Lorcan.

'I do it all the time, if I start something I don't like. It saves on money and the time it takes to stretch out a new canvas.'

'But could you do it in a way to hide the painting below and then be able to reveal it at a later date?'

'Yes, it would need a lot of skill to make sure the original painting wasn't damaged – but definitely possible.'

Feeling more excited than ever, Amelia got out the gallery guide from The National Gallery that Benedict Geissler had had in his camper van. She flipped to the right page then thrust it at Lorcan, pointing at the lost painting of Lucrezia Borgia.

He looked at the image for a moment and Amelia waited. It took another minute or so until Lorcan let out an expletive and then looked at Amelia's cat painting.

'What the... Oh my God! It's... But how...'

'Dotty always said part of the appeal of the painting was how incongruous the frame was, as if the painting was really trying to punch above its weight!'

'Because the real painting this hid was by one of the best Florentine Renaissance artists and worthy of this type of frame.'

Amelia got out her phone and googled the image of the

painting, zooming in on the ornate surround and put it beside the painting her godmother had bought in a charity shop. It was identical, right down to the little nick in the bottom right of the frame.

'Would you be able to see if the painting is definitely underneath?' Amelia asked Lorcan.

'Yes, you can do infrared scanning, there's multi-spectral imaging technology, all sorts of ways science can determine what lies beneath. Hidden works are found all the time, by the likes of Van Gogh, Picasso, even da Vinci.' He picked up the painting and very lightly ran his fingers over the surface. 'Look, see the slightly cracked appearance on the surface, I'm pretty sure that there's an oil painting under this, as it draws out all the moisture from the acrylic paint that covers it.'

'Is there something that can be used to do a quick check that doesn't rely on expensive technology?'

'Rubbing alcohol would remove the acrylic paint.'

'Have you got any here?'

Lorcan paled slightly. 'But what if I ruined the painting?! A lost masterpiece found then destroyed in moments!'

'Maybe just a bit on the bottom?'

'But, Amelia!' Lorcan looked pained.

'We may not have long before the murderer gets away, possibly with two stolen paintings. And maybe another victim! We have to try!'

Lorcan pulled at his goatee and shook his head slightly as he looked at the painting before him.

'Just a tiny bit, Amelia. This section in the middle at the bottom, with her hands resting on a prayer book. I could try a bit there and see if the colours come up in a similar tone.'

Just then the door opened and Sally and Gideon came in. He produced the poster tube containing the portrait of Cesare Borgia from under his coat. Automatically, Gideon flipped the lock over on the door.

'The guests are on their second glass of champagne. Toby and Jack are poised to keep everyone busy with food and drink. What's going on?' Gideon asked as he and Sally came nearer. Lorcan had a bottle of something clear and spirity smelling which he was tipping onto a clean cloth.

'I may be about to ruin a priceless piece of art,' Lorcan mumbled before gently dabbing at the bottom centre of the painting, his hand shaking as he did so. The dark paint lifted almost instantly revealing bright white underneath.

'Is that meant to look like that?' Gideon asked in horror as they all leaned in closer to Lorcan.

'It is as if it's been covered by a couple of layers of titanium white, which is what I'd do if I was trying to disguise a 500-year-old painting. Here we go.'

And then, with tiny, gentle dabs from the cloth, another layer came through. This one was of a rich brown with little flecks of gold. Lorcan stood up and exhaled.

'That could be the spine of the book she's holding!' Amelia gasped.

Without a word, Lorcan resumed the painstakingly slow reveal, moving slightly to the right where more paint cleared away to reveal a pale creamy white.

Lorcan stood back and zoomed in on the image of the painting on Amelia's phone. 'That could be her fingers, resting on the book. Right, I'm not doing any more, it needs a proper restorer to carry it out, but I'm pretty certain, from what's been revealed, this is Ghirlandaio's panting of Lucrezia Borgia. Especially taking into account the other painting,' he gestured to the poster tube.

'Remember Vanessa said that when the police raided the rooms of the Romeo Robber there were only a couple of stolen paintings recovered; the rest were his own, far inferior works so the police thought they only had a small haul, but if they'd paid attention to all the pieces, they'd have found–'

'Millions of pounds worth of art he painted over,' Lorcan finished in wonderment.

'Bloody hell!' Sally said. 'I'm gone barely forty-eight hours and all this has happened!'

'It looks like we've finally reunited brother and sister,' Amelia said.

Amelia suddenly felt incredibly emotional to think the silly painting would soon be gone forever and wished her godmother, Dotty, was on hand to share the story with. Dotty would have revelled in the drama the painting was causing, and that she'd unwittingly bought a rare, concealed, Renaissance masterpiece. Amelia could imagine them sitting cosily together in the drawing room, either side of the fire in the wing-backed chairs, tears of mirth rolling down their cheeks at the absurdity of it all. The vision was so real a wave of grief hit Amelia like a physical blow and the image of the painting before her swam with unshed tears.

Wordlessly, Gideon put his arm around Amelia.

'So, what do you suggest we do? Have a last-minute special double addition to the exhibition! That would certainly make the front page of the *Wester Ross Chronicle*!' Gideon said.

'Well, it would be one way of flushing out the murderer!' Amelia said, clearing her throat and composing herself. 'But I think we need to be a little more subtle. I think we need to set a scene.'

'Oh?' Gideon said, interest obviously piqued. 'And would you need the skills of a fabulously talented, not to mention extremely handsome actor in the setting of this scene?'

'She will, but you'll do as a last resort,' Sally quipped and swiped him on the arm to show she was joking.

CHAPTER 45

By eight o'clock that evening, the ceilidh band was in full swing. The wedding guests, having drunk and eaten for most of the day, were attempting a Dashing White Sergeant.

It was almost as if there hadn't been a death, Amelia thought as she watched the guests giggling as they whirled each other around the area in the dining room that had been cleared for dancing. Even Terence was up on the floor, laughing uproariously, his kilt swinging, as he attempted a reel of three with Nisha and Betty but kept going the wrong way, causing them to bang into each other.

With the guests and most of the staff busy, Amelia went into the kitchen where Jack, Gideon, Toby and Lorcan were deep in conversation.

'How's it going?' Amelia asked, joining them at the table.

'Good, they all seem happy and distracted next door.'

'A bit too happy, don't you think?' Gideon said. 'I hope when it's my time, there's a bit of mourning, I'm not saying mirrors should be covered and everyone wears black for a year, but a little grieving would be good. A tear or two at the very least.'

'Maybe they're crying on the inside,' Toby suggested.

'Do you think they're assuming it's natural causes?' Gideon wondered. 'But regardless of the outcome, Vanessa is still dead!'

'There's no way it wasn't murder. And at least one other person knows it too,' Amelia said.

'But no one is acting any different,' Jack said grimly.

'It's cold,' Toby agreed.

'And, I don't know if anyone has thought about it, but where does that leave us if Vanessa was the Secret Guest?' Gideon said.

Toby shook his head. 'I really don't think we should be dwelling on that.'

'Well, she seemed rather annoyed with us, remember? What if she sent in a copy after that little exchange?'

'To be honest, Gideon, I'm not so sure Vanessa was the Secret Guest. I think she met her fancy men at those establishments, and that was her only connection,' Amelia said. 'She must have thought that was what we'd stumbled upon.'

Gideon pulled a face. 'I suppose. Where would she have found the time to write reviews, between conducting affairs, ruining the lives of actors and other agents and blackmailing her friends. There's only so much multitasking one woman can do.'

'But who else could it be?' Jack wondered.

'To be honest, I don't really want to know the sort of review we'd get with us being snowed in, having power cuts and being a real-life crime scene!' Toby said, taking a couple of trays of leftovers from the buffet and putting them on the table. Amelia pounced on some delicious looking prawn wontons.

'Well, the good news is, the Glencarlach Winter Festival Art Auction will be held tomorrow, and if you're right, Amelia, we can hopefully draw a line under everything,' Lorcan said, helping himself to a miniature pastry filled with beef and horseradish.

'And I spoke to Constable Williams,' Amelia said, not caring she was speaking with her mouth full. 'They're hoping the autopsy result will be in by the afternoon. If I'm right, he'll have Detective Inspector McGregor in tow, too.'

'Oh, deep joy!' Gideon said. 'He's such a ray of sunshine!'

Jack sighed. 'I'm worried this is going to backfire. We're up against a killer.'

'That's why we're keeping all this just amongst ourselves.'

'The inner circle,' Gideon added, reverentially.

'But we have to lure them out somehow,' Amelia pointed out, although she knew her plan was risky.

Just then the back door opened and a rather pale Kit walked in. 'They let me out!' he said with a tired grin, his eyes lighting up at the plate of buffet food on the table.

'Under strict instructions to take it easy or I'll be taking you straight back in again,' Sally said, following him in.

Toby patted Kit on the back as he drew out a chair for him.

'I used my connections to run Carlo's name against the next few ferries and flights. They've flagged them up and they'll ping me if Carlo or his registration number appears against a booking,' Kit said spearing a king prawn as he sat down.

Sally turned to him, appalled. 'Names? Flights? Ferries? Have you been investigating?' She narrowed her eyes suspiciously.

'All from my phone and a laptop a very kind nurse lent me whilst I lay in bed! It's what I do, cuz. Investigative journalist? Clue's kind of in the title.'

Sally gave him a withering look. 'If you do it again, I'll tell your mum.'

Kit rolled his eyes but didn't argue.

'Shall we put the first part of the plan into action? The band are due to have a break in about five minutes,' Amelia said, taking a step away from the delicious food.

Lorcan nodded and stood up as Jack reached under his seat and got the poster tube, handing it to Gideon.

'Is it in there?' Gideon asked.

'The copy is. I wonder if this was the same sleight of hand Geissler had planned.'

'And the original?' Amelia asked.

'Rolled up inside my welly boot in the wardrobe,' Lorcan said.

'And my poster is still in there too?' Jack checked, worriedly.

'Yes. But we've also put a tiny tracking device in there with it. We're hoping that if they know where it'll be for the next twenty-four hours it'll be one of the last things they'll take before leaving,' Amelia said, with a lot more conviction than she felt. 'I'll go and get Craig to bring in some more drinks to the dining room,' Amelia said. 'See you in five!'

Craig was restocking the fridge in the bar. The swelling on his face had definitely reduced but it still looked painful. He flinched slightly as Amelia walked up beside him, then smiled on seeing who it was.

'Let's take another couple of bottles through,' Amelia said. 'The band's due to go on a break in a moment and I'm guessing the wedding party will be thirsty after all that dancing!'

Craig began gathering glasses.

They timed it perfectly. The band had just announced the interval and had laid down their instruments to follow Toby through to the bar for refreshments as Amelia and Craig arrived in the dining room. A quick glance around the room confirmed that none of the guests were missing and that Lorcan had joined Evangelina and Nisha at one of the tables. Everyone seemed relaxed.

Just then Gideon burst through the door and made a beeline for Lorcan, calling his name and waving the poster tube above his head.

'Oh my God! Lorcan! I can't believe what I've done! Jack's going to kill me! It's that American football poster he wants you to frame, I must have gathered it up when I was helping you at the village hall with the exhibition and taken it home by accident! I just came across it when I popped back home!'

'Oh, don't worry, I'd totally forgotten about that!' Lorcan said walking over to Gideon and taking the poster tube off him. 'I've not had a chance to think about framing it yet, what with the exhibition–'

'And the auction!' Amelia interjected as she poured champagne. 'Don't worry, I'll speak to Jack,' she added. 'He'll be fine waiting. We may even have to hold on to it until we find a bigger house, especially as I'm not that keen on American football!' Laying down the glass she went and took the poster tube from Gideon and began walking out the dining room.

'Amelia!' Lorcan called after her. 'Just leave it in the bar for now, I'll take it home with me when I check out, and I'll take a look in the new year.'

'Sure,' Amelia said as she took the poster tube through to the bar and propped it up against the wall, in a very obvious spot. Her heart was beating wildly as she closed over the door and headed back to the dining room where everyone was milling about and chatting naturally as they waited for the band to return. She hoped their little performance had been natural enough to not be suspicious.

Now all they had to do was wait.

CHAPTER 46

27TH DECEMBER

Lorcan had been stationed by the front door of the art exhibition since the moment it opened. He'd refused all the complimentary teas and coffees the fair committee kept trying to foist on him. He didn't want to have to leave his post for a second as he didn't fancy explaining that the stolen Renaissance painting had been re-stolen while he was on a comfort break.

Sally was situated at the back fire exit – the only other way in or out – and was handing out a list of all the items which were to be included in the auction later. Halfway down was Amelia's Poirot cat.

Evangelina had arrived with Nisha and Terence and it had taken every ounce of Lorcan's self-restraint to not tell Evangelina what was going on; and to not kiss her. To be honest, the desire to kiss her was definitely outweighing the urge to catch her up on recent events, but to be on the safe side he did neither and kept resolutely behind the table, pretending to be busy by shuffling lots of paper and stapling things together.

Toby and Gideon arrived mid-afternoon. Without saying a word Gideon raised a questioning eyebrow.

Lorcan shook his head knowing exactly who Gideon was wondering about.

'Hasn't turned up yet, but don't worry, there's plenty of time; the auction doesn't start until five,' he said quietly.

Toby and Gideon went off to look at the paintings the people had handed in. Some were from those who attended his art classes; some were old family pieces that were of local historical interest to show how the Glencarlach landscape and harbour had changed over the years. There were two paintings from Lorcan and from another artist who lived and worked a few miles away. And as promised, Lorcan had included some lovely natural photographs of the locals. There was even a special exhibition from the children at the local primary school he helped out in. It was a glorious mish-mash of styles and skills with all the auction proceeds going to nearby charities.

Lorcan looked up and couldn't help but glance at the Poirot cat, focusing on the spot he'd hastily painted back over with acrylic, then used a hairdryer on to speed up the drying process.

'I see Amelia changed her mind about putting it into the auction,' Betty said swanning up to Lorcan.

'Ah yes,' Lorcan said. 'She was persuaded it's not the sort of art that's suitable for Stone Manor,' he said cheerily. 'And the charity auction is for such good causes. Do you think you'll be making a bid for it, Betty?' he asked.

A look of horror flickered briefly over her face before she smiled. 'Well, I have to be very careful with my purchases, being on a pension, you know. And I don't think it would fit with my other pieces, dear. Oh, I need a top up!' Betty patted Lorcan's hand and hastily made a beeline for one of the volunteers handing out tea.

'I think you've just upset her bohemian sensibilities!' Toby said with a smile as he and Gideon wandered back over.

Just then Kit came in, glancing around the room before joining Lorcan, Toby and Gideon, pushing his black hair out of his eyes. He looked very serious. 'Amelia's hunch was right,' he said taking his phone from his pocket and pressing a few keys before turning the screen towards them. 'Look at the name booked on tomorrow's ferry.'

They looked.

'Tonight's the night then,' Lorcan said as the others nodded in agreement.

Lorcan looked at his watch again. Less than two hours to go until the auction. He really did wish he could have a drink as he definitely needed something to help steady his nerves.

The Glencarlach Winter Fair Committee had decided to move the charity auction out of the rather cold and draughty village hall and into the Whistling Haggis, eschewing the hot water urns producing rather lacklustre tea and coffee for the far more appealing lure of spirit optics and draught beer. The official line was that people's generosity would flow more freely if fuelled by a whisky or two.

Those of a more cynical disposition thought Big Davey (also a board member of the committee) was looking out for his profits. No matter the reason, Lorcan thought the Whistling Haggis was a far preferable venue as he looked round the bar which was now standing room only. He could see that one of the booths at the back was taken by Amelia, Jack, Toby, Hamish and Kit.

Gideon and Sally had helped bring the paintings and photographs over the road for the auction and now they'd helped Lorcan set up, Sally joined Amelia at her table and Gideon stayed up front to be Lorcan's 'glamorous assistant' as he kept telling everyone.

Big Davey plonked a pint of export in front of Lorcan. 'It'll help wet your whistle,' he said with a wink and Lorcan took a very grateful swallow of his drink.

Lorcan, as chief auctioneer, all set with a gavel at the top of the bar, was ready to go as sheets of A4 paper with numbers on them were handed out to the tables to aid with the bidding.

All the guests from Stone Manor were in attendance at various tables. Right at the front, Evangelina sat with Nisha, and Lorcan really hoped her presence there wasn't just so she could add to her art collection. All this catching an art thief business was playing havoc with his love life. Or potential love life.

Right on 5pm, Big Davey rang the last orders bell to get everyone's attention and the auction was underway! First up was the schoolchildren's artwork as one by one parents and grandparents dutifully bid on their child's masterpiece.

'And I'm sure you will treasure Ryan's crayon depiction of Santa vs Godzilla for many years to come!' Lorcan said, banging his gavel down as a parent took ownership of the rather violent anime-inspired picture. 'And now we come to the work produced by our local artists whom I've had the pleasure of mentoring this last year. First up is *Harbour at Sunrise* by Jean Maddox.'

Gideon popped the painting by the popular shop owner on the easel and stood back to let the room see it. Jean clearly had a talent for art and Lorcan had found her a pleasure to teach as she took on board all his tuition and advice. Her painting elicited quite a bit of interest and two bidding parties quickly bumped up the price. Jean was delighted when Lorcan lowered the gavel on quite a considerable amount of money, as the owner of the yacht that had been most prominent in the scene went up to collect his lot and put a pile of money in the jar on the bar.

'Now we have handsome horse portrait of Solomon,' Lorcan said as Gideon put the painting on display. 'I'm going to start the bidding at fifty pounds.'

It soon rose in price, with Terence being one of the bidders. He'd clearly come with the view of getting it and there was quite an intense focus to him when he and another man went head-to-head over it. Eventually, Terence called out a huge jump in price and his fellow bidder indicated he wouldn't be continuing.

'Well, I suppose he has free rein to enjoy all his equine interests seeing as Vanessa's out of the picture now,' Gideon whispered to Lorcan as a triumphant Terence collected his painting. 'And maybe horses won't be his only pursuits,' Gideon added with a raised eyebrow when Terence paused to chat with Nisha, who admired his new acquisition and gave him a kiss on the cheek.

Next up were a couple of landscapes and simple watercolour of the church, which Rev McDade was delighted to purchase.

Lorcan could feel his palms grow clammy as Amelia's painting came closer to the bidding.

'And now we have a rather unique piece in our auction. The unusual subject matter of Agatha Christie's great detective Poirot depicted as a cat,' Lorcan said, surprised that he sounded so natural, as Gideon placed the painting on the easel. 'Now, originally Amelia hadn't intended to sell it. I'm afraid I must have mixed up the stickers – instead of getting me to change them back, Amelia has very kindly decided to continue with it for the auction.'

'Because I'll burn it if we don't get rid of it!' Gideon said loudly to the bar as everyone laughed.

They had decided to acknowledge the sticker change and go along with it so as not to arouse suspicion and Lorcan hoped it had all sounded plausible.

'But don't let my woeful lack of art appreciation put you off bidding for it! I think it just needs the right setting!' Gideon said.

'I'm going to start it off at ten pounds!' Lorcan said.

Getting into the spirit of her role, Lorcan saw Amelia hold up the piece of paper with her number on it. 'It's worth more than that! I bid twenty to keep it and torture Gideon!'

Lorcan laughed along as someone shouted out, 'Twenty-two.'

Then in a heart-stopping moment, Lorcan saw Carlo raise his number in the air and shout, 'Thirty!'

Lorcan was desperate to drop his gavel and shout out an immediate 'Sold' but he had to act naturally and try and bump up the price as he had with all the other submissions. He looked around the room. 'Come on, any advancement on thirty? It's an original!'

To his horror, Big Davey shouted out, 'Thirty-five!'

Lorcan's mouth went dry. This was not part of the plan! He couldn't risk his friend purchasing it! Not if it was a possibility he'd be murdered for owning it! Wordlessly he looked back round at Carlo and gave him a hopeful look. 'Do we have forty?'

'You can have fifty!' Carlo said with a laugh.

Lorcan whipped his attention round to the landlord but Davey pulled a face. 'Too rich for me!'

And it was with momentous relief Lorcan turned back round to Carlo and banged his gavel on the bar before anyone else could put in a sneaky bid. 'Poirot cat sold to number 27, Carlo Todero.'

CHAPTER 47

As it turned out, pretty much everyone headed back to Stone Manor at the same time.

'I never cared a jot about it when it hung on the wall behind the reception desk but that was before I knew what lay underneath. Now I'm bloody terrified they'll drop it!' Toby said as they saw Carlo stumble in the snow, causing the painting to slip slightly out his grasp.

'We have to pretend it's still the same awful, worthless painting as before and we've no idea what it really is,' Gideon said.

'It's not that bad!' Amelia protested.

'It is!' Jack, Toby, Gideon and Kit all replied.

Amelia hoped the bubble wrap Lorcan had used would be enough to protect it.

Lorcan, who'd already said he couldn't bear to watch it being carried so carelessly had gone ahead.

'Have you got a plan?' Jack asked Amelia as they walked hand in hand along the driveway.

'I do. Catch the bad guy.'

'Great. Then we can celebrate Christmas! And how do you propose to catch the bad guy?'

'Well, that's going to be a bit trickier.' She paused as her phone pinged with a text message. She was heartened to see that it was one of the two people she was hoping to hear from.

'Beniamino!' Amelia said as she read what he'd sent. Even in text Beniamino Vincenzi, the director at the helm of the Stone Manor documentary, was as effusive as he was in person. She scanned through all his greetings and well-wishes and suggestions they shoot another series before she got to the information she needed. 'Bingo! Beniamino *did* know Vanessa. She called him a few days before she arrived here to ask him about Stone Manor and to get the low-down on all the secret passages.' Amelia pocketed her phone, saying, 'Well, that solves *that* mystery!'

'It does?' Jack said.

'It does,' Amelia said firmly.

'And the rest of your plan?'

'The immediate plan is Lorcan's going to get Craig to set out some drinks in the drawing room and then go and check to see if someone's taken the bait and taken the painting from the bar.'

'I realise in the grand scheme of art, my poster isn't as worthy or as important, but I really hope, if they have removed the Ghirlandaio, they've left my poster.'

Amelia gave Jack's hand a supportive squeeze as they carried on. But even if the painting had gone, there was nothing else Amelia could do until she heard from Constable Williams. And if her hunch wasn't right... well, she'd be back at square one.

Back at Stone Manor, James steered everyone into the drawing room where the fire was roaring and Craig had set up some refreshments. Everyone seemed happy enough to sit around, making small talk before dinner. Lorcan came up to Amelia and whispered, 'The painting's gone,' then added to Jack, 'don't worry, your poster's still there and unharmed.' He mouthed

'Good Luck' to Amelia as he also went into the drawing room and took his place on the window seat.

Amelia's phone rang and she felt a frisson of excitement and fear when she saw it was Constable Williams. Part one of their plan had worked. Was she now on the right track with her next hunch?

'Amelia, Constable Williams here. I'm on my way.' There was a lot of background noise and it sounded like he was in a car. She could make out someone else talking over the noise of the engine.

'Have you got Detective Inspector McGregor with you?'

'I do. He's slightly sceptical that you've worked out what's happened but he's willing to hear you out.'

'It's quite a long-involved story but we think we've enough evidence,' she held up her crossed fingers to Jack.

'I'm sure you will have, Amelia.'

'So, are the results of the post-mortem in? Was I right?' She held her breath.

She could hear Ray give a slight chuckle down the phone. 'They are, Amelia! And, by Jove, how on *earth* did you work out what Mrs Maxwell would be poisoned with?'

'That's part of what I'll be explaining when you get here,' she said.

'Well, just make sure you keep everyone there!'

Amelia said goodbye then hung up just as Terence put his glass of orange juice down on a tray and came over to Amelia.

'I've decided I want to check out now, just in case the weather turns and we get snowed in again. We've heard nothing more from Constable Williams or that chap from Inverness. They've got my address anyway, so know where I am if they have any more questions. If I drive through the night I can get a clear run. I need to make arrangements for, you know...' He trailed off and then turned back to the group, 'Nisha, my dear? Are you wanting a lift to London? If Kit's going to be staying on for a few days he can keep the hire car you both came up in?'

'Thank you, Terence, I do need to get back and it's probably best you're not on your own at the moment,' Nisha said sincerely, placing her hand lightly on his arm.

'That's not too bad an idea. How about we do something similar?' Carlo said to Lucy. 'We can get home and take a bit more time getting ready for our honeymoon?'

'That sounds wonderful,' Lucy agreed. 'My husband has all the good ideas,' she said with a smile.

Ricky glanced over at Evangelina. 'I, uh, I think I'll do the same, I'm going to go and pack.'

Amelia's mouth went dry. This wasn't meant to happen! She needed to keep them all at Stone Manor until she had a chance to explain her theories to Constable Williams and Detective Inspector McGregor! But she hadn't thought to ask how long they'd be as no one was due to be checking out until the morning! Amelia glanced over her shoulder in the hope she'd see Ray driving up with the blues and twos on, but she was out of luck.

She couldn't let the murderer get away!

She needed to do something, and it had to be now. But what? She couldn't very well tell them all her actual theory on what happened to Vanessa!

Or could she?

It would certainly be one way to keep them enthralled.

CHAPTER 48

Amelia glanced at Jack and Toby, and nodded her head towards the door. Luckily Jack picked up her silent message and moved over so he was blocking anyone's quick get-away, ready to act as security if needed. Craig continued to hand out the teas and coffees and while everyone's attention was on him, Amelia dug into her pocket to find her phone and pressed a couple of buttons before surreptitiously placing it on the table beside her.

Amelia held off talking until Craig had gone round the room. Then she cleared her throat. 'I had planned on saying a few words before you all checked out, but because some of you are cutting your stay a little short, there's no time like the present.

'Obviously your stay is now coming to an end and it's been an eventful one for you all. As my brother, Toby, likes to point out, Glencarlach is normally a sleepy little village and so the events of the last few days have rocked our community. As well as the sad news of Vanessa passing, the church was broken into with some items being stolen. A man was murdered up at the folly.' Amelia paused as there were a few murmurs around the room at this as clearly not everyone had heard. 'Betty had an intruder; Carlo thought he'd been robbed; towels were stolen and turned up covered in blood; Kit was found near death; Lorcan was knocked unconscious in his studio; Jack and I were broken into; and there was the mysterious Mr Griffin who simply disappeared, leading many to believe he was behind some of the events during your stay.'

Amelia paused again as she took in the room before her.

'That's a lot of undesirable happenings for an otherwise quiet little community. Let's begin with the robbery at the church. Everyone agreed it was an awful thing to happen. The pantomime props and two valuable lanterns were stolen, along with, strangely, a large bunch of lilies. Teenagers having a laugh was the first suspicion. But the flowers? Hardly the thing teenagers steal during a crime spree.'

'Then of course there was the unexplained death of Benedict Geissler at the folly. At first it was presumed he'd had a heart attack but the post-mortem revealed something far more sinister. He was poisoned. With a lethal injection of potassium cyanide.'

There were a couple of gasps. Amelia definitely had everyone's attention now.

'Originally I thought all these strange happenings must be linked, and I was completely flummoxed – until I realised I was looking at different crimes. Benedict Geissler and Vanessa's death were connected but the robbery at the church was an entirely unconnected crime. Wasn't it, Ricky?'

Ricky's head shot up as Evangelina turned and frowned at him.

'How long had you and Vanessa been having an affair?' Amelia asked.

Nisha let out an exasperated sigh and shook her head as Evangelina looked on impassively. Terence too stared at Ricky, leaning slightly forward in his chair, waiting for the answer.

Ricky's mouth opened and shut a couple of times in surprise before he quietly said, 'About three years.'

'Evie,' Nisha said, looking at her friend in concern.

'I think both Evangelina and Terence had known for a while,' Amelia said, gently.

'You weren't the first, old boy,' Terence said to Ricky. 'You were the closest one to me that she picked though. That really twisted the knife.'

'Your little conversation on Christmas Eve about footwear didn't go unnoticed, Terence,' Amelia said. 'And obviously, Evangelina, you were carrying around the divorce papers to give to Ricky, an indication that something was seriously wrong. That's why you invited your best friend here. To act as moral support.'

Evangelina turned to Amelia. 'How did you know?'

'Vanessa had been adamant she needed to have a room directly next to the suite she and Terence shared. And it had to be north facing, for her art, which meant only one room was suitable. The other room next to their suite, the Marsh Room, was west-facing, which wouldn't do at all.'

'Oh, I'm in the Marsh Room,' Betty said to the group, helping herself to a shortbread finger and settling back into her chair.

'I was slightly concerned about giving Vanessa the Vargas Room because it was an interconnecting one, to the Simenon Room that had been specifically reserved by a Mr Griffin. But Vanessa didn't seem concerned, because that had been the plan all along. Ricky was Mr Griffin.'

There were a couple of gasps.

'The original Invisible Man!' Gideon piped up from reclining languorously on an ottoman.

'You were keen to receive a package from Amazon, and got quite agitated when it hadn't appeared. Then, when it did arrive a couple of days after you'd been expecting it, I saw you dump it, unopened, at the Christmas Eve nativity walk. I retrieved it from the bin and discovered the contents to be a torch, a wig, hat, fake beards and moustaches and glasses. These were amongst the items stolen from the church.

'Then, when you checked in as Mr Griffin, wearing the stolen pantomime disguises, it was after one in the morning, and our night porter was surprised that you didn't appear to have been battling through the elements. By this point Glencarlach had been cut off for many hours. You had no transport and you hadn't been whiling away your time in the Whistling Haggis. I believe you took advantage of a point when Davey wasn't at the reception desk and then made your way outside, where you could keep watch and "arrive" once he was back at his post. Although it was late, you didn't want to risk being inside the hotel in your disguise for too long in case someone recognised you. And I believe you were on your phone at this time, which was the light Betty saw in the grounds of the hotel. On getting to your room, you hung the Do Not Disturb sign on the door, unlocked the interconnecting door and waited for Vanessa to appear.

'Obviously you knew about the secret passageway that led to the cellar, as Vanessa contacted Beniamino Vincenzi, the director of our Stone Manor documentary. He told me he was only too happy to tell Vanessa about the secret passageways. A quick check showed the lock on the door at the cellar end of the passage had been replaced with another one that only you had the key to. It allowed for another way in as well as a quick get-away if you thought someone was likely to enter the room.

'But why steal the lanterns?' Gideon asked, sitting up, slightly. 'All phones have torches.'

Everyone looked to Ricky, who cleared his throat. 'Vanessa liked to roleplay. She was the damsel in distress and I was the wicked–'

'Oh God!' Nisha interjected in disgust. 'Vanessa playing a damsel? That would stretch anyone's role-playing skills!'

'But more interestingly than the lanterns being stolen, is the bunch of lilies. I wondered what you could have possibly gained from stealing them. Evangelina,' Amelia said turning to the actress, 'how are you feeling now?'

'Much better.'

'You see, I'd noticed a correlation between how bad your cold was and when you'd been in your room. It's well documented that you suffer from hay fever. As does Gideon.'

'I'm a martyr to the summer months,' Gideon confirmed.

'When I checked your room on Christmas Eve I noticed some yellow powdery residue on your pillows and headboard, which had come from the stamens of the lilies. Gideon was with me at that time and he too began sneezing. Ricky kindly got you a cold remedy, which he picked up from the pharmacy in the village. It's an over-the-counter one, readily available, that can cause drowsiness. It added even more drowsiness when Vanessa crunched up one of her sleeping tablets into it. Add to that a glass of wine and then a double measure of whisky–'

'Oh my God, *you* drugged me!' Evangelina turned towards Ricky. 'So, it wasn't a new natural cleaner you'd been using.'

Amelia shook her head. 'No.'

'Just my sorry excuse for a soon-to-be ex-husband. I can't believe it's taken me so long to get a divorce, you utter disgrace.'

'Had you not arranged to meet with Lorcan you would have slept on, waking up in the morning, no doubt feeling awful but none the wiser,' Amelia said.

'Were you trying to kill me?' Evangelina said to Ricky, barely able to conceal her anger. Lorcan came over, sat on the arm of her chair and rested a hand on her shoulder, and she covered his hand with her own.

'No!' Ricky said sadly. 'You don't really drink much so I didn't think you'd have alcohol with it.'

'You could have killed me just to carry on your sordid affair. We've been miserable for years! Why go through all of that instead of getting a divorce?'

'He just wanted to ensure you'd be asleep throughout his assignations with Vanessa. You mentioned you and Ricky had a thorough prenup. I'm guessing that there would be a penalty if adultery were involved?'

'Yes, in those early days, Ricky was convinced I'd have an affair.'

'Well, I knew there had been someone before me. Someone you were still clearly in love with when we met!' Ricky rallied, staring at Lorcan.

'And still am,' Evangelina said softly as she exchanged a look with Lorcan.

'Are you going to tell the police?' Ricky asked Evangelina. 'Or cripple me financially with the divorce?'

Evangelina looked at him coolly. 'I don't want any of your money, Ricky. I don't care if you had an affair. I have no interest in revenge. Strangely enough, I think you will suffer enough having lost Vanessa. I now just want out of this sham of a marriage.'

Ricky looked relieved but then turned back to Amelia 'What will happen to me regarding the robbery?'

Amelia hadn't a clue. 'Well, if Evangelina isn't interested in pressing charges, I'm pretty sure if you return the lanterns and send a very generous donation to Reverend McDade, Constable Williams will look favourably on you.'

Gideon got up from the ottoman and handed Ricky a piece of paper. 'Here's the account number and sort code for the church fund. Make sure you don't stint with the zeros. Think how much you would be out of pocket if the prenup had kicked in.'

Amelia raised a questioning eyebrow at Gideon wondering how he had the bank details for the church fund.

'Back in my drinking days, just after we arrived here, there was an incident with a bottle of vodka going through a stained-glass window, followed by a bit of blasphemy. I wanted to keep it on the hush-hush,' he whispered with a wink as he sat back down.

Ricky, meanwhile, had already got out his phone, opened his banking app and was keying in details.

'And of course, after Vanessa died, you were so worried about being caught in the Simenon Room, you panicked and packed all your belongings, and left, making it look like the mysterious Mr Griffin had something to hide.

'I believe it was the events on Christmas Eve that sealed Vanessa's fate. That and her love of blackmail. At one point we thought Vanessa was the Secret Guest, the anonymous hotel critic, who we know is staying at Stone Manor over Christmas. Many of the far-flung destinations Vanessa had visited were coincidently where the Secret Guest had also been. We had a couple of conversations full of misunderstanding and Vanessa thought we were alluding to her numerous affairs and thought we were trying to blackmail her. As she said, it was something she knew very well, that she was the master of. Clearly Vanessa had enemies. It was because of this blackmail that we had another red herring to deal with: Betty's intruder.'

Betty sat up in her chair and looked around the room expectantly. 'Was that you too, Ricky?'

'No,' Dan said, stepping forward. 'It was me.'

CHAPTER 49

Betty gasped as everyone turned to look at the Kings. Alice reached out and held her husband's hand supportively. Dan nodded to Amelia for her to continue. He hadn't been joking when he said he was sick of secrets.

'It wasn't your room he intended to be in though, Betty,' Amelia said. 'He was trying to get into Vanessa's other room to retrieve something of his he suspected Vanessa had taken. He knew it was the one next door to their suite, but he got the wrong side.'

'I'm sorry, Betty, I felt awful at scaring you,' Dan said.

'Just be thankful I didn't put a bullet through you!' Betty said, crunching down on another piece of shortbread.

'It explains why you made such a big show of going downstairs and asking Davey for tea and toast,' Amelia said to Alice. 'You wanted him away from the reception desk to give Dan enough time to search in Vanessa's room. Then, after the agreed amount of time, you went back upstairs and commented on Dan being asleep all the time.'

'Yes, it wasn't my finest hour,' Alice said.

'Was Vanessa blackmailing you over this item you needed back?' Carlo asked Dan.

'Yes,' Dan said and sighed. 'It was copies of an old business deal from a few years ago. It all ended up being legit but… I'll tell you all about it later.'

'The interesting thing about this contract wasn't the content, though, but the name of the other party involved. Mr Sebastian Calver,' Amelia said as she looked round the room, hoping for a reaction. A sea of blank faces looked back at her.

Regardless, Amelia ploughed on.

'On Christmas Eve, Vanessa told a story over dinner. It seemed just another one of her tales but looking back, there was a lot more to it. The story was of the Romeo Robber who was believed to have been behind the thefts of the artwork that hit London.

'Enter Mr Benedict Geissler. Mr Geissler worked for an art insurance company and his company paid out a small fortune on the thefts. There were a couple of near misses but they never caught the thief that targeted the wealthy art collectors of London. This thief was very clever and as a passable artist realised he could hide the paintings by covering them with his own work then pass them on through the black market. When the police finally had a tip-off, they found a couple of the stolen paintings but the rest they thought were averagely painted and worthless. For some reason, these worthless paintings weren't catalogued and held, and many somehow ending up on the market again. Or in charity shops.'

'The Poirot cat!' Betty interjected.

'Yes, Betty, the Poirot cat. Vanessa took a great interest in the little newspaper cutting of the hotel which had that painting in it. She must have remembered that painting from the time when she'd lived with the artist and unbeknownst to her then, the Romeo Robber. She did admit to having a wonderful memory. But Vanessa clearly recognised something else and thought she could get a little extra money by her usual means; blackmail.' Amelia thought back to the moment when Vanessa said she knew what Amelia had been hiding. Amelia thought she'd been referring to the dead mouse, never for a moment thinking it was a priceless lost painting.

'But Vanny didn't want for anything!' Terence exclaimed. He turned to Dan, his face quite ashen. 'I'll make sure I pay back everything she took from you.'

'I honestly don't think it was all about the money, Mr Maxwell. I think the power she held over people was the real reason behind the blackmail,' Amelia said. 'But Vanessa really thought she'd hit the jackpot over her next victim. Someone who could easily afford to pay whatever extortionate amount Vanessa planned on blackmailing them over.

'Now, let me get back to the Poirot cat painting. Vanessa wasn't the only one to recognise this painting. Benedict Geissler was also obsessed with the paintings stolen in London. Because of the failings of the Met, there was never enough funds to reopen the case but it didn't stop him investigating it in his own time and then devoting his retirement to bringing down the thief. And when he saw the newspaper article of Stone Manor he instantly recognised the ridiculous painting of the Poirot cat which he'd long suspected hid another painting.

'He arranged to meet me, refusing to come into the hotel because he couldn't risk being seen. Before he died he tried to tell me about the missing painting by the artist Domenico Ghirlandaio. I however having no background in art, had no idea what he was talking about.

'Luckily, we found enough to be able to piece together the missing information. There was currently an exhibition on in The National Gallery, showing the other famous Ghirlandaio painting, the one that was meant to be paired up the with the painting hidden under the Poirot cat.

'Mr Geissler had phoned Lorcan and asked him to do a copy

of the one in The National Gallery as he obviously knew it would be stolen. Lorcan had worked for Geissler previously and had done something very similar with a Manet painting to act as a decoy in a sting operation. But when Geissler didn't keep their appointment, Lorcan began to get anxious about having a copy of a painting that had recently been stolen.

'This all seems very far-fetched,' Carlo said, doubtfully.

'Not really,' Amelia said. 'There was a Post-it note on my desk with his name and number. Someone saw this and knew instantly why he was here. I suspect the murderer messaged him and arranged to meet him earlier, got there, came up behind him and injected the poison. There was enough to have killed him almost instantly and when I appeared a few moments later he was almost dead. I believe he just had time to throw his phone away, in case Lorcan or Kit could be traced from it and put in danger.

'Then Lorcan was knocked unconscious in the early hours of the morning. At first I thought it was Ricky who had possibly found out about his past relationship with Evangelina but it didn't fit. I believe the murderer overheard Lorcan had a selection of paintings from Stone Manor, and hoping to stumble across the Poirot cat let themselves into the studio to find it.'

'But I wasn't sleeping well,' Lorcan said. 'I got up early and went into the studio and disturbed the intruder. I thought it could have been someone searching for the copy of the famous painting I'd done for Benedict Geissler.'

'But how did Kit fit in with it all?' Nisha asked.

'Kit's an investigative journalist and had worked with Benedict before. And because of this he was the murderer's next intended victim. He left the café on Christmas Eve to make a few phone calls to try and find out what Benedict Geissler was working on and what had led him to Glencarlach.

'Someone obviously overheard him and followed him and hit him over the head to leave him for dead in the harsh conditions.'

'It must have been someone very big and strong to do that,'

Lucy said, glancing round the room and frowning before resting her gaze on DeShawn.

'That's a very good point. Not many could easily move an almost six-foot dead weight.'

DeShawn shifted uneasily as a couple of the guests turned to look at him and his impressive physique that had helped him in his football career.

'And then of course there was the break-in at the Gatehouse. Again, it was strange as nothing was stolen but the person who broke in was clearly searching for something specific. And they were; a painting stolen from The National Gallery in London a few days earlier and hidden in Jack's luggage for him to bring up here for them to steal back at a later date. The original painting of the one Geissler had asked Lorcan to copy.'

'I read about the painting being stolen!' Betty interjected.

'So did I,' Alaiya agreed. 'And is it here?'

'Oh my God!' Evangelina turned round and looked at Lorcan.

'Everyone was busy that night, though,' Dan said. 'It was when Jack gave us his talk about being a writer and Lucy had her hen-do.' He turned to Alice who nodded in agreement.

'Exactly. And that's what made me think the murderer must have had an accomplice.'

Now there was a little ripple of chatter as everyone looked at each other and discussed this new revelation.

Amelia glanced down the drive. The pillar lights reflected in the snow but there was no flashing light cavalry coming to help her. She had to carry on.

'But... I can't think of one person who could do this, let alone two!' Evangelina said to Nisha.

'But, you see, it makes perfect sense when you realise the subject of the paintings,' Amelia said, and once again everyone turned to look at her.

'The painting stolen from The National Gallery, that Lorcan also made the copy of, is of Cesare Borgia, and the painting covered up by Poirot cat is that of his sister, Lucrezia Borgia. Both painted in 1492 by Domenico Ghirlandaio.'

'So, a brother and sister are behind all this?' Alice asked.

'Yes, a brother and sister, whose father is Sebastian Calver, who was the Romeo Robber.'

'Calver?' Dan said. 'The same man I did the contract for? But I never heard from him again.'

'And I don't know anyone with that surname,' Terence said, 'let alone a brother *and* sister!'

'Ah well, you see, they changed their name by deed poll. Isn't that right, Lucy?'

CHAPTER 50

There was a moment of shocked silence until Lucy gave a little giggle then looked frightened. Clasping her hand to her throat in disbelief.

'What? Seriously? You think *I* murdered that man, Benedict... what's his name? Carly! Tell her she has to stop this nonsense!'

'This is ridiculous!' Carlo said. 'You can't possibly think my wife could have anything to do with murder! That's insane!'

'You may want to hear me out, as you are one of her intended targets.'

Carlo shook his head in disbelief.

'I agree, it does seem quite far-fetched until Constable Williams let me know the result of the post-mortem. Vanessa was indeed murdered.'

'What?' Terence interjected. 'No, it was her heart.'

'I'm sorry, Terence, but it wasn't. Vanessa was also poisoned.'

'Cyanide too?' Gideon asked, sitting forward, clearly carried away with the story.

'No, I had a feeling it would be something else and I was right. Vanessa was poisoned by *Digitalis purpurea*.'

'What's that?' Terence asked, looking from Amelia to Lucy.

'Otherwise known as–'

'Foxgloves.' It was Carlo who spoke, looking at Lucy in disbelief. He slowly removed his hand from her knee.

'And I believe you keep the poison in your silver locket, the one that you always have on you. The gift from your father, which is an exact replica of the ring that Lucrezia Borgia had many centuries ago when she poisoned her victims. And I'm sorry to tell you, Carlo, but I believe Lucy has been dosing you in small amounts for the last few months. Just enough to cause headaches, confusion, blurred eyes; all the symptoms you've been suffering from, which your close friends thought was down to early-onset dementia.'

'Oh my God! I thought it was your boyfriend that had the great imagination!' Lucy said. 'You should really start writing fiction too, Amelia.'

'It all fits, though,' Amelia said. 'I remember seeing you on Christmas Eve. You'd been looking at sledges outside Jean's shop when I ducked in for a coffee. You must have overheard Kit talking on the phone and realised he could easily be onto you. You followed him and waited until he was on a quiet stretch and then hit him over the head, ready to leave him for dead. Once you'd rolled him onto your newly purchased sledge he would have been easy enough to pull away from the driveway, where you proceeded to cover him with snow, assuming he'd die before being discovered.

'That's where the mystery of the towels come in. When it was suggested you all go sledging after the scavenger hunt, you realised you hadn't cleaned the sledge of Kit's blood. You took the towels from your room to clean it with, but then realised Carlo was distressed at the towels disappearing as he also feared he'd misplaced them, and couldn't remember where. So, to hush him up and to deflect any connection to yourself, you snuck into Dan and Alice's room and took their towels to replace the ones in your own room, letting Carlo assume he'd been confused.'

'But what about Lorcan being hit?' Evangelina asked.

'And your house being robbed?' Nisha added.

'That was a bit harder to piece together and where having an accomplice came in handy. The morning of Lorcan's attack was the morning after Betty's intruder. It was also when Carlo misplaced his wallet and our boiler broke down. Davey had been alerted to this because Carlo, an early riser, had gone for a shower. The water was cold. His first thought was that it was a fault with his room and went into their other room, which Lucy was using for her wedding preparations.

'When that shower didn't run hot either, he called down to report the incident to the front desk, got dressed then tried to get back into the room he shared with his fiancée but it had locked behind him. Mindful that his wife took sleeping pills and not wanting to disturb her unnecessarily, Carlo went for his walk and started work a little earlier than usual, but still kept to his daily routine. What he hadn't realised was that while Davey was checking the boiler out, Ms Carvalho slipped out and headed over to Lorcan's studio to try and find the painting of the Poirot cat.

'I'd like to think she didn't plan on killing you, Lorcan; she just needed to render you unconscious so she could escape and head back to Stone Manor without being rumbled. Knowing the painting wasn't at Lorcan's, the only other place it could be was the village hall, awaiting the exhibition. You broke in there, Lucy, and changed the red dot to a green dot, which meant it would go into the auction. Although it was Carlo bidding for the painting, I believe it was you who'd made the suggestion.'

Judging by Carlo's face, Amelia knew she was right.

'We know you were the one to steal the Ghirlandaio from The National Gallery, the one of Cesare Borgia. You were concerned that Geissler was onto you as he'd been in regular contact with your father in prison. Fearing you were being watched you pickpocketed Jack in London, stole his room key then hid the painting in a poster tube he'd be bringing back up to Glencarlach. Because, like your obsessive father you wanted to reunite the paintings. Cesare and Lucrezia Borgia. They were meant to be together forever, just like their father, Pope Alexander III wished. Then they would make their way to France where your father would travel after his release from prison and you could all be reunited. You mentioned many times how obsessed Carlo was with Jack's blog. It put him firmly in the frame, but obviously you followed it too.

'It must have been so frustrating to not find the portrait of Cesare Borgia you stole from The National Gallery in our Gatehouse. That's when we thought we'd hurry things along. So we made a big show of Gideon finding the poster tube that you knew contained the Cesare Borgia portrait.'

'But who could be her accomplice?' Carlo said, clearly still not wanting to believe the woman he loved could be behind it all.

'Her brother, of course. Craig.'

CHAPTER 51

A melia had been expecting some sort of explosion of anger or denial from her barman, but instead, Craig sat down on one of the free chairs round the fire.

'I'm sorry,' he said, looking up at Amelia, 'I didn't realise she'd go this far. I tried to stop her.'

'And you tried to warn me, didn't you? The letter telling me that all guests weren't as they seemed?'

Craig nodded. 'I needed you to be alert. I know it sounds ridiculous but I've really enjoyed my time here and I'd hate to think Lucy would hurt any of you.

'It was so hard growing up.' He sighed, closing his eyes briefly as if trying to shut out whatever memories had resurfaced. 'Our father was obsessed, as you say. He'd wanted to call us Cesare and Lucrezia but luckily our mother had more sense. She tried to protect us but when she died, obviously he had sole custody. And well, Lucy became as obsessed with Renaissance art, particularly Ghirlandaio, as dad was.'

'Craig! Stop talking now!' Lucy warned.

'I love you, Lucy, but you can't go on like this. You need help.'

He looked at Carlo. 'I'm sorry. I know I should have gone to the police but I kept hoping Lucy would stop.

'We'd drifted apart over the years. I needed to get away from the toxicity of my father. That's when I went travelling in my camper van. I'd hoped with my father in prison, Lucy could move on with her life, but then she called me one day. She'd seen the article in the paper about Stone Manor and knew it was where our father's missing Lucrezia painting was. She'd already hooked up with Carlo by this point. I guess she upped the ante for getting married, and picked here. I know Carlo is a huge fan of Jack but let's face it, if Lucy suggested they get married in a mud hut in Mongolia, Carlo would have agreed. I realised I had to be here on hand to keep an eye on her. And you kindly gave me a job,' he added, giving Amelia a brief smile.

'I stupidly alerted her to Geissler being here. James came to tell you he'd called. I panicked and told Lucy and I just knew she was going to do something awful. She wouldn't listen to reason so the next best thing was that I delay you as long as possible so you wouldn't get hurt.'

Amelia remembered she'd been trying to get away to meet Benedict and that's when Craig waylaid her with discussing the champagne order.

'Yes, I broke into the Gatehouse on my night off, when I knew Lucy had an alibi. I tried to not make too much of a mess. I had faith the poster tube would turn up somewhere and obviously when you did that little performance, I took the painting from the poster tube, not realising it was a fake.'

'You took Carlo's wallet. Hid them for a while and noted down his card details to book a ferry crossing in his name to make it look like he was guilty,' Amelia said.

'Yes.' Craig looked down at his hands and sighed. 'I tried to stop her killing Vanessa, I really did.'

'You broke the Campari bottle. Campari being so bitter would have easily hidden the digitalis but Lucy managed to give it to Vanessa anyway. Probably when they'd met in the small hours of Christmas morning to discuss blackmailing money.' Amelia now realised Vanessa's reference to it being 'almost time' wasn't that she thought it was Christmas; it was for her secret assignation with Lucy. 'I imagine Lucy agreed to the blackmail but poisoned Vanessa before she left. The poison took a little while to react, inducing the vomiting that Terence thought was just a hangover. Later, possibly feeling a little better, Vanessa left her room and popped down to the bar for another bottle of champagne to celebrate with Ricky, and that's when the poison finally had its fatal effect and stopped her heart.'

'You know it's very rude to talk about someone when they're in the same room as you,' Lucy said as all eyes turned to her. Amelia happened to see the glint of mother-of-pearl just as Betty shrieked, 'She's got my gun!'

Someone screamed. Carlo stood up to restrain her but Lucy was too far away.

'How...?' Amelia started to say. She'd locked the gun in the safe.

'How did I get the gun?' Lucy said, then rolled her eyes. 'Please! I stole a painting from The National Gallery; do you really think a poxy electronic keypad safe would get the better of me?'

'Put the gun down, sis,' Craig said, also jumping to his feet.

'What happened to it being you and me together, against all odds?' Lucy said.

'That wasn't me that said that. It was Dad,' Craig said desperately, holding his hands out as he tried to take a step forward.

'You don't deserve to call him that,' Lucy said spitefully, raising the gun towards Craig's chest.

There was a shout as Gideon leapt from behind, and with

sheer brute force pushed Lucy's hands down, away from her brother's vital organs.

'Gideon!' Amelia shouted as her heart jumped into her throat.

A shot fired.

CHAPTER 52

Gideon yelled and the shock of the gun going off caused Lucy to drop it. Quick as a flash DeShawn dived at her, knocking Lucy to the ground, managing to kick the gun away at the same time.

Amelia ran over to Gideon who was pale and shaking and clutching his lower leg where blood flowed freely. 'Why am I always the one to get shot,' he said through clenched teeth.

'Don't worry, the bullet isn't inside!' Toby said, pointing to the little gold pellet on the carpet as he hunkered down beside Gideon.

Everyone was up on their feet, talking at once and the room became lit up by a flashing blue light.

'It's Constable Williams!' Lorcan shouted.

'That's not really any fucking consolation to me right now unless they have an ambulance in tow!' Gideon said breathlessly before letting out a howl of pain.

Just then Constable Williams ran in through the front door, closely followed by Detective Inspector McGregor and a few other uniform officers.

'Did I just hear a gunshot?' Ray asked, taking in the scene.

'You need to arrest this woman,' DeShawn said as he stood up, dragging Lucy up with him.

'And me,' Craig said, holding out his hands, ready for cuffs.

'Did you get my recording?' Amelia asked.

'Yes, it was a bit patchy when we went through some black spots, but we got the gist, although we'll need a proper statement.'

'And I've also recorded everything on my phone!' India said, her normally white face pink with excitement as she handed her mobile over to one of the uniforms. 'Can I post it on TikTok when you're done with it?' she asked.

'Has someone phoned an ambulance yet!?' Gideon called out from the floor as Toby pressed Gideon's cashmere scarf against the wound to stem the bleeding.

Detective Inspector McGregor walked over as Lucy and Craig were taken away.

'Do you normally condone such unconventional and vigilante-like policing?' he said to Ray.

'We got our bad guys!' Amelia interjected.

McGregor didn't crack his face. 'You may think you've been clever, Ms Adams, but we frown upon members of the public taking the law into their own hands.'

'I was just trying to keep everyone here until you arrived,' Amelia said. 'I just couldn't help but get carried away with the moment.'

McGregor took a deep breath, as if to say something then changed his mind, then turned on his heel and marched down the steps of Stone Manor.

'Watch your back with that one, Amelia,' Ray said. 'He's pretty pissed off with our community-spirited provincial-style police work. Can't say too much, though, as you got there before he did. And he's got the London mob on his back about the painting. You do still have it, don't you?'

'Yes, safely rolled up and secured in a welly boot.'

'Excellent!' his bushy moustache quivered as he tried to hide a smile.

'Oh, and you'll need to give them that too,' Amelia said, pointing to the one of the Poirot cat. 'It's hiding another stolen painting.'

'But Lucy seemed so *nice!*' Alice said coming up to them, clearly in shock at the unfolding events.

'Everyone thought that, but I saw how angry she could become when pushed. She was enraged when she thought the wedding was going to be cancelled. I realised she was the one who'd beaten up Craig, too. He'd broken the Campari bottle and had gone against his sister's plans. He flinched one day when I came towards him and I realised there was someone he was scared of.'

'How did Vanessa know?' Alice wondered aloud.

'Vanessa clearly recognised something, according to the partially burnt out note I found in the fire. Maybe it was Lucy's necklace; she had been admiring it. Maybe she overheard us talking about Benedict Geissler and, with her excellent memory, recalled him from the investigation of the Romeo Robber. Maybe both. Vanessa was many things but stupid and unobservant weren't two of them. She must have traced Lucy and dug up the information on her, the way Vanessa normally did.'

'I really thought she loved me,' Carlo said, coming over.

'I think she did, but loved your Renaissance art more.'

'So, she thought she'd marry me, bump me off, then live happily ever after with my original da Vinci sketches,' Carlo said sadly.

They all watched as the police cars containing Lucy and Craig retreated up Stone Manor drive. Even Jingles had left the warmth of the hotel to sit on the top step and observe their departure.

'I'm surprised you didn't suspect me!' Carlo said.

'I did for a while. Kit even had your name flagged on the ferry and flight bookings as I was convinced you'd be hotfooting it to

France. But then I got Kit to trace Craig's name too and lo and behold, he'd booked a ferry leaving for France first thing tomorrow. I imagine that he was going to leave here tonight, take the paintings over and wait for Lucy and their father, when he was released from prison.' Although he had a toxic relationship with his father, I guess family stick together. Amelia still felt quite sad at losing such a good barman and member of the Stone Manor team.

'Looks like that Detective Inspector would be lucky to have you on the force,' Carlo said.

Amelia shook her head. 'No, I just seem to be in the right place at the right time.'

They were interrupted by a shout from the drawing room.

'People!' Gideon yelled. 'For the love of GOD, would somebody PLEASE call me a fucking ambulance!'

'Gideon, you're a fucking ambulance!' Kit, Toby and Amelia all shouted back.

CHAPTER 53

Lorcan stood on the top steps of Stone Manor, watching as the last of the police cars went down the driveway, making slow progress through the snow.

'What do you think will happen to them?' Evangelina said as she came and stood next to him.

'I have no idea. I imagine Lucy will go away for a very long time. As for Craig? I don't know. I suppose he did try and stop her...'

He looked down at Evangelina and he felt his chest do that funny thing where it seemed to crush his heart and he felt he wasn't getting enough oxygen to breathe properly.

'I meant what I said in there,' Evangelina said, 'about still loving you.' Her eyes searched Lorcan's looking for a reaction. 'The reason I didn't want to kiss you in the library, well actually I *did* want to kiss you, but I didn't because I wanted to give Ricky the divorce papers first. I wanted to close that part of my life before starting a new one.'

'Nothing to do with prenups?'

She laughed. 'Not a thing. And then everything seemed to spiral away from us.'

'Ah yes, that's because unbeknownst to you I was solving a murder. Artist by day, crime-fighter by night.' He smiled and turned so they were facing each other. He brushed a strand of hair from her face. 'So, this new life you want to start, does it involve moving up to a beautiful Scottish village known for its soaring crime rate?'

'It does.'

'And could it possibly involve living with a dashing, handsome, *super*-talented and not to mention hilariously funny artist, who is a bit of a superhero in his spare time?'

'Wow you escalated from crime-fighter to superhero fairly quickly.'

'I'm a fast mover. Actually, I'm really not as it's taken over fifteen years to *finally* get the woman of my dreams.'

'And I do think I want to be with a dashing, handsome, *super*-talented, not to mention hilariously funny artist who moonlights as a superhero. But you also forgot, who's often a bit of an eejit,' she teased, doing an impression of his accent.

'Oh, is that right!' Lorcan laughed, drinking in every inch of her face.

'Get a room, you two!' Gideon said as he and Toby came out of the front door.

'I'm taking him to accident and emergency,' Toby explained.

'I don't even qualify for an ambulance!' Gideon said huffily.

'Dr Kaur's phoned ahead; they're expecting us. The bullet just grazed you.'

'When you get shot, only *then* are you allowed to say something as insulting as "the bullet just grazed you" *JUST*!'

They walked down the steps, with Toby supporting Gideon as he let out a wail of pain each time he put weight on his injured leg. Toby bundled him into the back of the Stone Manor Jeep and pulled away.

'Maybe Gideon's right,' Lorcan said. 'Maybe we should get a room.'

'I like that idea,' Evangelina agreed, then looked back into Stone Manor. 'Although I don't really think I want one in there, no offence to Amelia. It's a beautiful hotel but I think I'd like somewhere a little quieter.'

Lorcan wrapped his arms around her. 'And where do you have in mind?'

Evangelina leant into him, circling her arms around his waist. 'There's a really lovely house, a couple of miles away, with a welcoming kitchen and an Aga, and views down the glen.'

'I know the place. Although, we have some unfinished business to deal with first.' He looked up at the mistletoe hanging above their heads. 'Have you heard the saying it's bad luck to ignore mistletoe.'

'No.'

'Funny, neither have I,' he said as he bent down to kiss her.

CHAPTER 54

28TH DECEMBER

'Merry Christmas!'
        'Merry Christmas!'
Amelia and Jack were sitting on the sheepskin rug, in front of the fire in the Gatehouse, a bottle of red wine and an array of opened presents between them. Jack had already put his framed signed poster of the book tour over the mantelpiece, absolutely delighted with his gift.

They chinked their wine glasses together.

'At one point I really thought we'd be celebrating Christmas after new year!' Jack said. 'Especially after McGregor pulled you in for questioning.'

Amelia groaned. It had been a very intense five-hour interview where he'd left no stone unturned, but she'd made it out with only a stern reprimand and a lecture about taking the law into her own hands.

'Thank goodness Lucy didn't go really crazy otherwise one of us might not have made this at all,' Amelia said, raising her glass and taking a sip of wine.

'How is Gideon?'

'Driving Toby mental. Turns out he didn't even need a stitch, just a big bit of gauze. He was really lucky, but he's more disappointed he won't have a scar for all his heroic efforts! But they're back at home, their real home and everyone has checked out.'

'Good,' Jack leant over and kissed Amelia lightly on the lips. 'Now wait here, I've another present to get you, one that I hid in case we got burgled again.'

Amelia sat back on her hands and listened to Jack rummaging through the drawers in the bedroom.

'Um, give me a minute, I can't actually remember where I put it!'

Amelia laughed as she thought back to the rest of the day. With the case being solved, all the remaining guests had understandably been in a hurry to check out. Terence was subdued but still insisted on giving Nisha a lift to London. She also disappeared then returned a few moments later with full make-up and perfume on. Amelia had a good feeling about them.

Kit was more than happy to stay on for a few more days to work on the story of Sebastian Calver and Benedict Geissler. He would be staying with Sally and Hamish and they'd all agreed to meet in the Whistling Haggis the next evening for drinks.

The Kings were next to check out, Alice and Dan clearly relieved to no longer be under the blackmailing sights of Vanessa. India, without her phone glued to her hand was actually a very chatty young woman and the three of them left in high spirits.

Ricky skulked off after paying and didn't look at anyone on the way out.

Carlo was unsurprisingly subdued.

The Johnsons also left, full of promises to return in the summer, when DeShawn's filming would have stopped, and they planned to coincide their stay with Sally's wedding just so they could meet up with Betty again.

'I've had the most wonderful stay,' Betty said as she checked out, with Hamish waiting to drive her to the ferry. 'I haven't had this much excitement in months! Not since the Danieli when a rather attractive and famous actor invited me along to an all-night poker game.'

'Really!'

'Oh, nothing untoward happened, he was far too young for me and I had to let him down gently, of course.'

'Wait, hang on, you were at the Danieli?'

'Yes, and quite a few other very famous hotels,' she said with a wink. 'Although I think for entertainment value, you can't really beat a *real* murder mystery, can you? And I'm sure the Secret Guest, whoever they are, will report accordingly!' she said with a wave as she headed out front, the fabric of her patchwork cloak billowing out behind her.

Thinking back to that exchange made Amelia laugh. Of all the people to be the Secret Guest, Amelia loved that it was Betty. Of course, all those years of hobnobbing with artists, actors, writers and politicians who took her away for long weekends and fancy meals meant she was in the perfect position to visit hotels and then do reviews.

When Evangelina checked out, she looked so happy and relaxed. She wasn't going far though, just to Lorcan's house and Amelia had a feeling she wouldn't be leaving. Lorcan had very kindly promised Amelia he would copy the Poirot cat painting as it held many sentimental memories for Amelia.

Amelia heard a triumphant 'yes' from next door and then a moment later Jack appeared with something behind his back.

'Do you know, when I was back in New York, I realised something.'

'What was that?'

'It was far too boring. New York just doesn't have the constant thrills and excitement of this place.'

'Maybe we should go there for a restful holiday?' Amelia said.

'There's been something I've wanted to give you since I got back.'

'Ooh, matron!' Amelia laughed.

'No, I'm being serious.' And he really did look serious.

Amelia sat up slightly. From behind his back, Jack produced a small velvet box.

'I bought you this. It was always top of my shopping list but there just wasn't the right time to give it to you, what with all the dead bodies and the crime solving, you know...'

'Yeah, they tend to get in the way.'

'But I figured, when would be more romantic than when we've just watched a police car drive away with two baddies handcuffed in the back seat. So...uh, so um, I was wondering, if you'd like to become my, um, if you'd like to, you know...' he sighed and rolled his eyes heavenwards. 'Shit, for a writer I'm suddenly unable to find the right words, or any words for that matter.'

He handed Amelia the little velvet box.

Time seemed to stop for Amelia as she opened it up. Inside, nestled on a scarlet silk cushion was the most exquisite ring, a square cut ruby, surrounded by diamonds.

'It's not as big as the Rubra Amora we found hidden here, but I thought it would be a nice reminder of that time we solved the mystery of Stone Manor.'

'It's exquisite!'

'And if you agree to marry me, we could spend the rest of our lives solving crimes and having you rescue me from perilous situations.'

She looked up at him, the reflection of the fire flickering golds and oranges on his handsome face.

'I can think of nothing better,' Amelia said, smiling.

THE END

ACKNOWLEDGEMENTS

I would like to say a massive thank you to Betsy, Tara and Clare, along with everyone at Bloodhound Books who helped with the production of the novel you've just read.

A huge outpouring of love goes to my amazing family. Pete, you have endless patience as I ramble on about plot arcs and characters. Your ability to rustle up a jambalaya at short notice as I finish off a chapter is awesome, as is your sixth sense for those moments when I need an Apricot Ricky. Thalia, Adeline and Oriana; you all keep doing you!

I had great fun writing this book as I've always loved spending a winter's afternoon by the fire, drinking hot chocolate and reading stories about Christmas. And snow. And being snowed in at Christmas, especially if there's a murder to solve. Just like my heroine, Amelia, I adore the novels of Agatha Christie and her writing has had a huge impact on me over the years. As did watching Scooby Doo as a child, which I now watch with my own children. Never underestimate the power of Scooby Doo.

I would also like to add a little historical note. Domenico Ghirlandaio was indeed a fifteenth century Florentine Renaissance artist. There is nothing in the history books to suggest that he ever met with any of the Borgias…..but then again there's nothing to say he didn't! So, this book is also for those art romantics, searching attics in the hope of discovering a lost Renaissance masterpiece. Never stop looking.

A NOTE FROM THE PUBLISHER

Thank you for reading this book. If you enjoyed it please do consider leaving a review on Amazon to help others find it too.

We hate typos. All of our books have been rigorously edited and proofread, but sometimes mistakes do slip through. If you have spotted a typo, please do let us know and we can get it amended within hours.

info@bloodhoundbooks.com

Printed in Great Britain
by Amazon

10825897R00222